springtime
at cherry tree cottage

Also available by Cathy Woodman

Trust Me, I'm a Vet

Must Be Love

The Sweetest Thing

It's a Vet's Life

The Village Vet

Vets in Love

Country Loving

Follow Me Home

Vets on Call

springtime

at cherry tree cottage

cathy woodman

PEGASUS BOOKS
NEW YORK LONDON

Springtime at Cherry Tree Cottage

Pegasus Books Ltd
148 West 37th Street, 13th Fl.
New York, NY 10018

First Pegasus Books hardcover edition April 2017

ISBN: 978-1-68177-361-2

10 9 8 7 6 5 4 3 2 1

Printed in the United States of America
Distributed by W. W. Norton & Company, Inc.

In loving memory of Dr Brian Chadwick, geologist,
bibliophile and wonderful dad

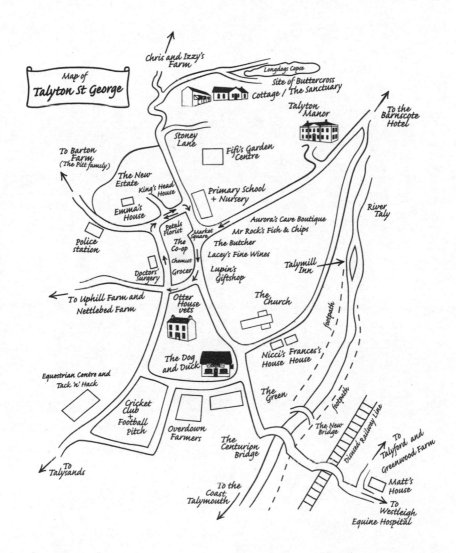

Map of
Talyton St George

Chris and Izzy's Farm

Longdogs Copse

Site of Buttercross Cottage / The Sanctuary

Talyton Manor

To the Barnscote Hotel

Stoney Lane

Fifi's Garden Centre

To Barton Farm (The Pitt family)

The New Estate

King's Head House

Emma's House

Primary School + Nursery

River Taly

Petals Florist

Market Square

Aurora's Cave Boutique

Mr Rock's Fish & Chips

Police station

The Co-op

The Butcher

Lacey's Fine Wines

chemist

grocer

Doctors' Surgery

Lupin's Giftshop

Talymill Inn

To Uphill Farm and Nettlebed Farm

Otter House vets

The Church

footpath

The Dog and Duck

Nicci's House

Frances's House

Equestrian Centre and Tack 'n' Hack

The Green

footpath

Cricket Club + Football Pitch

Overdown Farmers

The New Bridge

Disused Railway Line

To Talyford and Greenwood Farm

The Centurion Bridge

To Talysands

To the Coast, Talymouth

Matt's House

To Westleigh Equine Hospital

Chapter One

A Fresh Start

Christian Grey, eat your heart out. My horse is the original fifty shades and far more gorgeous. It's true that I have a whip and spurs somewhere amongst my belongings, but I've never had any desire to use them. I've never loved anyone even half as much as my beautiful grey boy. When I'm with him my heart beats faster and my blood bubbles with happiness. I don't have to pretend to be one of the lads at work, or make out that I'm having the time of my life in front of my ex, or act the perfect daughter to please my parents. I can be myself.

I lean forwards in the saddle and stroke Rafa's neck, running my fingers through his flaxen mane, which falls in waves down past his dappled shoulder. He smells of sweat, fly-spray and de-tangler, and his coat feels warm and slightly damp.

I sit up straight and ride on, squinting in the rays of the early-evening sun that slant between the branches of the gnarled trees bordering the lane. The ancient oaks are unfurling their leaves and the

1

blackthorn is frothing with blossom. It's late March and my favourite time of year, when the weather is getting better and the days start drawing out, meaning there's more opportunity to get out riding.

At the top of the hill where the scent of wild garlic and farmyard starts to fill my nostrils, Rafa sidesteps a shadow. I take a tighter grip on the reins and push him forwards with the pressure of my calves. He breaks into a trot and I begin to relax again as he covers the ground, the sound of his feet muffled by the grass that's growing lush and green between the stones and patches of tarmac.

I bring him back to walk. He shies for a second time, snorting as if to say, 'Scary monster alert. Let's get the hell out of here.'

'Oh no you don't,' I say, spotting the offending plastic bag that's drifting slowly across the ground in front of us. 'You are such a wuss,' I add lightly. That's what he's like, though. He doesn't care about trucks, rattling trailers or tractors, but show him a crisp packet and it's the end of the world.

'It's nothing.' I take a firm hold. 'There's no need to be silly about it.'

I focus on the scenery, trying to ignore the way his hindquarters are bunching up beneath me as he utters another snort, blowing air through his nose so hard that he makes us both jump.

At the summit of the hill, the lane bends sharply one way then the other before hugging the contour of the slope on the way down the far side. There's a bank of red earth to the right and a hedge to the left filled with hazel, pale yellow primroses and blue speedwell. I can hear the faint sound of church bells and water, a small torrent emerging from a culvert

2

below the hedge where the ground falls away. In the distance I can see glimpses of a river and the market town of Talyton St George.

When I hear the rumble of an approaching tractor, I decide to trot along to the next gateway to give it space to pass, but as we get closer, the scent of farmyard becomes more noxious. Rafa stops dead in the middle of the lane, his ears pricked, his nostrils flared and his head up like a giraffe. I make a clicking sound in my throat to ask him to move on, but he refuses to budge any way but sideways. As he starts to sidle up the bank, I give him a firm nudge in the ribs with my heels. He doesn't respond so I lean across and snap a twig off a nearby hazel, using it to give him a tickle on the flank.

I can hear the tractor moving closer, chugging up the hill. In desperation, I flick Rafa with the twig again, and with my legs flailing in best Pony Club fashion, we're away, at least as far as the gate where he stops abruptly, sending me halfway up his neck. I slide back down into the saddle, trying to regain my stirrups. His heart is pounding loud and fast. He's genuinely scared this time. He snorts for a third time. The echo, followed by a series of loud oinks, comes back from behind the hedge, and all is lost.

He plunges forwards, unseating me so I'm clinging to his withers. I grab at his mane and I'm just about hanging on until he bucks and I lose my grip on his slippery tresses. He tips me off into the hedge beside the gate and bolts towards the tractor, the clatter of his hooves fading into the distance.

Struggling to catch my breath, I extricate myself from the brambles in full view of an audience of sandy-coloured pigs. My burgundy sweat top is adorned with sticky buds and the knees of my cream jodhpurs are stained green. The screen on my mobile has cracked into little pieces, but I'm okay: my skull-cap is intact; no bones broken.

Cursing the amount of de-tangler that I used on Rafa's mane while getting him ready, I start to run after him, listening out for the sound of skidding wheels and the sickening crash, but it doesn't come. Instead, the tractor appears and draws up alongside me. The driver, a middle-aged man in a red baseball cap, leans out of the cab.

'You're going to have to run faster than that, my lover. Running faster than the wind, he was,' he calls in a broad Devon accent, dropping his aitches and rounding his vowels.

I thank him – I'm not sure what for – and keep running down the hill until I reach a crossroads with a wooden signpost and a grassy triangle in the centre. Rafa has left a circle of hoof-prints, as if he paused for a mouthful of grass.

I call his name repeatedly. There's no sign of him, no clue as to which way he went. I'm really panicking now, agonising about what I'm going to find. He could be lying in the road with a broken leg for all I know. My lungs are raw, my muscles are burning and my feet are killing me. I can't hear anything except a pulse of impending doom thudding in my ears.

And then I catch sight of two horses, a black one and a grey, heading my way along the right fork at the crossroads. My heart floods with relief, and my face with embarrassment as the rider of the black horse moves closer. He halts just in front of me, and looks me up and down, one eyebrow raised.

'I assume this is yours,' he says, handing me Rafa's reins.

'Thank you for catching him,' I say, still breathless. I check my horse's legs, running my hands over his knees and fetlocks. There are no cuts or obvious bruises. He's had a lucky escape.

'Is he all right?'

'He's fine.' I look up. The rider of the horse is male, most definitely male, and in his mid- to late twenties. He sits tall in the saddle, with his long muscular legs in dark breeches and leather boots wrapped around his horse's body, but it's his shirt that really catches my eye. It's flamboyant and rather ridiculous, made from cream-coloured cheesecloth with a ruffle down the front. He wears it with the top buttons unfastened, revealing the shadowy dip at the base of his neck and a generous view of the slab-like muscles of his chest. The sleeves are rolled up to show off his lean, tanned arms.

'How about you?' he asks. 'You look as if you've been dragged through a hedge backwards.'

'You aren't far wrong there, but I'm okay, thanks.' I'm carrying my riding hat under one arm and my shattered mobile in the other hand. Aware that I must have one of the worst cases of hat-hair ever, I run my fingers through my short dark brown crop in a vain attempt to give it some body.

'Are you sure? You've cut your lip.'

I touch my mouth, tasting the metallic tang of blood.

'It's nothing.' I try to make out his features, but his face is shaded by the peak of his hat; a helmet – like the polo players wear – not a skull-cap like mine.

'What happened?'

'He took a dislike to the pigs.'

'It's funny how some horses can't stand them.' The sunlight catches the rider's face, revealing strong cheekbones, a clean-cut complexion and a wicked smile. I can't help wondering if his long dark eyelashes might be enhanced in some way, and I'm pretty sure he's wearing a touch of pearlescent eye shadow and some lip-stain.

'It isn't *that* funny,' I say fiercely, sensing that perhaps, amid his concern for my health, this man who's riding around the countryside pretending he's Ross Poldark is laughing at me. There was a time when my friends and I would have found the whole idea of Rafa disappearing at full gallop without me hysterically funny too, but I start work tomorrow and I need to be in one piece.

'I'm sorry. My name's Robbie, Robbie Salterton.'

'I'm Flick. It's short for Felicity,' I say, testing out my right knee as I look around for a convenient place from which to get back into the saddle.

'You look as if you've taken quite a tumble,' Robbie goes on as I lead Rafa towards the bank. 'Are you sure it wouldn't be safer to lead him home?'

'No, really. I prefer to be on top.' Immediately, I wish I could unsay what I've just said . . .

'Oh, so do I,' he says, his voice laced with humour and suggestion, as I turn Rafa to face the way we came from, as well as to hide the heat in my cheeks. 'Let me give you a leg up.' Robbie is on his feet and at my side, his horse standing quietly without restraint. Before I can argue that it isn't strictly necessary, he's in position, ready to take my lower leg in his hands.

I take up the reins and bend my left knee.

'On the count of three. One, two, three . . .' Robbie propels me back into the saddle with seemingly effortless force, almost sending me off over the other side.

I regain my seat with as much poise as I can muster and slip my feet into the stirrups. He vaults easily on to his horse's back.

'Thanks again,' I say, as I'm planning a rapid escape to salvage the last remnants of my self-esteem. It's all very well falling off now and then, but why did it have to go and happen in the proximity of this gorgeous, capable and well-spoken stranger? All I want to do now is get away to check my wounds.

'Anytime,' he calls over his shoulder as he rides off in the opposite direction. I notice how his horse has a loose shoe, making a double clink as its hoof touches the ground.

Now, I should have thought ahead. Rafa's coat is dark with sweat. He's in an emotional state, and looking for reassurance and safety in numbers, so why on earth would he want to leave the other horse and return to face the pigs alone? When I ask him to walk on, he refuses, and I wish I'd hung on to the hazel stick. I growl at him and flick the loop of the reins against his neck, hoping that Robbie isn't looking behind him, but he still won't budge.

There are times when I wonder if owning a horse is all it's cracked up to be, and this is one of them. Horse and rider in perfect harmony. Not.

I hear the sound of hooves and Robbie's voice behind me.

'I should have thought to offer you a lead.' He chuckles. 'Don't say there's no need for it – I'd hate to think of you standing out here all night.'

I have no choice as he walks his horse up alongside Rafa, our stirrups clashing as we move along the lane.

'I'm sorry,' I say.

'It's no problem. I was riding what we call the square, which is really more of a circle. I can go back home either way.' He pauses. 'I haven't seen you around here before. What brings you to Furzeworthy?'

'Work.' I try to get Rafa to leg-yield towards the hedge, but he's like a limpet clinging to the other horse's side.

'Are you staying at Mel's?'

'That's right. How did you guess?' When I arrived at the B&B today, Louise – my new boss's wife – told me the place was a hotbed of gossip, but I didn't imagine that news travelled this fast.

'Actually, I saw the horsebox outside when I was driving by earlier.'

I glance towards my companion. He's grinning.

'I'm the farrier who's taking on his round,' I say, smiling back.

'I see. Mel did mention that he was sorting out cover for when he goes into hospital for surgery on his back. I didn't realise you were . . .' He hesitates.

'A woman?' I finish for him.

'I don't mean to sound sexist. I'm not like that,' he says, sounding somewhat bashful. 'I'm just surprised. I don't know why, when I've had a female vet and saddler before.'

I bet you have, I think. Going on his good looks and confidence, I reckon Robbie's the type who's had many women.

'This is the first time I've come across a female farrier,' he continues.

'There aren't many of us about – not yet, anyway.'

'I hope I haven't offended you.'

'Not in the slightest. It happens all the time.' I smile again. 'In fact, the most misogynistic clients I've come across have been women, and their attitude is more down to the fact they're disappointed because I'm not some fit guy with potential, rather than that they don't trust me to shoe their horses.'

'I think you're going to have an interesting time. Not in a bad way,' he adds quickly, 'but you know what horse people are like.'

'The farrier I trained with says there are three types of personality. Type A, who are the stressy ones, type B, who are the laid-back characters, and type H, who are completely mad about their horses – the sort who always have hay in their pockets, buy nothing but corn oil and carrots at the supermarket, and spend most of their wages at the tack shop.' I pause. 'Your horse has a loose shoe, by the way.'

'I have noticed,' he says lightly. 'Mel's been finding it hard to keep up. Nelson's overdue for shoeing.'

'He's lovely. He's a Friesian, isn't he?' He's tall and well built, like a carriage horse, and about 16.2 hands high – my height, the equivalent of five foot six at the withers, the point just in front of the saddle. He has a magnificent crest to his neck and a mane that's almost as impressive as Rafa's. His veins stand out from his gleaming black skin, as if he's so full of life that it's bursting to get out.

I can hardly tear my eyes away from this double vision of masculinity, man and horse.

'Yes, the Admirable Nelson – that's his full name – is a Friesian stallion. He's amazing, the best horse I've ever had.' Robbie's voice is filled with pride and affection as he reaches down to stroke his flank. 'Yours is a Spanish horse, isn't he?'

'My parents kept an Andalusian stallion at stud.' I have fond memories of the farm – I must have been the only child at school to think that it was perfectly normal to keep bags of colostrum next to the Mini Milks in the freezer. 'They bred Rafa from one of their mares.'

'They haven't got any more, have they?'

'Sadly not. They sold up a couple of years ago. My dad's retired, although he and Mum still have contacts in Spain, if you're serious.'

'I'll bear that in mind. I'm always on the lookout for horses like him. How old is he?'

'He's thirteen now, old enough to know better,' I grimace as he tenses beneath me, having caught the scent of pig as we move closer to their field. 'He was born the day before my sixteenth birthday. I was supposed to be revising for my GCSEs, but I knew from the way the mare was dripping milk that she was about to give birth. I couldn't go downstairs because my parents were entertaining, so I climbed out of my bedroom window and down the ladder I'd taken out of the garage beforehand.'

'Did you get caught?' Robbie asks.

'They found out when I crashed their dinner party, calling for help. Dad wasn't happy that I'd risked my neck, but Mum was more concerned about the foal.' I was remembering finding him lying in the straw, still wet from the birth. He'd been born black – he hadn't started going grey until he was a couple of months old.

'I watched him stagger to his feet.' He'd had knobbly knees and his long legs had seemed out of proportion to his body. 'When he went to his mother to feed, she went for him.' I remembered that too: the way she'd pinned back her ears and bared her teeth, her eyes filled with fury, while her baby had cowered in the corner of the stable, lost, confused and distressed. I hadn't been able to stop crying.

'What did you do?'

'I fed him colostrum from a bottle and then we tried him with another mare we had. She had a foal at foot, and wouldn't entertain taking on a second mouth to feed, so I took him on. I made him a rug and fed him with milk replacer from a bucket every two hours.'

'What happened to the exams?'

'I passed. I'd never have heard the end of it if I'd failed.'

'I've been around horses all my life, but I don't have any experience of hand-rearing one. I imagine it's pretty challenging.'

'Rafa had the other foal to play with. He was cheeky, but I made sure he had respect for humans. When he tried to kick out, I used to grab his hind legs and hang on to them so he couldn't do it. He was a quick learner. I put a halter on him, brushed him, picked up his feet, and did everything to make sure he grew up with good manners.'

'So what went wrong?' Robbie laughs, before sobering up quickly. 'I'm sorry. I didn't mean to offend you by criticising your horse.'

'No offence taken,' I say, although I do feel a little hurt.

'I know what horses are like. One minute, you're on top of the world, the next you're on the floor.' Robbie stares at me – intently, covetously – and

11

I wonder what he sees in me; a woman of twenty-nine with hazel eyes, slim yet fit, with killer guns that are well defined, but still feminine . . . then I realise he's looking at Rafa.

'These two would look amazing in an arena together. Can he do any tricks?'

'I do a bit of dressage with him, if that's what you mean.' I smile to myself at my mistake.

Rafa slows his pace and comes to a stop a couple of metres from the gateway, while Nelson walks straight on past. Robbie pulls up and waits. The pigs, which have been digging in the mud around the trough, come wandering across to investigate. Rafa puts himself into rapid reverse, stops and rears up, refusing to go forwards.

Robbie trots his horse back down the lane and manoeuvres him so he's alongside Rafa and facing in the same direction. Without warning, he leans across and grabs my reins.

'Do you mind?' I exclaim, but we're already on our way past the gate, with Nelson shielding Rafa from the sight of the pigs. Robbie releases the reins, letting me take back some kind of control as Rafa breaks into a jog.

'Thanks for that,' I say, bringing him back to walk. 'I feel really stupid now. No one's done that to me since I was about ten.'

'I didn't mean to make you feel bad. My father used to do it all the time with my mounted games pony, and in front of my friends.'

'I suppose it had the desired effect,' I say ruefully, as we hack side by side along the wide grassy verge that opens out ahead of us. I change the subject, not wanting to dwell on the fact that my horse appears to have transferred his allegiance to Robbie, temporarily at least. 'Have you had Nelson long?'

'Since he was a yearling. I backed him and brought him on. He's been a star ever since. I have other horses, but he's the best. He'll do anything for me: play dead; jump through fire . . .'

'Oh?' I'm not sure whether or not to believe him.

'I'm a stunt rider, qualified, insured, and a member of Equity. My brother Dillon and I are masters of Roman and liberty riding.'

'Enlighten me. I haven't a clue what that means.'

'It's where you control a team of horses, standing on their backs and using your voice.'

'What? No reins?'

'That's right. I can manage up to twelve at once.' His eyes flash with humour as he continues, 'That's on a good day, at home, when there's no wind to get under their tails. Dillon and I usually run displays with a team of eight. We travel to some of the agricultural shows, and we're booked to perform at an international event next year. We train every day. I'll show you sometime, if you like.'

Like, I think? I'd love it.

'A stunt rider? That's amazing. It explains a lot – the shirt, for example. Are you wearing make-up?' I have to ask.

'Do you think I've overdone it?' he teases.

'It's a little weird. I'm all for guys being in touch with their feminine side, but that seems a bit much.'

'It's part of the act. A reporter for the local newspaper came out to interview me and take some pics today. The *Chronicle* is filled with stories of rescued animals and local non-events, but any publicity is good publicity as far as I'm concerned. I'm hoping the story will get picked up by the nationals, to spread the word about what we can do with our horses.'

'Have you been in any films or on TV?'

'I've been a stunt double for –' he mentions an actor that everyone, even my mother, will have heard of – 'and my brother and I have provided horses for a few TV ads and a couple of one-off dramas. It's top secret, so I probably shouldn't be telling you, but I'm talking to a production company about a contract to provide horses and riders for a TV series.'

'Don't worry. I won't say anything.'

'I'm crossing my fingers that I'll have good news soon, because we could do with the money to build up the team. We need more horses.'

'How many have you got?'

'We have nineteen between us at the moment, plus my old games pony, but we could always do with more for our various equestrian activities. We train aspiring stunt riders and run confidence-building courses. We also break and school horses for trick riding, and I'm developing the concept of horses as therapy. I volunteered at a centre in Wiltshire to see how we could offer it at our place.'

I'm swooning in the saddle. If I were in a costume drama right now, I'd be begging for the smelling salts. At last! All my life – well, since I was about sixteen and first recognised the existence of boys – I've been hoping to find a man who is as mad about horses as I am, and I think I've just found him.

I wish circumstances were different, that I hadn't sworn off men for the foreseeable future and just shown myself up as the world's worst horsewoman. I give Rafa a pat, hoping there'll be time for the shame to fade before I see Robbie again.

We pass a tub of spring daffodils and a road sign that reads 'Furzeworthy', the name of the hamlet where I'll be staying for the next three months at least.

'You'll be all right now?' Robbie stops at the gate of Wisteria House, where there's a forged-iron B&B sign hanging from the wall that hides the house from the road.

'I'm fine, thank you.' All I need is a shower and a couple of paracetamol for my bruises.

'I'll see you tomorrow then.' Robbie swings his horse around with the merest touch of the reins against his neck.

'Tomorrow?' My forehead tightens.

'Hasn't Mel told you?'

I shake my head. 'I haven't met my new boss yet, only chatted to him on the phone.'

'You're booked to fix Nelson's loose shoe,' he adds cheerfully over his shoulder as he rides away.

That's awkward, I think as I dismount. I lead Rafa on to the drive, closing the wooden gate behind him in case he has any plans to accompany Nelson. I take him past the house, a former farmhouse, built from red Devon brick with a tiled roof and freshly painted white wooden window-frames. Woody branches of wisteria run from one side of the house above the main door and along the pergola at the front.

There's a soft-top sports car and a family MPV parked along the gravel, but no sign of a farrier's van. Beyond the vehicles, there's a pair of wooden loose-boxes – one for my horse and another for his gear and my tools – and a double garage and brick extension with a horseshoe hanging upside down above the door.

I tie Rafa up outside the stables, untack and hose

him down. He stamps his feet, taking a moment to appreciate the sensation of cold water against his skin. I remove the excess with the scraper and lead him out to the field next to the stables, where he goes straight down and rolls.

Grey horse plus Devon mud equals a peculiar shade of orange.

He hauls himself up and gives himself a thorough shake. He takes a mouthful of water and dribbles it out between his whiskery lips before heading off to graze.

'I haven't shod a stunt rider's horse before.' I lean against the gate. 'How cool is that.'

'Hello, Flick. What was that?'

I turn abruptly to find Louise immediately behind me. She's wearing a wrap dress that flatters her curves, and wellies that don't do anything for her at all. I flush to the roots of my hair at being caught apparently rambling on to myself.

'Oh, nothing. I was talking to Rafa. It's a bad habit of mine.'

'Come in and have a glass of wine.' Mel's wife has a ready smile, wavy blonde hair down to her shoulders and blue eyes. She's about the same age as me, yet she's settled with a husband and son, and the B&B, while I'm no longer sure what I'm looking for, or if I'll ever find it.

'Yes, why not?' I say, thanking her.

I leave the head-collar in the stable ready for the morning, and follow her into the back of the house. We pass through the boot room where Louise leaves her wellies, and I pull off my jodhpur boots and chaps before entering a proper country kitchen with an Aga, butler sink and dresser. There's a brown ceramic hen on the windowsill and yellow curtains printed with red roosters. There's a bottle of rosé, a flagon of cider, a couple of wine glasses and a toy train on the elm table in the centre.

'So you're in one piece,' Louise says. 'I've been worried about you, coming off your horse like that.'

'How do you know?'

'Well, apart from the grass stains on your knees and the bloody lip, Robbie called – he wanted me to make sure you were all right.'

'That's kind of him.' An image of the stunt rider on his testosterone-fuelled stallion jumps into my head and lingers there.

'That's my cousin all over. He's a lovely guy. A bit of a lad, maybe, but he'd do anything for anyone.' Louise picks up the wine bottle and gestures towards the sink. 'You're welcome to wash your hands. Would you like a drink? It's way past wine o'clock,' she adds when I hesitate.

It's true. I had dinner – or what she called 'tea' – at five with Louise and her son, Ashley, a quiet boy of about seven. He didn't utter a word the whole time, which I found rather disturbing. I wasn't a shy child.

'You can have cider if you prefer, but I wouldn't recommend the local brew unless you're actively seeking a laxative effect.' Louise smiles as I run my hands under the tap. There doesn't appear to be a towel so I let them drip dry. 'Or there's a beer in the fridge. Mel likes a lager when he gets in from work.'

'A beer would be great, thanks.' I don't want a hangover tomorrow. 'Isn't Mel back yet? I was hoping to have a chat with him.'

'He dropped in for his tea before going off with his brother for a couple of pints. They'll have gone to the

Talymill Inn or the Dog and Duck in Talyton. I shouldn't wait up if I were you.' Louise fetches a bottle of lager, opens it and passes it over to me. 'Please make yourself at home.'

I pull up a chair and sit down as she pours herself a glass of wine.

'I'm so pleased you've agreed to cover for Mel while he's getting himself sorted,' she begins. 'I hate to see him dragging himself out to work when he's in such terrible pain. A bad back is an occupational hazard, but we hoped he'd get away with it for a few more years at least. He's only forty-eight, after all: a spring chicken.'

I'd hardly describe a man in his late forties as a spring chicken, I think, as she continues. 'Sometimes he wishes he'd gone into dairy farming like his brother, but he wouldn't be any good at getting up in the mornings.'

'When does he have the operation?' I ask.

'Tuesday, the day after tomorrow. He had his pre-op checks last week so he's ready to go. I think he was half hoping they'd find something wrong with his heart or liver so he had an excuse not to go ahead.'

'Tony told me that you and Mel met while he was shoeing your horse.'

Tony was my ATF, or Apprentice Training Farrier. Based in Wiltshire, he's in his early fifties, and an experienced – if not always patient – teacher. I can recall his cutting remarks whenever I put the wrong shoes in the furnace, or dropped a box of nails. It was a fun, fast-paced, and sometimes pressured environment, and I loved it. In fact, I miss being part of the gang now. There were always three or four apprentices at different stages of training, and Tony. He's a mate of Mel's, which is how I found out about this job. He put in a good word for me and here I am.

'I'm one of those horsey women who fell for their farrier.' Louise runs her fingers up and down the stem of her glass. 'Mel was still married to his first wife, but they were living separate lives – pretty much, anyway.' I wonder if she uses that excuse to justify his infidelity and her involvement in breaking up a marriage. I can see why an older man would fall for her, with her caring outlook, sense of humour, and the beauty spot on her cheek. 'Everyone said it wouldn't last, but we've been together for nine years now, and married for seven.'

'You don't have a horse now?' I ask.

'I kept my mare until Ashley turned two and things started getting difficult. I couldn't manage any longer.'

It seems a little odd, I think, because Louise seems very much like the coping kind.

'I imagine that it's pretty time-consuming, running a B&B,' I observe.

'The business does well in the summer, but it's very quiet in wintertime. My parents run a small hotel not far away from here. They're my mother's pigs – the ones that gave Rafa the heebie-jeebies. Anyway, I've had years of experience in hospitality. It fits in well with looking after Ashley – and Mel, of course.' She pauses, checking the clock on the wall before turning back to me. 'Are you married, or engaged, or seeing anyone?'

'Oh no,' I say, revealing more than I intend in the forceful tone of my voice.

She smiles wryly. 'You sound like someone who's decided to remain single, come hell or high water. What happened? You don't have to say,' she adds quickly. 'I'm sorry, I'm such a gossip.'

'No, it's fine. I can talk about it now,' but before I can go on, Ashley cries out from somewhere upstairs. Louise raises her eyes towards the ceiling as he cries again.

'I'm afraid you'll have to tell me another time. I'm going to have to sit with him for a while,' she sighs. 'You're welcome to stay here, or take your drink into the snug or your room. Help yourself to another.'

I wish her goodnight and head for my room at the front of the house, one of the three en-suites that she uses for her bed-and-breakfast business. I look out of the window where I can just make out Rafa's grey silhouette in the darkness.

Louise's questioning has brought unwelcome memories of Ryan back to the forefront of my brain. A wave of regret washes through me as I recall the good times with my ex, the cuddles, kisses and companionship . . . And then the infidelity, utter devastation, and legacy of debt that he's left me with . . . I take a deep breath, count to ten and close the curtains, determined not to waste any more emotional effort on the waste of space who was once my fiancé. I can do it. I know I can. I'm over him, but I'm not ready to move on. I'm not sure that I ever will be.

I shower and change into my PJs before retiring to bed, but I can't sleep. Tomorrow, I'll be out on the road with an anvil, tools and van in my first job as a qualified member of the Worshipful Company of Farriers. I can't help wondering if Mel's clients will be receptive to having a female farrier to shoe their horses, or if I'll struggle to prove myself. I wonder, too, having demonstrated my complete inability to control my own horse, if I'll have to work extra hard to win Robbie Salterton over.

Chapter Two

Only the Horses

I wake to the sun's rays passing between the heavy brocade curtains and the aroma of sausages and bacon. I feel as if I'm on holiday until three alarms sound from my iPad, alarm clock and watch, bringing me to reality and the realisation that it's my first day in my new job.

The adrenaline kicks in. I jump out of bed and throw on a pair of jeans and a baggy sweater. I pad barefoot downstairs, past the snug for the B&B guests that's complete with a sofa and bookshelves laden with romances and thrillers. The corridor is filled with chicken-themed ephemera, including paintings, ceramic plaques and ornaments.

When I reach the door that's open into the kitchen, I pause to listen to the fierce sizzle of frying bacon and Louise's one-sided conversation with her son. I walk on by, my stomach growling as I put on my wellies and head outside to find Rafa. There's a black Toyota Hilux parked outside the garage that wasn't there last night.

I don't think Rafa is as pleased to see me as I am to see him. When I reach the far side of the field to catch him, he lifts his head and gives me a look as if to say, 'Can't I stay out today?' I'm tempted to leave him, but his belly is round with the lush spring grass and I don't want him overdoing it. Usually, I like to have him on full-time turnout by the beginning of April, but there's too much to eat out here. The pasture is a smorgasbord of grasses and herbs.

I bring him into the stable where I give him a tiny feed and a small hay-net. I'm down to my last couple of flakes of hay, never a good feeling. Rafa digs up the bed of shavings that I made for him the night before and takes a couple of mouthfuls of hay before resting his leg and closing his eyes. I leave him to snooze, although I doubt he'll sleep much with the throbbing of a tractor muckspreading in a nearby field, the cooing of wood pigeons and cawing of rooks, and the frantic clucking of one of Louise's backyard hens that's laying an egg.

I return indoors to brush my hair and do my make-up, adding a touch of foundation with SPF, mascara and lip-gloss, before returning downstairs for breakfast. I knock at the door into the kitchen – I'm not sure if I'm supposed to order breakfast here, or wait in the dining room that's set aside for the B&B guests.

'Come on in. There's no need to knock. We don't stand on ceremony.' Louise beckons me across to the table before attending to a pan on the Aga. Ashley is sitting in front of a bowl of Rice Krispies, his head to one side, as if he's concentrating on the noise they make as he pours milk on to them from a jug. The milk wells up over the rim of the bowl, spills on to the table and trickles towards the edge.

'Ashley, you're spilling it,' I say, at which Louise turns and grabs the jug from his hand.

'You're making a mess, darling,' she says, hardly raising her voice. She hands him a spoon which he drops on the floor – deliberately, I think. I pick it up, rinse it in the sink and wipe it with a tea towel printed with chickens. I put the spoon on the table within Ashley's reach. He picks it up and starts eating his cereal without saying a word.

'Did you say thank you to Flick?' Louise says, giving me a look of apology.

He doesn't look up, even when I sit down opposite him to eat a plateful of fried potato, bacon, sausages, egg, mushroom and tomatoes.

His mum sends him off to clean his teeth and fetch his bag for school.

'You'll have to bear with him, I'm afraid. He doesn't mean to be rude.'

'It's okay,' I say, although I do feel a little confused by his behaviour. It's as if he doesn't want to know me.

'He has problems communicating and processing information, which means that he struggles with any form of social interaction. He goes to Talyton Primary where he has a Learning Support Assistant, but we're under pressure to send him to a school for children with special needs instead.' Her eyes grow glassy with tears. 'Even though the other children do their best to include him, he knows he's different. It's very hard. Mel finds it particularly difficult to accept. He's a real man's man, very sociable and hardly stops talking. You'll see when you meet him.' She looks past me. 'You made it in time for breakfast, I see. Mel, this is Flick.'

'So the cavalry's arrived.' I turn to see a thickset man, dressed in a tweed jacket over a check shirt and jeans; he's walking stiffly over to the table, his back bowed. He shakes my hand, pumping it roughly up and down. 'It's great to meet you at last. Tone's told me all about you. What's he said about me?'

'That you're a top bloke.' Those were his exact words and I don't mind repeating them. Mel seems pleased.

'We've been mates for many years. He was best man at our wedding, wasn't he, Lou.'

'I'm surprised you remember,' she says cheerfully.

'Of course I remember.' He moves around behind his wife, slides his arms around her waist and gives her a bear hug. 'Getting shackled to you was the best day of my life.'

'Sit down, you charmer,' she says, turning to kiss him on the lips.

When he straightens up to pull up a chair, his belly seems to slump over the top of his belt. His head is shaved completely bald and his skull has a pointed appearance. He has massive arms, a ruddy complexion and a Roman nose. As he sits down, Louise places a mug of coffee and a cooked breakfast in front of him.

'I thought we'd better have a quick chat before you go on the road.' He smiles, revealing two gold crowns in his upper jaw. Louise hands him a bottle of ketchup. He squeezes half of it over his food and picks up his knife and fork.

'You can use the forge whenever you like – the key's under the stone trough, right-hand end. I've entered you for the Eagle Eye class at the spring Farm and Country Festival in a few weeks, so you might want to practise. I need you to represent my business while I'm out of action, and it's a good way to make a good impression and meet new clients.'

'I've had plenty of practice making shoes,' I say, amused. 'I didn't do much else before my exam.'

'Tone said you were pretty dedicated.' He takes a huge mouthful of food and chews for a while before continuing again. 'But you did have something to prove, being one of the few females in the profession. I reckon you'll stir things up around here.'

I can't help wondering, as I watch him eat, if I'm here to give him some kind of notoriety while he's out of action.

'I've got my surgery this week. I've put it off for as long as I can, but the pain's too much to bear—'

'On some days, he can hardly move,' Louise cuts in. 'On other days, he's fit enough to walk back from the pub after a few pints with his brother. There are times, like this morning, when it's hard to feel any sympathy.'

'Heartless woman.' Mel gazes fondly at his wife. 'Thanks for driving me back to fetch the pick-up this morning.'

'You've made me late for the school run.' Louise touches his shoulder as she leaves the kitchen to go and find Ashley. 'I'll see you both later.'

'Well, Flick, we'd better make a move.' Mel stands up slowly from his chair, one fist pressed into the small of his back. He picks up a book and a mobile from the dresser and hands them over to me.

'Here's the diary and the business phone – I can't be arsed to change the number.'

'Have you got a price list?' I ask.

'It's in the back – Lou printed it out for me. It's flexible. When a client pays in kind with cider, cake, or a leg of lamb, I'll cut a fiver off the bill, but don't let anyone take the mickey. It's payment on the day – cash, not cheques, and absolutely no credit.' He pauses, his eyes on my face. 'Don't look so worried. My clients are well schooled in my ways. As time's gone on I've been able to pick and choose. I'll admit there are some oddballs, but they're okay on the whole.'

He hands me a set of keys. 'These are for the Toyota.'

'Thanks. That's great,' I say, guessing that this is the end of my induction, but he follows me outside.

'I'll give you the guided tour.' He opens the tailgate of the truck to show me the set-up in the back: the aluminium-lined workspace with drawers and gas furnace, which consists of a metal box with a door in the front of it, fuelled by a propane cylinder.

'It has twin burners,' Mel says proudly. 'I've had it for a while. I replaced the ignition system and cleaned the jets the other day. I've loaded the drawers with shoes and nails. You should find everything you need: anvil, stand, vice, trolley, etc. I've sharpened the knives.'

'Thank you.' I have brought my own tools with me, apart from an anvil.

'The front isn't this tidy.' He grins. 'I didn't get around to that. I've been too busy trying to keep on top of things. The competition horses are back in full work and everyone's making the most of the good weather and lighter evenings. I'm not complaining, though – it pays the bills.'

I tuck the mobile in my pocket and open the diary to check where I'm supposed to be going first.

'What time am I supposed to be at Eclipse?' I ask, reading Mel's handwriting. 'It doesn't say.' It also doesn't say where – or what – Eclipse is.

'Oh, that's the Saltertons' place. There isn't a time – I always get there when I get there. It's just up the road.' He waves vaguely in the direction in which Robbie rode away last night. 'All the addresses are programmed into the satnav in the front of the truck.'

He closes the tailgate while I go around to the driver's door and jump in. There's a packet of sweaty sandwiches, a couple of chocolate wrappers and several empty cola bottles in the passenger footwell. A pen dangles on the end of a piece of string tied to a diary on the dashboard, and there are crumbs on the seats.

It's pretty disgusting, but it will do. I make a plan to muck it out later.

I fasten the seatbelt, switch on the engine and satnav, and I'm ready to drive off when Mel gets in too, grunting as he slides his bulk into the passenger's side. He glances across at me, one eyebrow raised at my surprise.

'I didn't realise . . .' I stammer.

'That I was coming with you,' he finishes for me. 'It's only for today, to help you out with the navigation and introduce you to the Saltertons.'

I wonder if he can actually let go; if he's one of those people who are unable to delegate. I don't blame him for being protective of his business, but it makes me feel as if I'm on trial. He reaches out and taps the dashboard, reminding me of my old driving instructor.

'Let's go. Turn left.'

'Left?' I pull up at the gateway on to the lane as the satnav is telling me to leave the unmade road and turn right.

'You don't need to listen to that thing.' Mel reaches forwards and turns it off. 'I thought I'd show you around, so you can get your bearings.'

'You really don't have to.'

'I hate sitting around. I'm one of those people who's on the go all the time.'

I have my eyes on the road, but I can tell from his voice that he's smiling when he continues, 'It drives Lou mad.'

The gears scrunch as I change from second into third.

Mel winces.

I drive on down the lane, taking care at the blind bends and praying that we won't meet anything coming the other way.

'It's fine. We have all day,' Mel says with sarcasm. 'Tone said you were a bit flaky behind the wheel.'

I'd love to be able to abandon my new boss in the lane and tell him to make his own way but, considering it's my first day, I decide it probably isn't the best move.

'Take the right fork at the crossroads,' he goes on. 'That takes us down into town. I'll show you where to buy the best sandwiches.'

He directs me through Talyton St George, a quaint little town, where bunting flutters between the antique lampposts, and some of the streets are so narrow that there's a one-way system to cope with the traffic.

'If you stop here.' Mel points to a row of shops.

'Where?' I ask, noticing that it's all double yellow lines.

'Just here. No one will mind, not for a few minutes.'

I park in front of the baker's and we go inside, where Mel introduces me to a middle-aged woman, dressed in white, who is serving at the counter. Plump and pillowy, with a dusting of powder across her cheeks, she resembles the floured baps in the basket on the shelves of fresh bread behind her.

'This is Cathy,' Mel says.

'Hello,' she says. 'Don't let this man lead you astray.'

'Oh, I won't,' I say, not quite sure what she means.

'Don't worry. Flick is one of the lads.' Mel reaches around my shoulder and hoicks me towards him as if we're best mates. 'She's taking on my round while I'm getting my back done.'

'I'm impressed.' Cathy picks up a pencil and notepad from beside the till. 'What can I get you?'

'Chili chicken in a wholemeal baguette. Deep fill,' he says with a wink.

'That's a given where you're concerned.' Giving him a flirtatious smile, she takes his money before I give her my order of cheese and pickle sandwiches.

Mel eats his lunch on the way back.

'Have you always lived around here?' I ask.

'I was born and bred on a farm, not far from here. My family's been in the dairy business for generations. My brother stayed on at the farm while my parents gave me a pot of money to put down a deposit on the property I'm in now. It was like an advance on my inheritance. My mother's still alive and kicking, but my father died a long time ago. He had a heart attack.'

29

'I'm sorry.'

'That's another reason why I've decided to go ahead with the op. Life is short and I want to live it to the full. I want to be able to do what I want, not be stuck in a wheelchair.' Mel's voice fades and I spot the first sign of vulnerability. 'The operation isn't without risk; I'm relying on my surgeon having a steady hand,' he continues quietly. 'I'm not looking forward to tomorrow.'

We enter Furzeworthy. There are some bungalows, a terrace of cottages rendered in pastel colours, a few detached red-brick houses and a tiny church with a graveyard of mossed stones, neatly mown grass and a yew tree, and that's about it. The nearest it has to a shop is a table outside one of the residences that has a 'For Sale' sign, some jars of honey and seedlings in pots, and an honesty box on top of it.

'This is the Saltertons' place,' Mel says.

I turn left at the sign: *Eclipse Equine: Liveries, Breaking and Schooling, Horses as Therapy. R. and D. Salterton. Home of the Eclipse stunt team.* From here, there's a long drive, bordered by post and rail fencing and a beech hedge. A few hundred metres along, a cottage appears. It's picture perfect, built from cob with a roof of golden thatch, and painted pale cream. It has diamond-leaded windows set deep in its walls and a door of dark oak. In front of it is a country garden filled with spring flowers, anemones, narcissi and hyacinths, but most obvious are the cherry trees, three of them growing in the lawn and laden with pink blossom.

'Is this it?'

I can't see any stables.

'No, keep going. That's where Robbie lives with his kid,' Mel says. 'Cherry Tree Cottage.'

Robbie has a child. I don't know why my brain registers that particular piece of information, and the fact that Mel doesn't mention a 'significant other', a wife or girlfriend.

The drive continues and, eventually, a house comes into view, a country house with a ha-ha separating a manicured stretch of grass from a sweep of rugged pasture. It's white and built in the Georgian style, with a double front, sash windows and a roof of grey tiles. It reminds me of the doll's house my father bought for me one Christmas. I unpacked and arranged the furniture and the dolls, and never played with it again, but it took pride of place on a special shelf in my bedroom.

I slow right down. The house stands slightly higher than the surroundings, with green hills behind it and views of the countryside, sweeping down to a wood and dropping away towards the Taly valley in the distance.

'It's pretty breathtaking, isn't it?' Mel says. 'The estate has belonged to the Saltertons since they made their fortune in shipbuilding a couple of centuries ago. They were loaded back then, but now they're asset-rich and cash-poor, and muddling along like the rest of us.'

'I don't think I'd care if I was lucky enough to live here.' The house is magnificent, but the cottage would be my dream home if I was given the choice. I've always wanted somewhere that's cute and quirky with oak beams, a wood-burning stove and a paddock for Rafa. One day . . .

'Carry on past the house and take the turning immediately beyond it. Neil – that's Robbie and Dillon's father – and Sally Ann, his wife, live in the big house.'

'Slow down a minute. All these names and relationships are a lot to take in.'

'Robbie's brother, Dillon, lives in the cider house, one of the converted barns,' Mel continues. 'Neil's tried his hand at keeping deer and ostriches, but the horses won out. The boys were stars in the Pony Club. They moved on from being key players in the mounted games team and tetrathlon to performing tricks and creating their own stunts. The rest is history.

'Neil keeps beef cattle and rents out some of the land to a local farmer, as well as overseeing the equestrian operation. Sally Ann looks after the holiday accommodation – they have several chalets scattered throughout the park – and she organises the displays and training sessions for the team. She also keeps the diary for the courses they run for anyone who wants to have a go at being a stunt rider.'

'It's quite an empire then.' My fingers tighten on the wheel as I suppress a twinge of regret and envy that Robbie's family are involved and supportive of each other, while mine has been fractured by the choices I've made and my parents' stubborn refusal to back down on their prejudices. I can hear my mother now, expressing her disappointment when I told her I was giving up my well-paid job in sales and marketing to learn how to shoe horses.

Don't come running to us when it all goes pear-shaped, when you're fed up with working in the mud and freezing rain, and your back's killing you. After all we've done for you, paying for the best education and supporting you through your degree, this is how you show your appreciation.

'Did you ever ride or have your own horse?' I ask Mel.

'No way. I had a go, but it wasn't for me. I spent my time driving tractors and running Talyton St George's YFC. The Young Farmers' Club,' he adds in explanation. 'It was a great way of meeting lots of single ladies. I broke a few hearts along the way, but some of them remain good friends of mine, especially the horsey ones who use me as their farrier.'

I'm uncomfortable listening to Mel brag about being a heartbreaker in his youth when he's old and married, but I have a feeling that his local knowledge is going to be more of a help than a hindrance. All I have to do now is to forge relationships with his clients and prove that I can shoe horses as well as anyone.

Chapter Three

New Shoes

I pull into the turning behind the house to find two massive dogs running out towards the Toyota. I brake and toot the horn. The grey rough-coated creatures stand in front of the bonnet with their mouths wide open, as if they're smiling.

'What now?' I look towards Mel for guidance as they wave their long tails.

'Don't worry about them. They'll get out of the way. Drive on.'

'I don't want to run them over.' It wouldn't exactly be a good start. I open the window and wave at them. 'Go away. Shoo!'

One of them walks along the side of the vehicle and stops to cock its leg up the wheel.

Mel leans across me.

'Robster, get your hounds under control, will you?' he bellows.

A figure moves out of the shadow of the overhang above the nearest block of stables that form one side of the yard. There are more stables and outbuildings through the gateway beyond. It's Robbie, without his hat this time. He has brown wavy hair, short at the sides and long on the top, and he's wearing a close-fitting grey T-shirt and stonewashed jeans that emphasise his broad shoulders and narrow hips. He strolls towards us with long easy strides, stopping beside the truck, where he stops and gazes at me, fixing me with his deep blue eyes.

Close mouth, I tell myself as a fly buzzes around my head.

'I'm sorry about the dogs. They wouldn't hurt anyone.' He calls them. 'Badger, Tatt, here.' They amble towards him and stand one at each side of their master. 'You know that, Mel,' he adds, glancing past me.

'I've been wary of dogs since I almost got bitten in the nuts,' Mel says crudely. 'That's one big advantage of being a female farrier.'

'If you're trying to say I have no balls, then you're wrong,' I say lightly.

'Ha ha, she's quicker than you,' Robbie says, smiling.

'So she should be. She spent three years at university, only to change her mind and become a lowly apprentice with one of my mates.'

'Drive on through and park anywhere you like.' Robbie points towards the gateway into the next yard, where I stop the truck alongside another more modern block of looseboxes made from breezeblock and clad with timber. There's a barn filled with bales of hay opposite, a pathway leading to the fields and paddocks beyond, and a larger-than-average arena with a rubber and sand surface.

I suppress a wave of 'yard envy', an affliction suffered

only by horse owners, as I get out of the truck and admire the facilities: plenty of rings for tying up, a dedicated wash-down area and floodlights. I open the tailgate, slip into my leather apron and lift out the anvil and trolley, setting up while Mel looks on and Robbie fetches his horse.

'Nelson's for new shoes all round.' He ties him to the baler-twine loop on a ring in the wall beside the nearest loosebox. 'How is that crazy horse of yours?'

'He's fine. It's me who's traumatised.'

'What else have we got this morning?' Mel asks.

'Scout – that's my brother's horse,' Robbie explains for my benefit. 'And then there's T-rex, but he's for a trim, that's all.'

'It's your lucky day, Flick,' Mel says. 'T-rex is a real sweetheart.'

'Do I detect some sarcasm in your voice?' I ask, relieved that I don't have to do all the Saltertons' horses at once. When I was working for Tony, he had a team of apprentices at different stages of training, so we could get through many sets of shoes in a day. It's a lot slower when there's only one of you.

'T-rex is your typical naughty pony,' Robbie says.

'So why is he named after a monster?' Mel jokes. At least, I hope he's joking.

'Is tea all right for everyone?' Robbie asks. 'Mum's got the kettle on.'

'That's good for me,' I say.

'Sugar, or are you sweet enough already?' Mel says.

'I'm more than sweet enough, thank you,' I say firmly, making it clear from the start that I'm not going to put up with any nonsense.

I turn my attention to Nelson, making a quick assessment of his general health and temperament.

Silky feather grows down from his fetlocks to partially cover his dark grey, almost black hooves. He looks well and he seems calm, the expression in his dark brown eyes bright with intelligence – but stallions can be unpredictable, so I treat him with extra respect.

I wonder if Robbie might want to get on with something else, but he stays, chatting with me and Mel. A few minutes later, an older version of Robbie, not quite as tall and with shorter hair that's greying at the temples, joins us with a tray of tea and biscuits. He places it on the roof of the Toyota, out of reach of the dogs, who are waiting for me to make a start.

Mel introduces me to Neil, Robbie's father.

'I never thought I'd see the day.' He removes his rimless specs and wipes them with a handkerchief from the pocket of his pale cotton trousers, before putting them back on so he can get a better look at me. 'I'm not sure this is a good idea. Women shouldn't be shoeing horses – it's dangerous. I'd hate to think that one of our horses had hurt someone.'

'Give her a chance,' Mel says. 'She knows her stuff.'

'Excuse me,' I say, speaking up. 'I am here.' A certain amount of curiosity is acceptable, whereas blatant sexism isn't. I still find it weird that when I was working in an office environment after my degree, there were all kinds of rules as to what constituted sexism and sexual harassment, but when I was out and about with Tony and the male apprentices, demeaning and lewd comments were encouraged – and the smuttier the better.

Robbie glares at his father. 'There's no need to look at Flick as if she's an alien. Women can do anything

37

they choose nowadays – you know that. I trust Mel's judgement.'

'It wasn't my intention to offend, but if I have . . .' Neil is well-spoken and in his fifties. His fraying blue and white striped shirt appears to be from the same era. Smiling apologetically, he reaches out for my hand.

'I find your opinion patronising, but I'll forgive you.' We shake hands. 'You men are all the same.'

'We're what?' Neil says, his eyes narrowing to slits.

'She's winding you up, Dad,' Robbie says.

'Oh, I see.'

'I think we've all been guilty of sexism at one time or another.'

'I've been harassed many a time,' Mel says. 'When I was an apprentice, a lady owner slapped me across the rump for walking behind her horse without letting it know I was there.'

I can't help smiling. I've been guilty of harassment on a small scale too. When I was in my teens, we had two farriers. I classed the boss as ancient – as in, about the same age as my father. His assistant was in his twenties, shy and handsome, and I used to fancy the chaps off him. He used to drink every mug of tea that I brought him until he must have been brimming over. My mum took every opportunity to put him down – he wasn't good enough for me because he was 'only a blacksmith'. I was destined for Maximilian, who played polo; even though, as I pointed out to her, he was clearly gay.

Robbie turns to me. 'What made you want to shoe horses anyway?'

'One of my first memories is the sound of the farrier on my parents' farm.' I recall the clank and hiss of hot horseshoes being dropped into water to cool, and the tapping of nails being hammered into the horses' hooves. 'When I realised I was going to die of boredom working in the corporate world of sales and marketing, those memories returned. From then on, I didn't want to do anything else. I resigned from my job, applied for a pre-farriery course and never looked back.' I pause. 'I'd better get on.'

'Yeah, sure. Go ahead.'

I approach Nelson and give him a pat. I pick up his forefoot and start to remove the shoe. It sounds painful to the uninitiated, but it's attached via bevelled nails, usually seven of them, to the wall of the hoof, where there are no nerves or blood vessels. This means that there's no blood involved and no pain for the horse. To keep the shoe on, the end of the nail that sticks out through the hoof is folded over. This is called a clench.

I use a hammer and a tool called a buffer to raise and cut the clenches, then when all the nails are straight, I grab the pincers to grip the shoe and gradually lever it off, starting from the heels and working round to the toe. Nelson is totally cool about it and stands like a rock.

As I work, I become aware that I'm being watched intently by Mel, Robbie and his father, and a fourth man.

I reach round to check that my jeans are belted snugly around my hips. No bum crack. I glance down at my chest, glad that I wore a polo shirt not a vest, so there's nothing to see there either.

As I'm bowed over, Robbie introduces his brother, Dillon. I glance up. He's fair-haired, blue-eyed, and a couple of years younger, and he's wearing a bottle-green shirt, black jodhpurs and long black riding boots.

'Hello, Flick. It's nice to meet you.' He's good-looking, but not as beautiful as Robbie. 'Can I trust you with my horse?'

'Of course you can,' Robbie says, sounding slightly offended on my behalf. 'I'm sorry about my family.'

'I know what it's like, having a horse of my own. You want the best people,' I say. 'It's all right. I've done my time – four years and two months, to be precise.'

'When did you qualify?' Dillon asks.

'Earlier this year.' I'm trying not to giggle because Nelson is nibbling at my clothes. I can feel him chewing at the belt on my leather apron and pulling up my top to reveal my loins. I let his foot down and straighten up. I give Mel a look, daring him to comment, but he merely nods with approval.

I move on to trim Nelson's hooves, which have grown just like human fingernails since the last time he was shod. Using the nippers I cut away clippings of horn, which the dogs fight over. Robbie intervenes, making sure Badger and Tatt each have a share to chew on.

Farriery is hard on the hands as well as the back, and when I said there was no blood involved, I meant from the horse's perspective, because when I'm preparing Nelson's fourth and last foot with the drawing knife, I manage to catch my finger. Blood pours from the wound and drips on to the concrete. In an attempt to downplay my self-inflicted injury, I scurry to the pick-up, grab a plaster from the first-aid kit in the glove compartment, and wrap it around my finger to stem the flow.

'Are you okay?' Mel asks as I return to pick up the hoof knife from the trolley. The horse shifts his bum round. Robbie pushes him back.

'It's just a surface wound.' I grimace.

'You're bleeding through the plaster,' Neil observes. 'Does that need a stitch?'

No way, I think, feeling like a complete idiot.

'It's fine,' I insist, as the plaster starts to peel away – the glue seems to have suffered from the heat.

I hear a roar as Mel starts up the furnace, followed by the chink of horseshoes. It's like a branch of Clarks in the back of the truck, with a range of prefabricated shoes of different sizes to choose from. He selects a new set in Nelson's size and puts them in the fire to heat up.

'I'll get you a fresh one,' Robbie offers, and before I can say it isn't necessary, he strides away and disappears into the first yard before returning a few minutes later. 'Allow me.'

I remove the original plaster and watch him apply another, much larger one with a cartoon printed on it, to my finger.

'Thank you,' I say, amused.

'I thought that Peppa Pig would make you feel better,' he says, and I do indeed feel a remarkable improvement in my condition, but it has more to do with his close and personal attention than a cartoon pig. 'You'd better not let Rafa see it,' he adds with a grin.

'Hey, give it a rest.' I laugh and give him a gentle push, my hand on his arm.

I fetch out one of the shoes from the orange heart of the furnace, carrying it away on the pritchel, a tool with a pointed end that fits into one of the nail holes.

I pick up Nelson's front foot and apply the shoe to the weight-bearing surface of the hoof to check the fit, triggering a series of crackles and a flurry of sulphurous smoke. I put the shoe down on the concrete and rasp away any bumps to make a flat surface for the shoe. When I'm happy, having given the shoe a couple of knocks with the hammer around the anvil (I'm being ultra-careful in front of my critical audience), I drop it into the bucket of water that Robbie brings.

The dogs try to drink from it.

'They're big dogs,' I observe.

'Irish wolfhounds,' Robbie says.

'Robbie had this big idea they'd be part of the stunt team,' Dillon says.

'It didn't quite work out though, did it?' Neil says.

'It turns out that I'm good with horses, but not dogs,' Robbie says. 'Not these two, anyway. As soon as you put them in an arena, they lose their heads. The only time we tried it was at the first show of last year, and I had to pay out a small fortune in compensation—'

'I think it was me who paid those bills,' Neil cuts in with a chuckle.

'What were they for?' I ask, wondering if Mel was right to be circumspect, and picturing a crowd of people with their limbs torn and bleeding after an onslaught by wolfhound.

'Several ice creams, three burgers and a picnic,' Robbie says.

'And a bottle of Bolly that they allegedly had over,' Neil grumbles lightly. 'If they ever go into the ring now, they're on leads.'

I fit the cooled shoe, hammering in the nails one by

one, then twisting the ends off and bending them over
with clenching tongs. Nelson starts to fidget towards
the end of the process – I'm not sure if he's uncomfortable or bored. Only when all four shoes are back on
do I tidy the clenches. With the horse's foot resting
on the tripod so I have both hands free, I rasp down
any sharp edges, along with the hoof wall where it
meets the shoe, to reduce the chance of cracks. Finally,
I tap the clips into place.

'Done,' I say happily.

'Thanks.' Robbie unties Nelson. 'Now I can take
him out to play. I'm going to school him for half an
hour. Why don't you fetch Scout, instead of standing there gawping, little brother?' He leads Nelson
away.

Neil and Mel hang around with Dillon, chatting
about business, horses and mutual acquaintances,
while I shoe Scout. Just as I'm finishing off, Robbie
reappears, accompanied by a young woman who's
leading a small dark brown pony with a sway back,
bony rump and flecks of grey around the eyes.

'Flick, this is Kerry.' Robbie introduces us. She's in
her early to mid-twenties – it's hard to tell because
she has a slightly weather-beaten look from long
hours working outdoors; but she's feminine and nat-
urally pretty, with a heart-shaped face, strong
cheekbones and long blonde hair tied back in a loose
ponytail. She's wearing a navy sweatshirt, purple
check jodhpurs and brown leather boots.

'She's our head groom,' says Neil.

'Your only groom, I think you mean,' she counters
as she ties the pony up.

'And quite a babe,' Mel says. 'Easily winner of Rear
of the Year.'

She smiles in a way that suggests she is quite used to his chat.

'She keeps us in order,' Dillon says.

'You mean she cracks the whip,' Mel cuts in.

She rolls her eyes at me.

'I get this all the time. They're so immature.'

'This is T-rex,' Robbie says. 'He's my first pony. He's in his thirties. He used to be able to clear over three feet with ease, and always came home with loads of rosettes. Unfortunately, he's a bit much for my daughter. Maisie's seven and nowhere near strong enough to handle him. She wants to ride off the lead rein, but I don't trust him to look after her.'

I'm not sure what to say. This is an area where we have nothing in common. I select a hoof knife, pick up the pony's foot and trim back his toe. He has tough little feet and I bet he's never needed shoes. As I pick up the other front foot, he fidgets, trying to pull away. I hang on quietly, knowing that once I let him go, he'll realise that he can get away with it. He goes up and down again, twisting my back as I take his weight. Robbie tells him off.

'Show him the rasp,' Mel says. 'Don't stand for any of that nonsense.'

I prefer to work cooperatively, so I wait for T-rex to settle, keeping hold of his foot. When he does quieten down, he realises that it isn't worth fighting and lets me trim and rasp his feet without further incident. I glance across at Mel, who's walking away with Neil, and I can't help wondering if telling me the pony was going to be really naughty was a wind-up.

Kerry is talking to Robbie, one hand on his arm. I hear him ask her to get Dillon to help her bring in some of the horses while he waits for me to finish with T-rex.

'I'll catch up with you in a minute,' he adds when she hesitates. It's enough to arouse my suspicion that their relationship might be more than that of professional rider and his groom, and my reaction – the briefest stab of disappointment – is enough to make me realise that I mind, even though I really shouldn't. I hardly know him.

'T-rex's had his pedicure,' I say. 'All done.'

'I'll take him back to his stable,' Robbie says. 'Thanks, Flick. By the way, that lot don't usually hang around when the farrier's here.'

'The novelty will have worn off by the next time, I hope.' I change the subject before he disappears. 'I don't know if you can help, but I'm looking to buy a few bales of hay.'

'Yes, of course. We still have tons of the stuff from the winter. How much do you want?'

'Ten would be great,' I say, thinking that I can store them in the spare loosebox at Mel's.

Robbie names a fair price.

'It's a bit cheeky of me, but could you deliver them too?'

'If you come and help me load the trailer –' a smile plays on his lips – 'and buy me a drink sometime.'

'Of course. Thanks, that's great.'

'I have a meeting tomorrow afternoon, but I'm free in the evening. Drop by at six.'

'I'll see you then.' I watch him lead the pony away before I return the anvil and trolley to the truck, and wait a few minutes for Mel to return so we can set out for the next yard.

We visit two more establishments, one north of a place called Talyford where I do two sets of refits. The shoes aren't worn, so I remove them, trim the hooves and put them back on until next time – six to eight weeks later, as long as the horse isn't doing too much road work. At the next and final yard, I replace a couple of sets of fronts – some horses can get away without shoes on the back.

On the way back to Furzeworthy, Mel talks about horses he has shod and the people he's met. He can talk for England, and I find myself switching off as I drive back through the lanes with a smile on my face because I'm going to see Robbie again tomorrow night.

'Flick, did you hear that?' he says, interrupting my thoughts. 'Are you listening to me?'

'I'm sorry,' I mumble. 'I was somewhere else.'

'I was asking you what you're planning to do after you've done this stint for me.'

'I thought you knew – I told you about my plans when I spoke to you on the phone. I'm going to buy a van and kit it out as a mobile forge so I can get my own round up and running.'

'Not here though,' he says sharply. 'Not on my patch.'

'I wouldn't dream of it.' I pause. 'Well, I might dream of it, but I wouldn't do it. I'm already on the lookout for an area where there's a shortage of farriers, perhaps due to retirement, for example.'

'I'm not going to retire in a hurry. I can't afford to. The doc says this op gives me a fair chance for a full recovery.' Mel falls silent and I glance across to check he's still alive. My new boss is big and loud, but he's also scared. 'I'd miss it if someone told me I could never do it again,' he says eventually. 'That's shoeing, not sha—'

'Okay, I get the idea,' I interrupt.

'I'm sorry. Remind me to mind my tongue.' He changes the subject. 'Do you fancy a beer on the way home?'

'I'm all right, thanks. I really should get back for Rafa.' I hope I haven't offended him by turning down his invitation.

'I'd forgotten you were one of those mad horse owners I see every day. Another time.' He's smiling. 'I expect Lou will have some chores for me to do. She wants everything done before I go into hospital. That's what marriage is all about, I suppose: penance.'

'I don't follow.' When I was going to marry Ryan, it was going to be the best day of my life, the start of a wonderful existence with my best friend, lover and – I can't quite bring myself to add 'soulmate', because he so obviously wasn't. Looking back, it was Sarah, my BFF, who was my confidante while I was with him. I feel a little guilty now. She had a lot to put up with.

'You'll find out when you get hitched,' Mel sighs.

I don't think there's much chance of that now, I muse. I can't imagine letting myself get that close to anyone again. In my experience, dating only leads to disappointment.

On our return to Wisteria House, I turn Rafa out and muck out the stable. I straighten his bed and sweep up outside ready for the morning. I notice that Ashley is watching. I offer him the broom. He shakes his head. I don't push it.

After a shower, I go down for dinner in the kitchen, where Louise dishes up ham, parsley sauce, peas and potatoes.

'I ate with Ashley,' she says. 'I hear you had a good day out with Mel.'

'It was great,' I say, sitting down at the table.

'What did you think of the Saltertons? Mel said you had quite a reception.'

'They're an interesting family.' I'm not sure how to go on. 'I didn't know Robbie had a daughter . . .'

'Oh yes, it's very sad. Maisie lost her mum.' Louise shakes her head very slowly. 'Carla and Robbie were teenage sweethearts. They were together for a few years until Carla fell pregnant – there was some kind of trouble from her parents over the pregnancy that made them split up. Carla died giving birth to Maisie. It was terribly sad. Tragic. She was young and so looking forward to being a mum.' Louise pulls a tissue from a box on the dresser and dabs at her eyes. 'It still gets to me. We were pregnant at the same time. Maisie was born a couple of months before Ash. She never knew her mother.'

She glances towards the back door, which is open on to the garden, where Ashley is playing with a toy digger in one of the flowerbeds. 'I won't say any more now. I don't want to worry him when his daddy is about to go into hospital. Anyway, Robbie's had to step up and he's been amazing, the best father anyone could wish for.'

I don't know what to say. Poor Maisie. Poor Robbie. It puts my problems into perspective.

'He deserves to be happy after what he's been through, and there's nothing I'd like more than to see him find love again, but I'm not sure that he will. He's never short of female attention, but he never stays with anyone for very long. I don't know if it's because he's stuck thinking that there's no one in the world who can match Carla, or if he's simply not met the right person.'

'I got the impression he and Kerry were close.'

'If they are, Robbie's keeping it very quiet.'

A doorbell jangles in the distance.

'I'd better get that. I'm expecting guests, so you'll have neighbours on your landing tonight. See you later.' She bustles away, leaving me with my dinner and my reflections on my first day at work. I gaze down at the Peppa Pig plaster that's peeling away from my finger, and my thoughts return to Robbie and a little girl who's lost her mother, which makes me wonder how I'd feel if someone called me to say mine had passed away when I hadn't spoken to her for weeks.

I pick up the business phone – I need to get mine repaired somehow – and call my parents.

'To what do we owe this honour?' my mum says sarcastically when she realises that it's me.

'I wanted to say hi and see how you and Dad were, and let you know that I'm okay.'

'That's nice, I suppose. How's Rafa?'

'He's settled into his temporary home.' The conversation is stilted and I'm not sure what else to say. 'He bucked me off yesterday. How's Dad?'

'You can ask him yourself. Here he is.' There's a crackling sound as she hands over the phone. 'It's Felicity.'

'Hello, how are you, stranger?' My father's voice is filled with warmth, making me feel guilty for not keeping in touch. 'Is everything all right?'

'All's well. I'm shoeing horses in a little place called Furzeworthy in Devon.'

'You're happy?'

'Very.'

'Well, you know how your mother feels about that.'

'I know, but I don't want to argue about it any more. I've made my choice and it's the right one for me. How are you, anyway?'

'So-so,' he says. 'The knees are playing up, but I can get about. Your mum and I are staying at the villa for a while.'

'I didn't know you were away.'

'You only have to ask.' His tone is sad rather than critical. 'You're more than welcome to visit us in sunny Spain.'

'I'd like to, but I can't at the moment—'

'Your job,' he cuts in.

'That's right. I'm covering for another farrier while he's in hospital having surgery.'

'Never mind. We understand that you're busy. Keep in touch, won't you? None of us are getting any younger.'

I wish him goodnight and cut the call, glad that I got in contact with them and wishing that we could return to a time when we had an easier relationship and I was their golden girl, but that can't happen. I can't rewind the clock.

Chapter Four

Irons in the Fire

I'm on my own today. It's a great feeling, not having Mel looking critically over my shoulder or having to listen to his incessant chat. I've mucked out the truck, and installed an air freshener. I have a packed lunch – Louise offered me a good deal, much cheaper than the bakery in town – and I can relax knowing that, by the end of the day, I'll have a stack of hay for Rafa.

Even though I have no intention of getting involved with anyone while I'm here, I'm looking forward to seeing Robbie again. Not only is he easy on the eye, but I think we could be friends.

With the address for Nethercott Farm programmed into the satnav, I head south on the road signposted to the coast. At the top of the hill, I catch a glimpse of the sea glittering in the morning sunshine, confirming that I am going in the right direction. (Having been sent down a lane in the dark and straight into a flood that wrecked the engine in Tony's van when I was an apprentice, I have an inherent distrust of satnavs.)

When I arrive at the farm, I have to get through the

gate into the yard and past a white Range Rover while an old fawn goat tries to get out, so I'm already stressed when I meet the horse owner, who is positively hostile.

'You aren't Mel.' Her hair is thick and glossy, her make-up more evening than daytime, and her cropped top shows off her tanned stomach and a jewelled blue piercing. She's older than me, in her late thirties or early forties.

'I'm Flick,' I say cheerfully. 'You must be Gina.'

'I was expecting Mel.'

I notice her looking down at my plaster, a blue one that Louise gave me to replace Peppa Pig. I hide it behind my back.

'He promised me he'd fit me in before his op,' she continues.

'He's having his surgery today.'

'I don't understand why he didn't tell me.' She shakes her head. 'I'm really not sure about this.'

'Do you want me to shoe your horse or not?' I ask.

'Obviously, my horse needs to be shod. He's a TB and has very sensitive feet.'

I sigh inwardly. From my experience, thoroughbreds are sensitive in every respect.

'Mel's a miracle-worker, the only farrier who's been able to keep shoes on him for more than five weeks.' She pauses, making her decision. 'I'll go and get him.'

She brings a chestnut gelding out of the loosebox in the corner of the farmyard and holds on to him.

'He hates being tied up. The first time I had him shod, he pulled back and the side of the stable came down. He was petrified – it made him ten times worse.'

'I'm not surprised. What's his name?'

'Rambo. He's an ex-racehorse.' She gazes at him adoringly. 'He only ran three times. He won once, was placed twice, and then he decided he didn't like racing – he didn't even get out of the stalls. My husband was part of a syndicate who bought him as an investment. Their loss is my gain.' She smiles. 'I'm retraining him to jump. He's going really well now.'

I look at Rambo's feet. He's flat-footed with low heels and it's a challenge to remove his existing shoes without damaging his crumbly hooves, but I get a new set on and Gina seems pleased with the result. Crossing my fingers that they'll stay on until my next visit, I pack the tools and anvil away while she returns the horse to the stable.

'I'll get the gate for you,' she says, reappearing.

'You mean the goat?' I say, but she doesn't seem to have a sense of humour. I open the diary to look at the price list. 'That will be . . .' I name the figure.

'Oh no, you've got that wrong.'

'It says here.' I run my finger along the line to show her.

She looks at me. 'Mel and I have an arrangement.'

'He's told me that everyone knows that it's cash on the day.'

'No, I said Mel and I have an *arrangement*.' She emphasises the word to make it clear that she isn't referring to money. I guess she's talking about payment in kind, but what kind?

'Look, I'll call him.'

'You can't. He's at the hospital and I have his business mobile.'

'I have his private number.' She takes her mobile out of the back pocket of her jeans. 'Give me a minute.'

She walks away until she's out of earshot. I stroke the goat until she comes back and hands the phone to me.

'Hi Flick,' Mel says.

'I'm sorry about this—'

'Oh, don't worry about that. I'm still waiting to go into theatre,' he cuts in. 'Gina is one of my specials.'

'She says you have an arrangement.'

'That's right,' he says smoothly. 'She's set up a bank transfer so it's fine. All under control. How is Rambo?'

'Okay, thanks.' My brain is racing. If they had set up a bank transfer, why didn't Gina just say so? Equally, why didn't Mel? 'Good luck,' I add.

'I'll see you in a few days.'

'Cheers,' I say, handing back the phone.

'Mel,' Gina says. 'Mel? Oh, he's gone.' She looks at me. 'Happy now?'

I nod. Happy, yes, but not satisfied that I really understand what's going on.

I say goodbye and repeat the game with the old goat at the gate while Gina looks on. Once outside, I reset the satnav for my next destination, where I shoe two ponies at a private house. On my way back towards Talyton St George, there's a call on the hands-free.

'Hi,' I say.

'Hello?' says a man's voice. 'Can I speak to Mel?'

'I'm afraid he's had to take some time off.'

'He didn't mention it last time I saw him.'

'He was supposed to have notified all his clients.'

'Oh well, I don't think admin is one of Mel's strengths,' the man says with humour. 'Do you happen to know who's covering his round?'

'Yes, I am.'

'You?' It's his turn to apologise. 'I thought you were

one of Mel's friends answering his phone. I'm Jack, Animal Welfare Officer for this area. I've picked up a pony abandoned in a field over at Bottom End and I'm taking him to the Sanctuary. I wondered if you could drop by ASAP to look at his feet. His hooves are so overgrown the poor thing can hardly walk.'

'I can be there within the hour.'

I'm going to drop into town to send my mobile away for repair, and pick up some cash from the hole in the wall to pay for the hay for tonight and, in spite of my straitened circumstances, treat myself to a cream tea at the Copper Kettle, the teashop in Talyton St George first. It's a bit early in the day for scones, clotted cream and strawberry jam, but working outdoors gives me an appetite.

'That's great,' Jack says. 'See you later.'

The call cuts out and I realise I've forgotten to ask him for the address.

When I'm in town, I find the postcode in the back of the diary and head to the Sanctuary. I follow a narrow lane, which peters out into a long gravelled track where the hedgerows press in on either side. At the end, there's a gate. I open it and enter, parking in front of a bungalow that's surrounded by tubs of tulips in bud.

I slide out of the driver's side of the truck, but before I can follow the sign that reads 'Visitors this way', a woman emerges from the bungalow. She's carrying a baby on her hip and I'm guessing from the blue dungarees and khaki sunhat that he's a boy. I'm not sure how old he is – a year, eighteen months, maybe. I'm no good at babies.

'Hi, you must be Flick. I'm Tessa, Jack's wife. I'm the manager here.' The woman tucks a stray lock of wavy, almost black hair behind her ear. The baby turns away from me and rests his head against her breast. 'Oliver, don't be shy.' She smiles warmly. 'He'll be all right in a few minutes.' He starts to cry. She puts her hand in the pocket of her overalls and pulls out a soother, pops it into her mouth and then the baby's. Silence prevails. 'Jack wanted to be here to meet you, but he's been called out to a car fire – nothing major.'

'He's a busy man,' I say, noticing that Tessa appears to have another baby on the way.

'He's a part-time firefighter. He's always on the go.' She pauses. 'I'll take you to see the pony. The vet's on his way to look at him too. Oh, here he is now. That's his car.'

The vet parks his silver four-by-four alongside Mel's truck. He jumps out and greets us with a brief smile. About thirty-five years old and five foot ten, he has a rugged appearance with short brown hair, hazel eyes and a square jaw. He wears a check shirt and grey moleskin trousers and carries a stethoscope tucked into his breast pocket.

'Hello Tessa, and . . .'

'Flick.' I hold out my hand. 'I'm the farrier.'

'Ah yes – Mel told me you were covering for him. How's it going?'

'Okay so far, thank you.' I hesitate, wondering if he's going to introduce himself. 'I didn't catch your name.'

'I'm Matt Warren from Westleigh Equine. Where's this pony?' he goes on. 'I'm sorry to rush you both, but I have to get back for one of the horses at the clinic.'

'He's this way,' Tessa says, and we follow her past

a kennel block and cattery to the far end of a barn, where there's a small lean-to stable. She stands back with the baby while the vet and I peer over the door. 'Jack says, please can you give us some idea of his age and breed, and check for a microchip. There's a head-collar on the hook. We had to take the one he was wearing off – it's left a wound across his nose.'

I take the head-collar and walk into the stable, where a chestnut pony with wary brown eyes, a white blaze down his face, patches of white where the saddle would sit if he had one on, and one white foot at the back is pulling strands of hay like spaghetti from the net hanging from the ring in the wall.

'Hello, boy,' I say quietly, my chest tightening when I notice the band of raw flesh around his nose. I buckle the head-collar around his neck and lead him over to the door.

'Bring him outside where the light's better,' Matt says.

I rub behind the pony's ears as I encourage him into the sunlight. He must be about 13.2 hands high – I can reach comfortably around his shoulders. His hooves are so overgrown that they remind me of Aladdin's slippers. I stand him just a few steps away from the stable door for Matt to have a look at him first. His ribs are visible and his coat is thick for the time of year and like a bear's.

The pony is happy for the vet to scan him for a microchip: there isn't one. He's reasonably cheerful about having his wounds examined and treated, and his girth measured so Matt can make a rough calculation of his weight, and fairly chilled about having his heart listened to, but before I can tie him up to look at his feet, he decides he's had enough. He tosses his head, kicks up his heels and canters off towards the paddock, with me in tow. As we reach the fence, he drops his head and tears at the grass, as if he hasn't eaten for a month.

'I couldn't stop him,' I say, trying to catch my breath as I check my hands for rope burn and drag him back.

'It's always the quiet ones,' Matt says. 'Has he some ID I can use when I'm writing my report? What shall I put? Chestnut pony?'

'He needs a name,' Tessa says.

'What about Blaze?' Matt suggests.

'I was thinking Paddington because he reminds me of a bear,' I contribute.

'That's a great idea,' Tessa agrees.

'Paddington it is then,' Matt says. 'What are Jack's plans for him?'

'If he can trace the owner, which is unlikely because he hasn't had any luck so far, he'll pursue a prosecution. The pony will stay here until he's ready for rehoming.'

'We'll see what happens then. I'm sorry to rush off like this. It's good to meet you, Flick.' Matt leaves as I fetch my knife, nippers and rasp.

'Don't let me hold you up,' I say to Tessa, who's waiting.

'If you're sure.' The baby has settled. He smiles at me and the soother drops out of his mouth. Tessa catches it before it reaches the ground. 'I've got pretty good reflexes now. There'll be hell to pay if he can't have it back.' Smiling, she pops it straight back into his mouth. 'Thanks for coming out to us today. I expect we'll be seeing you again at some stage, not that we take in many horses here. If ever you want a couple of rabbits or guinea pigs, or a dog, we're in-undated at the moment.'

'I'd like a dog one day, but I already have a horse and he takes up most of my spare time.' I put Paddington's foot back down and straighten up, rubbing the painful knots from the muscles in my back. 'I'll put him away when I'm done.'

When I've finished trimming his feet, I lead him into the stable, where he returns to his hay-net. He's a sweet pony, I think, and I can't help wondering what kind of life he's led, and what brought him to this.

By the time I get back to Furzeworthy, it's gone six, but Robbie doesn't seem to mind me turning up late. Dressed in a navy T-shirt, jeans and short boots, he waves when I arrive at the yard behind the house.

He's with Kerry and a bay mare of similar build to Nelson. Her coat gleams like a conker freshly split from the shell, and the tips of her ears, her knees and hocks, mane and tail are black. Kerry hangs on to her via a rope halter and aims a squirt of fly-spray at her. The mare strikes out with her front leg. Kerry jumps back and tries again from a safer distance. The mare rears straight up and slams her front feet back down on the concrete. Kerry swears and hands the end of the rope to Robbie.

He leads the mare forwards and asks her to move back again to make sure she's listening to him before he calls Kerry to continue with what she's doing. The mare flattens her ears and gives her handlers the evil eye. Robbie doesn't speak. Using pressure on the rope, he asks her to take a step forwards again, and rubs her neck when she obeys.

Kerry gives her another go with the fly-spray and, this time, she stands quietly with her head lowered.

Robbie turns and gestures for me to approach.

'Hi, Flick. Come and join us, if you dare.' He chuckles. 'Meet Diva, our new recruit.'

'She's rather beautiful,' I say.

'She's quite horrid,' Kerry says with feeling. 'Robbie, I don't know what you and Dillon thought you were doing buying her.'

'She has spirit, which is just what we need, along with bravery, courage and trainability.' He grins ruefully. 'We'll have to see if we can win her round to our way of thinking. If not, she'll have been rather an expensive mistake.'

'I'll put her away,' Kerry says as a car draws up on the far side of the yard next to the rear entrance to the main house.

'Thanks,' Robbie says.

'I'll talk to you about the other thing later.'

'Other thing?' He frowns. 'Oh yes, that. I'll check the diary.'

'I've checked. You are free that day – I've put a reminder on your mobile. You don't mind, do you?'

'No, that's fine. Whatever.' He pulls his mobile from his pocket and unlocks it with a password which means, I guess, that rider and groom are pretty close. Ryan and I never shared our passwords.

Robbie returns his mobile to his pocket as she leads the horse away.

'Daddy!' A girl dressed in school uniform – a royal blue polo shirt, grey pleated skirt and brown sandals – comes running across the yard from the car, while a woman – Robbie's mother, I assume – takes some shopping bags out of the boot.

'Maisie, this is Flick.' Robbie holds her hand tightly.
'Flick, this is Maisie.'

'Hello. I'm seven. How old are you?' She looks up at me.

'Twenty-nine.'

When she smiles, I can see the resemblance between her and her father in her high cheekbones and deep blue eyes. Her long hair is a lighter brown with a fringe and tied back in a ponytail.

Robbie sweeps her up into his arms. She giggles and clonks him affectionately over the head with her book bag.

'Did you have a good time at Ashley's house?' he asks.

'We made fairy-cakes.'

'I can tell.'

'How?'

'You have icing sugar stuck to your chin.' He rubs it away gently with a finger.

'Nanny's got some in the car for you. We put sprinkles on and fairy-dust and everything.' Maisie puts her arms around his neck and tips her head to one side. 'Can you help me with my sentences now?'

'You know Miss Fox only gave me three out of ten last time.'

'She gave you six. Please, Daddy . . .'

'I'll come and help with your homework as soon as I've taken some hay over to Wisteria House for Flick's horse.'

'And then can I have a ride on T-rex?'

'Not tonight. I've had a busy day.'

'You don't have to lead me.'

'You know very well that I do. There's no way you're riding him on your own.'

'But I really, really, really want to ride on my own.' Her lower lip wobbles and tears threaten to spill down her cheeks. 'Demi at school rides off the lead rein.'

'That's because she has a sensible pony. You know what T-rex's like. He's a—'

'Very naughty boy,' she finishes for him.

'That's right. One day we'll find you a pony that I can trust to look after you.'

I can't help smiling. Robbie seems more protective of his daughter than my dad was of me. When I was a child, he bought or leased me the best ponies and the most expensive kit: fitted tweed show jackets with velvet collars; canary-yellow jodhpurs; shiny leather jodhpur boots. I had long hair down to my waist and Mum used to plait it at the same time as she plaited the ponies' manes and tails, finishing it off with a ribbon to match their velvet brow-bands.

Some of the ponies were highly strung, and on the rare occasions that I came off, my father would pick me up, dust me down and drop me straight back on. He treated me like a princess, but one with attitude. I dismiss a twinge of regret. I wish my father had the same confidence in me now as he did back then.

'Can I help you with the hay?' Maisie asks.

'Not this time. We agreed that you wouldn't stay up late when you have school the next day,' Robbie says. 'I have to go – we don't want Flick's horse to starve, do we?'

'Don't be long.' She turns and skips back to where her grandmother is waiting.

'Who'd be a single parent?' Robbie sighs. 'Actually, apart from being utterly exhausting at times, it's brilliant. Maisie's the best thing that's ever happened to me.'

'She's lovely.' Like her dad, I want to add, my heart melting. Not only is he the ultimate horse-mad male, it's obvious that he loves his daughter to bits, too.

'This way.' He moves up to my side.

I sense the firm touch of his hand against my back as he guides me in the direction of the barn in the yard, beyond where the trailer, a double horsebox in blue aluminium with a cream top, is parked with the tailgate down.

'How many did you say you wanted?'

'Ten will be enough for now. There isn't much room to store them at Mel's.'

I follow him into the barn and watch him climb up the side of the stack.

'Watch out!' He pushes a bale from the top. It whistles past my ear and bounces across the floor. 'And again.' He continues until there's a heap of bales on the ground. He half slides, half jumps down and goes to pick one up. His T-shirt has ridden up at the back revealing a sheen of sweat across his lightly tanned loins, and the blocks of muscle on either side of his spine. He's wearing a worn leather belt and navy underpants with a bright pink band around the top.

Forcing myself to look elsewhere, I pick up another bale and carry it out to the trailer.

Robbie is fit and gut-wrenchingly gorgeous. There's no harm in looking, is there? Louise says he's single, but I don't know for sure if he's available, and I'm not interested in a relationship, but I can't help wondering what he sees when he looks at me.

He pauses from loading the trailer, a half-smile on his lips as he glances across. I catch sight of my reflection in the wing mirror of the four-by-four. I run my fingers through my hair, but there isn't much I can do about my dismal turnout. I've been wearing the same polo shirt and jeans all day, my boots are dusty and my fingernails are cracked and grubby.

Having loaded the trailer, I close the ramp and follow Robbie along the drive and down the lane in the truck. We pass the cottage again, where the cherry trees are in full bloom now, covered in the flouncy, candyfloss-pink blossoms that confirm that spring is here to stay.

'How was your meeting?' I ask as we unload the hay into the stable beside Rafa's.

'It was very promising. I showed the TV producer around the yard. He made all the right noises, but he isn't going to make a decision until he's seen a live performance. Unfortunately, or fortunately, depending on how you look at it, he isn't available – due to other commitments such as holidays and filming – until the Country Show.'

'Is that the same as the Farm and Country Festival that Mel's told me about?'

'No, that's in April. The Country Show is at the end of June. That gives us three months to train Diva as a spare for the team.

'I need this contract,' he continues. 'He's looking at hiring me as stunt rider and advisor on set, as well as four of our horses – Nelson in particular – and someone to give one of the actors a crash-course in how to ride.'

'Not literally, I hope.'

'Oh no. I'm pretty hot on safety. I don't want any of my horses getting hurt.' He pauses, resting one bale on top of another inside the stable. 'What kind of day have you had?'

'I shod an ultra-sensitive thoroughbred. That was stressful.'

'Not Rambo?' Robbie asks.

I nod. 'Do you know him?'

'Gina sent him here for six weeks of intensive training in the autumn. I'm not sure it made much difference.'

'She says he's getting on well.'

'That's quite gratifying to hear. I thought he might be too much for her.'

'After Rambo, I went over to the Sanctuary to trim a pony's feet.'

Robbie moves aside so I can throw the last bale on top of the rest.

'Have you ever thought of taking on a rescue?' I ask. 'I don't know if he'd make a riding pony, but he was very sweet and quiet on the ground.'

'Sophia from the Pony Club is keeping an eye out for a pony for us, one that's been through a family, been outgrown and passed down like an old pair of boots; one who knows their job.'

'Ponies like that are like gold dust. You could be waiting for ages.'

'I don't want any old pony. I need one I can rely on – it needs to be completely bombproof for my daughter.'

'I couldn't fault him. He struck me as the kind of pony who'd appreciate someone small to love him.'

'What's he like then?' Robbie sighs. 'Sell him to me.'

'He's about 13.2, chestnut with a white blaze.'

'A good horse is never a bad colour, so they say. How old?'

'Middling, according to the vet. Fifteen or sixteen. He seems to have plenty of life left in him.'

'Much as it sounds like a charitable thing to do, he's no use to me.'

'He has a couple of patches where a saddle has rubbed and the hair has grown back white, so he must have had tack on at some time.'

'That doesn't necessarily mean he'd accept a saddle now.'

'He might be useful as a therapy pony,' I suggest, determined not to give up just yet.

'I'm not sure that a rescue of unknown history fits the job description.'

'It's okay if you don't think he'll be suitable, but I liked him and he's had a tough time. I'd like to think of him having a better life with someone like Maisie to care for him.'

Robbie touches the corners of his eyes.

'You are bringing me to tears,' he jokes. 'God, Flick, you are very persuasive.'

I wish I was, I think. I wish I could persuade him not only to consider the pony as an option, but me as well, because although I'm virtually falling over myself in front of him, he's treating me as a new friend, one of the lads. He isn't looking at me with any hint of appreciation or attraction in his eyes. There's nothing to suggest that he's noticed that I'm a woman – and why should he, I ask myself, when I smell of horse and can throw a bale of hay as high as he can?

'What's this pony's name?'

'He didn't have one, so we christened him Paddington. I suppose you might want to change it,' I add when he stands in front of me, his mouth curving into a smile.

66

'What kind of name is that? Who chose it?'

'I did.'

'Paddington!' He laughs as he follows me out of the stable. 'Let me think about it.'

I close the door behind us. Rafa is in the adjacent stable, fidgeting to get out and scraping the floor. I take a couple of screwed-up notes from my pocket and hand them over to Robbie.

'Here's what I owe you for the hay, and I said I'd buy you a drink.'

'Don't worry about the delivery. It didn't take long.' As I suppress a twinge of disappointment, he moves up to pat Rafa's neck. My horse looks past him, tossing his head with impatience, as if to say, 'Stop wittering and let me out of here.' 'Have you ridden him past the pigs again?'

'Not yet. I've been too busy to take him out.' I pause, wondering when I'm next going to see Robbie – not because I fancy the breeches off him, you understand, but I could do with a friend to show me around.

My friends from school and uni are scattered across the country, and busy with their own lives. Even Sarah, who's been like a sister to me, is currently less available than she used to be because she's pregnant and moving house. We talk on the phone and keep up on Facebook, but it isn't the same as meeting face to face. 'How about going out for a hack sometime?'

'That would be great. I can't give Nelson a good gallop when I'm out with Maisie, and Dillon's not keen on keeping me company. Much as I love spending time with my half-brother, you can have too much of a good thing.'

'Half-brother?'

'Everyone thinks of us as full brothers,' Robbie explains. 'Although Sally Ann is my mum as far as I'm concerned, she isn't my biological mother. She's Dad's second wife. I don't remember my birth mother. I don't know if that's because I was too young, or because I don't want to remember her. She walked out when I was eighteen months old.' He bites his lip before continuing, 'People say she must have had her reasons, that she must have been deeply depressed or desperate to abandon her own child, but I'll never understand how she could do it.

'When I remember how small and vulnerable Maisie was when she was the same age, I couldn't have abandoned her. It's incomprehensible to me, and cruel.'

'You don't have to talk about it.'

'It's all right. It's ancient history. I'm over it.' A shadow crosses his eyes and I wonder if it really is something that you can recover from. 'Next weekend is Easter. Let's ride out on the Sunday if you're free. If it's a nice day, we can take the horses down to the river. I know where the water's deep enough for them to swim.'

'Won't it be too cold?'

'The forecast is for warmer weather, a mini-heatwave.'

'Okay, that sounds fun. Brilliant.'

'How about I meet you here at ten?'

'That's perfect.' I want to say that any time's fine with me, but I don't want to sound too keen.

I watch him drive away in a hurry to get back to his daughter. I spend an hour looking after Rafa. I turn him out, scrub the water trough until I'd be happy to drink from it myself, and make his day-bed, as I call it, ready for the morning. When I go indoors, I have the house to myself. Louise has left a note telling me to help myself to the fish pie that's in the fridge. She and Ashley have gone to her parents' for the evening. Mel has survived the op to fuse the bones in his spine and is in recovery. She's put the chickens to bed. Smiley face.

It's very quiet, too quiet for me. I Skype Sarah on my iPad, but she can only chat for ten minutes because her hubby has dinner ready on the table.

'He's such a hero,' she sighs. 'He's spoiling me to bits. I'm planning to be pregnant for ever.'

'You're incredibly lucky.' I watch her stroke her baby bump. She's tall, slim and elegant, with shoulder-length dark hair and hazel eyes. Her white embroidered loose-fitting shirt contrasts with her tan.

'I know.' She frowns. 'This sounds bad, but I'm glad it didn't work out between you and Ryan. You weren't right for each other.' She cocks her head. 'David's brother is back on the market . . .'

'Oh no.' I met him at their wedding. I made a horse-shoe especially for Sarah and David, a good-luck charm decorated with ribbons and flowers. David's brother is decidedly geeky and wouldn't know one end of a horse from the other.

'You aren't going to let one bad experience hold you back for the rest of your life? I know it's made you wary of men, but you can't let it go on for ever. I hate the idea that you're letting Ryan win.'

'It isn't about winning and losing.'

'I think it is. He's made you lose your self-confidence – when it comes to men, I mean, not in general.'

'He's made me question my judgement. Ryan took me for a ride, so to speak, and I'm not prepared to let that happen for a second time.'

'David's brother is a lovely man.'

'I'm sure he's very sweet, but he isn't my type.'

'Remind me, Flick. What is your "type"?'

An image of Robbie Salterton on a big black stallion comes galloping into my head, sending my ex-boyfriends, including Ryan, running for cover. I wonder how good the picture is at Sarah's end, if she can see me blushing, but I'm reassured by the fact that the detail is poor. She looks as if she's been airbrushed – I can't see the blemish on her chin that she acquired on a cross-country course when she came to grief as we did a pairs class on our ponies.

'I'm not sure now. Tall, outdoorsy, blue eyes, brown hair. Must like horses.' I smile. 'I'm getting carried away. I don't need a man. I need to sort out my finances first.'

'First? So there is hope then?'

'Maybe a little,' I admit.

'How is that going?' Sarah asks. 'Have you managed to reduce the amount you owe?'

'Hardly.' I shrug. 'Sometimes I feel like I'm drowning in debt.'

'I wish you'd accept a loan from us.'

'I couldn't. It's very kind of you, but I'm not going to replace one loan with another, and my dad's always told me never to borrow from friends.'

I change the subject to a less painful, less controversial topic. 'How was your scan the other day?' I don't really need to ask because I saw the pics on Facebook, but I want to show Sarah that I've been thinking of her. Her face lights up as she gives me an update on the baby's health and how many times she feels it – I should say 'her', because we know she's a girl from the scan – kick in a day. She talks about how hard it is to choose the right antenatal and parenting classes, and the difficulties of choosing a suitable name without offending anyone. She's going to be a fantastic mum. I love to see how happy she is. It makes me happy too.

I hear David calling her in the background.

'I'd better go,' she says. 'Keep in touch.'

'Will do.' I sign off and stare out of my bedroom window, where Rafa is having a moment, cantering and bucking around the paddock in the cool of the evening.

I can't wait to ride out with Robbie at the weekend. I'd love to have time to chat and get to know him better, whether or not it leads to anything else. I'll be spending a lot of time with the Saltertons and their horses this spring. I just hope the new mare behaves herself when it's her turn to be shod.

Chapter Five

Wet Shirts and Hidden Depths

It's Sunday morning and I could sleep for hours. I'm physically exhausted from working from eight in the morning to six or seven at night, including Good Friday and most of Saturday. It turns out that Mel has let his business slide, postponing visits until the horses' shoes are almost falling off, and he's expecting me to get it back on track. I'm not complaining, though. I'm loving the challenge and the pretence of being my own boss.

However, I'm already wondering how long I'll be needed here. Mel was in hospital for five days. He came home with painkillers and a string of physio appointments, and determined to be walking without sticks within three weeks. It sounds selfish, but I'm hoping he doesn't rush back too soon.

I drag myself out of bed and peer out between the curtains. Rafa is waiting at the gate. I throw on some clothes and head downstairs. I've missed breakfast with the family. Louise is in the kitchen, closing the zip on a cool-bag.

'Morning, Flick. We're off to see friends today. They have a caravan at Talysands and we're going to have an Easter egg hunt on the beach.' She smiles. 'I can't wait.'

'Have a lovely day.'

'I'm hoping that it'll take Mel's mind off the after-effects of his op,' she goes on. 'Anyway, what about you? Have you any plans?'

'I'm going for a hack with Robbie.'

'Oh . . . ?' Her voice rises and her eyebrows seem to hover in question, as if she's waiting for me to tell her more. Her eyes glint with a hunter's sense of closing in on their prey. 'He's rather gorgeous, isn't he?'

'I hadn't really noticed,' I mumble.

'Come on, you can't be the only unmarried – or married, for that matter – woman who isn't swooning at his feet. A handsome stuntman galloping around the countryside in tight breeches – what's not to like?'

Indeed, I think to myself. I just wish I knew how he saw me: as a girl or one of the lads?

'I'd better go. Mel and Ash are waiting in the car. Have fun.'

I say goodbye to Louise and grab some breakfast before doing my make-up, adding lip-liner and matte pink lipstick to show Robbie that I can do feminine. I select a pale blue V-necked T-shirt to reveal some cleavage, and close-fitting off-white jodhs that emphasise the length of my legs. On my way outside, I pull on a pair of long black leather boots to complete the look. They're a little tight around my calves, but today I choose style above comfort.

When I bring Rafa up from the paddock and pick out his feet, I notice that he's due for shoeing soon.

I brush him, tease out the knots from his mane and tail, and tack him up. Hearing the sound of a horse's hooves coming up the lane, I put on my hat, tighten the girth, and lead him across to an upturned bucket where I spring into the saddle.

'Hi,' Robbie calls from the gateway. 'Your escort awaits.'

'I'm ready,' I call back. I slip my feet into the stirrups and collect up the reins as Rafa moves away, keen to meet up with a fellow equine. I'd prefer him to have the company of other horses all the time, but I can't afford to turn down free livery. He whickers at Nelson, but Nelson doesn't take any notice.

'Not surprisingly, my horse is more interested in female company.' Robbie smiles as he fiddles with the lead rope that's tied around Nelson's neck – for emergencies, I assume. 'Like me,' he adds, but I think he's talking generically, not referring to me. 'How are you?'

'I'm well, thanks. How about you?' I'm not sure what to say, whether we'll have enough topics in common to continue a conversation, or whether we'll ride along in silence.

'It's been an okay few days.' He turns to whistle at the wolfhounds, who are dawdling with their noses in the hedge, before we ride down the lane, side by side. He's wearing jeans today, short boots, and another flowing shirt with ruffles down the front and ripped sleeves.

'What's with the shirt?' I ask. 'I thought it was a costume for your stunts.'

'It was the only clean top I could find. I haven't got round to doing the washing.'

I smile at the idea of a dashing stuntman doing

something as ordinary as the laundry, but Robbie seems subdued, as if he's preoccupied. I wonder why? Is it the TV contract? Is it something to do with Maisie, or his love life? I don't feel that I know him well enough to ask.

As we approach the pigs' field, Rafa starts to snort and skitter across the lane. Robbie moves to the inside and I keep pushing forwards, and we're past the gate before he knows it.

'He's a quick learner,' Robbie observes. 'Now that we're heading towards the river, do you fancy taking the horses for that swim?'

I hesitate.

His eyes crease at the corners. 'Don't tell me he won't go into water.'

'I used to ride him in the stream back on the farm, and we've done water jumps before.'

'What's the problem then?'

'Won't we get wet?' I glance down at my clothes, my best jodhs and leather boots.

'Well, it does seem likely.' His tone is lightly sarcastic. 'I always leave my saddle and boots on the bank. If you don't want to swim, you don't have to, but the weather is perfect for it. Nelson loves the water.'

I don't want to spoil his fun. I'd forgotten that he'd mentioned swimming.

'Okay, let's do it,' I say.

'Are you sure?'

'Sure . . .' He's right about the weather. It's unseasonably warm for the first weekend in April.

We continue down the lane into the valley and on to a clinker track with trees and bushes running along each side.

'This is the old railway line. We're getting closer to

Talyton St George. You can just see the church and the new bridge from here.' He points through the trees. I stand up in my stirrups, catching a glimpse of the river and the town. Nelson pulls up sharply. Rafa almost bumps into his behind.

'We go right here. There's a ditch a few strides after the turning,' Robbie says. 'Don't worry – it's tiny. Follow me.' Nelson is off at a brisk canter before I can ask exactly what he means by 'tiny'. Rafa plunges and I have no choice but to go with the flow, hanging on as we fly between the trees, ducking branches and keeping my toes in tight to his sides. Nelson takes off over a gaping hole in the ground and lands the other side. Rafa grabs the bit between his teeth and springs off the edge. He arches his back and leaps across to reach the other side and, by some miracle, I go with him.

The track opens up on to a wide-open space, where Robbie pulls up and waits for me to join him.

He's laughing. 'I don't know how you stayed on just then.'

'Me neither.'

We walk across a field, past a flock of sheep with their lambs, until we reach the river bank where we continue away from the town. Rafa spooks at an elderly man who's fishing under an umbrella.

'That's Nobby Warwick,' Robbie says when we're out of earshot, 'church organist, village drunk and poacher. Dillon and I used to wind him up when we were hanging around down by the river, meeting girls, drinking . . .' He grins. 'I'll never let Maisie come down here with friends – I know only too well what my brother and I used to get up to. Anyway, it means I know all the places where the river's deep enough for swimming.' He pulls up a few strides further along the bank and points to the water. 'This is Dead Man's Pool – so-called because someone drowned here.'

I gaze into the murky depths as he continues, 'A highwayman held up a stagecoach on its way to London. He made off with the loot, but the locals caught up with him. He abandoned his horse and ran into the valley, which was shrouded in mist. He fell into the river with jewels around his neck and gold coins in his pockets, and drowned. They never found his body.'

'Maybe he got away,' I suggest.

'It's said that if you look down you can see his limbs among the roots of the trees over there.'

'Ugh, that's horrible.' A shiver of fear runs down my spine as I picture the highwayman's arms and legs, pale and rotting away under the water.

'You're as bad as Maisie. It's only a story.' Robbie jumps off, loops his arm through the reins and unfastens Nelson's girth. He sweeps the saddle off his back and places it on a log beside a hummock of grass. He removes his hat and starts to strip slowly out of his shirt.

Time seems to stand still as he lifts the hem up to reveal his lean figure. The contoured muscles of his belly are covered with lightly tanned skin, and the smattering of dark curly hair that starts at his bellybutton fans out across his chest. He tugs the shirt over his head and throws it across the saddle, turning away for a moment so I can see his hard muscular loins above the waistband of his denim jeans.

I grow lightheaded at the sight of him, and it crosses

my mind that I could actually faint like a romantic heroine, and he could catch me in his arms and hold me against his naked torso, and recognise that I am a member of the opposite sex. But I wouldn't take advantage of my feminine wiles like that, would I? Not unless the situation became absolutely desperate . . .

Robbie whistles for the dogs, who trot up and sit on guard beside his belongings.

'Are you coming in?' He kicks off his boots.

'Of course.' I dismount and remove Rafa's saddle, leaving it beside Nelson's, before I look around for something that I can use as a bootjack.

'Come on then, matey,' Robbie says, his tone a mixture of amusement and impatience.

'Matey?' I exclaim.

'We are mates, aren't we?'

'Yes, but . . .' That sounds like something he'd say to his brother, or one of his male friends. 'Oh, never mind.'

'Hurry up,' he goes on.

'Just a minute.' I try catching the heel of one boot with the toe of the other and dragging it off. I have a go at forcing it off by pushing it down with both hands, but there's no way. My calf is firmly stuck. I look at the water. I can't contemplate wrecking my beautiful boots. I turn to Robbie. 'Um, this is embarrassing . . .'

'I'll give you a hand.' He unties the lead rope from around Nelson's neck and lets the end dangle from his noseband.

'Are you sure that's—'

'It's fine. I've taught him to ground tie – that's why I carry a rope.'

'I'm impressed. I'm not sure I could trust Rafa.' Keeping a firm hold on the reins, I sit down on the log beside the saddles as Robbie kneels at my feet, which is exactly where I would want him in different circumstances: bowed down in worship at my supreme womanliness.

I offer him my foot.

He wraps one hand around the toe and one around the heel and pulls sharply, taking me by surprise and tipping me backwards. I grab at the log and cling on, laughing.

'How did you get these bloody things on in the first place?' Robbie's laughing too. 'Are you sure they're even yours?'

'They've always been a bit on the tight side.' My face is burning and it has nothing to do with the heat of the sun. I've started work and muscled up since I bought them.

Robbie tries again and, eventually, the boots come off. He rests his hands briefly on his hips as I remove my socks.

'Are you ready now?'

'I think so.' I stand up and mount my horse from the log while he vaults on to Nelson. Rafa follows Nelson down the bank to a gently shelving beach of pebbles and red sand. Nelson enters the water and drinks. Rafa follows suit, lowering his head and burying his nostrils as a kingfisher flies past with an iridescent flash of blue. I cling on to his mane as he splashes with his front foot.

Robbie rides into the deeper water until Nelson is swimming; only his ears, eyes and nostrils, and his tail streaming behind him, can be seen above the surface of the dark pool in the riverbed.

'Flick, come on in,' he yells, leaning forwards on his horse's back.

'It looks cold,' I say, hesitating.

'It's a little chilly, but you soon get used to it.'

I send Rafa out into the pool. Suddenly, he loses his footing, and we're both in the water. I gasp in shock, but it's refreshing, exhilarating, exciting . . . As Rafa swims upriver, I slide off his back and let him tow me through the hot and cold currents of water. A fish leaps out and falls back in again, and a pair of ducks skim across the surface. I begin to relax. I've been so focused on my problems, on putting on a good show for Mel's clients, that I've almost forgotten how to have fun.

Robbie brings Nelson alongside.

'It isn't so bad, is it?' he says, heading towards the shallow water.

'It's great,' I agree, following him.

We ride up the bank and jump a small woodpile at the top before returning to where the dogs are snoozing beside the saddles. As the sun warms my body, I become aware that Robbie is staring at me, his brow furrowed. I glance down at my top. It's stuck to my skin, my bra clearly visible, and everything underneath looking decidedly perky. Keep looking, I think. I am a woman.

His lips curve into a smile before he turns away, his gaze following a group of teenagers who are strolling along the path towards us with their mobiles and a rucksack.

We tack up and put our boots back on. Robbie slips into his shirt.

'Normally I'd suggest we could ride back via the pub, but I promised I'd take Maisie riding this afternoon,' he says as we trot in the direction of the old railway line. 'It's her birthday.'

'I didn't realise. You should have said you wanted to spend the day at home with her.'

'She's with her grandparents today – not Mum and Dad, Carla's parents. She's due back later for a birthday tea.' I'm not sure how to react because I recall that, if it's Maisie's birthday, it must also be the anniversary of her mother's death. 'Mum's made a cake – in the shape of a princess – and I've bought her a doll that she wanted for her present.'

'How old is she? She did tell me, but I've forgotten.'

'She's eight. I can't believe it.' He pauses. 'It doesn't feel like eight years since Carla passed away.'

'I'm very sorry.'

'I met her down here by the river,' he says, and, with a jolt of unreasonable disappointment, I wonder if he deliberately chose to be here today to remember her. 'It was during the summer holidays when she was sixteen. I was a year older, and a bit of a rebel. In fact, I'd just been expelled from school.'

'You? What did you do?'

'I was a boarder at a top independent school – I only agreed to go because they had equestrian facilities. Anyway, much to my dad's fury, I was kicked out for drinking while on a school trip. I felt guilty for letting him down, but I hated it there and I didn't want to do A-levels and go to university. I came home and kicked about for a while. On the day I met Carla, I'd just "borrowed" a shopping trolley from the Co-op. Don't ask me why. I can't remember. It was some kind of prank. Don't tell Maisie any of this, will you?' he adds lightly.

'I won't,' I promise. 'What was Carla like?'

'She was the most amazing human being, generous, loving . . . I'll never forget her smile, the freckles across the bridge of her nose . . .' His voice fades for a second time. I notice how he swallows hard. 'I didn't know what to suggest to make sure I saw her again, so I offered to teach her to ride. We spent hours at home in the arena, whatever the weather. She was a natural.'

Is that why he doesn't appear to be involved with anyone else, I wonder? Has he really not had a serious relationship in eight years?

'Her parents disapproved. They weren't happy about her seeing one of the irresponsible Salterton brothers, or taking up what they felt was a dangerous sport.'

'Did they try to stop you seeing each other?' I ask, thinking of how my parents tried to guide me into seeing young men they approved of. Once Sarah overheard my dad at some social gathering, telling this guy I'd fancied for months that I was engaged. When I tackled him about it, he denied all knowledge, but I could tell he was lying. But by then, it was too late, and my potential paramour was going out with my cousin.

'They did at first, but when they realised I was serious about her, they backed off. She was all set to start a course in environmental science when she found out she was pregnant. It was then that the proverbial hit the fan. I couldn't see what the problem was. Carla and I talked it through and decided that she could delay going to university for a year. After that, I'd look after the baby during the week, and she'd come home at weekends.' He breaks off. 'It sounds completely naive now. I didn't realise that

82

caring for a baby is all-consuming; that you can't just put it aside for a couple of hours like you can with a horse or dog.'

I keep silent, listening to him talk against the sound of the horses' hooves and the squeak of leather tack, while the dogs lope along behind.

'I don't really understand what happened after that. Things went wrong between us. Her parents accused me of being controlling. They said I didn't want her to go away to study and that's why I'd made her pregnant, which was ridiculous. It was an accident. Carla didn't find out she was having a baby until she was six months gone.

'At about thirty-six weeks, she started feeling unwell. She was admitted to hospital with pre-eclampsia and made to rest. Her parents took over. I visited her, of course, but I was busy working, trying to get the stunt team going so I would have money to support us. We weren't living together, but my parents offered me Cherry Tree Cottage for when she came out of hospital – I did a room up as a surprise for her. We weren't a couple at the time. There'd been a few rows, but I always thought we'd make a go of it as a family.'

But she never came out, I think. I can feel the sorrow in his voice and the pain in the slump of his shoulders.

'I was away with the team when her condition went downhill. She had her labour induced, but her parents didn't let me know. Carla called me after they'd started her off, but by then she could hardly speak. I knew something was badly wrong, that she needed me. I raced back, leaving the horses with Dillon, but by the time I got there, it was too late. She'd had a fit and never regained consciousness, although I like to think she knew I was at her side when it was all over.'

'Oh, Robbie,' I sigh.

He looks across at me, straight in the eye, his expression dark with hurt.

'They wouldn't let me see our baby.'

'Who wouldn't?'

'Her parents. They blamed me, and in a way they were right to.'

'It wasn't your fault.' I wonder how many other people have said that. 'I'm sorry, what do I know?'

'I kicked off, of course. Then I was escorted away from the hospital by security. I went back in and was arrested and thrown into a cell for the night to calm down. Calm down? I've never been so angry and upset. My dad came down with a solicitor friend to bail me out on condition that he took me straight home.'

I can't imagine Robbie losing his temper, but nor can I imagine how anyone would feel at being denied contact with their newborn daughter at the same time as losing her mother, the woman he was in love with. I have no doubt that whether or not they were together at the time, he'd always loved her.

'The next day I found out that Carla's parents were claiming that they had no clue who the baby's father was – which is terrible, considering how that made their daughter look.'

I agree. It's outrageous. My parents haven't always been scrupulous with the truth, but I can't imagine them doing something that low.

'At first, I was absolutely furious and devastated,

84

because I'd lost both Carla and my daughter – Mum sat me down and made me try to see it from their point of view. They'd lost their only daughter and Maisie was part of her. I could understand why they were desperate to hold on and bring her up themselves. But Maisie was mine and I wasn't going to let her grow up thinking that I'd abandoned her like my birth mother did me. When Carla was lying unconscious in Intensive Care, I promised her . . .' His voice breaks. '. . . That I would care for our baby and love her for both of us.'

I wipe my eyes with the back of my hand. It's the pollen.

'I had to go to court to obtain parental responsibility and get custody. They even did a DNA test to check, although I had no doubt.'

'That must have been agony for everyone.'

'It was. I didn't want to fight, but I wasn't going to lose her. It took a long time, but the judge made it right. The day I held Maisie in my arms was the day I finally grew up.'

It takes me a moment to focus on where we're going.

'What happened with Carla's parents?'

'I made my peace with them. They take Maisie on holiday and have her some weekends, and they spend half the day with her on her birthday. We don't celebrate today, but we'll have a party tomorrow.' Robbie rides Nelson through a gap in the trees and into a field, planted with lush green wheat. I follow, keeping Rafa behind Nelson on the grassy track alongside the crop.

'That's enough about me,' Robbie says abruptly. 'How about you? What's your story?'

'There isn't much to tell really.'

'Have you any brothers and sisters, infamous relatives or significant others?'

'I'm an only child. My dad's so much older than my mum that everyone assumes he's my grandfather. I'm single and intending to stay that way.'

'Do I detect a trace of bitterness?' he says. 'I'm being ironic, by the way. Who was he?'

'One of the apprentices I met when I was with Tony, my ATF.'

'ATF?'

'Apprentice Training Farrier. My ex, Ryan, was a couple of years ahead of me.'

'I bet you fell for his massive guns,' Robbie says brightly. 'I'm sorry, I shouldn't make light of it. You were serious?'

'Not at first. We helped each other out a few times. I covered for him when he overslept. He put out the flames when I set my hair on fire in the forge. That's one of the reasons I keep it short.'

'You should retrain as a stunt rider – it's far safer.' Robbie opens the gate into the field. I ride through and he closes it behind us. 'What happened?'

'My hair grew back after a while.'

He chuckles. 'I meant what happened to you and this Ryan bloke?'

I smile at my ditziness.

'We moved into a house and made plans for the future – the usual couple stuff.'

'But? I detect that there's a "but".'

'Ryan always gave me the impression that he had money in the bank. When he qualified he bought a brand-new mobile forge and set up not far away from where Tony's based in Wiltshire. I was going to be his partner in the business after I'd passed my diploma exam.'

'Why did you break up, if you don't mind me asking?'

'We went on holiday to the Caribbean, staying in an exclusive resort on a banana plantation. It was a magical trip. On the last day, Ryan proposed on this beautiful beach with a ring wrapped in a banana leaf.' I'm remembering it as if it were yesterday. 'I was so excited. It was the most romantic thing anyone's ever done for me.'

'So you said yes.'

I nod, then correct myself, in case he's under any misapprehension. 'I didn't accept because it was romantic. I was in love with him.'

'I kind of guessed that. You seem quite . . .' He searches for an appropriate description, and comes up with something that a Jane Austen heroine would say about her hero. '. . . Honourable, like you'd always do the right thing.'

'I like to think so. I'm not afraid to speak out.'

The track widens and the horses walk out smartly, matching each other stride for stride.

'When we arrived at home, I discovered that he'd taken out loans, including the money for the engagement ring, in both our names. We had a massive row and things were never the same again. Ryan set himself up with a piece of posh totty who had her own place with several horses. I was gutted when I found out.'

'I assume that he didn't have the balls to tell you.'

'I found text messages on his phone – I watched him put the password in so I could type it in myself – that didn't have anything to do with shoeing horses.

When I confronted him, he tried to tell me there was nothing going on, but eventually he admitted he was seeing someone else.'

'I suppose it was better to find out sooner rather than later.'

'It was too late in a way,' I say, thinking of the debt that Ryan has racked up on my behalf. I'm too embarrassed to admit that I didn't keep on top of our finances. I didn't discover until too late that he'd cleared the money from our joint account. I started getting letters from the electricity and gas companies to inform me that the direct debits weren't being paid. The bank won't close the account until the overdraft has been paid off, and I can't persuade Ryan to repay half of the money. He's always got some excuse and now he's avoiding my calls completely. It's a worry I don't wish to share with Robbie.

He half turns his horse to face me as we reach the foot of a long hill. Nelson is on his toes, snatching at his bit and tossing his head.

'How about a gallop? I'll beat you to the telegraph pole.'

'We'll see about that,' I call back, as Rafa dances on the spot in anticipation.

He counts, 'One, two, three, go.'

And we're off!

I lean forwards like a jockey, standing up in my stirrups and letting out the reins as Rafa goes from 0 to 60 in seconds – okay, I'm exaggerating. It's probably about 30 or 35, less than a racehorse. For a while he's ahead of Nelson, but as we approach the top of the hill, his lack of fitness begins to tell, and I become aware that Nelson is gaining on us. I give Rafa a squeeze with my legs. He responds, lengthening his stride and fighting Nelson off. Nelson moves up again, his nose level with Rafa's shoulder, then his neck, and we're past the pole.

Laughing, I start to pull up.

'I make that a dead heat.' Robbie grins as he lets Nelson relax into a walk, holding the reins at the end of the buckle.

'No way. Rafa won it by a nose.'

'I don't think so.'

'I know so,' I say, determined to have the last word.

The dogs catch up with us and we move on, the horses puffing and blowing lightly, our clothes drying in the sun, as we return to Wisteria House, where Robbie says goodbye.

'I hope I haven't bored you. I don't normally open up to people like that, but you're easy to talk to.' He reaches out and touches my thigh, sending a shot of electricity right through me. 'That was fun. We'll have to do it again.'

'Thank you for showing me around.'

'Anytime.'

'Wish Maisie a happy birthday from me.'

'Will do.' He doesn't seem in any hurry to ride away just yet, as if something is holding him back. 'Oh, I know what I was going to ask you. I've spoken to Jack about that pony you told me about. I've arranged to go and have a look at him sometime. Maybe you could come with me. I thought you might like to see how he's getting on.'

I'd love to spend as much time as possible with you, I want to say, but I stick with, 'Yes, I'd love to catch up with Paddington.'

'Okay, I'll be in touch. I'll see you soon – I can't

remember when you're next booked to come to us to get some shoes on the new mare.'

'That could be interesting,' I say, sighing inwardly.

'She'll be fine. I'll be there – I'm sure we can do it between us.'

I smile wryly. I reckon he will bring her round with his caresses and sweet-talk. I know I'd soon succumb to them if he was inclined to try out his moves on me.

'Bye, Flick. Don't be sad about the race – maybe you'll beat me next time.'

'I *did* beat you. I told you. By a nose.'

He rides away as I turn into the drive. I smell of river water, and horse, and my hair is sticky under my hat, but I don't care. Robbie might have called me 'matey', but he's also noticed that I am a woman. Whether or not he's been deliberately playing it cool, he failed to disguise his appreciation of my figure. He isn't entirely as he appears, I think. Like the river, he has hidden depths.

Chapter Six

Nailed it

On Tuesday, I have time to shoe Rafa first thing in the morning before I head off to attend to some horses at the local riding school. I like to keep busy. It takes my mind off the thought of having to get shoes on Diva. Considering how she behaved with Kerry the other day, even picking up her feet will be a challenge. Most horses are happy to be shod, but I've met a couple who could only be done under sedation from the vet. I hope Diva isn't going to be like that.

I turn into a driveway, signposted 'Letherington Equestrian Centre'. I pass between a field sectioned into small paddocks with electric tape, and a warehouse-style shop called Tack 'n' Hack where I suppress the urge to stop and have a look because there's bound to be something, the latest horsey gadget or gizmo that I just have to have, although I can't afford it.

I drive on past a barn, through a car park, and on to a yard that's bordered on three sides by breeze-block and tile stables. It's tidy, but not spotless, with straw scattered about and a few weeds growing up in the cracks in the concrete, but the horses appear fit and well cared for. A brown one, with a white star on his forehead and a Roman nose that reminds me of my boss, looks over one of the doors, and a dapple-grey mare is tied up outside another. I jump out of the truck.

'Good morning,' I call, bringing a middle-aged woman marching across the yard towards me. Dressed in a cream blouse and tan jodhpurs, she has wide hips and a booty to rival Kim Kardashian's.

'I'm Flick.' The horses touch noses and squeal.

'You're the farrier.' She looks me up and down. 'I'm Delphi.' Her hair is streaked blonde and tied back, her complexion tanned and lined. Her accent is decidedly posh. 'I don't like chopping and changing because it's unsettling for the horses, but Mel's reassured me that you know what you're doing.'

'Where shall I start?' I ask.

'Willow needs a trim – all she does is a little light hacking. Dark Star is for refits all round – he's an eventer.' She waves towards the mare and the brown horse. 'They belong to one of our local GPs, Nicci Chievely. We call her the galloping doctor.' Delphi hardly pauses for breath. 'Then there's one of my dressage horses for a new set. And, as you're here, if you wouldn't mind having a look at one of the school ponies – she's lame and I don't want to bother the vet unless I have to.'

I can't help wondering if I'm going to be here all day.

'One of my apprentices will be round to help you in a while. I can't stop, I'm afraid. I'm taking a lesson in a few minutes.' She strides away, leaving a trail of expensive perfume in the air behind her.

I turn to the grey mare.

'Willow, let's have a look at those feet of yours.'

I spend the rest of the morning with Delphi's apprentice, Katie, a girl of nineteen who aspires to become an elite dressage rider, the next Charlotte Dujardin. She fetches me the other horses and provides me with a chipped mug of orange squash and soggy digestive biscuits. It's quite pleasant on the yard, apart from a few annoying flies. Mindful of Mel's instructions about taking payment at the time, I walk through into a second yard of cob-and-brick buildings, where the riding school ponies are stabled, and find Delphi in the indoor school beyond. She's finished the lesson and her pupils are running up their stirrups and leading their mounts away.

She takes me into a dark tack room where the air is thick with the scent of leather, saddle soap and camphor. She squeezes between the rows of saddles and bridles to reach the old desk in the far corner, on which there is a heap of paperwork. She takes a cheque from one of the drawers and counts out some cash from a biscuit tin.

'Mel doesn't accept cheques,' I say as she tries to hand it over.

Delphi frowns. 'Nicci *always* pays by cheque.'

'Thank you.' I take it, accepting that this is another of the exceptions he forgot to tell me about. 'Let me know if there are any problems,' I say, squinting as we move back into the sunlight.

She gives me a look. 'I hope that won't be necessary.'

Me too, I think, but I always mention the possibility. It's all part of the service.

'I'll see you in two weeks' time.' I checked the diary earlier – Delphi has a regular slot every other Tuesday.

'You mean Mel won't be back in harness by then?' she says sharply.

My heart sinks because I thought I'd won her round.

'He's had major surgery. He won't be back to work for at least twelve weeks.'

'Oh dear, I thought he was putting it on. I shouldn't have made such a scene when I found the girls rubbing liniment into his loins the other day.' Delphi snorts with laughter, sounding much like a horse. 'I'll see you again soon.'

I drive to the Saltertons' next, arriving at about lunchtime. The dogs walk across to greet me, their tongues lolling with the heat. I look around for Robbie. He and Dillon are in the arena with a group of horses, and Kerry is looking on from just inside the gate. I wander over to watch.

'Hi,' I say.

'Oh, hello,' Kerry says. 'Come and see the experts at work.'

'How is it going?' I ask. Robbie and Dillon, both dressed in dark breeches and yellow T-shirts with the Eclipse team logo across the front, are cantering around the arena in opposite directions, Robbie standing on Nelson's back and Dillon on Scout's. Each has a bay horse moving alongside. The sight gives me goose bumps.

'They're practising a new routine.' She smiles wryly. 'It isn't going too well.' She points towards Robbie, who carries a trailing whip, not to punish, but to guide the horse beside him; except that the horse has other ideas, spinning away from Nelson and attaching himself to Dillon's pair of steeds. Robbie and Dillon pull up.

'That's Turner,' Kerry says. 'He's a lovely horse, but not the brightest.'

'Let's pair him up with Scout this time,' Robbie suggests.

'It's a bit of a pain,' Dillon argues. 'Scout's always worked with Dennis.' Dennis is a bay horse who is part of the team.

'But Turner is very friendly with Scout.'

'They are field buddies,' Kerry says.

'Let's try it,' Robbie says. 'It's always better to work with a horse, not against him. It would save embarrassment later. Can you imagine him doing that in front of the paying public, let alone the TV producer and his associates?'

'I think we should stick to our guns,' Dillon says. 'What use will Turner be if he won't work without Scout to hold his hand? He needs to learn to be completely independent.'

'He hacks alone,' Kerry points out.

'That's all very well, but how will he react on set if some actor who's had a crash course in riding is on his back and he sees Scout in the distance?' Dillon says. No one responds. 'Yeah, exactly.'

'We'll work on that,' Robbie says. 'In the meantime, it wouldn't hurt to swap for the sake of the new routine.' He glances towards me, as if aware of me for the first time. 'Hello, Flick. I'll be ten minutes.'

'That's fine,' I say. 'I'm in no hurry.' I'm not in a rush to shoe Diva, although I know I'll feel a lot better when I've finished.

Robbie tosses the whip to his brother and they canter around the arena again. Turner seems more relaxed in his new pairing, matching his stride to Scout.

'That's better,' Kerry observes. 'It's pretty stressful, running a successful stunt team, and I sometimes wonder if we'll ever get it right. Perhaps I should try a show-jumping yard for a quieter life.'

'Would you prefer that?' I ask.

'Not really. At least, I don't think so.' She grins. 'Maybe I'll get a chance to be on the telly as an extra. It's my belief that you can always replace one stunt-man with another, but you can't do that with a groom. Robbie and Dillon couldn't do without me.'

'I suppose not,' I say.

'It's me who makes sure that everything is prepared before we leave for these events. It's me who remembers to black out the little patch of white on Scout's chest so that he matches Nelson, and it's me who checks that there's enough fuel in the horsebox the day before.' She moves to the end of the gate and picks up four head-collars that are hanging from the post. 'Are you done?' she calls.

'That's enough for now,' Robbie calls back. He jumps down from Nelson's back, landing lightly on his feet.

'I'll put them away then,' she says.

'Thanks, Kerry.'

'I'll give you a hand,' Dillon says, stepping across from one horse to the other and sliding off over Turner's rump.

Robbie moves to the gate and vaults over the top as Kerry catches the horses.

'I thought we might have to cancel,' he says. 'Kerry couldn't catch Diva in from the field earlier, but Dillon and I managed to round her up. She isn't nasty, just maligned and misunderstood.' He smiles ruefully. 'I expect that's what they all say.'

'Owners do tend to see their horses through rose-tinted spectacles.' I smile back, glad to be back in his company. He changes the subject. 'I wondered if you could spare the time to go and see this pony, then have a quick bite of lunch before you shoe Diva. What do you think?'

'Yes, that would be great. I'd love to.'

'Come with me then,' he says, and I follow him across the yard and jump into the Land Rover that's hitched to the trailer.

The wolfhounds watch us go, their expressions forlorn.

'The dogs don't look very happy,' I observe.

'They don't like being left behind.'

'How was Maisie's party?'

'I survived it. That's about all I can say.' Robbie grimaces. 'I was in hot water because I forgot to buy party bags. For a while, I was the worst dad in the world.'

Not for long though, I think, watching him smile fondly as he drives along the lanes towards the Sanctuary.

'So, what's it like so far, trying to fill Mel's shoes? Or perhaps it would be more accurate to say trying to fit them . . .'

'I am fitting Mel's shoes,' I point out firmly. 'I know what I'm doing. There's no trying about it.'

His eyes grow soft with regret and a little hurt, perhaps at being misunderstood.

'I'm sorry. It's all been rather stressful. The reversing warning on the back of Mel's truck has broken – I drove it into a fence this morning.'

'I know someone who can have a look at it for you.'

'Thanks, but I'll get it into the garage when I have five minutes.'

'Here we are.' He lets me jump out to open the gate at the entrance to the rescue centre. We meet Tessa outside the bungalow, without the baby this time.

'I'm so glad you've agreed to take Paddington,' she says.

'Take him?' I turn to Robbie as we stroll towards the paddock, where the chestnut pony is waiting at the gate. 'You mean you're going to give him a home?'

'I'm a sucker for a sob story,' he says wryly. 'Jack confirmed everything you said.'

'The wound on his face is healing well,' Tessa joins in. 'He just needs a good diet and some TLC.'

'We have plenty of grass at home; probably too much for a pony like him.' Robbie lets Paddington nuzzle the side of his neck. 'He seems very chilled.'

'He's been as good as gold,' Tessa says. 'Jack said you were looking for a therapy pony – he'll be perfect.'

'I'll try him under saddle too. He might turn out to be suitable as a riding pony as well. Maisie will adore him, whatever. She'll be able to groom him and lead him about in a way she can't with T-rex. Have you got the paperwork?'

'It's all ready for you to sign. Do you want to load him first then drop into reception?'

'Yes, let's do that. I'll fetch a head-collar. I've got one in the trailer.'

Paddington ambles straight in, ready for the trip to his new home, and Robbie signs the papers. When we arrive back at the yard, I lead Paddington out of the trailer and Robbie opens the door to the empty stable beside T-rex, who whinnies and kicks at the partition between the two boxes. Paddington whickers back.

We watch them looking at each other over their stable doors.

'Thanks for the tip-off. Now I have an extra mouth to feed.' His arm slides around my back, his hand resting on the curve of my waist as he pulls me towards him, giving me a brief squeeze.

My heart beats faster at being appreciated in a way that I haven't felt for a long time. I'm pleased for the pony too. I only hope he turns out to be what Robbie is looking for. As I glance up at the outline of his face, the wayward locks of hair that fall across the broad forehead, the straight nose and the strong jaw, I wonder if he could also be looking for someone like me if I should convince myself that I'm ready to move on. It's a long shot, though. I don't know that much about him, in the scheme of things.

He relinquishes contact and steps up to feed T-rex a couple of mints from his pocket.

'I shouldn't really. It makes him nippy.'

I smile when I notice him do the same with Paddington, who puts his head in the air and curls his upper lip, revealing his teeth as if he's never been fed treats before.

'Maisie will spoil him. I can't wait to see her face when she gets back from school.' He changes the subject. 'I'll put our lunch order in, then we can make a start on Diva. What would you like? A baguette with ham and pickle, cheese and tomato, chicken and salad, or any other combination thereof? Water, Diet Coke or orange squash?'

'Are you sure? I have food with me.'

'Have something fresh, for goodness' sake,' he insists.

Thanking him, I give him my choice and he disappears off to the house, while I slip my leather chaps over the top of my jeans, put my baseball-style cap on and apply sunblock to my arms. I keep a bottle in my survival kit with my shades, water and cold coffee to drink, insect repellent, a packet of digestive biscuits and some fruit, along with lip-gloss and antiseptic hand cleanser.

I lift the anvil and tools out of the truck, by which time Robbie is back with a tray of food and drink. The woman I recognise as Maisie's grandmother accompanies him. She's about fifty, with straight, shoulder-length strawberry-blonde hair, and wearing a maxi-dress in blues and greens. Up close, I'm surprised to find that she's less than five feet tall.

'Flick, this is Sally Ann, my mum. Mum, this is Flick,' he says, introducing us.

'It's lovely to meet you,' she says. 'Robbie's told me a lot about you.'

I notice how he blushes under the tan.

'So where's the new pony then?' she goes on, as Paddington's head appears back over the stable door. 'Oh, he's a funny-looking one with all that white on his face.' She moves closer to him. 'How could anyone bring themselves to hurt him? He's very cute –' she turns to me – 'unlike the mare. Good luck with her.'

Robbie leads Diva out of her stable and ties her to the ring outside.

'You have remembered that you're picking Maisie and Ashley up from school this afternoon?' Sally Ann says.

'It's okay. I won't forget.' He smiles. 'Not this time, anyway. I told you I was the world's worst dad . . .'

The big bay mare starts pawing the ground. Robbie touches her shoulder and she stops.

'I'll leave you to it. I have a load of admin to do indoors. It's a shame – it's such a lovely day.' Sally Ann returns to the house.

'Help yourself,' Robbie offers, and I take a swig from one of the bottles of Diet Coke. I have a couple of bites of a chicken-and-salad baguette before making a start.

Now that the mare is here in front of me, the nerves have returned. I take a deep breath. As well as teaching me how to shoe a horse, Tony also taught me never to show your fear. I make friends with her, giving her time to see that I'm not a threat, before I move to her shoulder and run my hand down the back of her leg. As I reach her fetlock, she lifts her foot. So far, so good. I catch her foot between my legs, take my hoof nippers from the trolley and start to clip away the excess horn. The wolfhounds grab the pieces and trot away with them, and I begin to relax. I repeat the exercise with the other feet, rasp the hooves smooth and measure her up for a set of shoes.

I glance at Robbie who remains close by, skipping out the stables to keep them clean during the day, and punching some extra holes in a pair of stirrup leathers.

'These are too long for Maisie as they are,' he says in explanation. 'As for Diva, I'm not saying a word. I don't want to jinx it.'

'Hot or cold?' I ask him.

He tips his head to one side, considering. 'She's

been shod before, according to her previous owner. Hot's better, isn't it?'

'It makes for a better fit.'

Robbie fetches a bucket of water while I heat the shoes in the furnace. I start with the near or left fore, picking up Diva's foot with one hand and holding a shoe with the pritchel in the other. I apply the shoe to the foot, briefly at first to get her used to the smoke and the smell. She shifts her weight slightly on to mine. I touch the shoe to the foot for a second time so it will leave a mark on the hoof to show me where to rasp away any unevenness.

As the smoke crackles and swirls, the mare pulls back and drops herself almost on to her knees. I can't hold her. She staggers up. The shoe and pritchel go flying, as does the trolley of tools, as I jump back to get out of her way.

'Are you okay?' Robbie makes his way to the mare's head; he grabs her by the head-collar and leads her a step forwards to reduce the tension on the rope.

'I'm fine.' I collect up the tools, the pritchel and shoe. I drop the shoe into the bucket of water. 'Let's try cold.'

'I'll stay with her.'

With bated breath, I try again, checking the cooled shoe against Diva's foot, while Robbie whispers sweet nothings into her ear. Whatever he's saying, it works, because she lets me nail the shoe on once I've flattened the toe slightly with the hammer to match the shape of her foot. I repeat with both of her hind feet, and move on to the last one, the off or right fore.

The shoe is the perfect fit. Holding the nails in my mouth, I lean into Diva's flank with the fetlock flexed and her hoof caught between my knees. I apply the shoe and tap in the first nail, using light taps to start it off and harder blows to drive it through the hoof, listening for the sound that tells me I've seated the nail in the right place.

The nails are shaped so they bend outwards and emerge on the sides of the hoof as they are hammered in, preventing them hitting the sensitive inner part of the foot. The first goes in fine, and the second. When I knock in the third one, Diva tries to pull her foot away. I hold on, take a breath and go for the fourth. As I'm about to make the first tap with the hammer, she leaps skywards and back down again. I've still got her. I drive the nail through and out the other side of the hoof and through the flesh at the base of my left thumb. My first thought isn't the pain. It's that I've just nailed my hand to the hoof of one of the most unpredictable horses I've ever met, and I've got to detach it somehow without upsetting her.

I take a breath as the pain takes over, searing up my arm and bringing tears to my eyes. I breathe out and focus on slowly disconnecting my hand from the nail, feeling it ripping slowly through my flesh. Robbie remains silent, keeping Diva calm.

'Done it,' I gasp as quietly as I can. I move away and examine the wound.

'Did you prick her or something?' Robbie asks.

'No, I pricked myself.' I look at the hoof to check there's no bleeding that would indicate I'd driven the nail into the sensitive part of the foot by accident. 'I'll replace that nail to make sure. I don't want her going lame.' I reach for the tools and pull it out before finishing the job.

The mare fidgets the whole time I'm cutting off the sharp points and clenching the nails. She shifts her weight on to me – it's killing my back – and she pulls back abruptly at least three times, twisting my spine in the process.

'Hey,' I scold, as perspiration drips from the tip of my nose. I'm losing it. I really am.

'Stand up,' Robbie says gently to Diva. 'This won't take much longer.'

The more I hurry, the more difficult and diva-esque the mare becomes. When I go to pick up a foot, she resists. When I insist, squeezing the back of her leg, she snatches it up and slams it back down.

'I'm done,' I say eventually. My joints ache, my back hurts, my hand is throbbing, my head is swimming and my knees are weak. 'Will you trot her up, just to make sure I haven't done any damage?' Aware that Robbie is gazing at my injured hand, I hide it behind my back, just as I did to hide my plaster from Gina when I went to shoe Rambo. It's ridiculous, but I'm burning with embarrassment. Why does everything conspire to make me look incompetent when I'm trying to prove myself?

'It wouldn't be your fault if you had. Diva moved at the wrong moment.' He unties her and leads her away to trot her along the concrete and back.

'She looks fine, but if she goes lame in the next day or two, we'll know why,' I say as he leads her back into the stable and closes the door behind her.

'Are you sure you're okay?' He moves up close to me. 'You're looking very hot.'

'There, and I thought you'd never notice,' I say lightly as I sway against the trolley.

'Ha ha,' he says dryly. 'No, really, you look kind of clammy, as if you're going to . . .' I feel his arms around my back as he catches me. '. . . Faint.' He sits me down on a nearby bale of shavings.

'I'm all right,' I say, when he's squatting down beside me, holding my hand and turning it over to examine the puncture wound at the base of my thumb. My heart flutters fast and furiously, like a giant butterfly trapped in my chest.

'You need to get that looked at,' he says sternly. 'It'll be full of bugs.'

I try to get up.

'What are you doing?' His eyes are filled with concern.

'Packing up . . .'

'Oh no, not yet. You stay there while I get you a glass of water, then I'm going to take you down to the surgery to have that checked. You won't be able to shoe any more horses if you lose your thumb.'

'You're overreacting,' I protest. I don't want to sit waiting to see a doctor, but when I read the concern in his expression, I realise that it's me who's being silly. The wound is oozing and the surrounding skin turning red. 'All right, but I don't want to put you to any trouble. I can get to the surgery myself.'

'I'm going that way anyway. I have to pick Maisie and Ashley up from school.' He checks his watch. 'I can drop you off, fetch them, and come back to pick you up when you're done.'

'Don't I need an appointment?'

'They're pretty good. One of the doctors, or the nurse, is usually on site. Someone will see you.'

'That sounds like the voice of experience.'

'I'm often down there with Maisie. She's going through the medical dictionary from A to Z. We're up to J. The last time was I for infected toenail.'

I stand up slowly. Robbie takes my arm.

'I'll help you to the Land Rover.'

105

'What about—'

'Your tools? They can wait. Come on,' he adds in a tone that brooks no argument. He opens the door and helps me into the passenger seat, where I wait for him to unhitch the trailer and fetch me a glass of water before we leave.

He drops me off outside the surgery in Talyton St George, where the receptionist registers me as a temporary resident, and ushers me in to see Dr Nicci in her consulting room.

Dr Nicci is in her thirties, blonde and blue-eyed. She's wearing make-up, a vibrant turquoise shift dress and heels. She looks up from where she's sitting at her desk with a sign reading 'I am at the stables' beside her computer. There is a gallery of photos on the wall, many of them with horses as their subjects, including one of her riding a big brown horse over a rustic fence on a cross-country course.

'Hello.' She pulls up some details on her screen. 'I'm Nicci.'

'I'm Flick,' I say.

'You're the farrier.'

'I met your horses up at Delphi's.' A shooting pain makes me grimace.

'I'm glad neither of mine were responsible for you sticking a nail into your hand. Take a seat and I'll have a look at it.'

'Thank you for seeing me without an appointment.' I sit down beside the desk. The doctor moves closer, pushing her office chair on wheels around with her feet.

'It's fine. I'm here this afternoon anyway.' She pauses, a twinkle in her eye. 'I'd rather be out riding though.'

'So would I.'

'Do you have a horse?'

'An Andalusian gelding. I like to hack and do some dressage with him. He doesn't like jumping.'

'I'm an eventer. I'm hoping to qualify for Badminton this year, but we will have to see . . .' She sighs. 'Dark Star is a different horse from when I first got him – Matt gave him to me as a Christmas present a couple of years ago. He was hard work – Star, not Matt – but now he's lovely, a genuine four-star competition horse.'

'Is that Matt the vet?' I ask.

'That's right. Have you met him?'

'Yes, at the Sanctuary.'

Nicci slips on some surgical gloves and examines my hand. She flushes the wound and applies a light dressing.

'I'm going to prescribe you a course of antibiotics because that looks as if it's already infected, and it goes quite deep,' she says. 'It goes without saying that you should keep it covered for now to keep the dirt out, and I'm advising you to take a couple of days off to give it time to heal. That's going to hurt.'

'It's hurting already, but I can't afford to take time off. I'm covering for Mel.'

'It's up to you. That's my advice. If the pain gets worse, you must come back immediately to have that wound flushed out under local anaesthetic.' She smiles. 'Matt says there are plastic shoes for horses. Perhaps you should try them with No More Nails from a DIY shop.'

'It would be a lot safer,' I say, amused. I thank her before I leave to pick up antibiotics from the nearby pharmacy. After I've queued there for twenty minutes, while the woman in front of me gossips with the assistant about a recent Parish Council meeting, I return to wait outside the surgery for Robbie. He turns up moments later with the two children in the back of the Land Rover. I jump in.

'Hi, Maisie. Hello, Ashley,' I say.

Ashley acknowledges me with a frown – which is progress, I suppose. Maisie bounces up and down in her car seat, clutching a reading book in one hand and a drawing in the other.

'Daddy says you hurt yourself.'

'I've been to the doctor. She says I'll live,' I respond, glancing at Robbie.

'And I'm having a surprise,' Maisie adds.

'What's that?' I ask, humouring her.

'I don't know because it's a *surprise*,' she says, somewhat scathingly.

'I'm sorry. My daughter's eight going on eighteen.'

'Daddy, tell me what it is,' she goes on. 'Please, please, please.'

'You'll have to wait until we get home.' Robbie pulls out to pass a motorhome that's been left parked on the pavement outside the teashop and sets off for Furzeworthy. Maisie doesn't let up about the surprise for one moment on the trip back.

'I'm sorry,' he says to me. 'I should have kept my mouth shut.'

He drops Ashley at Wisteria House, where Louise emerges for a quick chat. She looks into the Land Rover with a big grin on her face.

'What are you doing, Flick? Bunking off?'

'I gave her a lift to the doctor's,' Robbie says, and I show her the dressing on my hand and the packet of medication.

'I drove a nail through the base of my thumb.'

'Oh dear, these things happen. Mel put a nail in his knee one time. I often remind him of it when he's getting too big for his boots. I hope you're all right.'

'I will be, thanks,' I respond.

'He's hobbling around on his sticks at home, determined to be fit for the spring Farm and Country Festival which is in less than two weeks' time. I've told him he'd be better off staying indoors, but he won't have it.'

'Hurry up, Daddy,' Maisie calls from the back seat.

'I'd better get the dinner on,' Louise says.

'I'll see you soon,' I say. 'I've just got to pick up the truck.'

'You are going to stay for the big reveal?' Robbie says.

'Well, yes, I wouldn't want to miss it.'

'Is it a baby rabbit?' Maisie asks.

'No,' Robbie says, 'and it isn't a kitten either.'

She crosses her arms and pouts. 'It isn't fair. Flick knows and I don't, and I'm the one having the surprise.'

'Exactly,' Robbie says calmly. 'It won't be long now.'

As soon as we arrive at the yard, where he parks close to the new pony's stable, Maisie unfastens her seatbelt and struggles with the door. Robbie moves round to help her out.

'See if you can spot anything different.' He waves towards the stables, where Diva is chewing on some hay, spilling it across the ground outside. T-rex whickers, bringing Paddington to his door. 'Well?'

'It's a pony!' Maisie screams with delight and excitement, reminding me of how I used to react when my parents brought a new horse or pony on to

109

the farm. She starts to run across, then stops and turns back to her father. 'What's its name?'

'He's called Paddington.'

'Paddington Bear,' she cries, running towards him with her arms outstretched. 'Daddy, I can't reach.'

Robbie scoops her up so she can stroke the pony's face.

'What do you think?' He glances at me.

I want to say that I worry about the risks of feeding your child to the horses, but Paddington seems happy.

'He's lovely.' Maisie giggles as he ruffles through her hair with his top lip.

'Would you like to give him a brush?' Robbie lets her back down; five minutes later, Paddington is tied up outside the stable while Maisie stands on an upturned bucket with a body brush in her hand.

'Be careful not to tickle him,' Robbie says as we stand side by side, watching. 'Firm strokes, that's right.'

'All over?'

'Yes, all over.' Robbie reaches across and gives me a big hug, and my heart melts. 'I think I've made one little girl very happy.'

And this big one too, I think.

'I'd better go,' I say, checking my mobile.

'Oh no, come back to the cottage for some cake,' he says quickly. 'Mum's made a chocolate sponge.'

'Can I have some?' Maisie drops the brush back into the plastic box that serves as a container for the grooming kit.

'After you've had your tea. Let's put Paddington away – I'll turn him out next door to T-rex later.'

Maisie leads the pony back into the stable and removes the head-collar. He makes to barge out again, but Robbie beats him to it and closes the door, fastening the top and bottom bolts.

'I reckon he's looking for grass. He's a typical greedy pony. Let's go. I haven't even turned the oven on to warm up yet,' Robbie continues.

'It's all right, I'll eat Nanny's cake,' Maisie says.

Her dad shakes his head rather wearily as she runs ahead of us across the drive and opens the gate into the cottage garden.

'You're so lucky to live in a place as beautiful as this,' I say as I follow Robbie along the path of stepping stones that runs across the lawn between the cherry trees.

'I'm afraid to admit that I'm often too busy to notice. It is lovely.' He stops and gazes up at the brick chimneys topped with red pots that rise up through the thatch at each end of the building. 'I wasn't sure when I first moved in, but now it feels like home.'

He moves on and opens the front door. There's a neat stack of logs piled up to one side of the porch and a stone mushroom to the other, along with a gnome drinking from a tankard, and a plastic hound almost as tall as Maisie sitting on its haunches.

'I didn't think gnomes would be your thing,' I comment.

'Dillon thought I should have one. Come in.' He lets me through into the hallway, where one of the wolfhounds greets us with a low bark. The other is sprawled out on the leather sofa in the living room beyond. I follow Robbie and Maisie into the kitchen, noticing how he has to duck his head as he goes through the doorway.

'How old is the cottage?' I ask, taking in the

flagstone floor and the dark oak beams that run unevenly across the ceiling.

'Parts of it are over four hundred years old. That's the bread oven.' He points to the alcove set deep in the wall beside the fireplace. 'There's a larder through that door – it's always cool in there, it's a great place for keeping beer.'

'And cheese,' Maisie says, joining in.

'There's an Aga, but we only use it in the winter.' He moves across and switches on the electric oven. Maisie opens the back door to let one of the dogs out. 'Would you like to feed the chickens?' he asks her as five rather scruffy brown hens come scurrying towards us, hopping uninvited into the kitchen. 'They look a bit tatty, but that's because they haven't been with us long. They're ex-battery hens – they always take a while to recover from the experience, but they'll soon be laying eggs for us.'

'Don't you worry about the dogs?'

'They know better than to touch them.' Robbie turns away as Maisie fishes about in the cupboard under the sink and pulls out a container of chicken feed. 'What would you like to drink? Tea?'

'Please,' I say, as he takes two mugs down from the hooks above the window. There's a spider weaving its web across the corner of the diamond panes, and crockery piled up in the butler sink. The curtains need a wash and the potted fern on the sill needs some water. The house is crying out for some TLC.

'Take a seat.' He waves towards the wooden table in the centre of the room. 'That's if you can find one. Move the laundry to anywhere you can find a space. It is clean.'

I bundle up a load of crumpled shirts, dresses and

socks from one of the chairs and put them on the end of the table on top of some paperwork. I want to offer to help out in some way, but I don't want to hurt his feelings. He serves me tea and a slice of chocolate cake. He gives in and lets Maisie have some too before placing a tray of breaded chicken fillets and frozen chips in the oven. He pours peas and sweetcorn into a saucepan and puts it on the hob.

'All we need now is ketchup,' he says, hunting around in the fridge for the bottle. 'I can guarantee that there'll be tears before bedtime if there's no tomato sauce.'

I have to say that I'm impressed, even though Robbie's house turns out to be far more chaotic than I expected. Sally Ann and Louise help him out with Maisie, but he's more of a hands-on father than I imagined. It puts him in a different light. He's a domesticated, hardworking dad who can't have much time and energy left for dating and wild nights out. I find Maisie exhausting. She's always on the go, asking questions, arguing, and making the simplest task much more complicated than it should be. She's fed the chickens. They're pecking at the seed on the kitchen floor while she attempts to sweep up some extra feed that she spilled. As she brandishes the broom, which is taller than her, she knocks the dogs' water bowl over, and soon the floor is covered in a brown soup.

'I need a cloth, Daddy,' she says.

He hands her a towel from the laundry pile. 'Spread that out to soak up the water. I'll clear it up later.'

The saucepan boils over. I get up and turn the heat down.

'I should go,' I say. 'Rafa will be waiting to go out.'

'Thanks for coming to pick up Paddington with me. Maisie is completely made up. She doesn't care if she can't ride him. She's more than happy to groom him and give him cuddles. He's very sweet.'

'I won't say I told you so.'

'I think you just did. I've been thinking . . .' Robbie begins. I hold my breath, my overactive imagination putting virtual words into his mouth. *You are the most beautiful woman I've ever met. Let's get to know each other better. I don't normally take risks, but I'm willing to take a chance on you.* I bite my lip.

'. . . About Paddington,' he continues. 'I'd like to see if he'll make a riding pony for Maisie and I was wondering if you wouldn't mind helping me out sometime next week. I'm far too tall, but you'd be okay if you rode him with short stirrups.'

'I'm not sure.' I picture Paddington belting around the Saltertons' arena, bucking like a bronco and me flying off over his head – because it's bound to happen. I seem unable to keep my dignity in front of Robbie.

'I'll give you a lesson in trick riding with my horses in return. What do you think? Are you brave enough?'

'Of course I am.' I muffle the voice that whispers doubt into my ear. 'That would be great. I can't wait.'

A little while later, I return to Wisteria House. It's nine o'clock. Louise's car is on the drive and the lights are off. Rafa whinnies from the field when I walk past the gate and a bat darts silently past my ear. The moon bathes the countryside with a gentle blue light that's almost magical, and I make a wish: that Robbie would give me a clue that he fancies me just a little. He's seen that I'm a member of the opposite sex, but he's made no move on me to suggest that he'd act on it.

Chapter Seven

Why Walk When You Can Ride?

'Mel's staying in bed for a while – the painkillers are giving him a headache,' Louise says when I see her at breakfast on the Thursday morning, a couple of days after Robbie and I collected Paddington from the Sanctuary.

'What are you doing today?' I ask.

'I'm taking Ash and Maisie to school before meeting a friend for coffee at the garden centre. I lead an exciting life,' she jokes. 'We can have a chat over a drink tonight if you're free.'

'That would be great. I haven't any plans.'

'Not yet,' she smiles. 'That could change.'

'I doubt it somehow. There doesn't appear to be much in the way of nightlife around here.'

'I hope you aren't finding it too quiet. There are clubs in Exeter – that isn't too far away if you want a night out.'

'I think I'll pass on that for now – I'm not sure I'd stay awake much beyond ten.' I put my breakfast dishes into the dishwasher, pick up the business mobile, and my mended one which arrived by courier the day before, and go outside. When I'm saying goodbye to Rafa on my way to the truck, I receive a call from Robbie.

'Hi, I've got a therapy session this morning, but I was wondering if you were free over lunch to come and help me with Paddington. If you wanted to, you could stay and have a go at trick riding. I was supposed to be teaching this afternoon, but the rider's cancelled – I'm not sure if they're really ill, or if they've backed out. What do you think?'

'I could drop in at about one-thirty if that isn't too late.' I glance at my thumb. The antibiotics have kicked in and the bruising is going down. It won't stop me riding.

'That's perfect. I'll see you then. It shouldn't take more than half an hour or so with Paddington, and a couple of hours for the lesson. All you need is a hat and boots, good balance, common sense and a dash of bravery.'

'I have all of that.' I can't stop smiling. 'I'll see you later.'

'I'm looking forward to it,' he says.

I cut the call and race off to change into a pair of fawn jodhpurs. I get as many of the day's visits done in as short a time as possible before arriving at the Saltertons', impatient to have a go at trick riding but apprehensive about making a fool of myself. As I exit the truck, the wolfhounds come trotting over and the taller one of the two nudges me in the crotch in greeting.

'That's called being overly familiar.' I push him away and give him a pat.

'Badger likes you,' Robbie says.

Eyes front, I tell myself, as I notice exactly how tight his leggings are, leaving nothing to the imagination. It's a relief that he's covered up, I think, amused that I should even be thinking such a thing. It's because I've been so long without a man.

'I can't imagine you being nervous – you're the coolest guy—'

'Guy?!' I exclaim.

'I mean girl. You're the coolest girl I know. It was a slip of the tongue. I'm sorry, but that's how I see you. I can't help it,' he says earnestly, oblivious to how hurt that comment makes me feel. 'You're a laugh. One of the lads,' he adds adamantly – so adamantly that I wonder, just for one delicious moment, if he's having trouble convincing himself that that's how he feels.

But that seems like very wishful thinking. Apparently he still admires me for my manly qualities then, I think sadly. So much for the wet shirt.

'Are you ready for this? Paddington's in the stable – I've tacked him up. He went nuts when I put the saddle on, bucking and rearing.'

My heart plummets.

'He won't be any good for Maisie then.' I pick up my hat from the passenger seat in the truck, and ram it firmly on to my head. I don't think he's going to be much good for me either. I'm having doubts about what I've agreed to do. 'If he's completely wild when he comes out of the stable, I'm going to back out.'

'I wouldn't blame you.' Robbie rests his hand on the latch and turns to me with a twinkle in his eye.

'You're winding me up,' I say, relieved.

'He's been as quiet as a mouse. Look at him.'

I move to Robbie's side and look over the door,

where Paddington is standing with his eyes closed, resting one leg. He seems perfectly comfortable in a saddle and bridle with the reins tucked safely behind the stirrups.

'I think you'll struggle to get him to move at all.' Robbie opens the door and leads him out. 'I was going to suggest that I lunged him first to take the wind out of his sails . . .'

We walk with Paddington to the sand school. He grunts as Robbie pulls him up and tightens the girth.

'I'm afraid his knees are going to buckle when I get on him.'

'Come on, Flick. You don't weigh anything.' He smiles. 'Do you want to get on from the mounting block?'

I take over the reins and move the pony close to a set of wooden steps. I stand on the top and lean across Paddington's back. He doesn't budge, so I take up the reins, put my foot in the stirrup and swing my leg over his back. I sit down gently in the saddle and slip my right foot into the other stirrup, and sit there with my knees almost level with my chin.

'Frankie Dettori, eat your heart out,' Robbie chuckles. 'Let me take those down for you.'

'It's okay, I can do it,' I say, but without conviction. The belt-like leather straps will need adjusting so that the stirrups hang lower, but it's a slightly awkward manoeuvre, and I can't pretend I'm disappointed when Robbie ignores me and moves towards Paddington's right side. Okay, I think, if he insists on helping out with an operation which is likely to involve some touching of my inner thigh, then at least one of us will have enjoyed it.

Robbie is focusing firmly on the right-hand strap

while I attend to the left. His shoulders are tight and the muscle in his cheek is taut; once he's made the adjustment, he moves away abruptly.

Mesmerised by Robbie's proximity, I'm forgetting Paddington. I reach down and check the girth again. It's nice and snug. I give him a squeeze with my legs and he ambles slowly forwards. We walk around the perimeter of the school before I ask him to step up the pace. He shifts into trot, making the minimum of effort, and breaking wind several times, making me laugh. I change the rein and we trot in the other direction before I ask him for canter. It takes three attempts and then he's off like a pocket rocket, whizzing along at speed. Once he's done a circuit, I pull him up. He puffs and blows as I let him walk around.

'What do you think?'

'Looking good,' Robbie says.

'Thank you, but I'm referring to Paddington.'

'Very funny.'

I pull up and dismount.

'I assume that's enough for him for today.'

'I reckon so. Let's put him away.' Robbie takes over and I accompany him while he untacks Paddington and leaves him in the stable. I top up the water bucket from the tap outside while we chat.

'Thanks for that. I'd have needed roller-skates to try him out.' Robbie leaves the saddle and bridle on the rail outside. 'I'll turn him out later. It's Kerry's day off and Dillon's gone to pick up some bags of feed from Overdown Farmers.'

'I thought it was quiet.'

'Maisie's at school, and Mum and Dad have gone out for the day. They're going to pick her up on their way home.'

'You're lucky having such a supportive family.'

'I know . . . You've hardly talked about yours.'

'As I said before, I'm an only child. My parents said my appearance was a miracle. My dad had been told that he was unlikely to father a child because he didn't have very good swimmers. That's what he and Mum used to say when I was little. I didn't understand at first – for a long time, I had a picture in my head of lots of babies in armbands swimming about in a pool. Anyway, I was very much wanted.' My eyelids start to burn, which is ridiculous. I swallow hard, surprised to find myself growing emotional talking of my parents. I think of them in their younger days, my mum with long dark hair and wearing a bright red dress, walking hand in hand with a handsome man with rugged features, a heavy brow, and dark hair flecked with grey who looked old enough to be her father.

'My father was married when he met my mum. He was running a company. She was his PA. His family disowned him when he divorced and remarried. They said that it would never work, that she was a gold-digger, but they went on to have a good life together, united by their love of Spanish horses. I don't see them very often now, but it was different when I was growing up.'

Robbie waits for me to continue speaking.

'I was spoiled to bits. I had everything I wanted, but I also felt swamped with attention.' I feel sorry for Robbie as I recall how his mother left him. 'They were what people describe as helicopter parents. In fact, Dad did have a helicopter for a while. He sold his part-share in order to buy a particularly desirable stallion. A few years later, the same horse kicked my father, breaking both kneecaps and leaving him hardly able to walk.'

'How old is he?' Robbie asks.

'He's in his seventies. I feel bad about what's happened between us and I'd love to build bridges before it's too late, but . . .' I shrug. 'I have my pride. I need to show them that I can go it alone, that I don't need their money, and that I made the right decision for me.'

Robbie is frowning as I continue. 'My parents don't approve of my choice of career. They had high expectations and they've made it clear that I've let them down.'

'But you've done so well,' he exclaims. 'Look at you. You're good at what you do and you're going to make shedloads of money – well, not as much as a solicitor or a judge, but you don't have to depend on the vagaries of the TV and film industry, as I do.'

'They don't see it that way. In fact, I hardly get in touch with them any more because I can't bear to see their disappointed faces and listen to my mother's jibes about how I'll regret it one day, when my back goes and I'm working outside in all weathers. She goes on and on about how I'll never get married when my muscles turn to fat as I get older. She's pretty vain; when she was younger, she was what my dad describes as a stunner.'

'Like you,' Robbie says.

'I'm sorry?' Have I misheard?

'You're pretty stunning. Like mother, like daughter.' He smiles. 'You're blushing.'

'Thanks for the compliment.' I look into his eyes, searching for what he means by it. He gives me a long, smouldering stare. My heart beats so hard that it feels as if it's bursting out of my chest.

'When I said "looking good" earlier, I meant it. I was talking about you.' He has a half-smile on his lips when he turns away. 'Are you ready to try out some tricks?'

'What kind of tricks?' I say, flirting with him.

'You'll have to wait and see,' he says, flirting back. 'Let me get the saddle.'

I follow him into the tack room where he shows me a Western-style saddle with a metal horn at the front.

'This is a trick saddle.' He picks it up and we walk back towards the arena.

'What, no horse?' I say as he opens the gate.

'First things first. We're going to start with Woody.'

'What's that? Some kind of trick?'

'It's our pretend horse.' He points towards a wooden structure that resembles a horse's body on legs. It stands in the far corner of the school behind a set of jump wings and poles. 'It's cheap to keep and doesn't need shoes. You can give him a pat, if you like. He doesn't bite or kick.' Robbie slides it across the sand so it's away from the fence. 'Let me show you what you're aiming for.

'A lot of the tricks we do today were used in battle,' he goes on. 'You can employ them for attack or self-defence, hiding behind your horse's body while shooting at the enemy, or playing dead to reduce the risk of being shot at.' He takes a run-up and vaults on. He shows me the layover, the suicide drag, the mane drag, backbreaker, and reverse fender, until I don't know which one is which. He finishes his routine, standing perfectly balanced on the wooden horse's back and holding his arms outstretched. 'Your turn,' he sings out as he jumps down on to the sand, landing lightly on his feet. His brow glistens with a sheen of perspiration. His cheeks are lightly flushed. I'm amused and flattered at the way he's showing off. My knees grow weak too – from lust, not fear.

'Go on then. What are you waiting for?'

I summon my strength and take a run-up. I misjudge the distance and lose momentum, ending up halfway up the horse's side. Even hanging on to the horn on the saddle and thrashing with my legs, I don't make it, and I have to endure the indignity of making a second attempt before I scramble on top.

Robbie talks me through how to move to a crouch position, and from there to standing up. He explains how to do a laydown and I lie on my back at right angles to the horse's body, facing the sky.

'Keep your legs and shoulders up. Hold your body straight.' He presses gently on my abs, sending flickers of fire through my belly. I glance towards him. His pupils are dilated and dark with passion, his lips slightly parted. I'm not imagining it. There is definitely *something* going on between us. Not quite 'one of the lads' after all, then . . .

'No banana shapes,' he adds, his voice hoarse.

'I need to work on my inner core,' I say. I thought I was fit, but I'm not half as fit as my trainer. The trouble is that my inner core is currently a molten ball of longing and desire, and I'm finding it hard to concentrate. I want to kiss him. I need to feel his arms around me . . .

I force myself to focus on the lesson. Robbie shows me a couple of other moves before heading off to fetch Nelson and Scout. I sit sideways on the wooden horse waiting for him, my mouth half open.

'You can't stay on Woody. That would be cheating.' He laughs as he lets both horses loose in the school, a stick in his hand. 'Watch and listen carefully.' He calls Nelson to him and vaults on. I'm not sure how he signals to Scout, but he soon has them trotting slowly side by side with matching strides. I watch closely as he moves from a sitting position to a crouch and then to standing on Nelson's back. He sends the horses into a steady canter, and stands with one leg on each horse, travelling around the school.

My chest grows tight as I watch the three of them, moving as one with mutual trust. The horses aren't working under duress. They're enjoying it.

Robbie brings them back to walk, pulls up and salutes me.

'Show off!' I jest, trying to hide the fact that their performance has brought me almost to tears.

He jumps down between Scout and Nelson, landing softly like a cat, and gestures for me to join him.

'Now you have a go.' One eyebrow shoots up under his fringe as I hesitate. 'Relax. I'll be close by to hold your hand, metaphorically speaking. All you have to do is balance, go with the horses and remember to use your voice.'

'Horses, as in both of them?' I'm having severe doubts about my ability to balance on one, let alone two.

'You'll be too focused on using your voice to control them to worry about keeping your balance. If you're worrying about staying on top, you'll tense up and come off.' He doesn't give me time to argue. 'I want you to vault on to Nelson – he's as steady as a rock.'

'He's so big!' A little voice reminds me that I've vaulted on to Rafa's back before, and Nelson isn't

124

much taller. I take a few steps back, spring forwards and upwards, and pull myself on to his back. It isn't elegant, but I make it.

'I want you to do the same manoeuvre as you did on Woody, moving into a crouch as I walk Nelson along the long side of the school, and then, when you're ready, into a standing position. Remember to breathe,' he adds, as Nelson goes into walk.

I can't believe I'm doing this, I think, as I move into a crouch. That is fine, but when I start to straighten up and push myself up on to my feet, I notice I'm much higher off the ground, *much* higher. I wobble.

'Right, start talking to the horse,' Robbie instructs. 'I'll bring Scout alongside. When I say so, you need to push your weight on to your left leg and swing your right leg out.'

'That sounds like I'm doing the hokey cokey.' I soon discover that laughter and stunt riding are not compatible, and I lose my balance, tipping forwards and sliding back into the astride position.

'Try again.'

'I'm not sure I'm cut out for this.'

'Don't give up. You can do it.' Robbie's confidence is infectious, and soon I'm back on my feet, attempting to stretch between the two horses, so I'm standing with one foot on each of them. It takes three goes, but I make it eventually. 'That's it. You've got it.'

I keep the horses moving, walking side by side. It's great. I feel fantastic.

'Thanks, Robbie.'

'Don't thank me too soon. Keep focused.' He raises his voice as Scout on the outside starts to slow his pace. 'And don't forget to speak. You have to let the horses know what you want from them.'

It's too late. Scout comes to a complete halt and Nelson keeps going, and my thighs stretch and tear as I do the splits in the air and the ground flies towards me at an alarming rate. I land with a soft bump in the sand.

Robbie is trying not to laugh. It looks as if Nelson could be laughing too, nudging me with his nose, as if to say, 'What on earth are you doing down there?'

'Are you okay?' Robbie takes my hand and pulls me up. 'You were doing so well until you got to that corner.'

'I was so busy concentrating on staying upright that I forgot to speak.' I brush a load of sand off my bum. Fawn jodhpurs weren't the best choice.

'On you get.'

'What?'

'One more time.'

'You're a hard taskmaster.'

'It's the only way. I want my pupils to fulfil their potential. It's important for you to feel you've achieved something today. If you end the lesson now, all you'll remember is sliding off. Come on. Onwards and upwards.'

Ignoring the soreness in my muscles, I vault back on to Nelson. It's easier this time. I remember to keep both horses moving as I step across to balance one foot on Scout's back. They're responsive to every command and I soon have them walking around the school in both directions. I throw my arms in the air. I'm on top of the world.

'Okay, that's great,' Robbie says. 'Let's stop there.'

'Whoah,' I call and the horses come to a halt together. 'I did it.' I dismount and rub the horses' necks to show my gratitude.

126

'Well done. You're a natural.' Robbie moves in as if he's going to thump me on the back like he does his brother but, at the last minute, he reaches around my shoulders and wraps his fingers around my upper arm. My heart pounds as he hesitates for a second time. Standing perfectly still, I glance up. He's staring at me, his gaze travelling down my face, my neck, my breasts . . . I can hardly breathe as he leans in, his breath caressing my lips.

'Tell me I've got this right,' he whispers. 'I thought . . . I can stop. I mean, I don't want to wreck our friendship.'

'You've taken me by surprise, that's all.'

'I didn't think it would be that much of a shock to you. I've fancied you like mad almost since you first arrived in Furzeworthy.'

'Have you?' I frown.

'Pretty much since I found you limping along the lane without your horse. I wanted to whisk you up and gallop away with you.'

'I didn't think you were interested. You treated me like I was one of the lads.'

'I know. I was trying to avoid any complications. I thought if I could forget you were . . . a female farrier, I could resist, but I can't do it any more. You are just too gorgeous for words.'

'Don't speak then.' I tilt my head towards him and touch my lips to his, and we kiss. My head spins. I feel as if I'm dissolving into him.

'Daddy, I've been looking for you,' a small voice interrupts.

Robbie and I spring apart. I touch my mouth where just a moment ago his lips were in contact with mine. He groans.

'What are you two doing?' Maisie asks.

'We were in the middle of something.' He lifts her into his arms. 'Did you have a good day at school?'

'Yes.' She gives his nose an affectionate pinch.

'What thing? Were you kissing?'

'No, Flick thought she'd been stung by a wasp. I was checking she was all right. She's just had a lesson.'

'Did my daddy learn you how to be a stunt rider?'

'It's "teach",' Robbie says. 'You're supposed to say, "Did my daddy teach you . . . ?" '

'I've learned a lot today,' I say, 'but it's going to be a long time until I'm any good.'

'I'll have to give you a few more lessons,' he grins, and I smile back, because that is exactly what I want to hear. The more the merrier. 'Flick's been riding Paddington today,' he continues.

'Can I ride him?' Maisie asks. 'I wanna ride him.'

'Tomorrow. He's tired now and needs a rest. Maisie, please will you stay here with Flick while I put Nelson and Scout away? Health and safety.'

'Health and safety,' she echoes.

I stand beside her as he leads the horses away.

'Can I buy you that drink sometime?' I ask when we catch up with him at the stables. 'We used to go for a pint or two after work on a hot day like this.'

'Two pints?' Robbie looks at me, his eyes creased with humour.

'Not every day!' I exclaim.

'I'll see if Mum's happy to babysit tonight—'

'I'm not a baby,' Maisie cuts in.

'All right, I know, I'm sorry. Flick, I'll text you later.'

After I've left the Saltertons', it's another three hours before I finish work and get back to the B&B,

when I receive a text from Robbie to say that our trip
to the pub is on. I look after Rafa with Ashley looking
on. He accepts my offer of letting him help me lead
Rafa out to the paddock where, locked in his custom-
ary silence, he gives him a carrot. I decline Louise's
offer of a gossip over a drink. I shower, replace the
dressing on my thumb, and slip into a red skater dress
and pumps before Robbie picks me up. The fake tan
effect isn't great – I spend too much time in the sun
in jeans for my skin to have a natural glow. My knees
have turned out darker than my ankles, but Robbie
looks covetously at my legs, much as he looked at
Rafa the first time we met.

'You look . . . very different.' He opens the Land
Rover door for me. 'In a good way. Lovely . . .'

'Thank you. You look pretty good yourself.' He
smells good, too, of aftershave and fabric conditioner.
I resist the temptation to turn my head to kiss him. I
climb in and he closes the door.

'Maisie can't wait to ride Paddington,' he says as
we set off. 'I've left poor Mum trying to convince her
to have a bath before bed. She's amazing. I couldn't
have got through the nappy stage, the teething and
the tantrums without her. I'm referring to Maisie, not
me.' He changes the subject. 'I thought we'd try the
Talymill Inn along the river. The Dog and Duck's a
bit downmarket.'

'I don't mind which one. It's good of you to offer
to drive.'

'I've not been much of a drinker since I became a
dad. Hangovers and baby sick don't mix.' He takes
me along a road that runs parallel with the river and
pulls into a car park outside an old mill, a building
constructed from brick and tiles and smothered with

window-boxes and hanging baskets of greenery and flowers.

'This is it.' Robbie parks between a black convertible and an antique tractor. 'A couple of Londoners moved here and did it up before selling it on to the current owners. There's a beer garden at the back that runs down to the water, and a children's play area – Maisie loves it. I used to bring her here with the mums and tots when we were part of Talyton's toddler group. We'd have coffee and biscuits and chat about men and relationships and potty-training. It was embarrassing at times, but I wouldn't have missed it for the world. Maisie enjoyed the company of the other kids and I got plenty of help and support from the mums.' His face reddens. 'I was the only dad, so I received a lot of attention and the pick of the biscuits.'

It appears that neither of us is in a hurry to break the intimacy of being just the two of us in the Land Rover, but eventually we make our way inside the pub, with Robbie following along behind me to the bar where I order drinks.

'Mine's an alcohol-free lager, please,' he says.

'And I'll have a glass of rosé,' I say to the barman, wondering if I should be mixing alcohol with my antibiotics.

'You aren't drinking beer?' Robbie says quietly in my ear. 'I assumed you'd have a pint of real ale.'

'I'm not one of the lads now.'

'I can vouch for that.' He smiles and brushes my bare arm with his fingertips, sending a rush of heat right through me.

The barman rings up the price of the drinks at the till while I pull out my purse for some cash. There isn't any. I check inside my mobile phone case where I usually tuck away a twenty-pound note for emergencies, but it's gone and I remember that I spent it on my prescription and some other bits and pieces, including Polo mints for Rafa, at the chemist's. No problem. I pull out my card and hold it over the terminal for contactless payment, but the card is declined.

'How can that be?' I exclaim, although I know perfectly well. The account is empty and I've maxed out to the limit of the overdraft. 'It worked fine the other day.' I try it again with the same result. I'm starting to sweat because there are two drinks sitting on the bar and I have no way of paying for them.

'Perhaps you need a replacement card,' Robbie says. 'Let me pay for these. You can call the bank tomorrow.'

'Thank you. I'll pay you back as soon as I can.' I'll have to ask Mel for an advance on my wages.

Robbie pays and I pick up the drinks and carry them through the busy pub. We pass a group of women – I recognise Gina from Nethercott Farm among them – before we find a free table. I sit down opposite Robbie in the shade of a giant fern and watch the massive wheel turning in the white water in the mill-race that's been incorporated into the building behind a sheet of glass.

'Cheers.' Robbie picks up his lager.

We touch glasses and I take a gulp of wine, swallowing it down quickly. It's warm and metallic, like tea mixed with iron filings. I don't know why people drink the stuff – I smile to myself – unless they're trying to show someone how refined and sophisticated they are.

Robbie puts one finger to his lips and nods towards the group of women.

I listen. They are laughing and talking very loudly.

'Is it so wrong to flirt with your farrier?' says one of them – Gina, I think.

'You've made a bit of a habit of it,' says another.

'Have you heard? Mel's taken on a woman to cover for him while he's having his back done. I met her the other day.'

'I can't have that. I'll have to find somebody else. A female farrier couldn't manage my horse. Maverick isn't naughty. He's highly strung. He needs gentle handling and Mel is just the man to do it.'

'When I find an alternative farrier, I'll let you know,' Gina says. 'If you'll let me get a word in edgeways, I'll explain what happened. She came out to shoe Rambo the other day, and one of his shoes has already come off.'

My heart plummets. Of all the horses to lose a shoe, why did it have to be that one? Gina was sceptical when I arrived at Nethercott Farm. This will only have proved her point, even though I did nothing wrong.

'What about Mel?' the other woman asks. 'How will he feel if we all ... well, it feels like we're dumping him?'

'I can't help thinking that he deserves it,' Gina says, and although I'm angry at her comments about my competence, I reckon that her attitude has a lot to do with my boss not letting her know he was going for his operation. 'She's hopeless and I'm going to make sure all the horse owners in this area know it.'

'That's enough.' Robbie gets up and grabs my hand. 'Come with me.'

'I can stand up for myself,' I protest, although I'd rather leave it alone, but he's already letting the group know what he feels about their bitching.

'For those of you who haven't met her, this is Flick, my farrier,' he says, and the women fall silent. Gina sits fiddling with a heart-shaped locket on a chain around her neck. 'All of us know how careless horses are about their clothing, trashing their rugs and losing their shoes. It happens. You really shouldn't go around wrecking reputations when your own reputation is pretty fragile.'

'Excuse me?' Gina blushes.

'You know what I mean. Anyway, my new mare was trying to kill her the other day and, even though she had a nail through her hand, she carried on and finished the job. She's shod Nelson too, and everyone knows I wouldn't trust just anyone to look after him.' He pauses. 'And that's enough gossip about Mel. He's my cousin's husband, in case you've forgotten. I'd appreciate it if you had some respect for her feelings.'

'Everyone knows what he's like,' the other woman says.

'He's made some mistakes along the way. So what? We all have,' Robbie says fiercely. He glares at Gina.

I step forwards, linking my arm through his.

'Let's go back and sit down,' I say. 'It isn't worth it.'

'You're right,' he says, turning to me. 'Would you like another drink?'

'Thank you, but I haven't finished the first one yet.'

'I'll get another one in anyway. What are you having this time?'

'Okay, I'll try half a pint of the local real ale.'

Feeling guilty that he's paying for a second round,

I pop out to the Ladies to freshen up. I meet Robbie on the way back to our table. He's carrying two glasses.

'Enjoy.' He smiles as he places them on the table.

'Thank you.'

He pulls the chair out for me and I sit down, my mind in a flurry of anticipation. He takes the seat opposite and stretches out his long legs under the table. His calf sidles up against mine and there it stays.

We talk about music and our favourite box sets. Robbie's is *Game of Thrones*, but he can't watch it when Maisie is around. Mine is *The Wire*. As for music, I confess that my girl-crush is Taylor Swift. Robbie's musical tastes are varied, from the Beatles to Maroon 5.

'I listen to anything,' he says. 'We often leave the radio on for the dogs, and Kerry always has music on when she's on the yard.'

Kerry, I think. Now's my chance to ask.

'Are you and she an item?'

'Oh no. We're friends.'

'I'm sorry, I was being nosy,' I say happily.

'She's worked for us for over three years now. She's like part of the family.' He hesitates. 'Have you thought any more about your plans when you finish here with Mel?'

'Not really.' I raise one eyebrow. 'Are you trying to get rid of me already?'

He grins. 'Not at all. Rather the opposite, in fact.'

'I need to earn some money first, then I'll look for a second-hand van so I can strike out on my own. I want my own business. I like the idea of not having to depend on anyone else.'

'I have a friend, the guy at the garage, who buys and sells used vehicles. I can ask him to look out for something suitable. Have you got a budget in mind?'

'It has to be as cheap as possible, reliable, and not a rust-bucket. It doesn't matter about the colour.'

'I'll have a word with him when I take the Land Rover in for its MOT.'

We continue chatting for a while longer before setting out for home. As we travel along the narrow lane towards Wisteria House in the pale light of the crescent moon, I wonder what will happen next. Would Mel and Louise mind if I invited him in for coffee? Will he sweep me off to Cherry Tree Cottage for kisses and cuddles?

He pulls in beside the gate outside the B&B, leaving the engine running and the gearstick throbbing between us. He leans across and slides his arm behind my shoulders.

'Much as I'd like to, I'm afraid I can't stop now – I told Mum I wouldn't be later than eleven.' He smiles ruefully. 'I don't like to take advantage of her in case she doesn't offer again.'

I understand. Robbie has an unassailable commitment to his daughter. I'm not sure how I feel about it, though. When he said there was nothing going on between him and Kerry, I was relieved because it meant that he was free to see me, but now it seems that he isn't as available as I'd hoped.

'Are you free at the weekend?' he asks.

'This weekend?' I say stupidly, my heart hammering hard.

'I'm having a barbecue at the cottage to celebrate Mum and Dad's silver wedding anniversary. Everyone's invited. It's casual – wear what you like and bring a bottle. No presents, at my father's request.'

'It sounds a bit daunting, a family occasion.'

'Oh no, there'll be lots of people there.'

'What time?' I say, making my mind up.

'Any time after seven. All the horses will be out by then. Don't be late. I might need your help with the barbecue.' He inclines his head towards mine and presses his mouth to my lips, and I'm lost in his embrace until, eventually, he pulls away.

'I'd better go,' he murmurs, his reluctance to make a move evident in the tension in his face and his sigh of regret. 'I don't want to, but . . .'

'I'll see you at the weekend,' I whisper. 'Goodnight.'

'Goodnight, Flick.'

He waits for me to close the gate before he drives away. I walk past Rafa's paddock, where he comes ambling up to the gate at the sound of my footsteps on the drive. I give him a mint from my bag before I return indoors, where the house is in darkness and everyone is asleep.

Upstairs, I lie on the bed. A delicious tingle of anticipation runs from the top of my head to the soles of my feet as I dream of being in Robbie's arms with our mouths and bodies locked together. I can taste his kisses, smell his musky masculine scent, and hear the pounding of our hearts. I'm getting carried away. I'm ready, I think, for another relationship after Ryan, now that he's out of my system – emotionally at least, if not financially yet. I can say that now, though I still don't know how I'd feel if I ever saw him again. I smile to myself. I shouldn't have started reading the romance novels at Wisteria House for something to do in the evenings.

It's all very well dreaming, though. I have more pressing concerns. How am I going to cope without money? Working for Mel for three months or so isn't necessarily going to get me out of the hole I'm in. Not only do I have to repay my debts, I have to support myself and Rafa, and set up my own business.

I can't sleep. I turn on the iPad and surf the Internet for second-hand trucks, vans and furnaces to help me focus my mind on the future, and how I think I want it to be, but I can't help feeling that planning ahead is futile when I can't afford a round of drinks, let alone a truck.

Chapter Eight

The Healing Power of Horses

When I get Rafa ready on the morning of the barbecue, I ask him what he thinks I should wear tonight. He merely nudges my pocket to see if I have any treats. I hack him past the field where the piglets squeal and scamper about while the sows look on wearily as if they'd appreciate some peace and quiet. One of them stands belly deep in a muddy wallow beside one of the water troughs, her eyes half closed in the spring sunshine.

After I've washed Rafa down with Ashley looking on, I return him to his stable for the day. I grab a drink from the kitchen and Louise offers me cake before I go out again.

'It's carrot cake so it's vaguely healthy,' she observes as she cuts me a huge slice. 'I'm assuming you won't want dinner tonight as you'll be at the barbecue.'

'That's right. I should have said. I'm sorry.'

'No worries. Robbie mentioned it when I saw him in town today. Mel and I are going, and Ashley, although I'll bring him home early if he feels overwhelmed. I'm hoping he'll feel quite chilled because Maisie is there.' She smiles. 'It's a great night out. We go every year to celebrate some occasion or other. You and Robbie? Are you and he . . . ? Do I have to spell it out?'

'We're friends, that's all.' I turn away to read the headline on the paper on the table.

'You seem to be spending a lot of time together,' Louise tries again.

'It's because of the horses.'

'Sure,' she says wryly. 'As I've said before, he's a lovely guy, but he's wary of dating. He has to be because of Maisie. She doesn't need a constant stream of women passing through her life. Children –' she glances at Ashley, who is removing the wheels from a toy lorry – 'need stability.'

'I'm off to do a couple of trims,' I say, changing the subject. I drain my glass and eat the last crumbs of carrot cake before saying goodbye.

On my way, I drop into Talyton St George to buy wine from Lacey's Fine Wines and a bouquet of flowers from Petals as a small gift for Robbie's parents, using a credit card.

Later, I see to Rafa and call Sarah for a chat. She invites me to her and David's upcoming housewarming party and suggests that I bring a friend. I mention a particularly hot stunt rider and she's so excited for me that I'm afraid she might give birth there and then.

For my evening out, I choose a white cotton top with puff sleeves, caught in at the waist, revealing a hint of flesh, a pair of pale blue shorts to show off my legs, and deck shoes. I wear a silver necklace with a simple crystal pendant and put on some make-up.

Satisfied with my appearance, I drop into the kitchen to see if Louise, Mel and Ashley are about. Mel is at the table, eating beans on toast, Ashley is playing with Lego, and Louise is checking the B&B bookings in her diary. She looks up.

'You're keen,' she says with a gleam in her eye.

'We're running late as usual,' Mel says.

'Tell Robbie we'll be there soon,' Louise adds. 'Mel's had to have a snack in case he burns the steaks like he did last year.'

'And the year before,' he grumbles. 'There are some men who shouldn't be in charge of a spatula and grill, and Robbie's one of them.'

'Oh, don't be mean,' Louise says. 'At least he attempts something more complicated than beans on toast once in a while.'

'Why should I learn to cook when I have a beautiful wife who roasts and bakes like an angel?'

'Give over.' She flutters her eyelashes at her husband.

'It's the truth.'

'You wouldn't know the truth if it came and hit you in the face.'

'I don't know what you're talking about.' He straightens in his chair. 'Ouch! I'm not sure I'll be able to stay long tonight. My back's killing me.'

'Don't you dare duck out,' Louise cuts in. 'I had to have Sunday dinner with your brother and all his kids last week. The least you can do is return the favour and spend time with my family. It's Uncle Neil's silver wedding anniversary. It's special.'

'All right, I'll suffer,' Mel groans.

'Great,' says Louise, 'as long as you promise to suffer in silence.'

He smiles. 'You know me.'

'Yes, I do, only too well.'

'I'll be off then,' I say.

'If you wait, we can give you a lift,' Louise says.

'It's okay. I'll walk. It isn't far.'

'There's a space in the car for the way home, if you're coming back this way tonight,' she goes on, 'but if you aren't, I'll check on Rafa for you and bring him in tomorrow morning.'

'Thanks. Um, I'll see you soon.' I escape from the kitchen, grab my bag with the wine and present, and make my way to Cherry Tree Cottage, wondering if I'll be spending the night there. I won't take my toothbrush. I'm not that presumptuous, but I am quietly optimistic. Robbie is a red-blooded male. We're both adults. If a kiss should become a cuddle and lead on to something more, why not? We know where we stand. A springtime of friendship could lead to a summer of love.

Blue and silver balloons, tied with ribbons and dancing in the light breeze, are strung along the fence beside the Saltertons' drive. The sun is low in the sky and the shadows of the trees are lengthening as I walk past a row of cars and up towards the cottage. There are people I don't recognise congregated around a picnic bench at the end of the lawn, so I head for the house, past the cherry blossom that is scattered like confetti across the grass. The front door is open. I knock and walk on in, taking care not to trip on Maisie's riding boots, which have been cast across the flagstone floor. There's no one in the kitchen, but there are signs of recent occupation: two bowls of salad – one tomato and onion, one green; knives; chopping blocks; paper bags and cardboard boxes from one of the local farm shops. It looks much like a work in progress.

Through the window, I catch sight of Robbie in the back garden. Dressed in jeans and a short-sleeved blue shirt, he's standing over a barbecue on the patio, blowing on to the coals.

'You look like you could do with some help,' I call from the door.

'Hi.' He straightens. His eyes caress my body from top to toe and back again. 'I'd like to say that I have everything under control, but . . .' He holds out his hands. '. . . As you can see.'

I want to fall into his arms, but I notice that Maisie's on her way up from the bottom of the garden with a bucket and spade, and the two dogs, and I'm not sure how I'm supposed to behave.

'I thought I could cope, but I underestimated the amount of preparation. I'm in the doghouse because I forgot to wash Maisie's party dress, I was late firing up the barbie, and I haven't chopped the veg yet.'

'Daddy, I'm bored,' Maisie announces as she reaches us. She's wearing a sage-green shift dress embroidered with white daisies. 'Hello, Flick. You need a new pair of shorts.'

I panic. Have I torn them?

'They're too small, just like my school uniform.'

'Who do you think you are, the fashion police? They look great to me,' Robbie says bashfully. 'Just right.'

I tug at the hem.

'I don't think that'll make any difference,' he chuckles. 'You look amazing.'

The shorts are revealing – that was my intention – but, even so, my face flushes hot.

'Why are you going red?' Maisie says, not missing a thing.

'She's caught the sun because she didn't wear her sunblock.' Robbie gives me a conspiratorial wink.

'That's very naughty.'

'I think Flick could be quite wicked in all kinds of ways,' he teases.

'I don't know what you mean.' I tip my head to one side, hoping I look coquettish. I could certainly get wicked with Robbie. Hopefully tonight.

'Can I stay up late?' Maisie asks.

'If you're on your best behaviour.'

'I'll be good,' she says quickly.

'You can stay up if you're good too, Flick. Can't she, Daddy?'

He casts me a glance. 'Flick is a grown-up, so she can go to bed where and when she chooses.'

A second flood of heat rushes up my neck at the thought that I can also choose with whom.

'Go and wash your hands,' Robbie says. 'She's overexcited,' he adds as she disappears indoors. 'Like me.' He takes both my hands and pulls me in for a quick kiss. 'I'm glad you could come. I thought we could spend some time together afterwards . . . if you'd like to.'

'I'd love to,' I smile.

He releases my hands and takes a step back.

'What can I do?' I say softly. 'I could light your fire, if you like.'

'It's already alight –' he glances over his shoulder at the coals that are glowing orange on the barbecue – 'in more ways than one.'

'I'll prepare the veg.'

'Thank you.' Robbie shows me to the kitchen table

where I leave my bag and start cutting up courgettes, onions and mushrooms. 'Dillon's supposed to be here to give me a hand.'

'Are you talking about me?' Robbie's brother comes striding into the room and takes his brother in an affectionate stranglehold. I slide a cherry tomato on to a kebab stick as Maisie returns at speed to greet her uncle.

'It's time for a drink,' Dillon says.

'We have apple juice or cola,' Maisie says.

'There's beer in the larder and wine in the fridge.' Robbie extricates himself from Dillon's embrace and turns to me. 'There are a couple of bottles of rosé – I remembered.'

Oops, I think.

'I have a confession to make,' I begin. 'I'm not keen on wine. In fact, I hate the stuff.' Robbie frowns while Dillon looks on with interest. 'I didn't want you to think I drank pints all the time like one of the lads.'

'That's quite bizarre. You're a good actress ... or should that be actor? I really thought you were enjoying it.'

'You've made quite an impression on my brother.' Dillon grins as he takes a beer from the larder and snaps the lid off the bottle with his teeth.

'You have remembered you offered to babysit your niece tonight,' Robbie says.

'It's all right.' Dillon's eyes sparkle with amusement. 'I won't let anything get in the way of romance.'

'You also promised to keep your mouth shut,' Robbie adds.

'You're so easy to wind up, big brother,' Dillon chuckles.

'I wouldn't have to take everything so seriously if you weren't such an idiot sometimes.'

'You can rely on me.'

'Can I?' Robbie stares him straight in the eyes.

'You know you can.' A shadow of emotion crosses Dillon's face. I'm not sure if it's hurt, or offence, or a mixture of the two. 'I trust you with my life. I wish you could say the same of me.' He pauses as if to let his brother speak, but Robbie remains silent, his lips pressed together.

'Remember when we rode all the way to the quarry on the other side of East Hill,' Dillon continues. 'There was that drop into the water where I chickened out at the last minute and you went for it. And the gap between the rocks where you galloped straight through, even though it was only just wide enough for a horse. You had Nelson rearing up at the top of the fifty-foot cliff, bringing his feet down right at the edge and sending boulders crashing down the slope beneath you. I looked up to you. I was proud of you. I thought I couldn't have a better brother. Now look at you, with your folder of risk assessments. You're a wuss.'

'I have Maisie to think of,' Robbie says quietly.

'Hey, can I join the party?' I look up to find Kerry, wearing a short navy cocktail dress and heels, walking into the kitchen, where she makes a beeline for Robbie, kissing him on the cheek, before turning her attention to Dillon.

'Hello, Maisie. Flick, I didn't know you were coming.' She hardly gives me a glance, as if she's dismissing me altogether. I wonder if she has some kind of problem with me. Is she jealous of my friendship with Robbie, or my status as the Saltertons' farrier, or is she unimpressed with my outfit? My host said the dress code was casual, but I feel decidedly underdressed.

'I'll help myself to wine.' She takes a couple of glasses from the cardboard box on the worktop beside the sink.

'Allow me.' Robbie takes a bottle from the fridge, opens it and pours it for her.

'Thank you, hun. Let me get you a beer – you don't seem to be drinking.'

'No, it's okay. I'm on the wagon tonight.'

'You're becoming a bit of a Grinch,' Kerry observes.

'That's what I've just been telling him,' Dillon joins in.

'Thanks a lot,' Robbie says wryly. 'I don't want to be drunk in charge of the barbecue, that's all.'

'Gemma's with me, by the way,' Kerry says, handing a glass of wine to Dillon. 'She's keen to see you again.'

'Who's Gemma?' I ask Robbie, when Kerry and Dillon leave the kitchen together. 'I noticed how his face lit up.'

'She's one of Kerry's friends. She works with Matt at Westleigh Equine as a vet nurse. Dillon fancies her like mad, but she isn't quite so keen on him.'

'What about Kerry? Does she have a significant other?'

'She likes to play the field. I can't imagine her ever settling down.'

'I don't think she likes me,' I observe as Maisie, having heard voices, runs off to find out which guests have arrived.

'I like you,' Robbie mouths as people start to make

their way through the kitchen and out to the back garden. 'Let me introduce you.'

I meet Louise's parents, who run the nearby Barnscote Hotel. Her mother and Robbie's aunt, Elsa, is the person who breeds the outdoor-reared pigs. Neil and Sally Ann make their appearance soon after. Neil is wearing a blazer and grey flannel trousers, while his wife looks glamorous in a long fuchsia dress and jacket. Louise, Mel and Ashley turn up too, along with a number of others, including Matt and Dr Nicci, the Fox-Giffords and the Barneses, who all happen to be clients of Mel's. It's a great party – I shouldn't have worried because, even if we have nothing else in common, we can talk horses all evening.

I hand over my gifts to Sally Ann.

'You shouldn't have,' she says, giving me a hug. 'I'm so glad you could come, especially after what you've done finding Paddington for Maisie. She loves that pony. We all do.'

Feeling a little awkward among this close band of friends and family, I hang out with Robbie, assisting with the barbecue. The sausages and burgers begin to sizzle, the wine and beer and conversation flow, but there's no sign of his daughter, which is unusual. She isn't usually far away.

'Where's Maisie?' I ask. 'I haven't seen her for a while.'

'She and Ashley went off with Dillon.'

'Dillon's here,' I point out. He's leaning against the wall of the cottage with a bottle of beer in one hand and one arm around a girl.

Robbie's mood changes. He approaches his brother, his eyes glinting with irritation.

'Where are the kids? You're supposed to be looking after them.'

'I don't know. They can't be far away.' Dillon shrugs and the girl steps aside.

'They need constant supervision. You know that.'

'We used to play out all the time. We survived.'

'There's danger everywhere, the horses, the pond . . .' Robbie bundles him up against the wall, the sinews of his neck taut with barely suppressed fury. 'Where the f— are they?'

Choking, Dillon pushes his brother backwards.

'If you let me speak . . . they were with the pony.'

'Which one?'

'Paddington.'

'How many times do I have to tell you?'

'They won't come to any harm,' Dillon argues, as a high-pitched scream penetrates the dusk.

'What's that?' Robbie says urgently.

There's another scream and another. Robbie's face is white. He turns and tears down the drive towards the yard with Dillon in hot pursuit. I follow, my breathing sharp and painful. Paddington's stable door is open. The light is on. Robbie disappears inside.

'They're okay,' he shouts. 'Maisie and Ash – they're fine.'

'Where's the pony?' I ask.

'He can't have gone far,' Dillon slurs.

'You better hope he hasn't.' Robbie looks up from where he's squatting down in the shavings with Maisie's arms around his neck. Ashley stands in the corner. I want to comfort him, but I know he hates being touched.

'We were playing,' Maisie sobs. 'I was the therapy person and Paddington was helping Ashley to talk.'

'You know you mustn't do anything with the ponies without a grown-up. It isn't safe.'

'Ashley loves Paddington.'

'We all do, but that doesn't mean you can just set yourself up as an equine therapist. Where is the pony?'

'I don't know. He ran away.'

'Dillon, take Maisie and Ashley back to the cottage. Flick and I will look for Paddington.' He turns to me as the children walk away with Dillon in tow. 'Where would he go? Think like a pony.'

'Let's try the feed room.'

'He can't get in there. It's locked.'

'There's a bolt across—'

'You don't think . . .?'

We head for the corner of the yard and, sure enough, the door is wide open.

'He broke in, the cheeky sod!' Robbie grabs my arm. 'Listen.'

I can hear the clanging of metal bins being knocked about, followed by rustling and chomping. As we look inside, a white face looms out of the darkness.

'Come here, Padds.' Robbie laughs as he dives into the feed room and puts an arm around the pony's neck to pull him away from his impromptu supper. 'No takeaways. You'll get tummy-ache.' He leads him outside and back to his stable, hanging on to his mane and holding a small scoop of feed in front of him as a bribe. He closes the door on him and slides the bolt across, along with the kick-over bolt at the bottom which Paddington can't reach.

'All's well that ends well,' I say cheerfully.

'We haven't started yet. Come here.' He glances

around as he pulls me close for a kiss, his lips on mine, his hands running down my back, his fingertips grazing the skin above the waistband of my shorts and moving down to my buttocks, giving them a squeeze. I melt into him as the sun goes down over the hills.

'Robster! Ash wants to know if you've found the pony.'

Robbie and I jump apart at the sound of Mel's voice. I don't know why. It isn't as if we're doing anything wrong. It's just that I want to keep it to ourselves for a while. Robbie catches my eye and grins as he turns the light on from outside Paddington's stable. It's our delicious little secret.

'He's safe,' I say. Louise and Ashley are following close behind Mel and come to join us. Ashley looks over the stable door and Paddington walks across to greet him with a touch of his whiskery muzzle against his cheek.

Louise reaches out her hand. Robbie shakes his head.

'Leave them be,' he says quietly.

'I don't like it,' Mel mutters from behind me. 'Ash doesn't do horses.'

I think from the way that he sometimes hangs around when I'm looking after Rafa that Ashley likes him, but I keep my mouth shut.

'Sh,' Louise says.

'Padd-ing-ton.' Ash squeals and I make to move towards them, afraid that the pony is going to react with a nip or head-butt, but Robbie holds me back, his hands on my waist.

'They're okay,' he whispers.

I watch, holding my breath as Ash reaches up and

strokes the pony's face. He squeals again, then bursts into laughter.

'Oh-mi-God.' Louise turns and grasps Mel's arm as Ash laughs again. It's a bubbling sound, like the river flowing over the stones in the shallows, fresh and clean and new.

'It's a miracle,' Louise murmurs.

Robbie pulls me closer so I can feel his body pressed against my back, his chin resting on my shoulder and his cheek against mine.

'It's proof of the healing power of horses, if anyone should need it,' he says for Mel's benefit, I think, as Mel stands aside like a brooding shadow beneath the overhang. The emotion in Robbie's voice shatters me. I can't hold back the tears at the sight of the bond between a boy and a very ordinary pony who's turned out to be quite extraordinary. Robbie hands me something from his pocket, a tissue.

'Thank you.' I dab at my eyes and continue to watch until eventually Paddington steps back from the door and Ashley turns to face his mum.

'Padd-ing-ton,' he says.

'I know,' she says, a sob catching in her throat as he reaches for her hand. 'Let's go and find Maisie.'

We walk up the path to the cottage, Louise and Ashley strolling along with me and Robbie while Mel limps a few paces behind.

'Horses are emotional creatures and, because they're herd animals, they're experts at communication,' Robbie says. 'I've been trying to persuade you to give equine therapy a go for ages—'

'It isn't necessary,' Mel cuts in. 'I don't want my son wasting his time talking to animals.'

'Our son,' Louise corrects him. 'I want him to

be happy, unlike his grumpy old dad. Is your back troubling you today? We can go home if you prefer.'

'I'm fine,' he says snappily.

'He needs to eat,' Louise says. 'He's like a bear when his blood sugar's low.'

'I'd be more than happy to work with Ash for a couple of sessions a week.'

'I can't see the point,' Mel insists. 'I don't want my son messing about with horses. He'll end up galloping around the countryside in a flowing shirt, or show-jumping like a girl.'

'You've got that wrong. There are lots of male show-jumpers and the tight breeches are very masculine. It takes confidence to wear ruffles. Flick agrees with me.' Louise looks towards me for support.

'Only because she fancies Robbie,' Mel says. 'I don't know any other bloke who can carry off the romantic-hero look, and even then he looks like a complete –' he swears – 'when he's wearing make-up.'

'Thanks a lot,' Robbie says lightly.

'I don't want to talk about this now,' Mel says. 'Where's the grub? I'm starving.'

Maisie comes running along the path to greet us, with Dillon in close pursuit, perhaps contrite after what happened with the pony.

'Did you find Paddington?' she shouts.

'Yes, he broke into the feed room. He's a very naughty boy,' Robbie says. 'It's lucky that his belly rules his brain. I was afraid that he'd got out on to the road and had an accident.'

Maisie looks up at her father, the moon reflected in her wide eyes.

'Did you let him out, Maisie?'

'Nooooo,' she says, holding her hands behind her back.

'Are you sure about that?'

'Nooooo. I mean, yes.'

'Can I see your nose getting longer? Are you getting a black spot on your tongue?' Robbie asks.

'Everyone knows that isn't true,' she says confidently.

'Why are you crossing your fingers behind your back?'

'Because it keeps you safe when you tell a lie,' she says slowly, the revelation dawning on her that she's dropped herself right in it. 'I won't go into his stable again without you being there.'

'I know you won't, darling.' He smiles. 'Now, let's go and have some food.'

'There isn't very much left,' she announces.

'Why? Have you eaten it all?'

'Granddad took over the cooking—'

'Don't tell me. He burnt the sausages,' Robbie cuts in.

'He put the rest of the meat from the kitchen on the picnic table, and when he turned round it was all gone.' Maisie turns her head quickly from one side to the other. 'Zoom! Just like that. Badger and Tatt stole the chicken and the steak and the lamb. All that's left is sausages and sardines. Nanny isn't very pleased. She says she's trying to feed the five thousand on a few fishes and lots of burger rolls, but there aren't five thousand people here, are there, Daddy?'

'Granddad shouldn't have put food at nose height. Surely he knows that by now?'

'They ate a packet of butter with the paper on once.

153

We told Nanny that Dillon took it.' Maisie chuckles behind her hand. 'She believed us.'

'Or she pretended to.' Robbie smiles ruefully. 'Mr Rock's will still be open for fish and chips. Flick, are you coming with me?'

'I wanna come,' says Maisie.

'You're with us,' Louise says quickly. 'You can make a list of what everyone wants and we'll text it to Daddy.'

Soon we're on our way to Talyton St George in the Land Rover. The streets are quiet, apart from a middle-aged woman in a mac being towed along by a giant dog that's even bigger than the wolfhounds.

'That's Mrs Dyer, the butcher's wife,' Robbie says as we pass her and stop on the pavement just past the fish and chip shop, where the shutters are down. We pull up close by so I can read the note on the door.

'"Closed for one week. She who must be obeyed has booked us on a cruise when I'd rather be here eating chips and drinking beer."' I can't help laughing. '"Sorry for the inconvenience."'

Robbie doesn't see the funny side. 'Mr Rock's is never closed. Now what am I going to do?'

'Is there an Indian or Chinese?' I've seen a florist's, a pharmacy and a boutique. It doesn't look very promising. The antique streetlamps flicker in the dusk.

'There's supposed to be a curry house coming soon.' He sighs as he turns the engine back on. 'I'll see if Mrs Dyer will open up as a special favour.'

She is most obliging. Mr Dyer has apparently already retired to bed, but she has some steaks, sausages and burgers in the walk-in fridge to the rear of the shop. She weighs and wraps them, adds a couple of large marrowbones for the dogs, and Robbie pays with his card.

'Thanks,' he says. 'You've saved my life.'

'A big do, is it, my lover?'

'It's my parents' wedding anniversary.'

'How lovely.' Mrs Dyer gazes at me. 'And this is your young lady?'

'She's the farrier,' Robbie says, sidestepping the question.

'Oh, yes. You're staying with Louise and Mel.' She looks at my arms as if she's comparing them with hers. 'You don't look strong enough to handle them big horses.'

'It's brain that counts, not brawn,' Robbie says.

'I believe you, my lover. How's that lovely daughter of yours?'

'Maisie's fine.' He checks his watch. 'We'd better get back before there's a riot. It's been lovely talking to you, and thanks for opening up especially for us. I'm very grateful.'

'Anytime, dear. Do tell Sally Ann to let me know if she still wants half a hogget for the freezer.'

'Will do.' He picks up the bags and I hold the door open for him.

'I have a question,' I say, when we're back in the Land Rover.

'Go on,' Robbie says flirtatiously.

'What's a hogget?'

'It's a sheep that's older than a lamb and younger than mutton.' He grins. 'And there I was thinking you were going to ask me to . . .' He leans towards me.

'I was assuming that I didn't have to ask . . .' I move in for the kiss. I can hardly breathe and my chest is

155

tight. The lack of oxygen sends my brain into a spin, until all I can focus on is clinging on to him, one hand tangling through his hair and the other grasping at his shirt. A light goes on, illuminating the inside of the Land Rover. I pull away. Robbie groans.

'It's Mrs Dyer – she's watching through the window.' He sits back and turns the key in the ignition. 'We'd better not linger any longer. People will talk.'

We return to the cottage with the meat for the barbecue. Dillon takes over the cooking while Robbie proposes a toast to Neil and Sally Ann. He stands on the patio at the rear of the cottage, which is illuminated by a string of coloured lights, and taps a bottle of Prosecco with a spoon to call the guests to attention.

'Has everyone got something to drink?'

'Let me do that,' Kerry says, pushing in and taking the bottle. She flashes her cleavage in Robbie's direction. 'Do you like my outfit?'

'It's a bit different from your jodhs,' he says awkwardly, 'but very . . . nice. The dress suits you.'

'I didn't realise you were rushing off to buy meat. I could have come with you.'

'It's all right. Flick offered.'

'I see.' She stares at him, her eyes narrowed.

'What's that supposed to mean?'

She shrugs. 'You'd better get on . . .' She turns her back on him and – with a false smile on her face – proceeds to top up the guests' glasses.

Robbie might not see it, but I'm pretty sure Kerry has feelings for him. But frankly who can blame her, I reflect somewhat smugly, my heart fluttering as the memory of his kisses returns to me.

I fetch myself a beer and a glass from the kitchen and join the party.

'Hello and welcome, everyone,' Robbie begins. 'Thank you for joining us as we review the most beautiful love story that began over twenty-five years ago.'

'Oh, please don't remind us how old we are,' Sally Ann giggles as she holds on to Neil's arm. 'It doesn't seem possible.'

'The presence of so many family and friends just shows what kind of people my mum and dad are,' he continues. 'My brother and I . . . where are you, Dillon?'

He moves into the circle, dressed in an apron and armed with tongs and a spatula.

'We want to thank you for being the best parents ever. We've put you through a lot of hassle over the years.'

'Hear, hear,' says Neil.

'But you've always been here for us, through various accidents when we pushed the boundaries just too far with some of the stunts.'

'You and Dillon were on the "at risk" register, we took you into A&E so many times,' Sally Ann says.

'I can't believe you had the patience to teach us to drive,' Robbie says.

'How many cars did Dillon write off?' Neil puts his finger to his lips and rolls his eyes as if he's counting. 'Four?'

'And you've been the most amazing grandparents to Maisie. On top of that, you've kept us fed, organised and in horses. Your belief in us and the Eclipse team has never wavered—'

'Oh, it has a few times,' Neil cuts in.

'Not now, darling,' Sally Ann says, touching her throat.

'That's right, keep him in order,' Dillon laughs.

'Whatever has happened, good or bad,' Robbie says, 'you have always been there for each other. You are the most loving and devoted couple I have ever met. Your love for each other and for your family is incredible, and Dillon and I count ourselves as very lucky to have you as our parents.' Robbie hesitates. 'I think that's enough from me. Let's raise our glasses to the happy couple. To Mum and Dad, Sally Ann and Neil.'

'To Sally Ann and Neil,' the guests murmur above the chinking of glasses as Robbie finishes his speech.

'Congratulations on twenty-five years of happy married life, and our best wishes for another twenty-five, and more.'

'We'd like to thank our wonderful sons for this fantastic party,' Neil says. He turns to Sally Ann. 'When I first met my lady here, I knew she was very special. Within a week, I was sure she was for keeps, and before a month had passed, I had proposed. She turned me down three times—'

'I wanted to be sure,' she interrupts, 'and you've proved yourself to be the best husband anyone could have.'

'I'd be lost without you, love of my life.' He kisses her to applause from the crowd.

The party continues well into the night as we eat our way through a mountain of burgers and salad, followed by Sally Ann's home-made ice cream and a slice of anniversary fruit cake, created and decorated by star baker Jennie Barnes, and I find myself wishing that everyone was thinking more about getting up for their horses in the morning than downing more food and drink. However, Mel and Louise are the first to make a move, taking Ashley, who's fallen asleep with Badger on the sofa indoors. Maisie is still on the go, charging around with Tatt, pretending that he's a pony.

I stand beside Robbie on the lawn beside one of the cherry trees to wish the guests a safe journey home.

'She's never going to sleep tonight,' he sighs.

I'm beginning to understand how the commitment of having a child might have made some of my good friends drift away, temporarily at least.

'She seems to have enjoyed the party. I don't know how you do it.'

'Bringing up Maisie is a bit like having a horse.' His voice lightens. 'It's 24/7. Kids and horses thrive on routine, regular feeds, exercise and grooming. And they both need shoes. Maisie's always needing new shoes.' He grows serious again. 'She was supposed to stay with Dillon tonight, but he isn't sober, so Mum has offered.'

'But it's their anniversary.'

'The actual date is next weekend. They've booked a romantic getaway to a castle in Scotland towards the end of the summer. I thought maybe you'd like to stay for coffee.'

'There's a lot of clearing up to do.'

'That can wait until morning. You don't think I'm expecting you to stay to tidy up?'

'What are you expecting me to stay for?' I say archly.

He smiles, his eyes alight with desire.

'I thought we could get to know each other better.' He pauses. 'Flick, I'm desperate to hold you in my

159

arms. I can't wait for everyone to go home and leave us in peace.'

As if on cue, Sally Ann walks over, holding Maisie's hand.

'I think it's time we left. Thank you, Robbie, for a wonderful evening . . . and speech. I can't wait to see what you do for our fiftieth.'

'Thanks for having Maisie tonight.' Robbie hugs her.

'It's the least we can do,' Sally Ann says. 'Goodnight.'

'Goodnight, Daddy,' Maisie says, as Robbie bends down to kiss her. 'See you in the morning.'

'Not too early. Nanny needs her beauty sleep.'

'And her lotions and potions and a lot of wishful thinking nowadays,' Sally Ann laughs.

'Beauty comes from the inside,' Maisie says slowly.

'That's quite right, darling. Now, come on. It's time for bed.'

'Can I have a story?'

'Not tonight. You've stayed up late enough as it is.' Sally Ann leads Maisie away and the rest of the guests start to disperse. By 1 a.m., everyone has left, and silence has descended over the cottage. Robbie makes sure the barbecue has gone out while I put a load of glasses and plates into the dishwasher and turn it on.

'Flick, leave that,' he calls. 'Come out here for a minute.'

I join him in the garden where he's standing on the patio, looking up at the deep navy sky.

'There's the Milky Way.' He points up to the pure white swirl of stars above our heads and slides one arm around my back. 'It reminds me how magical the galaxy is, and how small and insignificant our lives are.'

'It certainly makes you think,' I say, leaning against

160

him and absorbing his warmth in the cool night air. 'But I don't want to think tonight.'

He turns and gazes down into my eyes. 'What do you mean?'

I lean up and touch my lips to his.

'I don't want to rush you.' His voice is hoarse. 'I don't want you to do anything unless you want to.'

'I want to,' I whisper.

'You want to go to bed?'

'Oh yes, more than anything.'

He wraps his arms around me and pulls me close. His eyes are smiling as he kisses me, gently at first, and then with urgency and passion. I respond. I can't get enough of him.

'Let's go upstairs,' he mutters. He takes me by the hand, and we walk through the cottage, past the sleeping dogs and up the creaking stairs to the bedroom where he closes the door behind us.

Chapter Nine

In Your Arms

The next morning when I wake it takes me a moment to realise where I am. I can hear birds singing, the sound of a tractor and a horse whinnying – its voice is too deep to be Rafa's. There are other noises too: the sound of breathing, and the growl of an empty stomach, not mine, and the rising tide of my pulse as memories of the night before come back to me.

'The first time I get to have a lie-in for months and they're silaging.' Robbie pulls a pillow over his eyes.

'Hey, do I look that bad the morning after the night before?' I say lightly.

He tosses the pillow on to the floor.

'Oh-mi-God no, you look more gorgeous than ever.' He cuddles up against me, moving his hand over the curve of my waist. The contact moves on to a kiss and soon we're making love, slowly this time, revelling in the intimacy and freedom of being just the two of us alone together.

Afterwards, I lie in Robbie's arms, feeling as though I'm on another planet where nothing else matters,

162

until a knocking sound from downstairs brings me back down to earth.

'I'd better see who that is.' He gets out of bed and wraps a sweatshirt around his middle like an apron before moving across to open the window.

'I'm sorry, Maisie wanted to see you,' Sally Ann calls up. 'I thought you'd be up by now.'

Robbie glances back in my direction. I know what he means. He's been up already.

'Nice butt,' I mouth at him.

'Maisie,' he calls down. 'Go back to the house with Nanny and I'll be over for breakfast in five minutes.'

'All right, but don't be late,' she cries.

Robbie closes the window, walks back to the bed, and leans down to hug and kiss me. 'I have to go. I wanted to cook you breakfast, but it seems it isn't to be.'

'Another time.' The bliss of having woken up with him soon overwhelms the disappointment of being rushed away.

'Oh, definitely.'

I drag myself out from under the duvet and slip into my clothes.

'I'll call you later. We'll arrange to meet up sometime this week if you're free. And if you want to,' he adds tentatively.

'Of course I do,' I say.

'I've got a busy week. It's the Farm and Country Festival next weekend – Dillon and I are taking the horses and putting on a Roman-themed display. We're booked for six performances, two each on Thursday, Friday and Saturday in the main arena.'

'That sounds exciting.'

'Nerve-wracking. We've put some new stuff into

the routine and it needs more practice. Dillon keeps ducking out of training. He's always got some excuse.'

'I'll come and watch. Mel's entered me for one of the farriery classes on the Saturday so I'll be there anyway. I wish he'd asked me first, but I think he wants to show me off. I hope I live up to his expectations.'

'I'm sure you will.'

'I'm going to have a couple of evenings in the forge to check that I can still make a decent shoe from scratch.'

'Perhaps we could go for a hack early in the week. Give me your mobile number then we don't have to keep in touch via Mel's business phone.'

'Of course. I'll text you.'

As I leave, with Robbie making sure that the coast is clear, he smiles softly and my heart lurches, and I know that it's too late to go back to being just friends. We need to talk about where we're going, if that's what we both want. I realise there are all sorts of complications, but I can see what the summer could be like if we carried on seeing each other. I wouldn't be averse to being with Robbie every night, drifting off to sleep in his arms and waking up nestled into his chest each morning.

I walk quickly back to Wisteria House where Louise has brought Rafa in from the field. He scarcely gives me a second glance. I slip back into the house and head for the kitchen to thank her because, even though I told her not to worry about it, she's cleared the droppings from the paddock.

Hearing voices, I hesitate at the door. I can see Mel at the table. I guess that Louise is at the Aga.

'There's nothing wrong with our son. You treat him

like he's "special" so he behaves like he's "special".'
Mel makes speech marks with his fingers, two on
each hand.

'You know very well—'

'Shut up, Lou. You don't have to lecture me.'

'All Robbie's saying is that Ash could benefit from
therapy. Please, Mel. You saw him last night. This
could make all the difference.'

'I've told you before. It's no use chasing rainbows.'

'Now you're admitting that there's something not
right. You're contradicting yourself again. Let me take
him for one session and then we'll see.'

'The answer is no. It won't make any bloody
difference.'

Not for the first time, I think how insensitive
Louise's husband is. He's definitely not a type H
person. He doesn't love horses, and I'm not sure what
he thinks of his son.

'There was a time when you'd do anything for me,'
Louise says flatly. 'I'm going to take him anyway.'

'Oh, do what you want. You always do.' Mel stands
up and scrapes the chair across the tiles with an
ear-splitting sound like chalk being dragged across a
board. He grabs his sticks and pushes past me without
saying a word.

'I'm sorry about that.' Louise looks up from a frying
pan filled with mushrooms.

'Are you okay?' I ask.

She nods.

'Thanks for poo-picking,' I go on, changing the
subject.

'I enjoyed it.' She smiles weakly. 'It's therapeutic.
If you ever want me to look after your horse again,
just let me know.'

'One of my friends has invited me to a housewarming party one weekend, so I'll bear that in mind, as long as you're sure.'

'Of course I'm sure. You're welcome.'

I spend the rest of Sunday in a daze. It's drizzling and grey, but I ride Rafa down to the river, where I let him splash around in the shallows while I watch a family of fluffy brown ducklings swimming frantically, trying to keep with their mother. Pictures of Robbie keep flicking through my mind like a slideshow: Robbie in his flowing shirt, leading my horse along the lane; Robbie in his wet shirt and jodhs, water dripping from his hair and down his face after our swim in the river; Robbie in close-up, his mouth on mine and his eyes half closed as we kiss under the duvet in his bedroom. I think about schooling my horse on the way home, but it's no use. I can't concentrate on anything. My attention span is now officially shorter than Rafa's.

I text Robbie, just to say hi and let him know that I'm thinking of him. He texts back to say that he'll call later. He sends a smiley face and two kisses.

After dinner with Mel, Ashley and Louise, who is also dealing with the unexpected arrival of a couple of B&B guests, I decide to practise making shoes in the home forge.

'I can give you some tips,' Mel offers as I leave the table.

'No, thanks, I'll be fine,' I say quickly. The last thing I want is my boss watching me.

'What are you going to tackle first?'

'Just an ordinary concave shoe with quarter clips.'

'Let me know how it goes. I want to be sure that we're ready to show the competition what we're made of.'

'Is it really that serious?'

Mel looks me straight in the eye. 'Deadly,' he says.

No pressure then, I think as I head outside to find the key under the stone trough to unlock the forge. I put some music on my phone and get started. I work with a bar of steel, heating and hammering it into shape while waiting impatiently for Robbie's call.

Twenty minutes later, my phone rings. I put down my hammer and tongs and the shoe I've made, and sip some water as I move away from the fiery heat of the furnace, the mobile to my ear. It's Robbie.

'I'm sorry, Flick. I can't make it tonight or tomorrow because I'm snowed under with last-minute preparations for the show and working with the mare, and I've just found out that Maisie has parents' evening. I know it's a long time, but how about next Sunday for a picnic? My daughter will be with her other grandparents, Nanny Dee and Granddad.'

'That sounds great. I'd like that.'

'There's nothing I'd like more than to be holding you in my arms right now,' he adds softly, making the butterflies dance in my stomach.

'Have a good evening.'

'And you. See you later.' I gaze at my mobile for a while after the call has ended. A picnic, just the two of us, no Maisie. It sounds like a date. I smile. It is a date. I suppress a twinge of anxiety, though. We need to talk about where we are going. It was supposed to be a casual fling, but I'm struggling to contain my emotions. I'm looking forward to the show and Sunday night far too much, and I'm worried that I'm getting in too deep, because even if it finished right now, it's too late. I'd be absolutely gutted.

I know it's mad to feel like this. I thought I could handle a light-hearted fling. Other people do. Sarah had many brief encounters before she met the man who became her husband.

I wonder if I should back off now, make my excuses and run for the hills.

I put my mobile down on the windowsill and return to the anvil. I pick up the shoe I've made and examine it. There's something not quite right about it and I don't know how to fix it. Dissatisfied, I return it to the furnace until the metal is glowing when I remove it, and drop it over the pointed end of the anvil. I hit it repeatedly with the hammer, getting into my rhythm, flattening out the imperfections and changing the curve at the toe. It's better, I think, dropping it into cold water, but it isn't one of my best efforts.

I close up the forge and return to the cottage. When I go to bed, I can't sleep for thinking about Robbie and the night before. Although I'm expecting to feel exhausted the next morning, just now I'm full of energy and raring to go.

Louise and I chat over breakfast on Monday.

'Mel's sleeping, so all is well,' she says. 'What are you up to today?'

'I have four horses to shoe somewhere north of Talyford. It's an eventing yard. The Dysons.'

'Oh yes. They're all right.' Louise smiles. 'They called to check you out. It's all right. Mel said you were okay.'

Okay? Is that all, I wonder?

'I'm going to the Fox-Giffords' after that,' I continue. 'One of their horses has lost a shoe.'

'You'll meet Sophia then. She must be in her seventies now. She's horse mad and comes across as a bit odd to me, to be honest. She married into the Fox-Gifford family; they own most of the land around Talyton St George.' She smiles again. 'More than the Saltertons. Mel's been their farrier for years.

'Her son Alex owns Talyton Manor vets and his wife is one of the partners at Otter House, the small-animal practice in town. Old Fox-Gifford, Sophia's husband, is no more, which is no loss to some of us. Local legend has it that Sophia gave birth to her son while she was out hunting. I'm not sure if it's true, but Alex could ride before he could walk.'

'Thanks for the info. How about you? What are you doing?'

'I'm taking Ashley for a therapy session with Robbie and Paddington after school. I know I shouldn't get too excited, but he seems to have a special bond with that pony. It's my dream to see Ashley able to join in at school. He'll never be top of the class or live completely independently, but there's a glimmer of hope that he'll be able to lead a fulfilling and happy life.'

I think back to my parents. All they wanted for me was to lead a life that fulfilled their ambitions and brought them happiness.

'Ashley's very lucky to have you fighting his corner.'

'Why don't you come and see us if you finish work in time? The session's booked for four.'

'I don't know. I expect Robbie would prefer peace and quiet.'

'He won't mind. Go on.'

'I'll see,' I say, thinking that I'd love a chance to

catch up with him today. I fetch my work boots and some change that I find at the bottom of a handbag, and head out to the truck.

Shoeing the eventers is miraculously uneventful and I carry on to the Fox-Giffords' afterwards. From what Louise has said, I'm expecting to come across a place like the Saltertons', but when I get to Talyton Manor, I find a grand old house that looks decidedly shabby. There are tiles missing from the roof; the white render is cracked and pieces have fallen away. The yard is in a better state. There's a barn conversion to one side with long windows and hanging baskets outside, and a row of stables with steps up to a hayloft. Opposite the barn is a horsebox in purple livery, a four-by-four, and an ancient Bentley.

As I park in front of the first stable, a pack of seven or eight dogs – Labradors, springer spaniels and maybe some springadors – come flying out of the house. They swirl around the truck. A liver-and-white spaniel jumps up and rests its front paws against the driver's door. I toot the horn and a woman emerges from the house, waving and yelling at the dogs, who turn tail and trot away.

Slightly unnerved, I get out of the truck.

'Don't worry. They're perfectly harmless.' I'm assuming from Louise's description that the woman is Sophia. She's tall and elegant in breeches, leather boots, a pale blue shirt and tweed waistcoat. Her silver hair is stiff with hairspray and her face lined with fine wrinkles. 'It's Hero who's lost his shoe. He moves close behind and sometimes treads on a shoe, pulling it *orf*.'

She slips a head-collar on to the horse standing in one of the stables and leads him out.

'He's a lovely-looking creature,' I say.

'His conformation leaves a little to be desired.' Sophia ties him up. 'He has sickle hocks and a jumper's bump, but he's brave and bold, and has a magnificent jump on him. He's by one of the top stallions and out of our own mare.'

I move up and stroke Hero's shoulder. He seems chilled. I pick up his foot, the one without a shoe. He's chipped the toe, but the nails have come out cleanly without causing any real damage. The old shoe is worn and twisted. I grab the anvil and tools from the back of the truck and fit a replacement. Sophia brings tea. It's cold and milky, in a grimy mug with cracks and a horsey motif. I rest it on the shelf beside the forge, amongst the iron filings and general crud.

'I think it's admirable that you've become a farrier,' Sophia says as I rasp around the hoof, making sure the clenches are smooth. 'It would be absolutely marvellous if you could come along for a day with the Pony Club to encourage the girls to think about farriery as a profession. So many of them want to be vets. And, while you're here, you can test them for their farriery badges.'

I hesitate, unsure what excuse to make, but it seems that it's too late and Sophia has interpreted my dithering as agreement.

'Thank you so much. I'm very grateful. You've taken a great weight orf my mind, stepping in for Mel. We're having a half-term rally in the middle of May and the Salterton boys are going to give a trick-riding demonstration.' She smiles ruefully as I'm thinking: It will be okay, because Robbie is going to be there. 'It makes me slightly nervous, having them galloping around without tack when I'm promoting health and safety around horses. You're welcome to stay for the whole day – we'll keep you fed and watered.' She gives me a date a month away. 'I'll be in touch nearer the time.' She pays me in cash, and I leave her sweeping the yard, surrounded by dogs.

I wonder what I've let myself in for.

I check the time. It's three thirty, so I have plenty of time to pick up some apples from the greengrocer's in town – for me and Rafa to share – and to drop by at the Saltertons' for four.

When I get there, Robbie, Paddington and Ashley are already in the arena. Maisie is sitting on the fence, perched on the top rail with her legs swinging as Louise stands close by to catch her in case she should fall.

'Hi, Flick,' Louise says over her shoulder. 'You made it.'

'Don't tell Mel. He'll say I'm not working hard enough,' I say, smiling. 'How's it going?'

'They've just started.' She nods towards the chestnut pony whose coat gleams in the sunshine.

Ashley, dressed in a riding hat, blue sweatshirt and blue trousers, is brushing Paddington's mane, but my attention is drawn to the object of my affection, who is holding the pony by a rope, stroking his forelock and talking quietly so we can't hear him. He's wearing a black T-shirt, jeans and short brown boots, and the sight of his broad shoulders and muscular chest reminds me of how much I want to curl up in his arms again.

'Maisie, sit still,' Louise says. 'We don't want you falling off.'

I rest one foot on the lower railing and lean against the fence to watch while absorbing the warmth of the afternoon.

Ashley hands the brush back to Robbie, who tucks it in his back pocket before asking him a question. Ashley shades his eyes and nods slowly. Robbie leads Paddington to the corner of the arena and stands him beside the mounting block.

'Oh-mi-God, he's going to get on,' Louise exclaims softly, placing her hand over her mouth.

'He's going to ride bareback,' Maisie says.

'I never thought he'd be brave enough to give it a go,' Louise says as her son climbs up the steps and stands on top of the block. 'I'm too scared to watch.'

'He'll be all right,' Maisie sings out.

Ashley leans on to Paddington's back and swings his leg over the top. He sits up slowly with his fingers entwined with the pony's mane. Paddington is completely unconcerned when Robbie asks him to move forwards. Ashley frowns. His body stiffens.

'He wants to get off,' Louise says quickly.

'No, look,' Maisie says as the pony takes another step, and another, following Robbie around the arena.

Ashley starts to relax, his legs hanging down against the pony's sides. He lets go with his hands and holds them up high in a gesture of triumph and wonder. Robbie lets out the rope so that Ashley is riding a large circle around him. Paddington walks round with his head lowered.

'I don't believe it,' Louise says.

'It appears that the other evening at the barbecue was just the beginning,' I say, a lump forming in my throat.

A few circles later, Robbie decides that pony and rider have had enough and leads them back to the gate. Maisie flings herself off the fence. She lands on her knees and bursts into tears, more from the shock than any pain, as it turns out; she's soon up again, bossing Ashley and Paddington around.

'Stand,' she says to the pony. 'Now you can get off, Ashley.'

'Leave this to me,' Robbie says, helping him to dismount and handing him the rope. Maisie opens the gate and Ashley leads the pony out across the yard, with Maisie trotting alongside, telling him how to hold the rope and what to say to Paddington. The pony knows perfectly well where he's going – straight off to his stable where there's a hay-net waiting.

'He's a natural,' Robbie says. 'He has perfect balance.'

'There's no way I'm letting you teach him any tricks just yet, so don't even think about it,' Louise says. 'I'd better get Ash home so I can cook dinner for the guests. They've ordered fish and chips – home-cooked, of course.'

Ashley is reluctant to leave the pony and give up his hat, but Robbie promises he can come back soon, and he relents and leaves with his mum. Maisie runs across the yard to hold on to the dogs by their collars while Louise drives away, leaving Robbie and me outside Paddington's stable.

'It doesn't always work out like that,' he says. 'Ashley's making rapid progress, thanks to our new therapy pony. I reckon he could turn his hoof to almost anything.'

'I hope you don't mind me dropping by. Louise suggested it.'

'No, that's fine.' He lowers his gaze slightly, giving himself an air of endearing shyness. 'Any excuse to see you.'

We stand looking at each other. I can feel the heat

spreading across my face as I read the intensity of the desire in his eyes. Suddenly, he shuts it off, just like that.

'I wish I could spend some time with you this evening, but I have to get on. I'm sorry. Maisie . . .'

Maisie again, I think, my heart sinking. I wish he was free to drop round for coffee, or to invite me over to Cherry Tree Cottage later, but he doesn't ask and I'm not able to suggest it because I know what his answer will be. He can't leave Maisie home alone, and he isn't prepared for her to stumble across the two of us in a clinch – and why should he have to explain the nature of our relationship to her when we don't even know that ourselves, not yet anyway?

Just as I'm wondering if we'll ever have the opportunity to find out, or if he even wants to, he ducks towards me and kisses me on the cheek.

'I couldn't resist,' he smiles. 'I'll see you soon.'

'You certainly will.' I watch him stride across to Maisie and the dogs before I head back to Wisteria House in the truck, where I find bad news waiting for me in the form of a letter from the bank. It's a reminder that I've reached the overdraft limit, and confirmation that I cannot close the joint account I opened with Ryan until it's paid off in full.

I check my other account online. I don't know why I bother, because I already know that I've hit the limit on that too.

I break out into a cold sweat. I have another three weeks until Mel pays me, Rafa needs his annual jab and a visit from the dentist to check his teeth, and I'm due to transfer the next repayment on the loan that Ryan took out on my behalf when we were together. I go and find Mel and ask him over a beer in the garden if he can let me have some of my wages in advance.

'I'd like to help you out,' he says, hesitating.

'That's great, thanks,' I say, jumping in quickly. 'I really appreciate it.'

'I think you bamboozled me into that one,' he sighs. 'What's it for, the horse?'

'How did you guess?' I say, happy to let him think that.

'Cheers.' Mel touches his beer bottle against mine with a cool chinking sound. 'Perhaps you should go back into management – you'd make more money.'

'I was in sales and marketing, and no, no amount of money would make me go back.'

'How do you think you're getting on here? Is it working out?'

'On the whole. It could be better. I mean, there are still some people out there who don't want me shoeing their horses.'

'You mean people like Gina.'

'I'm sorry. She was in the pub the other night. Rambo's shoe had come off and she was going to find somebody else to put it back on. I hadn't got round to mentioning it to you.'

'Don't worry about it. These things happen. I think I've calmed her down.'

'You've seen her?'

'She called me. You can't win them all, Flick.' Mel grins. 'Just mind you don't go nailing yourself to another horse before the weekend. That shoe you left in the forge was almost perfect.'

'Was it? I thought it was rubbish. It wasn't one of my best efforts.'

'You know something: when I gave up being a

perfectionist, life became a whole lot easier. You should try it.'

In spite of my predicament, I smile to myself at the idea of Mel giving me advice when he hardly knows me. I finish my beer before I take Rafa an apple. He crunches it between his teeth, releasing its fragrance as I call Ryan. My ex's mobile is switched off. I leave a couple of choice voicemail messages, but without any expectation of a response. It isn't fair. I slip my phone back into my pocket. How am I ever going to clear the debt on my own? I wrap my arms around Rafa's neck and bury my face in his mane, my heart breaking at the thought of being forced to sell him to start paying off my debts and cut my outgoings. I couldn't do it. I'd rather die.

Chapter Ten

Hammer, Anvil, Forge and Fire

It's the morning of my visit to the spring Farm and Country Festival and my heart is on fire, a burning ball of longing in the centre of my chest, at the thought of catching up with Robbie. It's been five long days since I last saw him, fourteen hours since he last texted with the times of the stunt team's performances. I know, I'm sounding pathetic.

I pull myself together as I sit in the truck, which is stuck in the double queue of traffic to get on to the showground, outside the city of Exeter and about twenty miles from Talyton St George. I check my reflection in the wing mirror – I took some time drying my hair, applying foundation, mascara, eyeliner and a semi-matte lipstick, wanting to appear practical but feminine. I settled on an outfit of a low-cut cotton blouse in fuchsia, and my best pair of black jeans, which are straight-cut and high-rise to avoid the risk of builder's bum, an affliction that I've discovered to my cost isn't exclusive to construction workers.

I glance to my left, aware that I'm being watched. An elderly man in a flat cap and brown coat gives me a thumbs-up as he drives slowly past in a muddy Land Rover towing a livestock trailer. I give him a wave. He grins. A cow's nose appears between the slats of the trailer bearing the sign 'Devon Red Rubies'. I assume it's referring to a breed of cattle I haven't heard of before.

Eventually, I arrive at the showground, and make my way to the exhibitors' car park where I find a spot not far from the Saltertons' horsebox. It is massive, designed with living quarters behind the cab and stalls for twelve horses. It's painted in navy livery, with the Eclipse stunt team logo and a row of galloping horses picked out in silver across the front, rear and sides. There's an awning, too, with a pasting table laden with bottles of water and cool-boxes, and a Range Rover, which I believe is Neil's, parked beside the hedge.

When I get out of the truck, I can hear the distant rhythm of a marching band, the crackly tones of the announcer over the loudspeakers, and the low bellow of a cow or bull. What with the sight of acres of white canvas and the scent of crushed grass and burnt onions, I could almost be ten again and with my parents, my dad throwing the tack on one of the ponies, and mum fussing about the neatness of the knot in my tie.

The sound of Neil's voice brings me back to the present.

'Hi, Flick. It's good to see you. I can't stop – I'm titivating.'

There are eight horses – four black, two bay and two grey – tied up, four to each side of the lorry, with

Nelson closest to the back. Neil is brushing their manes and tails, and painting their hooves with oil. Sally Ann is at the bottom of the ramp at the rear, tearing the plastic straw from a carton of juice. She sticks it through the top and gives it to Maisie.

'Now, sit there, please. Nanny has a lot to do before Daddy and Dillon can take the horses into the ring.' Her hair is frizzy, her dress is crumpled, and her bra straps are looping down her arms, but she's smiling. 'How are you, Flick?'

'Good, thanks.'

'We're running late. We had a flat tyre on the lorry, today of all days, but we're here now. It's only half an hour until the boys are on.'

'Can I give you a hand?' I ask.

'I'm not sure. Kerry's repairing a tear in Dillon's cloak with a needle and plaiting thread that we borrowed from one of the show-pony people. Robbie's doing his make-up and Dillon . . . I don't know where Dillon is. God, this is so stressful. I always say I'll never do another one, yet here I am, a glutton for punishment.'

'You can tell that my darling wife is stressed – she's talking nineteen to the dozen.' Neil peers up from underneath Nelson's belly. 'You could go and see if Robbie's ready. He's in the lorry. Tell him to get his skates on. It's their penultimate performance at this event. If the boys don't put on a good display, the organisers won't rebook them for next year.'

When he says 'boys', I'm not sure if he's referring to his sons, the horses, or both.

I climb the steps into the living quarters of the lorry at the same time as Kerry is leaving with a cloak thrown over her arm. She acknowledges me with a small smile. The wolfhounds are sitting with their hindquarters on the bench seats and their front paws on the floor, panting hot hair. Robbie is sitting between them, with various pots and potions lined up on a tray and a round magnifying mirror on his knees. He's wearing a dark vest that reveals the contours of his muscular arms, and tight leggings – or are they 'meggings', I'm not sure? I can hardly look. Focus on his eyes, I tell myself. Don't look down, no matter how compelling and fascinating the view. I clear my throat.

'Your dad wants to know if you're ready.'

He looks up with a lash-thickening wand in his hand.

'I'm not sure I'll ever be ready. This isn't going well. We're going to have to be better prepared for the Country Show in June when the TV guys are watching.' He pulls a wipe out of the packet on the tray and starts to dab mascara from his cheek.

'Hey, you're making things worse. Let me do that.'

'You?'

'You sound doubtful. Don't I always look amazing?' I say, flirting with him. 'I am suitably qualified too, being a girl, in case you hadn't noticed.'

'Oh, I'd noticed. Come and give me a kiss.'

I lean down to kiss him full on the lips before drawing back slightly to study his face, with the cobalt-blue eye shimmer and circles of blusher, and I can't help grinning. 'You aren't going for the natural look then.'

He smiles ruefully. 'It isn't supposed to be subtle. It has to convey a sense of theatre.'

I take a tissue from my pocket to smudge the blusher on his cheeks, blending it so he looks less of

181

a clown and more of the Roman emperor to suit the theme of the display. 'Who usually does your make-up?'

'Kerry's the expert, but she's clearing up some other disaster.'

'Let me do your mascara,' I offer.

He hands me the wand. Our fingers touch. An electric shock passes between us.

'Is that static, or a dart of lust?' I say. 'It's what happens in romantic novels. I'm reading one at the moment. Louise has lots of them on the shelves at the B&B.'

'Does she?'

'Maybe they're Mel's.'

'I doubt it,' Robbie says, with a hint of a smile.

'I was joking.'

'Did he come with you?'

'Louise is going to drop him off so he doesn't have to stand around all day. She says she'll let Ashley have a look at the tractors if she thinks he can cope with the crowds.' I load the wand with mascara. 'Now, look straight at me.'

'You have got a steady hand today?' he teases.

'Keep your head still and look down at your knee.' I reach across and gently place my thumb on his eyelid, lifting the lashes slightly. 'Relax.' I touch the wand to the root of his lashes and flick it upwards to spread the mascara evenly along their length. I move my thumb to the outer corner of his eyelid to catch the lashes there. I'm aware of his breathing and how his knees press against my legs as I lean in. It's intimate. Erotic.

I repeat the exercise with the other eye.

'Keep still, otherwise you're going to end up

looking like a panda on horseback. Do you need any lipstick?'

'Please,' he says, pouting.

I chuckle as I take the lip-brush from the pot on the tray. I cup his chin with one hand, feeling the roughness of his stubble against my skin. I press the lipstick to the centre of his upper lip, moving it to the left and then the right. I repeat with his lower lip.

'Now, go like this – draw your lips back. Like this!' I dab them with the tissue before reapplying a second coat.

'What do you think?' I hold up the mirror.

'That's perfect. Thanks.' He gets up and pulls a dark cloak out from underneath one of the dogs. He flings it around his shoulders and fastens it at the neck. 'What time are you down at the shoeing section?'

'I'm not sure. It's sometime this afternoon.'

'I'll come and watch with Maisie.'

'Oh no, don't. You'll make me nervous.'

'I can't imagine that. You seem pretty cool-headed under stress.'

I hesitate, expecting him to leave the lorry with me, but he sits down again.

'I hope it all goes well in the arena.' What else can you say to a stuntman to wish him luck? Is it like urging an actor to break a leg? Break your neck, more like. A tiny shudder tremors down my spine at the thought of Robbie coming to grief. Stunt riding has to be one of the most dangerous professions in the world. No matter how carefully you prepare, you can't eliminate every single risk.

'I'm just going to take ten minutes,' he says.

'I'll leave you to it.' I return outside where I find

Dillon dressed up just like his brother. The pale sweat from a severe hangover glistens through his make-up. 'Robbie says he'll be with you soon.'

'He's meditating. He does it every time.' He sips from a bottle of water.

'Someone's had a heavy night,' I observe.

'Just a bit.' He checks the decidedly non-Roman timepiece on his wrist. 'He'd better stop faffing – we're supposed to be on our way to the collecting ring.'

'I'm here.' Robbie appears at the door. 'You'd better be able to stand on the back of a horse, little brother. And get that watch off. How many times do I have to tell you?'

'All right. Keep your hair on.' Dillon hands his watch to his father for safe-keeping.

I think back to Mel's comment about perfectionism. I can sympathise with Robbie – it must be infuriating when your brother and teammate doesn't care as much as you do. I watch as Kerry, Neil, Robbie and Dillon take two horses each and start leading them away, while Maisie walks along behind them, holding Sally Ann's hand. I buy a coffee and a programme to check the times for the farriery classes en route to the main arena. I find a good vantage point at the end of a bench in one of the stands.

Robbie and Dillon are waiting with the horses in the collecting ring while Neil sets up a pair of vertical hoops side by side along the centre of the arena. The announcer introduces the Eclipse stunt team.

'Whatever you do, folks, don't try this at home!' he says as the music begins, stirring, mysterious and with a rhythmic beat that reminds me of the soundtrack to *Gladiator*. Robbie and Dillon make their grand entrance, sitting astride Nelson and Scout and carrying flowing scarlet and gold standards. Six horses trot freely alongside them to the centre of the arena, where the riders stop and salute the crowd before planting their standards in the ground.

Robbie moves to one end of the arena and Dillon to the other, where they move their horses around in circles at a steady canter before taking to the standing position. The crowd cheers and the music builds as each rider moves on to the back of two horses, one foot on each.

I can hardly watch, but there is something utterly compelling about the display. I don't know what it is, the athleticism of man – especially Robbie – and horse working in harmony, the skill and danger involved, or the sheer beauty of the performance, transporting me to another place and time, but I have a lump in my throat.

They gallop their teams of horses towards each other, raising their arms as they pass at speed. Dillon loses contact with his second horse, but regains his poise almost instantly so you'd hardly notice.

The music quietens while the brothers bring their horses together at a slow canter, performing a spiral pattern in and out again. Kerry opens the rope across the exit to the collecting ring and lets the free horses out, leaving Robbie and Dillon riding Roman-style on two horses each. As they canter around the arena side by side, Neil lights the wrapping on the hoops, setting them on fire. The music rises to a crescendo as the brothers ride at the hoops in opposite directions, galloping straight through them, their mounts apparently oblivious to the smoke and flames. The crowd roars. Robbie wheels round and gallops back to rejoin Dillon for a lap of honour, side by side, before flying out into the collecting ring.

When I walk past the ring, I notice that Kerry and Neil are catching the horses while the intrepid stunt-men are surrounded by teenage girls and their mums, wanting selfies.

I don't stop. I make my way to the shoeing section, pushing my way through the crush of people to find Mel. He's sitting on a director's chair, which looks quite precarious for someone who's recently undergone spinal surgery. He leans forwards, resting both hands on one end of a wooden stick, carved with a horse's head. It's so hot that the roof of the shelter, which is made from a metal scaffold and canvas, seems to be dripping with sweat, yet Mel manages to look cool in a navy blazer and long trousers.

'Hey, Flick. You made it.'

'I'm not late, am I?' My forehead tightens.

'No, you're here with time to spare. The demo's running a little slow. One of the other farriers is demonstrating how to shoe a pony from start to finish.' Mel clears his throat. 'I thought I'd better give you the heads-up – your ex-boyfriend is here.'

The pungent scent of burning hoof and overheating sheep from the marquee next door fills my nostrils.

'Ryan?' I should have been prepared. We move in the same circles, but it's more of a shock than it should be. 'Are you sure?'

'I was making myself known to some of your fellow competitors. I introduced myself and he told me he'd trained with Tony. I mentioned I'd taken on one of his apprentices, and of course, he knew all about you.' Mel points the end of his stick towards the workstations set up at the rear of the covered area. 'He's over there with his wife.'

I feel like I've been hit in the chest with a hammer. Wife? It's been four months since we split up. How could he move on so quickly and so definitively? And how could he afford to get married? The bastard! I bite my tongue.

'Let's hope you beat him, eh?' Mel says, as if he's read my mind.

'Oh, I'll make sure I do.' I feel even hotter now. I wish I didn't care, but the sight of my devious ex puts me in turmoil.

'That's the spirit.' Mel struggles to his feet. 'Right, the demo's finished. You're on next. Let's get this party started.'

It's hardly a party, I think, the nerves beginning to take over.

Ryan is moving towards me, dressed in a red vest, jeans and work boots. He's two years younger than me and a couple of inches under six foot, a fact that's always rankled with him. He's good-looking, but nowhere near as gorgeous as Robbie, and I'm happy to observe that his sandy-brown hair is thinning on top.

So what originally attracted me to him, I wonder? It wasn't love at first sight; more a friendship that grew as I discovered his sense of humour, generosity and willingness to help me out while we were out on the road together with Tony and the other apprentices. Okay, so he changed, or I got it wrong.

He appears to have a grandmother surgically attached to one of his massive arms. She has long dark hair left loose, a deep mahogany tan, and crow's feet. She must be at least forty-five, and that's being charitable. She's wearing a white blouse to match her perfect teeth, pale jodhpurs, and long black boots with spurs. I wish I didn't feel so mean about her. It wasn't her fault that Ryan and I broke up. It was his choice to be unfaithful.

'Hello,' Ryan smiles. 'Nat, this is Flick. Flick, this is Nat, my wife.'

'Congratulations. I wish you all the luck in the world.' I address this to Nat because she's going to need it. 'You look a little sunburned, Ryan. Have you been somewhere nice?'

'We've just got back from St Lucia.'

'We got married on the beach,' Nat adds.

Bile rises in my throat. That's where we went on holiday. That's where he proposed to me. I wonder if his new wife – who looks as if she exists on skinny lattes and salads – knows that. Part of me wants to tell her, but it won't make any difference. It won't make me feel any better. There's an awkward silence before Ryan speaks again.

'Mel tells me you're working for him.'

'It's only temporary, a stopgap before I set up my own round,' I point out coolly.

'If you're just half as successful as I am, you'll do well.' Ryan nuzzles Nat's scrawny neck, making me feel sick to the stomach.

'I see you've found yourself a cougar,' I comment when he joins me with the other entrants for the Eagle Eye class, waiting for Mel's instructions.

'Well, you know what they say about older women,' he says brightly.

'No, I don't actually.'

'They have the benefit of experience.'

'And money, I assume.'

188

'What do you mean by that?'

'Oh come on, we both know you didn't pay for the wedding.'

'I contributed.'

'Perhaps you'd like to contribute to paying off our debts and the overdraft.'

'I'm sorry, I can't at the moment. The flights alone cost an arm and a leg.' He pauses as my blood begins to boil. 'If I had some spare cash, I'd offer to help you out.'

'We both spent the money. We're jointly liable,' I point out.

'I know, but the loans are in your name and the bank can wait.'

'Sure,' I say bitterly. What did I expect?

I become aware of Robbie's presence. He's standing with Maisie, watching us intently.

'It wasn't all my fault,' Ryan whispers. 'I admit I could have handled the break-up better, more kindly, but it would have happened whatever. We weren't right for each other. I think you were in love with the prospect of us working together, not me. You were too busy for me in the end.'

'I was preparing for my exam,' I say, outraged, 'and you were never at home because it turned out you were with *her*.' A fresh tide of anger and regret hits me. 'And now you're here, making out that you've made it, when everyone knows that you're only where you are today because you've taken advantage of other people.'

'Isn't that the way of the world? I wanted us to help each other out, but you wouldn't let me. You were always wanting to do everything on your own, and your way. You can be too independent, you know.

It isn't attractive.' Ryan delivers his final blow. 'It doesn't come across as terribly feminine.'

'While sponging off women instead of standing on your own two feet makes you look soooo manly,' I say sarcastically. 'You're a complete wuss. You never take responsibility for anything.'

'Flick, is everything okay?' Robbie steps up beside me.

'It's fine,' I say firmly, as Mel calls for quiet and introduces the judge, a retired Fellow of the Worshipful Company of Farriers, who is dressed in heavy tweeds. He makes a speech, welcoming everyone to a celebration of farriery that will show off the medieval craft of making horseshoes, before Mel takes over again to read out the rules for the first class.

'You have fifteen seconds to look at the foot, followed by twenty-five minutes to make a concave hunter shoe with a toe clip to fit.' He smiles cheesily. 'Are you ready? Let's shoe.'

'May the best man win!' Robbie calls across.

'Flick's a lady,' I hear Maisie correct him.

'May the best farrier win,' says Mel. 'First up –' he pauses for effect before continuing – 'Felicity Coleridge.'

'Good luck,' Ryan says from beside me.

I glance down at my hands, which bear the evidence of hours of practice in the forge, remembering though how Tony used to diss our handiwork. A 'That's just about okay' from Tony was high praise indeed.

A little grudgingly, I wish Ryan luck too.

I move away and, having looked at the foot on a rather bored-looking grey cob, I head for my workstation, keeping a picture of the shape and size imprinted on my memory.

I take a bar of steel, heat and cut it. I mark the bar just off centre and hold it with tongs over the horn of the anvil so I can bend the white-hot glowing toe with overlapping blows of the hammer. I get into a rhythm, my ears ringing with the hollow sound of metal against metal, and I start to lose myself.

Once I've started to shape the toe, I create the edges of the heels and check that the shoe is the same thickness all over, working quickly as the metal changes colour from yellow to orange. I slide it back into the fire and wait impatiently for it to become malleable enough to work with again.

When it's ready, I mark the positions of the nail holes with the stamp before ramming the end of the pritchel straight through with blows from the hammer. Time must be running out. I'm not sure I'm quick enough. I redouble my efforts.

I draw out the toe clip and rasp the heels until they're smooth.

'One minute left,' Mel says.

Ryan has finished. He stands, watching me, his arms crossed, his expression smug.

I make one last check and I've finished too. My shirt is sticking to my back and my cheeks are burning with the heat.

Ryan strips off his singlet and uses it to wipe the sweat from his face, chest and armpits.

'All shoes are to be cooled and labelled, and left for judging,' Mel says. 'Labels and pens are here on the table.'

Ten minutes later, he gathers the shoes in a bucket and carries them across to the grey cob, walking slowly with his stick to allow the judge to keep up. I can't help thinking that they make a pretty good ad for spinal surgery: the judge the 'before' and Mel the 'after'. The judge stoops to lift the cob's foot and check each of the seven shoes against it. He struggles to stand up again, slips on a pair of horn-rimmed specs and makes notes on a clipboard before deliberating for what seems like hours on his decision, as the temperature continues to rise and the sheep next door bleat wearily.

From a distance, all the shoes look pretty similar, although I can't help thinking that Ryan's is larger than the others, which means he misjudged the size of the horse's foot. I smile to myself. It isn't the only thing he's ever overestimated. I recall him with the other apprentices, bragging about the size of his—

'Here are the results of the Eagle Eye class.' Mel takes a piece of paper from the judge and reads out the names in reverse order. Ryan is fourth. 'And in first place is none other than our own Flick Coleridge.'

'I suppose I should congratulate you, but they got it wrong. The old bloke should have gone to Specsavers,' Ryan mutters.

Mel basks in our shared triumph. 'Come and collect your prize.'

A hand on my back propels me forwards.

'Go and get it then,' says a familiar voice.

'Robbie.' I turn and flash him a smile.

'Well done,' he says.

The judge presents me my prize of a shiny new drawing knife, a Dartington glass tankard and a certificate, and a whiskery kiss on both cheeks, before I return to where Robbie and Maisie are waiting. Maisie relieves me of the tankard.

192

'That'll be perfect for your beer,' Robbie observes. 'If I didn't have to get the horses home later, I'd suggest we stay and celebrate. By the way, who's the bloke you were talking to?'

'My ex, Ryan. I wasn't expecting to run into him here.' I glance across to where Ryan's wife, Nat, is flicking through her mobile. I have a feeling that she's going to give him his comeuppance one day, but it doesn't matter to me now. There is some truth in what Ryan said earlier. The break-up wasn't entirely down to him. I played a part in it too. I pursued my career at the expense of our relationship. He felt neglected and, even though I was aware that we were drifting apart, I didn't do anything about it except nag and niggle. I'm glad he's moved on. He's married so there's no going back, even when, in my lowest moments, I've thought that I'd like to. I change the subject.

'You and Dillon were brilliant earlier.'

'It takes practice, attention to detail and a dash of creativity, I hope.'

'I don't know how you do it.'

'Me neither, sometimes. It's been a long three days and we have more shows coming up over the summer. It's great, though – I've never felt so good about the team's prospects.' He pauses. 'Are you still up for the picnic tomorrow? I'll be free at eleven – I'll pick you up—'

'I wanna come,' Maisie interrupts.

'Another time,' Robbie says.

'What can I bring?'

'Nothing. It's my treat.' He removes the tankard from Maisie's grasp and returns it to me. Our fingers touch and linger, and all I want to do is lean in and kiss him, but Maisie is here, pulling at his shirt and demanding an ice cream. 'I'll see you tomorrow.' His gentle smile makes my stomach turn in the best possible way. 'Bye.'

'B-b-bye,' I stammer as I watch him walk away with Maisie skipping along by his side. I can't wait to see him again.

I spend a while longer with my fellow farriers and an hour wandering around the showground looking at the horsey stalls. I spend money I haven't got, using my credit card, on a purple-and-black glitter lead rope for Rafa.

All in all it's been a good day. I've upheld Mel's honour in the shoeing contest, I've faced up to Ryan without collapsing in a heap and, best of all, I have a few hours alone with Robbie to look forward to. Will we decide to remain friends who fell into bed together? Or will we choose to commit to having some fun during the summer? My head tells me to go for the sensible option, while my heart yearns for the riskier one.

Chapter Eleven

The Cherry on the Cake

On a perfect sunny Sunday morning in the middle of
April, I hack Rafa out before Robbie arrives. I shower
when I get back from the ride and slip into a yellow
blouse and navy crops, keeping it casual, I think,
although I feel far from relaxed inside. As I head
downstairs, I hear Louise letting someone into the
house.

'Flick,' she calls. 'Robbie's here.'

'I'm on my way.' I grab the bottle of elderflower
fizz that I bought yesterday at the festival from the
fridge and meet him in the hall. He leans in and kisses
my cheek, his fresh scent of shower gel and tooth-
paste igniting a flame of longing in my belly.

'You're looking very bright.'

'Is it too much?' I gaze at his outfit of a khaki shirt
unbuttoned over a dark vest, black cargo shorts and
loafers, relieved to see that he appears to have made
an effort too.

'No, you look lovely,' he says quickly. 'Shall we go?'

'Enjoy your day out.' Louise appears in the front

doorway with a hen in her arms. 'This is Tansy – she's our resident escapologist. I'm on my way to put her back with the others. Will you be wanting dinner, Flick, or will you be late?'

'I'll be back.' I'm willing myself not to blush, but my cheeks aren't getting the message . . . I turn and walk outside, Robbie close behind me.

'I wondered if you could do me a big favour,' he begins, hesitating on the doorstep. 'It's a little cheeky of me, but Nelson's not quite right after yesterday. I thought you might be able to use your hoof-testers on him to put my mind at rest, if nothing else. I mean, it may be nothing.'

'I'll get them,' I say. 'We can go and do that now.'

'If you're sure.'

'Of course I'm sure. I know how I feel when I think there's something amiss with Rafa.' I return to fetch the keys to the truck. 'I'll drive round.'

'Okay. Follow me.'

We park in the yard at the Saltertons'. All the horses are out, having a day off, apart from Paddington and T-rex, and we have to go out to the field to catch Nelson and bring him back to the stables.

'I'll trot him up first.' Robbie runs alongside Nelson, trotting him across the concrete. The horse's hooves send up sparks as he powers past me. 'What do you think?' Robbie pulls him up and pats his shiny neck.

'He looks pretty good to me.' So does his handler, I muse, thinking wicked thoughts.

'During yesterday's second performance, he felt pottery, as if he wasn't picking his front feet up properly. The ground's very hard because we've had no rain and I'm hoping he's just picked up some bruising.'

'I'll have a look at his feet.' I fetch the hoof-testers, a set of large pincers.

'He isn't right,' Robbie insists.

I run my hands down Nelson's leg and feel for the pulses at his fetlock, and any heat or swelling, but there's nothing obvious. I pick up his foot and squeeze it in various places with the hoof-testers. When I pinch the middle third of the frog, Nelson reacts slightly, trying to pull his foot away.

'That hurts,' Robbie says.

'It does, but it isn't excessive.'

'Is it an abscess?'

'I can't see any trace of one.'

'I'll call the vet out tomorrow. It's better to be on the safe side.'

'It's probably nothing.' I echo his opinion from earlier on because I don't want him to worry, but I can't help feeling concerned that it's something far more serious.

'Thanks. I'll turn him out and we'll go for that picnic.'

I wash my hands under the outside tap while I'm waiting for him.

'Where are we going?' I ask when he returns.

'I was planning on going over to East Hill. We can sit and look at the sea . . . or each other . . .' He grins.

'Let's go. It won't be that long until I have to be back for Maisie.'

He drives me through the countryside towards the coast, and up to the top of a steep hill covered with trees, gorse and heather. We stop in a clearing under the beech trees and get out of the Land Rover. I take the bottle of fizz, while Robbie brings a picnic hamper and rolled-up blanket. We walk along an avenue with

Devon banks on each side, and green boughs forming an arch overhead. As the land flattens, the avenue opens out into an expanse of rough grass and scrub.

'I can see the sea,' I say, looking towards the horizon, where the hill slopes away sharply to another plateau and the cliffs and deep blue-green water beyond.

'It's a great view, isn't it?' Robbie says, keeping his eyes fixed on me.

We move on through the unfurling fronds of bracken and set up our picnic in the grass away from the beaten track. We sit down side by side. Robbie opens the hamper and passes me a plate.

'This is civilised,' I say.

'Don't sound so surprised,' he says, smiling. 'I know how to behave. Would you like a sandwich? Salmon and cucumber or chicken salad?'

'I'd like to try both. Did you make them?'

'I've been up for hours, getting this ready.' He offers me sandwiches from two plastic boxes. 'I even cut the crusts off.'

'Thank you.'

We eat. The food is delicious and I'm starving. I rest my empty plate on the blanket, slightly concerned because we appear to have run out of things to talk about. Robbie is unusually quiet. I wonder if he's worried about his horse.

'I expect Nelson will be all right,' I begin eventually. 'Maybe I could shoe him with some pads next time.'

'That isn't a bad idea. Thanks for having a look at him.'

'I told you, I'm happy to. It's an unusual thing to do on a date – if it is a date,' I say. 'We haven't really talked about where this is going.'

'This?'

'Us.' I shouldn't compare him with Ryan, but my ex was hard to pin down at times. Robbie gazes at me, one eyebrow raised, and I suddenly realise that he might think that I've overstepped the mark. 'I don't mean – I'm not making any assumptions,' I go on quickly. 'I just like to know where I stand, that's all.' I pause, waiting for him to respond. 'Was it a one-night stand?'

'Of course not. We're here, aren't we?'

'But?' I sense there's something wrong.

'Your ex. You seemed upset yesterday when you were talking to him.'

'Are you asking me if I still have feelings for him?'

'It's none of my business, but—'

'No, fair enough. I have nothing to hide. I hadn't seen him since we broke up and I was upset to find he'd just got back from honeymoon with his new wife, the woman he cheated on me with.'

'So it still hurts?' Robbie's eyes are downcast.

'No, I was shocked because they had the wedding on St Lucia where he proposed to *me*.'

'So you aren't really over him yet?'

'I don't love him any more. I *am* over him. I am *soooo* over him,' I repeat.

'Okay, I believe you. Here, have a cake.' He offers me a Bakewell tart. I take it and pick the cherry from the top. 'He sounds like a complete bastard!'

'I'm a little wary of getting involved with anyone because of what he's put me through.' I pop the cherry into my mouth and enjoy its sickly sweetness as I recall the predicament that Ryan has left me in.

'I understand.'

'I'm not sure if you can ever really "know" someone. Your parents would probably contradict me on that.'

'Does that mean you're turning me down?' Robbie bites his lip.

'When you say "turning you down", what exactly are you offering?'

'I'd like to get to know you better, Flick.'

'You do realise I won't be hanging around here for long?'

'Yes, you've said, but so what? The ideal scenario for me would be for us to take things slowly and quietly, and have some fun together for as long as you're here in Furzeworthy. We can go on some dates, take the horses out . . . What do you think?'

'It sounds perfect.' Almost perfect, I think, wondering how to deal with the consequences if I should fall head over heels in love with him, or vice versa. It's a risk, but one I'm prepared to take.

'I'd like to keep it from Maisie for now, if that's all right. She needs consistency.'

I nod, wondering how we'll be able to do that when she doesn't miss a trick. It's a fair request but one I'm unfamiliar with – I haven't been out with a single dad before.

'So, what's next?'

'A hug would be great,' I say quietly. I put the tart down as Robbie slides across the blanket and slips one arm around my back, taking my hand with the other. I lean against him as he pulls me close, his fingers caressing mine. I turn, seeking his lips, and we end up lying on the blanket, side by side and tangled together, with the buzzards soaring overhead in the cloudless sky. Yes, I have problems, but with

Robbie at my side I can sort them. I just don't know how yet.

'I wish I could take you back to the cottage this afternoon,' he whispers, his breath hot and damp against my ear.

'Oooh, so do I.' I turn and kiss him again. I can't get enough of him.

'I'll have to organise a sleepover – perhaps Louise will have Maisie for a night or two.' He rolls on to his back and checks the time on his mobile. 'We'll have to go back soon,' he sighs. 'You can see that I'm not great boyfriend material, a single parent with dogs and horses.'

'It's all right. I don't mind kicking around on the yard with you.'

'That's nice.' He rests on his elbow and runs his finger down to the tip of my nose.

'Shall we go now?' I ask.

'As soon as we've decided when I'm going to see you next. How about going for a ride one evening? I'd like to ride Diva out in company.'

We settle on a day later in the week.

'What about next weekend?' I ask, assuming he needs to plan well in advance for childcare.

'Actually, I could do with some help on Saturday afternoon, if you're up for it. It's the school fete – the PTA voted to hold it early this year so it didn't clash with any other local events like Pixie Day and the Country Show . . . Anyway, Paddington's going to give pony rides. It's a doddle.'

'Okay, why not?' It wasn't really what I'd been envisaging, Robbie and I spending time together in the presence of half the inhabitants of Talyton St George, but at least I'd see him. 'I realise that I'm running a little ahead of myself, but how about the weekend after that? A friend of mine is having a housewarming party in Hampshire on the Saturday night – would you be able to get away?'

He glances away and flicks a fly from his arm.

'I don't think so, not that weekend. I've got a lot on, lessons booked, a training session . . .'

'Never mind. I'll have to go on my own after all.' I try not to sound too disappointed as we help each other on to our feet. I can't help wondering if he's hiding something from me. He seems shifty.

'I'll need a bit more notice next time.'

'I doubt that there'll be a next time. I don't think Sarah has any intention of moving ever again. It's been stressful for her, wondering if she's going to be in her new house before the baby arrives. She's my best friend. I've known her for years. I wish I could introduce you to her. You'd like her . . .' I stop abruptly. Maybe I'm being presumptuous, wanting to show him off to my friends.

As we pack up and stroll hand-in-hand back to the Land Rover, I resolve to slow down and live in the moment, in case this moment is all that we have.

We ride out together later in the week after Matt has been to look at Nelson. He advises rest and anti-inflammatories for a week or so, and investigations if he's no better. Matt also calls at Wisteria House to give Rafa his annual vaccination.

Robbie and I take Diva and Rafa on the circular route. It's Diva's turn to be scared of the pigs, but Rafa is a star, giving her a lead and walking straight past, even though they're snorting and snuffling behind the hedge. I learn that it is just about possible to snog on horseback, and Robbie and I put in a considerable amount of practice to improve our technique.

The time seems to pass more slowly, the closer it gets to Saturday afternoon, but eventually it comes. At two minutes past one – I'm careful not to be early and appear too keen – I arrive at Cherry Tree Cottage, where the roses are in bud amongst the lupins and ornamental poppies. I slip my shades on top of my head, get out of the truck and walk up the path.

'Hello, Flick.' Maisie comes running from the front door. 'Paddington's going to my school today.'

'I've come to help.' I look down at my clothing – a fitted floral blouse, blue crops and canvas shoes – and wonder if I should have brought my boots.

Robbie emerges from the cottage. He greets me with a smile and my heart somersaults.

'It's good to see you,' he says warmly.

The feeling is entirely mutual. I want to throw my arms around his neck and shower him with kisses, but I remember to restrain myself in front of Maisie.

'Have you seen Louise?' he asks.

'She's on her way. She was loading some books and toys into her car for the second-hand stall when I left.'

'Good. She's taking Maisie with her.'

'I want to stay with you, Daddy.'

'We've talked about this. You've been a great help so far, but Flick's here now. I'll see you at the fete.'

'I wanna ride Paddington.'

'You're going to let the other children ride him, remember? You get to ride him anytime you like. Look, here's Louise. Wait a minute. Have you got your purse?'

Maisie looks up at her father as Louise pulls in on the drive.

'I have two pounds.'

'Don't spend it all at once. We'll see you there.' Robbie leans down and gives her a kiss. 'Be good.'

'You be good too,' she says.

'Aren't I always?' he grins, and flashes me a glance as Maisie skips off towards the car. A tiny shiver of longing darts down my spine as I recall how good he is with his hands, among other things.

'Where is everyone else?' I ask as we walk to the yard and Louise drives away.

'Mum and Dad have gone to visit my grandfather. They were hoping to take Maisie with them, but she wanted to go to the fete. Kerry's taken the afternoon off to go shopping. I have no idea what Dillon is up to – probably sleeping off a hangover. He didn't come home last night so Kerry and I had to do all the horses this morning.' He sighs. 'I despair.'

'What can I do?'

'You can bring Paddington over to the trailer, while I fetch some water and a hay-net for later.'

We load the pony into the trailer. He gazes over the breast bar, his ears pricked forwards and his forelock looking bouffant.

'He's having a bad hair day,' I chuckle as Robbie moves up behind me.

'I don't mind what he looks like as long as he's quiet and reliable. I took T-rex to the fete last year, but he couldn't cope for more than an hour.'

'I'm surprised you took him at all.'

'I led him the whole time. He doesn't dare take advantage of me.'

'I'd like to take advantage of you,' I say, my heart pounding faster as I turn to find Robbie's arms encircling my waist. His hands settle on the small of my back and his fingers slide under my blouse, caressing my skin. His lips find mine and we're kissing in the front of the trailer with Paddington looking on.

It's like I imagine heaven must be, being in his arms. I don't know where I am or what time it is, and I don't care, but eventually Robbie draws back, his breathing hard and fast, his eyes shining with lust and regret.

'We'd better make a move,' he says, and I smile at the thought of making moves with him. It's crazy, but he makes the sun shine in my heart. I turn to get out through the groom's door, ducking my head. He follows, closes the door and fastens the catches.

'Thanks for offering to help out today,' he says. 'Maisie loves her school. They're raising money for an outdoor classroom.'

'I think you twisted my arm, a bit like Sophia Fox-Gifford did the other day,' I respond.

'You didn't take much persuading.' He propels me towards the passenger door of the Land Rover with a touch of his hand on my buttock. 'Have you been volunteered for a Pony Club rally then?'

'I'm afraid so.'

'It isn't that bad.'

'She said you and Dillon would be there.'

'That's right. I'll take Nelson as long as he's okay.'

'How is he doing?'

'It's hard to say. I'm going to have Matt out again to check on him during the week. I don't want to take any chances.'

'I'll be crossing my fingers for you,' I say. I jump in and we set off for Talyton St George.

The school is a grey stone building with tall windows and a playground at the front. When I've driven past before, there have been children out skipping and playing football and hopscotch. Today, the playground is filled with various stalls, including a fortune-teller's tent, Jennie's Cakes, the Talyton Animal Rescue tombola, and second-hand books and toys. In the small playing field behind the school are a bouncy castle, a goal-scoring competition and a coconut shy, along with apple bobbing and some craft tables. There are people everywhere – grandparents, carers, mums, dads, children and babies.

'Remind me to stay away from the bouncy castle. The last time I had a go, Maisie accidentally gave me a black eye.' Robbie parks and unloads Paddington, or rather Paddington unloads himself at speed. 'Hey, steady on.' He hangs on tight to the lead rope.

'He's on his toes,' I observe. Paddington's eyes are almost popping out of his head at the new sights, sounds and smells, but he soon calms down.

Maisie's teacher shows us to the corner of the field, where there's a sign saying 'Pony Rides'. Within minutes we are surrounded by children wanting a ride, or just to stroke the pony. He's in his element, loving the attention.

We settle into a routine. Robbie leads while I walk alongside the riders. Some have natural balance, while others are less secure in the saddle. I catch at least three as they're about to slide off Paddington's back, one of whom is laughing too much to hold on, giggling at the sound of the pony breaking wind as he makes his way along the grass and back.

Towards the end of the afternoon, when even the wasps congregating in the dregs of orange squash have slowed to a faint buzz, we give Paddington a quick break to graze in the shade of the hedge.

Maisie arrives with Louise and Ashley. She's wearing a plastic tiara with red, green and blue jewels and cuddling a fluffy pink rabbit. Ashley carries a toy car.

'It's Padd-ing-ton.' Ashley strokes the pony's shoulder. Paddington lifts his head and breathes down Ashley's neck. He giggles.

'I don't know how I'll ever thank you,' Louise says.

'Don't thank me,' Robbie says. 'Thank Paddington.'

'I'll buy him a ton of carrots.'

'A bag will do. He's supposed to be on a diet. Look at his belly,' Robbie says. 'He looks like he's pregnant.'

'Paddington can't have a baby,' Maisie chuckles. 'Silly, Daddy.'

'We came over to tell you we're going home,' Louise says.

'We're having pasta for tea,' Maisie says, before changing the subject yet again. 'Look at what's on my head.'

'You look like a princess. Where did you get that from?' Robbie squats down beside her.

'Louise buyed it for me.'

Robbie looks up.

'I hope you don't mind. I haven't got a little girl of my own to dress up. I love buying sparkly things for Maisie.'

'Kerry can borrow it for the wedding.' Maisie takes it off and places it on her father's head, before turning to Louise. 'She's going to a wedding with my daddy. They might be getting married,' she adds in a hopeful tone.

'I'm going to a wedding with Kerry, but there's no way we're ever getting married,' Robbie says.

'Oh?' Maisie looks crestfallen. She retrieves her tiara and puts it back on at a slant.

'Come on, Maisie. Ashley wants to go home,' Louise says. 'I'll see you later.'

'Thanks,' Robbie says. 'I'll collect Maisie at seven.'

'Bye, Daddy.' I watch Maisie walking across the field with Louise and Ashley before I turn to Robbie, who's apparently decided to call it a day. He runs up Paddington's stirrups and loosens the girth. I stare at him, my heart thudding with disappointment. I knew there was something wrong. I knew he was hiding something from me.

I lead the pony back to the trailer while Robbie takes the money we've collected to one of the teachers.

'That was a good afternoon of fundraising – I'm happy with that,' he says when we're on our way home. 'Are you okay? You seem a bit quiet. Have I said or done something to upset you?'

I pick at a loose thread on my blouse. 'What's this about you going to a wedding with Kerry?'

'Oh, that. Her friend's getting married and I agreed to go with her as her plus-one. It was arranged a while ago.'

I know from the slight hesitation and the tone of his voice that he's being economical with the truth.

'It's next weekend, isn't it?' My voice sounds flat. I feel let down. 'That's why you can't come to the housewarming.'

'I'm sorry I didn't tell you. I thought it was easier if I didn't mention it,' he stammers. His face is red. 'When I said there was nothing going on between me and Kerry, that was true, but we used to have a . . . I don't know how to describe it . . .'

'You were friends with benefits,' I say for him. 'It sounds like you still are.'

'We don't sleep together any more. I promise.'

'It doesn't matter.' I bite my lip.

'I'm glad you feel that way. I was afraid . . .' He reaches out and runs his fingers down my arm as he drives. I flinch.

'What's wrong?'

'You lied to me.'

'Not exactly. I didn't say anything because I didn't want you jumping to the wrong conclusion. Flick, I didn't want to let Kerry down, and I didn't want to spoil what we have.' He swears lightly. 'I know it's meant to be light-hearted and a bit of fun, but I knew you'd be upset.'

'I thought you knew better than to mislead me.' I stare across at him.

'I've said I can't let Kerry down – I promised I'd go with her.'

'You knew about Ryan. You knew how I'd feel about being lied to.'

'I didn't lie.' He drops the visor to shield his eyes from the sun.

'You can put it how you like, but you weren't totally straight with me.'

The hurt and betrayal come rushing back.

'I don't think I've done anything wrong.'

'It doesn't matter what you think.'

I have zero tolerance for little white lies, no matter how well meaning the spirit in which they were intended. Since Ryan dumped me, I've become the human lie detector. I wasn't expecting him to cheat on me, so I wasn't suspicious, even when he was texting and keeping his mobile with him, taking it

209

into the bathroom or sliding it under the pillow in our bed. He told me it was his clients getting in touch and he couldn't afford to miss a contact while he was building up his business – our business. When I discovered that he was seeing someone else – it was her perfume that gave him away – I accused him of having an affair. He was sarcastic at first, saying, yeah, of course. It wasn't long before he confessed that it was only the once and a mistake because he was under a lot of stress, especially because I kept accusing him of doing wrong. Later, he admitted he was leading a double life.

I won't put myself through that again. I won't share.

'When we agreed that we were dating but it wasn't serious, I assumed we were going to be exclusive. It seems that I assumed too much.'

'We are exclusive,' he protests. 'I don't sleep around. I'm not like that. I'm telling you the truth.'

'How do I know what's true or not?'

'Just because Ryan let you down, doesn't automatically mean I will. You're being unreasonable. Oversensitive,' he adds.

'Oversensitive?' I exclaim.

'It seems to me that you're overreacting.'

'Hardly. I lost everything when Ryan cheated on me – my fiancé, my financial security and my future.'

'Oh, woe is me.' Robbie's tone is harshly sarcastic. 'He did you a favour. He freed you to find someone who's worthy of you. You're a lovely woman, Flick. You deserve better than that idiot.'

I'm only half listening to him, my mind focused on making the right decision.

I utter a chuckle of irony. 'All that creeping around

that night of the barbecue, and the farce in the bedroom on the morning after. It made me feel really cheap, that you were ashamed of being associated with me, but I went along with it for Maisie's sake.'

'And I'm really grateful for that. I'm sorry you felt like that, but I can assure you that was never my intention. I assumed you understood.'

'I understand it now. You wanted to keep everything low-key, as in "secret", because of Maisie, and then I find out that you're actually carrying on with Kerry. You weren't worried about your daughter. You were worried about Kerry finding out.'

'You've got the wrong end of the stick. I don't want to get Maisie all mixed up before I'm sure of someone. And I said I'd go to the wedding with Kerry as a favour. Honestly.'

'You could have told me. If Maisie hadn't blurted it out with the tiara, I'd never have known.'

'I didn't realise she had such a thing for weddings and finding her dad a wife.' Robbie pulls into the yard and reaches one hand across to touch my thigh. I push him away. 'I thought we were friends, more than friends. I've apologised and explained my position. Why don't you believe me?'

'Because you've admitted that you were deliberately hiding something from me. It's dishonest. I know it shouldn't matter to me that you are going to a wedding with Kerry, because we agreed we weren't committed to each other as such, but it's . . . oh, I don't know.' My voice tremors when I go on, 'It's made me feel bad, when I want to be happy.'

'So what are you saying?' Robbie asks slowly. His expression is dark, with I'm not sure what – anger, pain, irritation – but I don't care. I thought he was different. 'I take it that tomorrow's cancelled.'

I swallow back a sob of disappointment.

'I'll carry on shoeing your horses, but I don't want to see you again.'

He bites his lip. 'Okay, it's your decision. It's a shame. We could still hack out together.'

'No, Robbie,' I say firmly. 'Whatever it was, it's over. It's better that way.'

I return to Wisteria House without staying to help turn Paddington out, and I spend some time with Rafa for some equine therapy with a sensitive and emotional creature, not a man. It's for the best. I can focus on the future without distractions, and I'm a temporary fixture here anyway. I was a fool to think that a casual fling would work for me. I touch my chest. I've had a lucky escape. My heart isn't broken, just bruised.

Chapter Twelve

No Foot, No Horse

I'm grooming Rafa outside his stable on the Sunday morning after the fete when Robbie rides up and looks over the grey stone wall outside Wisteria House.

'Hi,' he calls from Diva's back. 'How are you?'

'Okay, thanks.' I pause from scrubbing at the mud on my horse's shoulder with his rubber currycomb. I tap it against the stable, knocking out a cloud of dust. 'And you?'

'I've been better.'

'How is Nelson?'

'Matt's coming out to see him again in the week.'

I don't probe any further. Obviously, he's showing no sign of improvement.

Someone shrieks, 'Look at me!'

It's Maisie, but I can't see her at first. A white face with pricked ears appears through the honeysuckle and brambles that clamber across the top of the wall, followed by Maisie's hat and eyes as she stands in her stirrups, balancing precariously.

'You're off the lead rein,' I say, avoiding Robbie's gaze.

'Yay!' She punches the air. 'We're going down to the river. Do you want to come?'

'I won't, thank you.'

'I'd really appreciate it if we could arrange to talk sometime,' Robbie says. 'Would you be able to come over for coffee or tea later this afternoon? Maisie's going to play with a friend.'

'I wanna stay and see Flick.'

'You've agreed to go to Chloe's. Please, Flick.'

'No, I'm all right. Another time.'

'Oh, go on,' Robbie joins in. 'I was hoping that you might have forgiven me.'

'I don't want to discuss it,' I say, swapping the currycomb for the body brush. I'm happy with my horse. I don't want to revisit the day before. What's done is done.

'What are you and Flick talking about?' Maisie frowns and hauls on Paddington's reins as he takes a mouthful of leaves from the tree that overhangs the wall.

'Nothing,' Robbie says.

'That's a fib. It must be something.'

'It was inconsequential chat.'

'What's that?'

'Never mind. We're talking about the price of fish,' he says.

'Oh?' Paddington turns his bottom towards Diva, making the mare flatten her ears.

'No kicking.' Robbie pushes her away.

'What sort of fish?' Maisie asks.

'Salmon, mackerel . . . all kinds.' He flashes me a brief smile. 'Are you sure we can't persuade you to come with us?'

'Quite sure,' I say. 'Good luck with the vet, by the way.'

Robbie thanks me for my concern and the two of them ride away along the lane. Rafa fidgets, wanting to go with them, and I feel a little mean for spoiling his fun. He would have enjoyed the company of the other horses.

As the sound of two sets of hooves fade into the distance and one of Louise's chickens clucks to announce that she's laying an egg, I wonder why Maisie's revelation about Kerry and the wedding bothers me so much. We weren't a couple. We were two mates having a good time, that's all, and today Robbie looks far from the romantic hero, with his tired eyes and tatty old sweat top. I'm trying to make him appear less attractive, but he's still as gorgeous when he looks slightly wrecked . . . no, more than ever.

I tack up and take Rafa for a ride, walking him past the pigs and down to the river where I find two sets of hoofprints, one large and one small, where Robbie and Maisie have paddled their mounts around in the shallows. I canter over a couple of logs on the bank before heading away to the long hill for a good gallop. It clears my head, and on the way home I make a mental to-do list for the week. I have plenty of work with a couple of new clients on top of the regulars. I haven't heard anything from Gina about Rambo, so I'm assuming she must have found someone else, another local farrier, to put his shoe back on. I need to speak to Louise to see if she's happy to look after my horse next weekend when I'm at Sarah's for the housewarming. I can leave him out in the field so she doesn't have too much to do.

On my return to Wisteria House, I turn him out with his fly-mask on before tidying up. I'm cleaning his tack when Louise appears with Ashley.

'Coffee,' she says, handing me a mug.

I take it, wondering what I've done to deserve waitress service.

'I made it,' Ashley mumbles.

'Oh, well done.' I taste it. 'It's perfect.' I look up. He looks away, his cheeks flushed. 'I was wondering, if it's okay with your mum, if you could help her look after Rafa for me next weekend.' I glance at her, hoping I haven't overstepped the mark.

'Is this for the party at your friend's?' Louise says.

I nod. 'If it's a problem, please say so. I can make alternative arrangements for him.' I'm not sure what, but I'll find a way.

'No, it's okay. We haven't got anything planned. What do you think, Ash?'

He looks up at his mum, his face lighting up.

'How is Paddington?' I ask.

'He . . .' He hesitates. '. . . We did trotting with Robbie.'

'Wow, that's brilliant.'

'He's doing remarkably well,' Louise says. 'Now we'd better leave you to it. I have beds to make and rooms to clean.'

'Thanks for the coffee.'

I finish off and put the tack away, placing the saddle on the stand with the numnah and girth on top, and reassembling the bridle and hanging it up. I have a shower and get myself some lunch. Mel appears in the kitchen to make a hot drink.

'How are you doing?' I ask.

'Not bad since I've found out that I'm not needed

216

at the next Pony Club rally,' he says. 'I hear on the grapevine that you're doling out the badges.'

'Yes, I thought I was doing a talk.'

'All you have to do is entertain them for an hour or so. Get them identifying the tools and saying what you use each one for. Don't let them handle them. One of them dropped a hammer a couple of years ago and broke their toe. One of the mums took them to hospital for an X-ray and a splint, and they were back in the saddle the next day.'

'I hope they behave themselves.'

'Sophia keeps them under control. If you run out of things to do, tell them the story of the Devil and the blacksmith, and why it's okay for farriers to hang horseshoes upside down. They love it.'

'Thanks for the tip. Um, do you know what happened with Rambo? I've been meaning to ask.' I haven't really, but it seems like a good time.

'I did it. I put the shoe back on.'

'What about your back?'

'It didn't take long. I have to start somewhere.'

'Perhaps not quite so soon, though.'

Mel sighs. 'You women are all the same. You sound just like Lou, telling me what I can and can't do.'

'It won't be long before you don't need me any more. Should I start looking for another job?'

'No, no. I couldn't do a full set, not yet.'

That's a relief then, I muse as he sugars his tea.

'I'll see you later,' he goes on, leaving the kitchen. I'm still not sure what to make of him.

I drive to the garden centre on Stoney Lane, on the edge of Talyton St George. I could do with some retail therapy, but maybe not this kind, I think as I walk – between rows of ornaments, garden furniture and pet

217

memorials – to the entrance, where the automatic door slides open into a humid world of fragrant and colourful plants, mingling with the scent of roast dinners and coffee.

What do you buy for a housewarming present? I survey the range of options, from beaten copper-effect cut-out wall decorations in the form of swirly trees and strange creatures (either hares with short ears or deer with long ones), to mirrors with ornate be-jewelled borders. I examine the lamps with their patterned shades and ceramic bases, and wonder if Sarah would like one. She'd find it funny, but it goes against the grain, wasting money on something she'll car-boot or throw in the bin, when I'm of limited means.

I wonder about making a plant-holder from horse-shoes, but decide that might look a bit cheap so, in the end, I choose a plant, an olive tree in an earthenware pot for the patio. I pay for it on my credit card and leave it outside Rafa's stable for the following weekend.

Later, when I'm watching TV in the snug, I check my mobile to find a text from Robbie.

Hope you had a good day. You're welcome to drop by any time. Don't be a stranger xx

I text back, wishing him goodnight, and then I hear nothing more from him until the Wednesday, when I receive a phone call while I'm driving between Uphill House and Nettlebed Farm. I answer on the hands-free.

'Hello, Robbie, how are you?'

'Oh, bearing up,' he says.

'What's wrong?'

'I wondered if I could ask you a favour.'

'You can ask . . .'

'It's about Nelson. Matt's been over this morning. He's gone back to the hospital to collect the X-ray equipment for this afternoon. It's rather short notice, but I was wondering if you could be here. Seeing as it's foot-related,' he adds quickly.

'What time?'

'About three thirty.'

'I can do that.' I make a quick calculation and decide that I can postpone one of my visits by an hour or so. 'Wouldn't it be better to have a chat with Mel? He has more experience of corrective shoeing than I do.'

'No, no. It isn't just about the shoes. I'd like . . . I need someone who understands how I feel about Nelson to be here.' His voice trembles and breaks. 'I'm terrified that it's going to be bad news, the worst.'

'Oh, Robbie, I'm sorry.' A lump forms in my throat as I imagine the dreaded conversation with the vet, the one I imagine having every time Rafa has a runny nose or mark on his skin. 'Of course I'll be there. I'm on my way to do a couple of trims, then I'll come to you.'

'I don't know how to thank you.'

'You don't have to.' Promising to see him soon, I drive on to Nettlebed Farm, past the ticket booth and into the petting farm. I park outside the visitors' centre and go inside to find Stevie, the owner and manager, a tall, well-built woman in her early thirties, with brunette hair and brown eyes. She's wearing make-up, royal blue overalls and navy wellington boots decorated with red and white dogs. She greets me, offering me a brew and cake from the tearoom.

'Normally I'd love some, but I'm in a bit of a hurry today.'

'Never mind. Next time, if you're willing to have a repeat battle with our donkeys.'

'They can't be that bad,' I say, smiling.

'Oh, you'll see. I've brought them in in advance – they hate being caught and they're quite handy with their teeth and back legs, so be careful.' We walk across the drive from the visitors' centre, which bears a sign reading 'The Shed', to a farmyard with cob-and-thatch outbuildings, including a couple of stables. Stevie shows me to the furthest one.

'They're tiny,' I say, looking over the door to find two miniature geldings, one a grey dun with sorrel highlights and one black.

'They have more than enough attitude to make up for their small stature,' she says wryly. 'I acquired them from Delphi Letherington. Do you know her?'

'I shoe her horses.'

'I won't say too much then. Suffice to mention that these two – Sneezy and Grumpy – were supposed to be fantastic with children, but it turns out that they prefer to eat them. I can't use them for petting. They're purely decorative. I should have sent them back, but when it came to it I couldn't bring myself to. They have a lovely life here – I envy them.'

'I see.' They stand less than a metre tall at the withers, so they don't appear to be particularly challenging adversaries, but when Stevie enters the stable to grab the grey dun by the rope she's left attached to the head-collar, he swings his rump towards her and kicks out. She's ready for him, taking advantage of the element of surprise by grabbing the unsuspecting black one instead and leading him outside for me to make a start.

He's so low to the ground that I feel as if my back will break as I bend down and grapple with his feet. He stamps, kicks, nips and tries to run away. There isn't a moment when he isn't making some attempt to thwart me, and the second donkey is just as bad. It takes me an hour and a half to get their feet done. They might be stubborn, but I'm more determined than they are.

'My husband Leo is one of the Talyton Manor vets. He keeps an eye on them, but hasn't the patience to deal with them when they play up. I'm sorry they took so long, but you're better with them than Mel,' Stevie says, as I rub the knots out of my back and collect up my tools. She pays me in cash and I carry on to Furzeworthy, where the sight of Cherry Tree Cottage reminds me of Robbie; as if I need a reminder, because he is never far from my thoughts.

Having parked on the yard and greeted the wolf-hounds, I say hello to Dillon, who is leading one of the team's horses across to the wash-down area. Kerry is unloading bags of feed from the Land Rover.

'Robbie's with Nelson,' Dillon says, nodding towards the stable, where Matt's four-by-four is parked outside. 'Have you two had a falling-out?'

'Not really. We've decided to stay friends, nothing more.'

'I thought you'd got a bit of a thing going at the barbecue.'

'It wasn't serious, just a springtime fling.' I glance towards Kerry, who's paused to answer her mobile. I don't think she can hear us.

'Okay, I'm sorry if I've embarrassed you.'

'It's fine.. You haven't.'

'Um, we could go out sometime if you fancy it,' he says, giving me a long hard look. 'I wish you didn't look so shocked. Now that Robbie's out of the picture . . .'

'No, Dillon.' I'm not sure how I feel. Surprised? Flattered? 'Thanks for asking, but you aren't my type. Do you usually go about asking your brother's cast-offs on dates with you?'

He grins. 'Occasionally. It's always worth an ask. It's all right. I'm not offended.'

Blushing, I walk across the yard to Nelson's stable, where Robbie is leaning against the door. He turns at the sound of my footsteps. His shirt has come unbuttoned, revealing a hint of the six-pack beneath. The familiar rush of attraction takes over, my skin tingling as I recall the touch of his mouth.

'How is it going?' I ask as Matt emerges from the dark interior of the building with his X-ray machine.

'I'm not sure, and there's part of me that doesn't want to know,' Robbie says. 'I'd really rather not be here at all.'

'I know.' I reach out my hand, but he turns away to help Matt, taking a plug from the electrical socket outside the stable, so he can put the equipment back in his vehicle.

'We'll have a look at the pictures while Nelson snoozes. He's had quite a lot of sedation.' Matt sets up his laptop and examines the radiographs before talking us through them.

'Is it bad news?' The muscle in Robbie's cheek tightens.

'It isn't the best, but there are things we can do. It's navicular syndrome. Both of Nelson's front feet are affected. It's basically pain that's caused by changes in the bones, tendons and ligaments in the back of the heel.'

'I was afraid it was something like that,' Robbie says, his hands in his pockets as we gaze at the screen.

'It would explain why he was fidgety to shoe,' I observe.

'What can we do? I need him sound. He's my lead horse.'

'I know,' Matt says quietly. 'If you'd said to me that this was a recent thing, and you wanted to use him as a quiet hack, I'd say great, he'll do okay for a while. However, he's in full work, he's already moving short-strided, and this is a progressive condition. I'm being straight with you. The prognosis for a return to the team is guarded.'

'That's pretty much the worst news . . .' Robbie's voice fades as what the vet is saying sinks in.

'We can investigate further with an MRI which, in my opinion, will confirm what we can see on the X-rays. We can try a shot of a bone-remodelling drug – he'd need to be in the hospital for twenty-four hours for that. We can change how he's shod to make sure the bones are lined up properly, taking some of the pressure off the heels. We can go for a surgical option, but there are no guarantees for a return to full athletic function.'

'What would you do if he was your horse?' Robbie says, clearing his throat.

'I can't tell you what to do for the best, but I'd go for corrective shoeing, painkillers and a controlled exercise regime to start with.'

'And if he doesn't improve or he gets worse?'

'Let's cross that bridge if and when we come to it.'

'Okay, let's go with what you suggest.'

Matt turns to me. 'If you can get some egg-bar shoes and pads on him soon, that would be great.'

'No problem,' I say, glancing at Robbie, who nods his assent. 'I'll order them and let you know when they arrive.'

'I'll leave you with some bute to put in his feed,' Matt says. 'Call me if you have any questions, otherwise I'll drop by and see him a couple of weeks after he's been shod.'

'Thank you.' Robbie shakes his hand.

Matt packs up his equipment and puts it back into his car, before counting out some sachets of painkiller into a plastic bag and writing a label for it. He hands over the drugs and drives away. Robbie puts them away in the feed room. When he reappears, Kerry is with him, her arm around his back.

'I'm so sorry,' she says.

'He picked his moment,' Robbie says, returning to where I'm watching Nelson. His coat is dripping with sweat and his nose is almost touching the floor, after-effects of the sedative. 'What am I going to do about the performance at the Country Show? What about the TV contract? I'm a horse short.'

'You don't know that for sure.' Kerry gives me an ultra-sweet smile, but I am not deceived. 'I'm sure Flick will be able to save the day.'

'Corrective shoeing is only part of it,' I point out, but Robbie already understands that.

'I'm really depressed about this.' His voice cracks. 'There's no show, no team without Nelson. I can't do it without him.'

'I know.' To me, Kerry's tone is grating rather than

soothing. I don't like the way she's muscled in to console him. It should be me who has an arm around him. 'One step at a time. There's still a good chance he'll be sound enough for work. There was a horse on my previous yard who had navicular – he was back doing high-level dressage within a couple of months.'

I refrain from mentioning the ones I've seen who had to be retired, as Kerry changes the subject.

'Just to let you know before I forget, I've booked us that room for the weekend. There was only one left – the luxury suite with a king-sized bed. I can't wait.'

'What did you do that for when I asked you to talk to me first?' Robbie's eyes darken with annoyance.

'Because I didn't want to risk having to go to a different hotel from the rest of the wedding party because we'd left it too late to book. You said you were going to do it, but you never did, so I took it on myself.' Kerry moves aside. 'I'll tack Diva up for you, then I'll do the water buckets on the yard so I can keep an eye on Nelson while you're riding.' She walks away, and I'm left with Robbie and a rising tide of anger. I know he's upset, but I don't hold back.

'I'm glad I didn't come over to the cottage to talk the other day. As I suspected, it would have been a complete waste of time—'

'She did that deliberately to put me in a bad light in front of you,' he cuts in.

'She's done me a favour. She's only gone and confirmed what I thought and you denied, that you're still sleeping together. Go ahead and make the most of that king-sized bed. See if I care.'

'Flick, it isn't like that.' He runs his hands through his hair in apparent frustration, but I can't help wondering if it is an act. He's a showman as well as a stunt rider. He knows how to put on a performance. 'I'll sleep on the floor, or in the Land Rover.'

'You can do what you like,' I say snappily. 'It doesn't matter to me.'

'But it does,' he says, holding out his palms, 'otherwise you wouldn't be like this.'

'Like what exactly?' My hands are on my hips, my fingers pressing against my bones.

He swears out loud. 'You're behaving like a stroppy mare.'

'What did you say?' I want him to repeat it, because I can't believe what I thought I heard – from Robbie, of all people.

'I didn't mean to make that remark – it just came out,' he blunders on.

'So you were thinking it anyway.'

'I didn't intend to offend you.'

'Well, you have, and I don't wish to talk about it any more.' He's as bad as some of the other males in my life with his sexist attitude. 'I'm sorry about Nelson. Really, I am. I'll be in touch when I have his new shoes.' I turn and walk away. It's all I can do. Why on earth did he ask me for my support when he has Kerry? I feel used and fed up and all I want to do is get away, but Maisie comes running across the yard from the house. She's wearing a Pony Club polo shirt, jodhpurs and short boots, and carrying a pink sparkly crop.

'Flick, it's you.' She throws herself at me, giving me a hug. 'Are you coming for a ride with me and Daddy soon?'

'I don't think so.' I hesitate before remembering that none of this is her fault, and give her a hug back. 'I might see you when I come back to put Nelson's special shoes on.'

She lets me go and runs off to her father. I don't look back.

Chapter Thirteen

The Way the Wind Blows

First thing on the following Tuesday afternoon, armed with special broad web shoes, plastic pads and sealant, I drive over to the Saltertons', past Cherry Tree Cottage and into the yard. Robbie is in the arena. I walk across to the gate, hesitating for a moment, my heart beating lightly as I spot him in his flowing shirt and jeans, working with Diva. He sends her off at canter in circles around him, using just his voice and the movement of his body.

I'm not sure if he's aware of my presence or not, but the mare slows to a walk, halts and rears up. He sends her away again, before turning towards the fence and letting her come to him. She's blowing lightly and her coat has a sheen like beaten copper.

'Chuck me that halter, Flick.' Robbie strokes the mare's neck and looks towards me. 'It's on the gatepost.'

I pick it up, open the gate and take it in for him. He slips it over the mare's head and leads her into the yard. I walk alongside.

'How are you getting on with her?' I ask.

'She's quick to learn, but inconsistent. I've been working with her at least once a day, sometimes twice. She'll try to lull me into a false sense of security by doing everything I ask of her in one session, then turn into a monster the next. She jumped out of the arena yesterday.'

'Do you think there's any chance that she'll be ready for the Country Show? When is it again?'

'It's less than seven weeks away now. It isn't just that. I'm hoping to take her to the Pony Club rally the weekend after next. Oh, I don't know.' He shakes his head. 'Kerry's taken a couple of days off, so we're short-handed. It would be handy if you could get Nelson out while I put Diva away,' he adds as Neil walks around the corner with the dogs.

'Don't let my son make you do all his work when it's him who's upset our groom. Did he mention that she went off in a bit of a strop? He's good with horses, I'll give him that, but he hasn't a clue how to handle women.' He gives me a long look. 'Is that sexist?'

'You were implying that women can be handled rather like horses,' Robbie points out.

'Goodness, no. I wouldn't say that. If anything, they're much less easy to break in.' Neil smiles. 'Look at you two with the long faces. You really need to lighten up a bit. It was a joke – what you call a wind-up. Anyway, it's lovely to see you, Flick. I hope you can help Nelson. He hates me, but I don't like to see him suffer.'

Neil walks on past, whistling for the dogs.

'I'll get the horse out,' I offer. 'It's no problem.'

I take Nelson out of his box while Robbie puts Diva away. Nelson trips through the door and shuffles round like an elderly man when I turn him to tie him to the ring outside.

'Can I help you with your anvil or something in return?' Robbie says, opening up the back of the truck.

'Thank you. How is he?'

Robbie puts the tool trolley on the ground. One of the hammers drops out.

'About the same,' he says morosely as he picks it up. 'I'm hoping for a miracle.' He moves across and puts his arms around the stallion's neck. The horse responds by turning his head and nuzzling at his shoulder. 'I keep asking myself, why Nelson? I've always been so careful not to overwork him. I've kept him as fit as possible to reduce the chance of injury, and yes, there have been times where I've had to work him on hard ground – I mean, you can't cancel a live show – but it hasn't been what I'd call over the top.'

The bright sunlight reveals the dark shadows around Robbie's eyes, and the contours of his cheeks, which appear more prominent, as if he's lost some weight.

'It isn't your fault. It's one of those things.'

'Maybe.' He shrugs.

I start to pull the first of Nelson's front shoes off.

'Did you enjoy the party at the weekend? I was thinking of you,' Robbie says.

'It was great, thanks.'

'How was your friend, Sarah?'

'She's fine.' She seemed very well, dressed in a yellow maternity dress and flats, and completely absorbed in preparations for the imminent birth of her baby daughter. 'She looks ready to pop.' I feel awkward suddenly, remembering that Robbie doesn't have fond memories of pregnancy and birth.

'When Ashley came for his therapy session yesterday, he told me that he looked after Rafa for you.'

'Yes, Louise offered. I know she's very experienced, but I still didn't like leaving him.' I had been lucky. Mel had let me take the truck and – because Rafa had nibbled the leaves off the plant I bought for Sarah – Louise had given me a jar of home-made strawberry jam and roses from the garden to give her instead.

I recall the conversation as she'd wrapped the flowers in tissue paper and cellophane.

'Mel and I are going out tonight,' she said. 'Sally Ann's coming over to sit with Ashley, so she'll make sure he gives Rafa his bedtime carrot. We've made a few changes to try and get our marriage back on track.'

'I didn't know it was off track,' I said hesitantly.

'You must have noticed that we don't always get along.'

'I wouldn't have said you were very different from other married couples I know.' I couldn't help wishing I had someone special to argue with now and again.

'Maybe not.' She turned the ring on her finger. 'Now that I'm confident that Ashley can cope with me going out for two or three hours, we're going to have a regular date night. Tonight we're off to the pub to hear some live music.'

'Enjoy,' I said.

'You too,' she'd said, and I'd thrown a few things into a bag and driven to Sarah's house in a small village in Hampshire.

Returning to the present, I pull the second of Nelson's front shoes off and shave a tiny amount of horn from his feet. I spend some time making sure that the weight-bearing surfaces of his feet are level, and that the feet are what we call 'balanced'.

As I work, I think back to the party. It had been a welcome distraction from the images that had flicked through my brain of Robbie and Kerry smiling from her friend's wedding photos and sleeping in a king-sized bed. I glance towards him now and again – his face is impassive as he keeps an eye on the stallion. Am I being unreasonable? Would he really keep two women on the go?

I'd talked to Sarah about how I felt about him, and she had consoled me, assuring me there were plenty more fish in the sea. The trouble is that I want so much more than a fish. She introduced me to David's geeky brother again, and her new neighbour, who's a personal trainer, over a glass of Pimm's, but there was no spark of attraction. The neighbour, Simon, was a laugh. He said that Sarah had told him I was a blacksmith and he was relieved to find that my guns were smaller than his. We chatted for much of the evening in the garden where the trees were adorned with strings of white lights. By midnight we were arm-wrestling across the breakfast bar in the kitchen, with Sarah looking on.

When I'm satisfied with Nelson's hooves, I fetch the new shoes from the truck to show Robbie.

'These are in the style Matt suggested. They're designed to spread the load across the wall of Nelson's feet. I'm going to leave his heels longer, to take the pressure off the back of the foot, but we've decided against wedges for now.'

'So he won't be getting the high heels he wanted,' he jokes.

'What is he? The world's first cross-dressing stallion?' I can't help chuckling at the thought and I start to relax in Robbie's presence.

I shape the first shoe and return with it on the pritchel. I pick up Nelson's foot and apply the hot shoe. The horn burns and crackles. Small sparks fly up in the swirling smoke. I take the shoe off, put it down and rasp the bearing surface smooth, using the non-singed areas as my guide.

Robbie brings me a bucket of water. I drop the shoe in. It bubbles and the tiniest wisp of steam rises into the air.

'How about your weekend?' I ask. 'How was the wedding?'

'I didn't go,' he begins. 'I took Maisie to the Mayday celebrations in Talyton instead.'

'Oh?'

'I couldn't. I know I told you that I was obliged to keep my word, but when it came down to it, it made more sense to stay at home. I wanted to prove to you that there's nothing going on between me and Kerry, so I asked Dillon to go in my place. She was not happy when I told her about the change of plan.'

'I'm surprised you did that after all you said about not letting her down.'

'I was hoping that it would make a difference.'

'It doesn't to me, not really.' Except that it does a little, I think to myself. It won't change our status, but it feels good that he thought I was worth dropping Kerry for, because I can't imagine that she was happy about the new arrangement.

'To us?'

'There is no us.' I look away with a pang of regret

at the expression of hurt in his eyes. 'I'd rather forget what happened and move on.'

'Please listen to me. Is it really that easy for you? You can make out you're one of the lads, that you don't care, but I know you better than that by now. You were right about Kerry. I didn't realise how she felt. I didn't see that I was stringing her along.' He blunders on. 'I really thought she was cool about the situation between me and her. She said she was. She told me she didn't want anything serious.' He shrugs. 'I don't understand people who don't say what they mean, or mean what they say.'

I gaze at him.

'I thought I was doing the right thing,' he continues. 'I didn't want to hurt anyone's feelings, so I let the casual relationship I had with Kerry drift into a kind of certainty on her part.

'If you didn't care about me, you wouldn't be upset, would you?' he adds hopefully.

'That's true.' I chew on my lip as I breathe his scent of leather and musk, and study his hands, which are turned palm-up towards me, as if in supplication. I love the gentle strength in his long fingers and the way the sinews of his wrists expand into muscle in his taut, tanned forearms, which disappear under the loose material of his shirt. 'I've already said that I'll be on my way when Mel is fit again. Let's leave it at that. Friends?'

'Friends . . .' he echoes.

I turn away and fit the two front shoes with pads and silicone gel.

'I hope Nelson's happy with his insoles,' I say, when I'm smoothing the last of the clenches. I let the horse's foot down and start to collect up my tools.

'I just want him back in work. As well as putting Diva through an intensive training programme, I'm looking for another lead horse at the same time. I'm not having much luck though. Horses like Nelson are few and far between. If you hear of anything that might be suitable when you're out and about, think of me.'

I think about him all the time, I muse.

'Of course, you could also consider loaning or selling Rafa,' he adds.

'Robbie!'

'No. That's okay. It was worth a go. He's a lovely horse.' He hesitates. 'Me and my big mouth. I should learn to keep it shut. I'm afraid I've hurt your feelings again.'

'I'm fine,' I say, more annoyed than upset. He knows I'd never sell him.

I catch sight of Sally Ann parking her car outside the house. Maisie jumps out with her satchel and book bag.

I wheel the tool trolley back to the truck and Robbie carries the anvil. On the way back, Badger wanders over, his claws clicking on the concrete. He nudges me in the crotch. I push him back and stroke his whiskery face.

Dillon walks across the yard with a wheelbarrow, spilling dirty shavings across the yard on his way to the muck heap.

'I don't know how many times I've told him,' Robbie sighs.

'He asked me out the other day.' I could keep it quiet. It doesn't make any difference and it isn't any of Robbie's business, but I want him to know. Friends shouldn't keep secrets from each other.

'Did he?' I notice his brow furrow and his hands clench. 'He's such a—'

'It's all right. I turned him down. I didn't think you'd care anyway.'

'Of course I care. He's my brother and he's being disloyal, hitting on you so soon after . . . well, you know what I'm talking about. I know what he's like, and the last thing I want is for you to get hurt.' He lowers his voice. 'He knows how I feel about you.'

'As a friend,' I say, reminding him of our agreement. 'Please don't have a go at him. I never had any intention of accepting his offer.'

'Okay. I'll try to pretend it didn't happen.'

'Thank you.'

'In the spirit of friendship, why don't you stay to watch Maisie ride? She'd love that. Can I tempt you? We can have tea together later.' He smiles softly. 'It's all right. I haven't got any ulterior motive for asking you round to the cottage. I could use some adult company for a while.' He tips his head to one side. 'I have fish fingers and chocolate-chip ice cream. Oh-mi-God, I'm such a kid. I can go and get something more sophisticated in town.'

I can feel myself melting at the thought as he tries to draw me back in, but it's no use. The core of resistance deep inside me remains intact. I won't go back to Cherry Tree Cottage. When I'm on the yard, I can stay strong, but I'm afraid that if I spend the evening with him, I'll weaken.

'It's all right, thanks, Louise is expecting me back for dinner, but I'll stay for a while to watch Maisie ride. I'd like to see how she's getting on with Paddington. I'll start getting him ready if you like.'

'We'll do it together. I'm under control,' he adds,

but the glint in his eye and the depth of his breathing suggests that perhaps he is not. It confirms that I'm making the right decision. It's impossible for us to be 'just friends'.

I stay to watch Maisie ride the pony. Having changed out of her school uniform into a pink T-shirt, pink-and-navy spotted jodhpurs, hat and boots, she flaps her legs against the saddle as she bosses Paddington around the arena, asking him to trot and canter. Paddington breaks wind every time he changes gait, making her burst out laughing. Robbie and I set up a course of four jumps made from colourful plastic wings and stripy poles.

Maisie sets out at a canter, jumping them one by one. Paddington appears to be enjoying himself.

'Put them up, Daddy,' Maisie calls as she pulls the pony up for a breather.

'They're fine at this height,' Robbie calls back. 'Remember what Nanny said about pride coming before a fall . . .'

'Yeah, yeah,' she says wearily.

'Where are you getting this attitude from? School? You're eight years old, not eighteen.' Robbie softens. 'I'll put the red one up.'

I put the jump up, just a couple of inches. Maisie sets off at full speed. Paddington breaks wind, not once but twice, and whizzes over the jump and off to the far side of the arena, losing his rider along the way. Maisie tumbles on to the sand, landing on her knees.

'Uh oh,' Robbie says, running across to her as Paddington ambles back, drops his head and nudges her as if to say sorry. 'How did that happen?'

Maisie grins. 'I farted.'

'Ha ha! Very funny.'

'I did.'

'How did that scare him when he farts all the time?' Robbie laughs. We're all laughing.

'Daddy, don't say that word. Nanny's coming,' Maisie says. 'She says it's rude.'

'What's been going on here?' Sally Ann asks as she turns up at the gate. 'You're too young to start doing stunts.'

'It wasn't planned exactly,' Robbie explains, hanging on to Paddington's reins with one hand and helping his daughter up with the other.

'I can't believe that I still worry about you all,' Sally Ann says. She asks me how I am and for my opinion of Nelson's feet before waiting with us to watch Robbie drop Maisie back into the saddle.

'How many times have you fallen off?' he asks her.

'Three,' she says, grinning and showing off a new gap where she's lost another of her baby teeth.

'So you have some way to go until you can call yourself a proper rider,' Sally Ann joins in.

'Four more falls to go,' Robbie says.

Maisie's face crumples and she bursts into tears. Paddington turns his head and nudges her foot.

'I don't want to fall off again,' she wails. 'It isn't very nice.'

'Nothing that's worth having comes easy,' Robbie says, looking at me. 'Go on. Take Paddington over the jumps once more and then we'll call it a day.'

Sally Ann covers her eyes as Maisie kicks Paddington into action, turning him from donkey to racehorse in less than two seconds. He flies over the jumps and Maisie stays with him as he gallops back to the gate and slides to an abrupt halt, flinging his rider over his shoulder and towards the ground for a second time. On this occasion, Robbie catches her by the arm, slowing her fall so that she lands on her feet. I'm expecting her to cry at the indignity of coming off twice in less than five minutes, but she gives Paddington a pat, and says, 'That's four times.' She counts back from seven on her fingers. 'Three more to go. Yay!' She looks up at Robbie. 'How many times have you fallen off? Fifteen times?'

'At least twenty.'

'Did you ever hurt yourself?'

'I broke my collarbone once, but most of the time I bounced.'

'What about you, Flick?' She turns to me.

'I'm afraid I've lost count. I haven't broken any bones, although I did bump my head and have to spend a night in hospital with concussion. I was wearing a hat, but I fell really hard against a cross-country fence.'

'Were you riding Rafa?' Maisie asks.

'No, I had another pony then, a chestnut one like Paddington, but without the white bits. He was called Mister.'

'Mister what?' Robbie says.

'Just Mister.'

Maisie is frowning as the information sinks in. 'That's weird,' she says, and I sense that I've gone down in her estimation even further than when I turned down her invitation to join her and her dad out riding the other day.

Robbie helps her back on for a second time and she rides Paddington quietly around the arena.

'I think the pony's found his feet,' he says.

'I hope he isn't going to turn out to be difficult,' I say.

'He behaves perfectly with Ashley. He's just begun to play Maisie up because she's started to get very bossy. He's good for her.'

'As long as he doesn't frighten her,' Sally Ann says.

'She's fearless, like her dad,' Robbie smiles.

'I'd better get going,' I say. 'If there's any problem with Nelson's new shoes, let me know.'

'Thanks, Flick,' he says warmly. 'I appreciate it.'

I wave goodbye to Maisie and bid farewell to Sally Ann. I make my way back to the truck and head back to the B&B.

Whatever I'm doing, even when I'm driving, thoughts of Robbie continue to drift into my mind, precious memories of the day he gave me the lesson in trick riding, the satisfaction I felt, having managed to get shoes on Diva, the joy I felt seeing Maisie's face when she first met Paddington. And – I bite my lip – the taste of his kisses and his tender touch as he made love to me. I swallow hard against rising grief. It's ridiculous. It was never supposed to be anything more than a casual fling. I had no expectations beyond friendship and a bit of fun. So why am I so upset? Why – after what happened, or didn't happen with Kerry – am I still obsessing over Robbie Salterton?

I miss him. I miss his warmth, friendship and humour. I could drop by to see him while I'm hacking out. I could text or call him and invite him to join me, but I wouldn't because, knowing he's seen me naked and exposed, not just physically, but emotionally, it feels awkward. He made me feel wanted, desired, beautiful and feminine. I can't pretend I have no feelings for him and go back to the way we were. It's impossible.

Chapter Fourteen

Hammer and Tongs

It's been a couple of days since I last saw Robbie. I texted him to ask how Nelson was with the new shoes and pads, and he replied that he was about the same, but there was no personal chat. I keep telling myself that I'm all right about it. When I ride past Cherry Tree Cottage, the tulips are blooming bright red and yellow, but ordinary everyday life has lost its colour.

I keep busy with work, and on Thursday, having finished an hour earlier than I anticipated, I drive back to Furzeworthy. I've been to Delphi's where I've shod three of her big dressage horses, prima donnas who barely gave me a glance, as though I was the Saturday girl in a shoe shop. The riding school ponies stood quietly with their heads down and eyes closed in the sun, and the yard's smelly tomcat looked on.

I'm thirsty, and desperate to shower away the scent of sweaty horse. After that, I have plans to raid Louise's fridge before I take Rafa out for another hack because when the going gets tough, the tough get riding.

Back at Wisteria House, I park outside the forge alongside a white Range Rover. Louise's MPV is missing, but I remember her saying that she'd be out. The sports car is under cover.

Rafa puts his head over the stable door and whinnies.

'We'll go out soon,' I tell him as I check his water and hay.

I enter the house around the back and push the kitchen door open. There's no one around, which is good because, although I'm welcome, it still feels a bit strange helping myself. I raid the fridge for cous-cous salad, ham and a carton of fruit juice. As I close the fridge door, I hear Mel's voice coming from the living room. He's talking to someone, but I don't suppose it will matter if I interrupt him for a minute – I could do with having a word with him about a horse he's been managing with the vet.

I bang a jar of mayonnaise on the table to warn him of my presence and move through the open door.

'Hi.' Oh no . . . 'I'm sorry,' I say, reversing in haste, but I'm not sorry for catching them out. I'm sad for Louise because her philandering husband, who is supposed to be recuperating from spinal surgery, is sitting on the sofa with his trousers down around his ankles and a semi-naked woman riding astride him. If she were on her horse, she'd be doing the rising trot, up and down. She screams as she pulls her blouse closed and grabs a cushion to cover her modesty, except that the cushion is quite small and she isn't sure which part of her modesty to cover.

'Oh Mel, you said . . . You said there was nobody home.' She's almost in tears.

'Gina, I almost didn't recognise you without your jodhpurs on,' I say harshly, my cheeks hot.

Mel pulls her close and she buries her face in his hairy chest.

'You're back earlier than I expected,' he mumbles.

'Gina came round to give me a massage.'

'Look, I don't care what she came here for. I'll leave you . . . er . . . to it.' I swear under my breath. All that lazing around with his feet up while Louise half kills herself doing the cooking, housework and child-care. It's outrageous. Disgusting. He's married and a dad. How could he? The trouble is, I know from experience that some men don't have any problem with declaring their love for two women at the same time.

Picking up my spoils from the kitchen table, and rather put off my food, I head for my room where I take some time to process my thoughts about what I've just seen. When I look back at the plate, the food has gone, and all I'm left with is the slightly bitter flavour of charred peppers. I wish I could rewind the recent events, but you can't just un-see something like that.

My instinct is to tell Louise straight away, to enlighten her about what a prick her beloved husband is, but she isn't here so it will have to wait. I have a quick shower to cool down. I change into my jodhs and a clean T-shirt before going to ride Rafa, by which time the Range Rover has gone.

I'm brushing Rafa's tail, untangling the knots with my fingers, when a shadow falls across my shoulder. I turn to find Mel, holding his stick in one hand and

243

resting his fist in the small of his back. I'm not inclined to respond with sympathy.

'I'm sorry about earlier,' he says. 'You won't say anything to Lou, will you?'

'I'm not promising anything. Louise has been great. She's a friend.'

'In that case, be a good friend and keep your mouth shut.' His complexion appears pale beneath his tan. 'The last thing I want is for her to get hurt.'

'It's a bit late to start considering her feelings, isn't it? Really, Mel. Do you think I was born yesterday?' I release Rafa's tail. The hair fans out around his hocks. 'I know you shoe her horse for nothing. I'm not stupid.'

'I love my wife and my son. It would break Lou's heart if she ever found out. Don't you have a conscience?'

'Don't make me laugh!' I say with sarcasm.

'What good would it do if she knew?' He tries another tack.

'I'd want to know, if I were her, so I could make a choice: to be with a man who didn't love me and respect me enough to keep it in his trousers, or move on, no matter how painful it was, to find someone who adored me so much he'd never entertain shagging another woman.'

'You sound like one of those soppy romance novels my wife reads. One man for one woman for the happy-ever-after.' He groans. 'Well, take it from me, life isn't like that.'

'You make me feel sick,' I counter. 'Whether or not you feel the urge to stray –' an image of the tomcat at Delphi's comes into my mind as I glare at him – 'isn't the point. If you're committed to someone, you don't act on it. It's a measure of a decent human being.'

'You don't understand what it's like. A man has needs.'

'Oh, cut the crap.'

'I love Lou.' He is livid with me or, maybe, just maybe, he's angry with himself.

'Besides, I'm not going to mention this to Louise,' I go on.

'I notice the tension go out of his shoulders as he breathes a sigh of relief.

'Thanks,' he says curtly. 'I appreciate it.'

'You're going to tell her,' I add, and his ire returns, but I don't care. I hate the easy duplicity of people like Mel and my ex, Ryan. Rafa's ears flick back as he detects the rising tension between me and my boss. 'Trust me, I will speak out if you don't.'

'You wouldn't!'

'Oh yes, I will.'

'You bitch. That's bloody blackmail.' His eyes darken. 'I thought you were a laugh; one of the lads.'

'You're wrong. It's all very well having a bit of banter when you're out and about, but to take it further when you're married to a lovely woman who clearly adores you, and you have a son who looks up to you, is . . . horrible. Despicable.' I recall how happy Louise was, telling me about date night and how they were working at their marriage.

'Is that it? Have you finished?' Mel crosses his arms.

'No, I haven't,' I snap. 'What about Gina? How must you make her feel when you have sex with her in return for shoes? It's like prostitution.'

'Now you're being completely ridiculous.'

'Am I?'

'Who are you to judge? It's just an arrangement we had. Gina knew I'd never leave Lou for her. She didn't want to walk out on her husband to shack up with me. It wasn't hurting anyone. What the eye doesn't see and all that . . . For f—'s sake, it worked for us.' He leans in close to me so that I can see the bubbles of white spit on his lip. 'What you saw wasn't meant to happen. I finished it with Gina the other day. She came round because she was upset and one thing led to another and . . . it was one for the road.'

'Do you really think I'd believe that?'

'It's the truth.'

'You wouldn't know the truth if it came along and bit you on the bum.'

'Leave it alone. If you so much as utter a word to Lou, I'll send you packing. You'll be out of a job with nowhere to live, and no place for your beloved horse.'

I let the words fly past me.

'You can't possibly carry out that threat. You'll have no one to look after your round.'

'I won't have a round soon if you carry on,' he growls.

I feel slightly sick as he stares at me, the blood vessels bulging at his temple, his eyes flashing; even his stubble seems to bristle with anger, and he seems suddenly to come to a decision.

'You're fired!' he exclaims. 'Pack up your stuff and go. I don't want to see your face again.'

'What?' I stammer. 'This minute?'

'Yes, now. Get the f— off my property.'

'You can't do that. You have to give me notice.'

'I don't think so.'

'You were supposed to be giving me a contract.'

'I'm glad I didn't get round to it now.' He shrugs.

'All we had was a verbal contract, the proverbial gentleman's agreement.'

I can see that his mind is made up and a cold chill settles in my stomach.

'What about my horse?'

'What about him?' Mel scowls. 'I'm sure you'll find someone to take him in. Half my clients are threatening to change their farrier, thanks to you.'

My forehead is tight, but I keep my voice even. 'I didn't think I'd done a bad job.'

'Quite the opposite. They think you're the dog's bollocks. *Oh, Flick, she's so wonderful.*' Mel adopts a mocking, effeminate tone. *'Don't hurry back to work, Mel. She's more than capable.*' He pauses. 'You wreck everything, wherever you go. Kerry's resigned because of what happened between you and Robbie. You're hardly as pure as the driven snow.'

'Resigned?'

'She walked out on the Saltertons yesterday, gave them five minutes' notice.'

'Well, it had nothing to do with me.'

'That's what you say. Now take your horse and go.'

'But what about all my gear?' I hired a horsebox to move it all before.

'I'll stick everything in the loosebox. You can collect it when it's convenient. Now, piss off. Get out of my sight.'

'But where am I going to go?'

'I don't know,' he says curtly. 'It isn't my problem.'

'Jennie's expecting me first thing in the morning. They need the ponies shod for Pony Club camp.'

'I'll work something out. Give me the mobile and all the keys, house and truck.'

I hand them over. I wonder about phoning Louise

or standing my ground, but he's so mad I'm not sure what he'll do. He walks across to the forge and leans against the door, staring at me. I go into the cottage and throw some clean clothes into a suitcase, along with my toothbrush, make-up and chargers. I take it to the stable where I make up a hay-net and a feed in a bucket with a lid on top. I throw everything into the wheelbarrow, lining it with a plastic bag first. I tack up Rafa and slip his head-collar over his bridle under Mel's brooding gaze.

A few drops of rain start to fall, and I'd like to think that he'll come over and tell me that he's calmed down and I'm welcome to stay, at least for tonight, but he's like a statue, immobile apart from the muscle tensing in his cheek. I hold the end of Rafa's lead rope, and the handles of the barrow, and set out. Rafa snatches a mouthful of hay on the way out past the cottage.

'Hey, you need to ration yourself.' I rearrange the feed bucket that's precariously balanced on top of our belongings. 'They're your provisions, for however long it takes us to find somewhere to stay. Where are we going?'

Rafa blows through his nostrils, as if he hasn't worked out the seriousness of our situation. We are homeless, or should that be 'stableless'? And although I've often worried about how I'll be able to afford livery for him, I've never been in this position where we have nowhere to go.

At the gate, I don't know which way to turn.

There's Cherry Tree Cottage and the Saltertons' place, of course. It isn't far and they have room for another horse. I wonder if Robbie still has a space in his bed – not that it matters. Whatever we had is over.

I thought that the last time we met was one of my lowest points, but this is worse. My heart is in my boots. Tears stream down my face as I make the decision to walk in the opposite direction, past the pigs and towards the river.

Raindrops patter against the leaves of the trees above. I glance up into a dirty grey mattress of cloud. It's going to be dark early tonight, and it won't be safe to be on the road for much longer. My clothes are getting wet and my horse is looking distinctly unimpressed as the rain trickles down his ears. I wonder if Sarah can help. I can borrow a lorry to take my things and Rafa back to Hampshire. I reckon I can beg a space on a livery yard where she keeps her horse, while she lets me have a bed for a couple of weeks and I find another job. I try my mobile. There's no signal.

In the meantime, I can let Rafa graze under the hedge beside the old railway line overnight, while I rig up a temporary shelter. I have to smile at my fantasy of turning an empty shavings bag into a tent. In the morning, I can head into Talyton St George and call Sarah from the phone-box – there's one by the church.

I can't bring myself to turn to my parents. I can hear my mother's voice saying, 'Told you so. If you'd stuck at the office job, you'd be managing director by now. Now look at you. You're a mess. I'm ashamed to have you as my daughter. How am I going to tell my friends that my clever, beautiful little girl, who showed so much promise, who had everything she ever wanted, has ended up without even a roof over her head?'

As I continue down the lane, the comforting sound

of Rafa's hooves reminds me to look on the bright side. We're alive. We have each other. I still have my career. I can find work. I can make life better. He turns his head and nudges my arm, as if to ask me how.

'It's all right,' I say as we walk on towards the crossroads, where we stop on the grassy triangle. 'I'll find a way.'

I let him have a few mouthfuls of grass. It's still raining. I can hear the sound of water rushing along the culvert and the rattle of a trailer being towed along the lane. I push the wheelbarrow on to the triangle. The wheel catches on a tuft of grass, and it tips, spilling its contents, just as a Land Rover approaches, flashing its headlights.

The driver pulls up and leans out of the window. It's Robbie.

How embarrassing. I squat down and pile my belongings back into the barrow, but somehow, although they fitted before, they don't any more, and I turn to find Robbie at my side with the bucket in his hand.

'I hear you've been evicted.' He takes the lead rope from me.

'How do you know?'

'Mel called to ask me if I'd pick you up and take you back to the farm.'

'Oh?' I find it hard to believe.

'He said he didn't care if people spread rumours about how he'd made a poor dumb animal suffer, but he didn't want anyone to think he'd be cruel to a horse.'

Which would be quite funny, I think, if I wasn't still close to tears. I bite my lip.

'What the hell did you do? Actually, don't answer

that right now. Let's get your horse into the trailer. It isn't safe to be on the road without lights.'

We load Rafa and the wheelbarrow into the trailer. Robbie closes the ramp and moves back to the Land Rover, where he holds the passenger door open.

'In you get then,' he says when I hesitate. 'What are you waiting for?'

'If you can take Rafa, I'll find a B&B in town.'

'Don't be silly. You're coming back with me.'

'I don't know that it's such a good idea. What about Maisie?'

'She's staying with her grandparents – it's an Inset day at school. They took her to the petting farm. I'll make up a bed in the spare room for you . . .' His voice trails off as if he's remembering when we slept together, wrapped in each other's arms. 'Come on. Get in.' He reaches out and touches my back, sending a shot of warmth through my core. 'You're soaked through. You'll catch pneumonia like that.' He reaches past me and grabs a coat from the seat. 'Here, have this.'

He drapes it across my shoulders and I clamber in. Rafa paws at the trailer floor, making it shake.

'Let's go,' Robbie says. 'I think we're keeping him up.'

He turns the trailer around the triangle and we travel back to Furzeworthy. I put my hands in the pockets of his coat, absorbing his scent.

'It's very kind of you to do this. I'll look for somewhere tomorrow.'

'Actually, it could be quite fortuitous all round.'

'What do you mean?'

'Kerry left us yesterday.'

'I'm sorry . . .' I feel partly responsible.

'It's a complete disaster.' Robbie sounds cross rather than defeated. 'Kerry knows exactly how we work. She can do everything from getting eight horses ready single-handed to make-up. I can't see how we'll find someone like her and get them trained up in time.

'Anyway, with our only groom gone, we're short-handed. If you could muck in and help for a few days while we advertise for a replacement in return for board and lodging, it would make my life a lot easier. It's the busiest time of the year for us, and we're a man – I mean, a person – down.'

'I'm sorry about Kerry. I didn't think she'd leave.'

'It's all right. It wasn't your fault. I thought it was down to me, but it turns out that she would have left anyway. She'd been headhunted by one of the show-jumpers she met at the festival. She's gone to a yard in Dorset. It's annoying, but there's nothing I could do to persuade her to stay.' He sighs as he changes gear. 'This will give you a chance to build bridges with Mel.'

'I don't think that will be possible. I walked in on him and another woman.'

'Oops,' Robbie says.

'Is that all you can say? Oops? They were having it away on the sofa in the cottage. They were at it hammer and tongs.'

'I suppose that's rather appropriate for a farrier. He is a bit of a one for the ladies.'

'So that's all right, is it?' I exclaim. 'He's married to Louise, whom I count as one of my friends. He's being unfaithful. It *isn't* right, and I told him so to his face . . . once he was fully dressed,' I add quickly. 'I said I'd tell Louise unless he did it first.'

'I see.' Robbie pulls into the drive and continues up past the big house to the yard, where he parks and turns off the ignition. 'Was that wise?'

'Obviously not, but I can't turn a blind eye. It isn't fair on your cousin. If someone had told me Ryan was seeing somebody else, I'd still have been devastated, but it would have been better than spending those extra months wondering why we weren't getting on, and letting him rack up more and more debt in my name. If I'd known, I'd never have ended up in the situation I'm in now. I'm up to my neck.'

'I didn't realise . . .' Robbie bites his lip and turns to look at me. 'So that's why you were so angry and upset at the show. I thought it was because you still had feelings for him, despite you denying it.'

'I denied it because I don't. I used to think that I was in love with him, but no more. He was fun to be with for a while, but he had a bad habit of pretending to be someone he wasn't.'

'Don't we all do that? To fit in?'

'You're a bit of a philosopher.'

'Maybe. How bad is the debt?'

'I've been paying off a fixed amount each month, but basically I'm skint.'

'Horses are expensive,' Robbie observes.

'Tell me about it, but there's no way I'm letting Rafa go. It would kill me.'

'I know how you feel.' He pauses. 'How much do you owe, if you don't mind me asking.'

'A few thousand.'

He whistles through his teeth. 'That isn't great.'

'I was planning to put most of the money I'm earning working for Mel . . .' I correct myself. '. . . Was earning, towards paying it off.' Warm wet tears roll

253

down my cheeks at the thought of my predicament. I'm grateful that he doesn't comment. 'I don't know what I'm going to do. I guess I won't be setting up my own business for now. I can't afford a mobile forge and the bank won't consider giving me a loan. I'll have to look for another job, and quickly.'

'I imagine you're paying a lot of interest on top.'

I nod. 'I looked into consolidating my debts, but it didn't make sense - the interest rate and monthly repayments were going to be more than what I'm paying now.'

'I'm sorry. Ryan seems to have got you into a bit of a pickle.'

'He wasn't entirely to blame. I should have kept an eye on our finances.'

'Yes, but it's no wonder you're wary of stepping into another relationship,' Robbie says as we turn into the drive. 'It seems that he's derailed your life.'

'You could put it like that. It's going to take me for ever to get back on track, so to speak. When I say that, I mean the financial part. My heart's mended. Seeing him at the festival took me by surprise. It was a shock to discover he was married, but I didn't feel jealous or hurt. I didn't look at him and think: I want you back. I was angry with him.'

'Considering what you're going through, I'm not surprised that you decided to confront Mel. But, I mean, wouldn't it have been in your interest to keep your mouth shut? I understand how you feel about infidelity – I wouldn't stand for it myself – but haven't you rather shot yourself in the foot?'

'It was the right thing to do,' I say mutinously. 'I thought you'd be on my side.'

'We both want to make sure Louise is okay. We have

different ways of going about it. Please don't tell her about this,' Robbie tries again. 'She's my cousin. I'm very fond of her.'

'I still don't see why I shouldn't.' However, I recall how happy she seemed when she was telling me about their plans for their date night. If I make this revelation, I will destroy any chance of them continuing to work on their marriage. It seems as though I'm damned if I do, and damned if I don't.

'I spoke to Mel a little while ago, man to man. He said he was terminating the arrangement he has with his bit on the side.'

Which is what he was attempting to tell me after I caught him in flagrante, I think.

'Perhaps they gave him too much anaesthetic. I reckon that major spinal surgery and the thought that your life is about to change makes you think about what you're doing and where you're going. He's realised he has to work on his marriage if they're going to stay together, and he can see what he has to lose if Louise divorces him.'

'That's very philosophical of you, but I don't see why he should get away with it scot-free.'

'He hasn't though, has he?' Robbie argues. 'He's kicked you out so he hasn't got anyone to work for him. Isn't that enough for you, or do you think he should be hung, drawn and quartered, or dragged through the divorce courts, whichever is worse? Is it fair to put Louise and Ash through that?'

'Doesn't Mel deserve it?'

'Life's too short for revenge and retribution.'

I lean back into the seat. I'm exhausted. My arms, my back and legs ache. My heart is sore because even when I try to do the right thing, I seem to end up doing wrong. I had Louise's best interests at heart, yet Robbie seems to think I should have kept my mouth shut.

He parks the Land Rover in the yard.

'Where would you like Rafa? In or out?' he asks.

'I think he'd be better in a stable tonight, if that's okay.'

'Of course it is. If you want to bring him out, I'll throw a couple of bales of shavings down in the stable over there.'

I open the ramp at the front and lead Rafa straight out on to the yard. He's damp, but warm behind the ears. He whinnies, and some of the other horses shout back from the paddocks.

'He can have the stable next door to Paddington. We're keeping him in on a calorie-controlled diet because he's getting too fat on the grass. Diva's in too.' Robbie fills a couple of buckets from the tap while Rafa is settling in, snorting at his new surroundings. He wheels the barrow into the shelter of the barn, returning with my suitcase.

'What about the flat?' I ask. 'Couldn't I stay there?'

'There's been a mains leak in the kitchen. There's no water at the moment and the floor needs stripping out, so it isn't an option I'm afraid. As I've said, you're more than welcome to stay with me and Maisie and the dogs.'

We walk together to the cottage, following the warm yellow glow from the porch-light and brushing past the roses, which shower us with glistening droplets of water. He unlocks the door.

'Go on in,' he says, letting me pass. 'You know where the bathroom is. I'll find you a towel.'

My forehead tightens.

'You look like a drowned rat. You need to get out of those clothes and into the shower.'

I wish that he was about to offer to scrub my back but, much as I'd love it, we've gone past that. At least, I think so . . . I walk upstairs, with Robbie following close behind me, feeling a frisson of guilt for wishing that he had his eyes on my behind. I stop at the bathroom door and wait for him to hand me a towel from the airing cupboard.

'Thank you,' I say.

I am chilled to the bone, and shaking with emotional shock. It isn't every day that you get the sack. I step inside the bathroom and close the door behind me. I strip off my wet clothes and stand in the cubicle and fiddle with the shower controls. No water. Cold water. Scalding water. I switch it off.

'Are you okay in there?' Robbie's voice. 'I forgot to show you how to work the shower – it's a bit quirky.'

'You can say that again.'

'Would you like me to show you? I promise I won't look,' he says lightly when I don't respond.

'Just a minute.' I pick up the towel and wrap it around my middle. I glance down. It's more of a hand towel than a bath sheet, and there's no shower curtain to hide behind, just a sliding glass screen. 'Come in.'

I'm aware that he's close. I keep my eyes averted, so as not to give him any clue as to how I'm feeling: naked, vulnerable, and wanting nothing more than for him to take me in his arms and hold me against his warm body. I notice in the reflection in the mirror above the basin that he's frowning and I wonder if he feels the same. His arm slides past my bare shoulder, sending shivers of goose bumps across my skin. He hesitates. I hear his breathing catch. I hold my breath.

There's definitely something going on. I can feel the electricity running between us. Is he going to kiss me? Would I resist if he did?

'Let me take your towel,' he says gruffly. 'It'll get wet.'

I unwrap it and thrust it into his hand.

There's a soft click as he turns the dial. A shower of water envelopes me with a welcome heat and Robbie disappears, leaving me with a sense of disappointment tinged with relief, because giving in to the temptation to kiss and cuddle would have made the situation more complicated than it is. We slept together and made an attempt to move forward together and it didn't work out, but I can't see how I'll cope with being 'just friends' when I'm lodging with him at Cherry Tree Cottage.

I wash, turn off the water and start to dry myself, remaining in the cubicle for privacy because I'm not sure about getting dressed. I have no clean clothes, and even the wet ones have gone from the bathroom floor.

'I've brought you some clothes from your suitcase. Unfortunately, they've got wet in the rain. I chose the driest from the middle, but if you think they're damp, I can put them through the tumble-dryer. There's a sweatshirt and jeans . . . and underwear.' I can just make out Robbie's silhouette through the shower screen. 'No, these are too wet. Can I lend you one of my shirts as a cover-up?'

'If you wouldn't mind, but not one of the see-through ones,' I call after him as he disappears again, returning with a crumpled shirt that he hangs over the towel rail.

'I'll be downstairs,' he says, hurrying away. 'Tea?'

'That would be great, thanks.' I emerge from the cubicle and pick up the shirt, one very much like the one he was wearing when I first met him. I slip it on and fasten the buttons at the front. It's flimsy, but not see-through, and the ruffles cover my chest. It's long too, reaching partway down my thighs. I check my appearance in the mirror, run my fingers through my hair and head down to find Robbie.

He's in the kitchen, his back to me as he pours tea from a pot into two mugs, one with the Eclipse team logo and another reading 'World's Best Dad'.

'Hi,' I say gently. 'Thanks for the shirt.'

He turns and looks me up and down appreciatively. 'You look much better in it than I do. Take a seat.'

He places a mug of hot tea in front of me and we sit opposite each other at the table, as if we're deliberately keeping a safe distance between us. A mobile buzzes. Robbie passes my phone across the table.

'I found it in your pocket. It seems to have survived the rain,' he says.

I check to find a text from Louise.

Hi Flick. I'm sorry about my husband. He told me what happened and how Robbie's taken you and Rafa in for the night. I'm sure we can sort this out, if we all sleep on it. See you in the morning. xx

I text back.

I'm sorry too. I'll be round to pick up the rest of my things between 9 and 10 am if that's okay. x

She replies.

We'll talk then. xx

He hasn't told her, has he, I think?

I look across at Robbie.

'Louise wants me to talk to Mel. She thinks we can resolve everything and start again, but I'm not going to. I can't go back.'

He frowns.

'Are you absolutely sure about this?'

I nod. 'I don't want to go back to work for him. It isn't just about me walking in on his extramarital activities. He resents the way his clients have started asking for me. He's afraid I'm going to take business away from him eventually. I wouldn't. I'm not like that.'

'What about the saying, every man for himself? If they want you to shoe their horses, you should go for it.'

'I don't have my own forge. Though if I did, I might just consider it, out of revenge for how he kicked not just me, but also my horse, on to the streets tonight.' I shake my head and then look straight at Robbie. 'Thanks for putting us up.'

'It's no trouble. I've said so. There's a spare room here. I'll make up the bed for you.'

My heart scrunches into a tiny ball as he makes it clear that we will be sleeping apart.

'Would you like a nightcap? I've got some brandy – for medicinal purposes and cooking.' He doesn't give me the option to refuse, getting up to find two glasses and a bottle of alcohol from one of the cupboards. He pours me a generous measure and pushes the glass towards me. 'There you are.' He sits down again, stretching his legs out, and making contact with mine, his jeans rough against my skin. 'I'm sorry,' he says, withdrawing quickly, as if he's stepped on to burning coals.

260

'It's okay. I don't mind.' I hesitate. 'Actually, I could do with a hug.'

'Do you think that's wise?' His eyes are on my neckline, where the collar of his shirt dips away to reveal the curve of my breasts.

'I'm not sure . . .' The brandy slides down my throat, radiating rays of warmth through my body.

'I don't think we could stop at a hug, do you? And if we did end up in bed, you might not be terribly happy about it in the morning. I don't want you having any regrets. As you've said yourself, it's complicated.'

I shake my head as I remember the last time he held me in his arms. 'You're probably right.'

'This is one occasion when I *know* I'm right,' he says with a smile. 'I don't want you to wake up and change your mind again. I have feelings too, and I'm not sure I can cope with any more drama. I have enough of that in my life already.'

I guess he's thinking of Diva and Maisie.

'Let's see how we feel in the morning in the cold light of day. If it makes you feel any better, you were right about Kerry as well. I feel like I've been a bit of a bastard.'

'Can you be "a bit" of a bastard? Isn't it all or nothing?'

'What do I know about anything?' He tries and fails to suppress a yawn. 'I'm shattered. It's been a long day – Diva was being a diva again. Let me show you to your room.'

I follow him upstairs, past the bathroom, the door with the sign reading 'Maisie's Room', and the room where Robbie and I spent our precious night together, to the next and last door on the landing. He turns the brass handle, pushes the door open and turns on the light.

'I haven't been in here for a while,' he says, moving inside to open the window and close the curtains. 'It probably needs airing.' He clears the bed of papers, boxes, and what appears to be laundry, placing everything on the polished oak floor. I watch, leaning against the cool cob wall, listening as the door slowly creaks closed and the water drips from the roof outside, splashing on the stones outside. The room is painted white and there's a child's cot folded up and leaning against the dark wardrobe, which matches the beams that run across the ceiling.

'Can I do anything to help?' I ask, as I inhale the musty scent of dried rose petals and vanilla.

'There are sheets and covers in the airing cupboard in the bathroom,' he says. 'I have a spare duvet somewhere.'

We make the bed up together before he retreats to the door.

'Is there anything else you need? Would you like a wake-up call?'

'What time do you normally start on the yard?'

'Between seven and seven thirty. I can't start too early because I have to wake Maisie and take her to the house for breakfast before school. It's unfair to expect her to sit around for hours while I'm doing the horses, and I can't leave her here home alone. But tomorrow, her grandparents are dropping her straight to school, which makes a change.'

'Okay, I'll do Rafa beforehand.'

'Don't worry about that.' He smiles ruefully. 'The money isn't great, I'm afraid, not much more than board and lodging. That's probably one of the reasons why Kerry left. She thought she wanted to be a stunt rider when she arrived, but she's more into jumping and eventing.'

'Thanks, Robbie. I'm just glad to have a roof over my head.' The rain continues to patter against the window. 'This is a lovely room.'

'I keep it shut up most of the time, unless we have friends to stay. It's a shame really.' He hesitates with his hand on the doorknob. 'In the morning you'll see that it looks out on to the cherry trees . . . Sleep well,' he adds.

'Goodnight.' I watch him close the door behind him, then turn off the light and slide into bed under the fresh-smelling duvet, still wearing his shirt like a caress against my skin. How can I sleep when I've lost my job? How can I possibly have peace of mind when I'm under the same roof as the gorgeous and generous Robbie Salterton?

Chapter Fifteen

The Price of Fish

According to my phone, it's gone eight when I wake up, wondering what I'm doing in a strange room, wearing somebody else's shirt. I sniff at the cotton. It smells of fabric conditioner, the one I associate with Robbie, and then I remember what happened last night and how I'm supposed to be ready for work.

I jump out of bed and open the door to find a neat pile of my clothing on the landing alongside a mug of cold tea. I dress quickly in a navy polo shirt and jeans, clean my teeth, and rush out of the cottage and down to the yard to find Robbie.

He's walking towards the stables with a couple of head-collars slung over his shoulder.

'I'm so sorry I'm late,' I say, joining him. 'I feel terrible.'

'It's fine. There isn't an award for employee of the year,' he jokes. 'You're here in time to help me turn Rafa, Diva and Paddington out and bring the rest in. Did you sleep okay?'

'I did. I wasn't expecting to.' Rafa whinnies at me and the sun comes out.

'You're welcome to go and see Mel anytime today.'

'Thanks, I need to pick up my things.'

'So you aren't going to try to get your job back?'

'No, as I said last night, I'm through with it. He'll have to cope without me. He was confident that he'd find alternative cover and it won't be long until he's back on the road.' I gaze at Robbie who's frowning, as if he thinks I'm making a mistake. 'I need to move on.'

'As long as you're sure. You're welcome to take the Land Rover – the keys are in the ignition.'

Robbie and I turn Paddington out with T-rex and put Rafa and Diva into adjacent paddocks. They touch noses, then start necking over the fence, nuzzling each other.

'Love at first sight,' Robbie says. I'm aware that his eyes are on me, not the horses. I blush, sensing the tension between us. 'That's a surprise. Perhaps Diva will be less stressy now that she's found a friend. She puts the others off by squealing and pulling faces at them.'

I take a pic to send to Sarah. A text comes straight back.

Aww, sweet! On the way to the hospital. Wish me luck xx

'What's up? Is Mel begging you to come back?'

'My friend's in labour. I'll be on tenterhooks all day.' I break off abruptly.

'You can talk about it in front of me,' he says. 'Life goes on. Does she know if she's having a boy or a girl?'

'A girl.'

He smiles gently as we start walking to the barn to collect the mucking-out tools. 'I don't think I could have coped with a boy. Maybe one day . . .'

'Do you want more?' It hadn't occurred to me before that Robbie might not only want a mum for Maisie, but more children too.

'I'd love Maisie to have a sibling or two. She'll make a great big sister – as you saw with Paddington, she's more than bossy enough.' He starts to walk back to the yard. 'Shall we make a start on the mucking out?'

'Of course. I shouldn't be standing around chatting.' I follow him to the barn where he opens the door and reaches inside for a shavings fork. As he hands it to me, our fingers touch and my body bursts into flame. Slowly, he leans in and brushes his lips against mine. I reach out and grasp his arm to steady myself, and somehow the fork ends up clattering to the floor, and he pulls me roughly into the shelter of the barn, closing the door behind us. I put my arms around his neck as he draws me close, pressing the length of his body into my curves. I want him so badly that I can hardly breathe.

'Robbie,' I mutter. 'Remember what we agreed last night?'

'Yes, but there is one enormous problem with that.' A big issue springs to mind immediately, something hot, hard and throbbing its way into my consciousness.

'It's that I fancy you like mad and I can't keep my hands off you. There, I've said it.' He holds himself still. I can see the pulse at his neck, marking time as he waits for me to respond.

'You know I won't be here for long . . .'

'So you've said a hundred times.' A shadow crosses

his eyes as a swallow flies across the rafters above. 'We could go back to before, if it's what you want too. We can spend time together, mess around with the horses – we could teach Rafa some tricks . . . We'll be exclusive – that's as important to me as it is to you. And we'll not worry about the future, just take it day by day. What do you think?'

'It sounds good,' I say, 'but what about Maisie?'

'I'd rather she didn't know.'

'Oh? I kind of hoped we wouldn't have to tiptoe around in secret.'

'It's better that she's clear that we have no ties and that you aren't a permanent fixture. She'll be sad when you leave anyway. I'd rather not confuse her.'

'You mean you don't want her to know that her dad sleeps with women.'

He shrugs. 'It sounds like a double standard, but she's too young to understand adult relationships. As far as she's concerned, love and romance is about princes bringing glass slippers and princesses lying waiting to be woken by a handsome hero.'

'That all sounds rather politically incorrect. Aren't there princesses who go around kissing a lot of frogs before they find "the one"?'

'I don't want Maisie to think that it's okay to sleep around.'

'Isn't that a little hypocritical? I mean, it's unusual nowadays for someone to meet and stay with the same partner for life.' I hesitate, noticing the look on his face. 'It's all right, I understand. You don't want her to have to grow up too soon.'

'That's right. I want her to have a childhood.' He touches his nose to mine. 'Do you think we can do this?'

267

'I guess it adds to the experience,' I say with a small inward sigh. 'It's just that when I'm with someone, I want to shout it from the rooftops.'

'I'm not that special.'

'Oh, you are.' I tilt my head for a kiss, and stand there locked in an embrace until the sound of Sally Ann's voice rings out from the yard outside.

'Where is everyone this morning? Robbie?'

With a growl of frustration, he releases me, and we emerge blinking into the sunlight with wheelbarrows and tools.

'Oh, there you are,' she says. 'Dillon didn't come home last night and there's lots to do. Flick? What are you doing here? No, there's no need to tell me. I can guess.'

'It isn't how it looks.' Robbie explains about Mel giving me the sack, although he doesn't give the reason, just says that there was a misunderstanding. 'Flick's going to help us out in return for board and lodging until everything's sorted out.'

'You can stay in the big house, if you like,' she says, turning to me. 'Neil and I are rattling around in there.'

'She's staying in the cottage with me and Maisie,' Robbie says hastily.

'Thank you for the offer though,' I say. 'It's very kind of you.'

'So, what are your plans?' Sally Ann asks.

'I'm going to collect my belongings today, then I'll start looking for another job.'

'There's plenty of breakfast to go round – you must join us later.'

I thank her again before Robbie and I make a start. We chat while we're mucking out the stables that were occupied the previous night.

'How is Nelson?' I ask as I make banks of clean bedding around the edge of Rafa's stable.

'He's far from being right,' Robbie says from the doorway. 'I've started him in light work so he doesn't drop too much muscle, but he doesn't like the hard ground, even with the pads and new shoes.'

'Don't expect too much too soon.'

'I'm trying to be patient, but I've got to have him right to have any chance of getting the TV contract confirmed. I don't think I can do it without him. We could use Scout as our lead horse, but he hasn't got the same presence as Nelson. You and Matt are giving me the "let's wait and see" scenario. What do you really think? You must have seen other horses with navicular. How many of them come sound enough to work? How long should I continue to flog a dead horse?'

'Well, for one, he isn't dead yet, and two, I'm not that experienced – it's Matt you should be talking to.'

'I need you to be straight with me.' He lowers his voice. 'I need you to confirm what I think I already know, that he's had it. He'll never be fit enough to be part of the team again.'

'I can't say that. There's always a chance.' I start to wilt under the pressure of his gaze. 'A very small chance . . .'

'Thanks for being honest with me,' he says gruffly. 'I needed to hear that.'

We empty the wheelbarrows on to the muck heap, then have breakfast with Dillon, who has made an appearance at last. We return to the yard.

'What next?' I ask Robbie.

'It's time for some team practice,' he says. 'We need Scout, Dennis, Turner and Carlton and some music.

I don't think the horses take any notice of it, but it helps me and Dillon. It's always good for the horses to get used to noise anyway. When I was doing a display with the Pony Club as a kid, there was a twenty-one-gun salute going off while we were waiting in the collecting ring. The ponies went ballistic – I don't know how everyone stayed on.'

I smile at the thought.

'Is this like a full dress rehearsal?'

'No.' He grins. 'I don't want the hassle of doing my make-up. I'm going to try Dennis out as lead horse today.'

It's my job to have the right horses ready at the right time and make sure that there's music playing through the loudspeakers on the perimeter of the arena. Luckily, Kerry was somewhat OCD about organisation, employing labels and colour-coding, so it's easy to match the tack to the horse.

I take ten minutes out to watch the brothers working the horses. I'm not sure that Dennis is up to being lead horse. He is more of a follower than a leader, hanging back when Robbie brings him and the other horse in the pair alongside Dillon's two, making it hard for him to keep his balance. I'm beginning to see how much Robbie relies on Nelson. He isn't going to be easy to replace if it comes to it.

I can see too why the TV producer would pick Nelson as the lead actor's mount for the series. Dennis is lovely, but he doesn't possess the same charisma and verve.

Robbie and Team Eclipse have a big problem on their hands . . . or should that be hooves?

When they return to the yard, I wash the horses down, pick out their feet and put them in their stables, where most of them have a good roll in their beds. Scout looks over his stable door afterwards, his mane adorned with pale cream curls of wood-shavings.

We stop again for lunch, when I finally get round to collecting my belongings from Wisteria House. I apologise to Louise for not letting her know I was going to be late.

'Never mind,' she says, as she opens the front door to me. One of the hens, bereft of feathers, sits perched on the banister behind her. 'I'm here all day anyway until it's time for the school run. It's good to see you.'

Mindful of my recent conversation with Robbie, I decide to keep my mouth shut.

'I'm sorry about my husband. I don't know what gets into him, but he speaks first and thinks later. He seems to have some idea that you're seducing his clients ready to steal them away when you set up your business, and he's still smarting a little about the horses as therapy sessions for Ashley. He seems to think that you influenced me when it's clearly not true. It was my decision.'

'I'm not stealing his clients, really I'm not.'

'I know. I've sat him down and given him a lecture – I've told him you're a decent person with ethics, so you wouldn't do any such thing. He was still mad last night, but he's calmed down today.'

'Where is he?'

'He's gone out with the truck – I told him not to, but would he listen? It isn't even six weeks since his op, yet he reckons he's fit enough to shoe a couple of quiet ponies by now. I expect he's preparing his apology right this minute.' She hesitates. 'You are

271

bringing Rafa back this afternoon? Ashley missed him this morning. We both did.'

'I'm sorry, I'm not coming back.'

'Mel didn't mean whatever he said or did to offend you. We need you.'

'I can't work for him any more.' Even if I can't tell her the real reason for the blow-up, I can vote with my feet. I can't stand by and pretend nothing's happening. I'd feel like a fraud. 'Robbie's offered me a temporary job.'

'What? As a groom?'

'I'm going to cover for Kerry's absence until they employ someone permanent.'

'That's such a waste.'

'It's only short-term, while I work out what to do next.'

'Fancy my cousin doing that. Whatever happened to family ties? Mel can't keep his round going without you.'

'He'll have to find someone else. I feel really bad about letting you down because we're friends, but—'

'Let's see, shall we,' Louise says bravely. 'Perhaps you'll feel differently in a day or two.'

'I won't change my mind.'

'Okay, if that's how you feel. I'll tell him I tried.' She smiles a small smile. 'I suppose I shouldn't be surprised. Why would you want to come back here when you can stay with Robbie at the cottage?'

'It does have its attractions, but that isn't my reason for being there. Robbie's lost his groom and his lead horse is lame. He needs all the help he can get if the team is going to have any chance of winning the TV producer over,' I say. 'Is it all right if I grab my things, only I'm on my lunch break and I don't want to be late back?'

'Of course. Go on up.' Louise steps aside, allowing me to pass. The hen remains on the banister as I make a couple of trips up and down the stairs to fetch the remainder of my belongings from my room. I clear the rest of Rafa's bits and pieces – except for a couple of leftover bales of hay – from the stables, and close the doors on the Land Rover.

Louise turns up to wish me goodbye.

'Don't forget us,' she says, giving me a hug.

'I won't,' I assure her.

Back at Cherry Tree Cottage, Robbie is waiting for me.

'I didn't give you a key,' he says, fishing about in his pocket. 'Here's the spare.' He presses it into my palm. 'Can I help you unload your things?' I open my mouth to explain that there isn't much to do, when he goes on, 'I should have made that a statement, not a question. Come on, I'll give you a hand.'

We take my personal possessions into the cottage and up the stairs to the spare room, before delivering the rest of the horsey items – including a broom, various rugs and purple buckets – to the yard.

'What next?' I ask.

'Kerry used to make up the evening feeds and hay-nets, and do any other odd jobs. Don't look so alarmed – I won't leave it all to you, but I do have to make some phone calls and answer a load of emails first.'

I feel the brief touch of his hand on my back and he's gone, leaving me to muddle along until he joins me later.

Maisie's other grandparents – Carla's mum and

dad – drop her off at about four. We're just finishing on the yard. She's over the moon to see her father – laughing, jumping up and down, words spilling from her mouth.

'Yesterday, when we went to the farm, we saw the donkeys, and I stroked a rabbit and Grandma got butted by a baby goat.'

'Slow down,' Robbie chuckles. 'It sounds like you've had a fantastic time.'

'We had Marmite sandwiches and ice cream and crisps.'

'All at once?'

'No, Daddy. Don't be silly.'

'How was school today?'

'Boring.' She turns to me, frowning. 'What's Flick doing here?'

'She and Rafa are staying with us. Now that Kerry's gone, she's going to help with the horses for a while.'

'Is Flick your girlfriend?'

'She's a friend. She's sleeping in the spare bed.'

'In Mummy's room,' Maisie finishes for him.

Robbie looks at me. 'Yes, in Mummy's room.'

'Like Rachel did,' she goes on.

'Indeed.' Robbie takes Maisie's hand. 'It's time we went home to cook some tea. It's such a lovely evening that I thought we'd light the fire outside. Flick, would you mind locking up the feed room and closing the gate before you join us?'

'I can go into Talyton St George for food,' I say.

'No, don't. You're more than welcome.'

'I'll catch you up.' I take ten or fifteen minutes to make sure the yard is secure, and I think about what Maisie has said. I feel at little sick at the thought that I'm sleeping in the dead ex's room, and uneasy that Robbie still describes it as 'Mummy's room', even after eight years. And who on earth is Rachel?

I give Rafa a carrot to say goodnight before making my way to the cottage, where Robbie is lighting a fire in the fire-pit in the back garden while Maisie collects sticks from the flowerbeds and under the trees.

'Hi,' I say. 'Is it okay if I use the shower?'

'Go ahead,' he says. 'Help yourself. You don't have to ask.'

I feel awkward though, more so since the conversation with Maisie.

'Are you all right?' he asks.

'I'm fine.'

'I should think dinner will be ready in about an hour. Don't tell Maisie, but I've put the potatoes in the oven in advance. Are baked potatoes with ham, cheese and salad all right? My cooking isn't up to my cousin's.'

'I'll be back to help shortly,' I promise, but when I return to the garden where the air is filled with the scent of wood-smoke, he seems to have everything under control.

'Would you and Maisie mind bringing the salad out from the kitchen?' he asks, reaching into the dancing flames in the fire-pit with a set of tongs to pull out a potato wrapped in foil.

Maisie sticks out the tip of her tongue as she concentrates on carrying the bowl of lettuce and tomato safely outside, while I keep the dogs at bay. She places it on the garden table, alongside a platter of ham and cheese.

'I've forgotten the drinks,' Robbie says.

'I'll get them if you tell me where to find them.'

275

'I'll show you,' Maisie says.

We drink elderflower cordial with our meal. Maisie talks about Paddington, Miss Fox, her schoolteacher, and compares her father's baked potatoes favourably with the Marmite sandwiches that she had for lunch at the petting farm the day before.

'That's high praise indeed,' Robbie murmurs, before he helps her get ready for bed, making sure she's showered, cleaned her teeth and got her uniform ready for the morning. I wait somewhat impatiently for him to read her a story. This morning, all I wanted was to be alone with Robbie to kiss and cuddle, but now I need some answers.

While I'm waiting, my mobile lights up with a text from Sarah:

Our beautiful baby girl, Isla Beatrice, was born today at 3.46 pm weighing 7 lb 3oz. All is well. xx

I text her back, congratulating her and David on Isla's safe arrival.

Eventually, Maisie goes to bed, and Robbie returns to the garden, where he sits down and gazes into the glowing remnants of the fire.

'What are you thinking?' I ask quietly.

'How wonderful this is, being here with you. I know it isn't the best of circumstances, but every cloud and all that.'

'Are you sure about me staying here, only I don't want to intrude or cause upset because I'm staying in Carla's room?'

He turns to me. 'We call it Carla's room, but she never slept in it. I should probably redecorate, but I've never got round to it because Maisie likes spending time in there, playing with her toys . . . I moved on a long time ago,' he adds, answering the unspoken question in my head, 'but she still has an emotional attachment to it.'

'And this Rachel? I hope you don't mind me asking . . .'

'She's an ex-girlfriend. I hadn't thought about her for a long time until Maisie mentioned her name. To cut a long story short, I met her when Maisie was about four. We got together very quickly; she moved in and slept in the spare room when we fell out. It was a mistake. Maisie was devastated when Rachel left. She thought we were going to get married. It was heartbreaking.'

'I'm sorry.'

'She was a lovely person, bubbly, good-looking and great with Maisie.' He looks wistful. 'They had a special bond, and it wasn't fair that my daughter had to suffer when we split up. Rachel wasn't into horses and, although she worked shifts – she's a nurse – she couldn't understand why I spent almost every waking hour on the yard. It's too late now, but I wish I'd handled it differently. I haven't seen her for at least three years, in case you're wondering,' he goes on. 'You have no reason to be jealous.'

'I'm just sad that it didn't work out – for Maisie, anyway.'

'But you don't like it, I can tell.'

'I'm sorry, I don't want you thinking that I'm some crazy obsessed girlfriend.'

He grins. 'Actually, I quite like the idea that you like me enough to have promoted yourself.'

I frown.

'You said "girlfriend".'

'Did I? Oh-mi-God.'

'Don't apologise. I love the fact that you want me to yourself.'

I move closer to him, the embers warming my cheeks. Carla, Rachel, Kerry and the others: they don't matter. It's my turn now.

'Kiss?' he murmurs, sliding his arm around my back.

'Oh yes,' I breathe. I look up into his eyes as a light comes on and a silhouette appears in one of the windows above.

'Daddy! Flick! I can see you.' There's an explosion of giggles.

'Maisie, you're supposed to be asleep,' Robbie calls, letting me go. 'Go back to bed.'

'I need you to tuck me in,' she says.

'I'll be up later.'

'Now?'

'What did I just say?'

'Okay . . .' The curtains close and the light goes off. Silence falls.

'I'll go up and check on her in half an hour or so,' Robbie says.

'She keeps you on your toes,' I observe. 'You don't get a moment's peace.'

He smiles. 'I know, but I wouldn't have it any other way. Shall we go inside and see what's on the telly? I usually watch something for half an hour or so to chill, nothing too challenging. I like a good crime drama or comedy. How about you?'

'I'll probably fall asleep. I'm not sure I can stand the pace.'

'The sooner you get back to shoeing horses, the better.' He pauses. 'I suppose you can't do much without the equipment.'

'I have a few tools of my own, but I need an anvil and forge as well. I can order shoes on credit, I think. Anyway, you'll have Mel and his replacement to look after the team, won't you?'

'I want you to do them. Diva's good with you. I don't want to set her off by having some big burly bloke brandishing a rasp at her, and I'd like you to continue with Nelson and his remedial shoeing. I'd rather not have anyone else.'

'You'll have to one day,' I say regretfully.

'I'm talking about for the time being. I imagine you need a van like Mel's – I can call my friend at the garage to see if he knows of anything suitable.'

'Thanks. That would be great, but it'll have to be incredibly cheap.'

'There's an old anvil at the back of the barn. You can have that. I don't know how we acquired it. The local am-dram group have borrowed it for one of their productions before.'

'I'd be very grateful for the loan. That way I can do some cold shoeing at least.'

'You can keep it. Dillon and I thought we might be able to use it as a prop one day, but we don't need it.'

We move indoors. In the sitting room, we sit down on the sofa side by side, without touching. We start to watch a quiz show on TV, but each time I glance towards him, he catches my eye.

'You aren't concentrating.' I give him a gentle nudge.

'Neither are you.' He rests one hand on my shoulder and his fingers caress my skin. I turn to face him as his breathing deepens, matching mine. The temptation is too much to resist.

'Let's go to bed,' he whispers.

'Are you sure?'

'Maisie will be asleep by now.' He stands up and helps me on to my feet. I make a play of falling into his arms, and we kiss until Robbie guides me towards the stairs and up to his room where we fall into bed.

Much later, we're woken by a wail. 'Daddy, where are you? I'm scared.'

Robbie and I sit bolt upright.

'We must have fallen asleep.' I scramble to get up, trying to unscramble my brain at the same time.

'I'll go,' he says, almost falling out of bed to reach the door, where the doorknob squeaks as it starts to turn. 'Maisie, wait there.'

I dive back under the duvet and lie flat like a starfish.

'I had a bad dream,' Maisie sobs. 'I wanna sleep in your bed.'

'Oh dear. Let's get you back to your room. You're getting too grown-up to sleep with Daddy.'

'It was really scary.'

'I'll tuck you in with teddy and wait with you until you're asleep. I'll tell you the story of the dream-catcher.'

'Okay,' she says eventually. 'Can I have a biscuit too?'

'No, no biscuits.'

'Can I sleep with Flick?'

'We mustn't disturb her. She's had a long day with the horses.'

And a short night with Robbie, I think, curling my toes at the delicious memory of our lovemaking. I listen for the sound of his footsteps padding across the landing, and the sound of a door being pulled shut. I peep over the top of the duvet to check that the coast is clear, before getting up, sweeping up the trail of clothes I left earlier, and making my way back to my room.

'Ouch!' I exclaim, as a pain shoots through my big toe. It takes me a moment to work out that I've stubbed it on one of Maisie's toys on the landing.

'What's that noise? Is it a ghost?' I hear her ask her father.

'There's no such thing. Please try to go to sleep.' I can hear the desperation in his voice. He's shattered, yet patient. I don't know how he does it.

I head for bed. I leave the light on and make an inspection of my room. This time, I take a closer interest in the feminine touches: cream curtains covered with pink roses; a marquetry box – inside is a necklace of semi-precious stones set in silver with a tiny card, reading, 'To my darling Carla, love you for ever, RS'; a pair of small leather riding gloves. I pick up a unicorn from the floor, one of Maisie's soft toys, I assume. I sit it on the dressing table where it watches over me as I slip between the cold sheets and fall back to sleep.

The next afternoon, when I'm wondering how Robbie and I will ever be able to organise spending time alone together, I arrive back at the Saltertons' with groceries that I've picked up in Talyton St George as my contribution to the household. Robbie is watching Maisie ride Paddington in the arena. He waves me over.

'What do you think?' he says.

'She's doing very well,' I say, as Maisie canters a circle, which comes to an abrupt stop as Paddington manages to stumble into walk.

'They're as ready as they ever will be for the rally.'

'When is it? Remind me.'

'Next Saturday. A week today. By the way, if you're interested, I've organised for Maisie to go to one of her friends for a sleepover afterwards. We can go out for a meal—'

'Or stay in,' I say.

Grinning, he leans across the gate and kisses me on the cheek.

'Daddy, you're kissing Flick,' Maisie shouts. She flaps her legs and Paddington breaks into a lazy trot, heading in our direction.

'I'm being friendly.' Robbie gives me a wink as Paddington stops beside us. 'Don't let him halt by the gate, otherwise he'll always want to do it. We don't want him getting into any bad habits.' He slaps the pony lightly on the rump to move him on. 'It's time to stop now.'

'Aw, do we have to?'

'That's enough for today – Paddington needs to conserve some energy for Pony Club.'

Maisie dismounts and I open the gate for her to lead Paddington back to his stable. She untacks him and puts her arms around his neck.

'So cute,' I say.

'I know,' Robbie sighs. 'I can't help it.'

I give him a gentle shove.

'Daddy, what are you saying?' Maisie asks.

'Nothing.'

'I expect you're talking about the price of fish again,' she sighs. 'I never want to be a grown-up.'

'It has its compensations,' Robbie says, amused.

I smile to myself because I have to agree with him. His eyes caress mine, and even though my head says that this is for fun, not for ever, my heart is filled with a rush of something deeper than desire.

I'm staying at Cherry Tree Cottage and Robbie and I have agreed on an exclusive but light-hearted relationship for as long as it lasts, and I'm over the moon. There is just one fly in the ointment: the presence of a certain rather endearing eight-year-old.

Chapter Sixteen

St Dunstan and the Devil

We're up early for the Pony Club rally the following Saturday. I catch all the horses and bring them into their stables for the day, while Dillon whizzes around on the quad bike with the trailer, clearing the fields of muck. I haven't seen Robbie since last night when we went to bed – in separate beds. Maisie is an extraordinarily light sleeper – she can hear a spider run across a carpet.

'Where's your brother?' I ask as Dillon stops to let me lead Paddington and T-rex past him.

'He's on daddy duty.' He grins. 'He can't find Maisie's hairnet, and Sophia won't let anyone with long hair ride without one.'

'I hope she doesn't expect you to wear one while you're doing the demo.'

He laughs as I walk on past him. Paddington makes a dive for the grass alongside the path, pulling up a mouthful of daisies and red clover. I keep him on a tight rope the rest of the way to his stable.

Having given feeds to the horses that need them, I

head inside the big house to find Robbie in the kitchen, plaiting Maisie's hair. She's holding a compact vanity mirror at arm's length, tipping her head from side to side and sticking her tongue out at her reflection.

'Please keep still,' Robbie groans, as first one and then another hairband snaps. 'Mum, have you got another one?'

'In the pot on the windowsill.'

'You're hurting me,' Maisie says. 'And that one's the wrong colour,' she goes on when Sally Ann passes him a replacement.

'I don't know why you're worrying about it,' Sally Ann says. 'It's the same colour as Paddington's lead rope. Help yourself to breakfast, Flick. There's coffee in the pot.'

I take two slices of toast, mushrooms, eggs and baked beans. I think it's going to be a long day.

'How's my favourite niece?' Dillon comes in from outside, wiping his boots on the mat on the way in. He ruffles Maisie's fringe as he moves past her.

'Hey, don't do that. It's taken me half an hour to get it right.' Robbie picks up the hairbrush from the table. 'What do you think?'

'It isn't as good as when Louise does it, but you're getting better, Daddy. You'll get there in the end.'

'Well, thank you for the vote of confidence,' he says in a lightly sarcastic tone.

'Thank you for my doing my hair.' She grabs the end of her plait and twirls it in a circle like a propeller.

'Don't do that. I don't want to have to start all over again. Now, Flick's going to help you give Paddington a bath while I hitch up the trailer and load all your kit, barring the hairnet that I still can't find. What have you done with it?'

'Paddington ate it,' she says with a cheeky grin.

'When?' Robbie exclaims.

'He didn't!' says Sally Ann.

'I showed it to him one day, and it went in his mouth and never came out.'

'Oh dear,' Dillon says gruffly.

'What are we going to do?' Robbie runs his hands through his own hair.

'You carry on,' Sally Ann says. 'I'll pop down to the chemist in Talyton when it opens at nine and buy a new one, and spares. I can drop over to the manor with them on my way home.'

'Thanks, Mum. You've saved my life.' Robbie moves around the table to give her a hug. 'I don't know what I'd do without you.'

'Neither do I,' she smiles gently, and a lump forms in my throat as I try to recall when I last felt that close to my mother. It's been a long time.

I finish my breakfast and put the plate and cutlery in the dishwasher before going outside with Maisie in tow. As we approach Paddington's stable, she skips on past me, opens the door and clips the rope to his head-collar before leading him out and tying him up. She turns on the outside tap and unwinds the hose.

I pick the shampoo and a sponge from the bucket of lotions and pampering potions. I open the lid and take a breath of the fresh scent of strawberries and cream. Maisie aims the end of the hose towards Paddington. The water loops over the top of his back and hits me straight in the chest.

'Ugh, turn it off,' I shriek, but she continues to spray me. I move around the pony and grapple with her for the end of the hose. 'I'll hold on to this while you rub the shampoo into Paddington's coat.'

'What's going on? I heard you shouting.' Robbie's eyes settle on my T-shirt, which clings to my chest. 'Would you like me to take over?'

'It's all right. I might as well finish the job now.'

'I accidentally on purpose sprayed Flick with water,' Maisie giggles.

'So I see. I think you should say sorry to her.'

'Sorry.' She opens the shampoo bottle, tipping it so it drips on to the ground, making bubbles in the puddles.

'You're spilling it. You'd better hurry up. Sophia will give you a black mark if you're late.' Robbie gives me a furtive smile. I reckon we work well together, with me in the role of good cop and him as bad cop. I find myself wanting to substitute the word 'cop' with 'parent', which feels odd when Robbie is Maisie's dad, and I'm merely helping out.

The hose chases the dirty suds out of Paddington's coat and down the drain.

I find myself wondering what sort of mother I'd make, if I ever had children. A strange sensation grips my chest, a pang of longing as I watch Maisie's small hands scrubbing the pony's shoulder with shampoo because she can't reach his withers. I didn't think I wanted one before, but I would like a baby. One day . . .

'Have you shampooed Paddington's tail yet?' I ask, having discovered previously that asking usually has a better outcome than telling Maisie to do something. She turns her attention to his tail. I look across the yard. Robbie is loading my tools into the trailer. My heart melts because it's the little things he does that show me how he cares about me. I watch him walk back from the barn, carrying the anvil. How will I even begin to tear myself away from my temporary lover and his funny and loving little girl?

Robbie drives the Land Rover and trailer to Talyton Manor. Outside the house, there are croquet hoops set out on the lawn. In the paddocks beyond, there are a couple of courses of show-jumps, and rows of horseboxes with a marquee.

'It looks as if you'll be doing some jumping, Maisie,' I say.

'Yay,' she says from the seat behind mine. 'Paddington loves jumping.'

'I think we're all going to have a lot of fun today.' Robbie reaches out and gives my thigh a sneaky squeeze.

I glance across. He catches my eye and winks. He isn't talking about Pony Club.

He chooses a spot to park on the field, making a third line behind the earlier arrivals. I jump out and open the door for Maisie, who lands on the grass with a big smile on her face. There are children of all ages, parents and ponies everywhere, and Sophia is in the thick of it, dressed in a hacking jacket and breeches, and yelling instructions.

She walks across to us to give us a programme for the day.

'Welcome to the fray. If you aren't sure about where you're supposed to be, just ask.' She looks past me. 'Ah, Robbie, I'm so glad you and Dillon agreed to take part.'

He greets her, kissing her lightly on the cheek.

'Maisie's in the yellow ride with Niamh, Chloe and Harriet.' Sophia checks her list. 'There's tea, squash and other refreshments available all day from the marquee, where Jennie's in charge of the catering. All rides must be lined up on the field by the pond at ten o'clock sharp.'

'We'd better get a move on then,' Robbie says as she walks away. 'Sophia can be ferocious, but her bark is worse than her bite. I've always looked up to her. I was captain of the mounted games team for several years, and she was one of the few who didn't tell me not to go into stunt riding because it was too dangerous,' he adds. 'She still rides, but only out hacking with her grandkids. I don't know what would happen to the Talyton St George branch of the Pony Club if she should ever hang up her boots.'

I unload Paddington from the trailer while Robbie helps Maisie into her body protector and jacket, and Sally Ann drops by briefly with the hairnets. I tack the pony up, fastening up the throatlatch on his bridle and tightening the girth on the saddle. By ten o'clock, there are four rides of children and ponies immaculately turned out and standing in a row in front of the pond for Sophia's inspection and an introduction to their instructors. Robbie and I stand watching until they're sent off for their morning activities.

'Paddington is looking amazing,' I say.

'It's hard to believe we got him for nothing. He isn't exactly showy, but he's more than a match for the other ponies.'

'I hope he behaves himself.'

'He'll be too knackered to do anything naughty. Haven't you read Sophia's schedule? The ponies have four hours of being ridden, although they do get a rest while the kids learn about stable management, tack cleaning and farriery, and watch the stunt-riding demo.'

'Which horses are you bringing?'

'I'm going to have to work with Diva while Dillon works with Scout. It'll be more low-key than usual – I'm a little stuck without Nelson. As you know, I've had Diva in training and she's doing okay. I'm planning to use her as our lead horse for now, mainly because I can't rely on her to stick with the team – she has too much of a mind of her own. We've had a couple of hairy moments, but nothing I can't handle.'

'Do you think she's ready, though? I don't like the idea of you getting hurt.'

'I didn't think you cared,' he smiles.

'Of course I do.'

'I think we should leave them to it and go and eat cake. I'm starving.' On the way to the marquee, Robbie asks me when I'm doing my talk.

'Immediately after lunch.'

'Would you like some immoral support?'

'Don't you mean moral?'

He chuckles, but I don't laugh with him. Much as I love holding hands, kissing and making love with him out of range of Maisie's radar, as if we are doing something immoral, I'd like to think more seriously about 'us'. I'm finding it increasingly difficult to keep it casual. It's all very well keeping reminding myself that there's nothing in it, no future, but my emotions keep welling up inside me, like water bubbling from an endless spring. Robbie is perfect. He adores his daughter and his horses. He's kind, funny, generous, and – best of all – he gets me. I'm falling in love with him.

'What are you thinking?' he asks softly.

'Nothing.' This isn't the time. 'I'd better get my tools out of the trailer.'

'I'll carry the anvil,' he offers.

'I can manage.'

He grins. 'I know. You're so bloody independent.'

'I'm not. At the moment, I'm dependent on you and your family.'

'That isn't true. We couldn't run the yard without you.'

'So you're no closer to finding a replacement then?'

He shakes his head. 'We've had some enquiries but, to be honest, I'm in no hurry.' He stands beside me, his fingers curling around mine as he lowers his voice to a husky whisper. 'It's selfish, but I like having you around.'

'The feeling's mutual,' I murmur.

He releases my hand, and we walk inside the marquee, where several women are organising the catering for the week. Jennie, who made the cake for Sally Ann and Neil's anniversary, looks up from where she's making sandwiches. She wipes her hands on her apron and nods towards the end of the table.

'There's tea in the urn and cider cake in a tin under the table. Grab a mug and plate, and help yourselves.'

'You see, it isn't such a bad day out,' Robbie says when we're sitting outside on the lawn with refreshments. 'Try some of this.' He cuts off a small piece of cider cake and offers it to me. As the sweet flavour of spiced apples floods my mouth, I give him a chunk of lemon drizzle cake in return.

'I'm going to check out the Victoria sponge next,' he says, jumping up. 'Can I get you something else? Or do you want the same again?'

'You choose.' I hand him the plate. 'I fancy something with chocolate this time?'

'I fancy you,' he grins.

He returns with a triple chocolate muffin, sits down and breaks it up. He slips a piece into my mouth. The chips are soft and semi-liquid in the heat. One sticks to my lip. Robbie smears it with his fingertip. Holding his gaze, I lick it off. His pupils flare and darken with lust and I wish we were alone.

'I can't wait until tonight,' I whisper.

'Me neither. Maisie will be tucked up at Chloe's house and we'll have the cottage to ourselves at last.' He reaches out and strokes my arm, sending shivers down my spine. Something vibrates in his pocket. He checks his mobile. 'I'm going to have to love you and leave you. Dillon needs me back at the ranch. Our groom is slacking.'

'What did I forget to do?' I say, wondering what I've forgotten. I thought I'd left everything ready – travel boots, hay-nets and water.

'I'm teasing. You're doing a great job. Dad and Sally Ann have had to go out to some meeting so he needs a hand loading. I'll catch you later.'

'You bet,' I say.

'Good luck with the talk. You might need it.'

'It won't be that bad, will it? You're making me nervous.'

Alone with thirty Pony Clubbers, I feel that I have reason to be apprehensive. I have my tools and the Saltertons' anvil between me and two rows of young people, Maisie and her friends in the front, and some world-weary teenage girls at the back. I hold up the items one by one and go through what they're called and what I use them for, before dividing the audience into groups and getting them to identify everything, making sure I have someone who looks vaguely responsible to take charge of the knives, pincers and hammers.

After they've done that, I run through a day in the life of a farrier. They ask me if I have a horse and I tell them about Rafa, or rather Maisie takes over in a proprietorial way, as if he is her horse, not mine.

'He's grey,' I say.

'With dapples,' she adds.

'He loves hacking and dressage.'

'My daddy says he'd love to do tricks with him.'

'Unfortunately he can't, because he's my horse,' I point out. 'Moving on, what shall we do next?' My session is supposed to be an hour long and it's already feeling like the longest hour of my life.

'Tell us a story about blacksmiths,' Maisie pipes up.

I try to think of a suitable subject, but some of the stories are unrepeatable to an audience of a sensitive disposition, and I don't want to ruin my image as cool female farrier by telling them about the occasions when I've run nails into various parts of my body, or been booted into the shavings by a grumpy horse. I recall Mel's comment about the story of the blacksmith and the Devil.

'Okay, I've got one. Gather round.' I wave my arm, and the riders move in closer.

'What's it called?' Maisie asks.

'It's called St Dunstan and the Devil . . .'

One of the teenagers groans.

'Boring,' says another. 'We're too old for stories.'

'Is it funny?' Maisie asks.

'No, it's dead scary,' I say. 'Does anyone knows who St Dunstan is?' No one does. 'He's the patron saint of blacksmiths. He worked at his forge, shoeing horses in the daytime, and playing on his harp in the evening. One evening, he was playing his instrument, when a man dressed in a long dark cloak turned up at the forge and started to make fun of the music. He howled like—'

'Like this?' One of the teenagers breaks into a high-pitched howl, at which the others join in.

'Just like that. Spookily,' I say when the cacophony has faded. 'The blacksmith noticed that the man had cloven hooves under his cloak and that he had a limp.'

'Didn't he have horns on his head?'

'Dunstan must have been pretty dim if he didn't notice.'

'Maybe it was dark,' laughs yet another. 'Was it dark?'

I feel like they're ganging up on me. I couldn't be a teacher.

'It was the hooves that gave the Devil away,' I say firmly. 'Dunstan offered to solve his sore foot by making him a shoe. The Devil agreed, thinking he was going to have a soft silk slipper, but the black-smith nailed a hot shoe to his foot.'

'Ouch,' says one.

Maisie and her small friends sit wide-eyed, cross-legged as if they're at school.

'The Devil was in agony, and begged St Dunstan to take the shoe off. Dunstan said he wouldn't unless he promised he'd never enter a place with a horseshoe above the door. He was in so much pain that he agreed. Dunstan pulled the shoe off and the Devil hopped away, and was never seen again.' I rack my brain to think of something to fill the ensuing silence. 'Blacksmiths are the only people who are allowed to hang a horseshoe up with the heels pointing downwards.'

'My mum says that the luck runs out unless you hang them the other way up,' says the cocky teenager.

'Ah.' I can't help feeling smug at being able to have the last word. 'There's no danger of that because it's the blacksmith who gives the shoe its luck.'

'What a load of old bo—'

'Sh, it's the CEO.'

Someone giggles and Sophia appears.

'I don't expect to hear bad language at the Pony Club,' she scolds. 'Now that Flick has scared the young ones half to death, it's time to find out how much you remember and who will be awarded their badges.'

She explains that I should ask the children some questions to check their knowledge and understanding of the topic of shoeing horses. She provides me with certificates and badges and leaves me to it. Everyone passes – even a couple of the teenagers who inform me afterwards that they've already got their Farriery badge, having received it from Mel the year before.

When I've finished, I have to wait for Robbie to turn up with Dillon and the lorry to put my tools away. One of the teenagers – the difficult one, Olivia, with the make-up and her shirt hanging out – insists on waiting around while the others go to check on their ponies.

'I'd like to know how you get to be a farrier,' she begins. 'I want to work with horses, but I don't want to do the exams to become a vet or a physio.'

'It isn't an easy option – it's hard graft.'

She nods. 'How do I sign up?'

'How old are you?'

'Fifteen.'

'My advice would be to get your GCSEs and find some work experience. If you still like the idea, you can apply for an apprenticeship. Does that answer your question?'

'Yeah, thanks. Can I help you put your tools away?'

'It's kind of you to offer, but I'm waiting for Robbie to turn up with the lorry.'

'Robbie Salterton?'

'That's right.'

'Do you shoe his horses?'

'Yes,' I say.

'It must be amazing to work with the stunt team.'

'It is. I get to shoe all kinds of horses. It's never boring.' I recall that I don't currently have the means to do any shoeing at all, and I'm gutted that it's going to be some time before I've sorted out some way of starting again, but I put my angst aside because, for once, I'm very aware that there's more to life than career—

'I said, Robbie and his brother are here.' Olivia's voice brings me back to earth. 'I'll go and see if I can help them.'

I glance towards the drive where the lorry is pulling in. Robbie is at the wheel. Dillon gives me a wave. They stop by to pick up my tools and the anvil before parking on the field. I help them unload the horses and wait for them to get ready.

'What the . . . ?' I say when Dillon appears, dressed in a long blonde wig, false eyelashes, lipstick, and a flowing gown with balloons tucked in the top.

'I'm Princess Leia. What do you think of my

heaving bosom?' Laughing, he hitches the balloons up to create a colourful cleavage.

'It's . . . I'm speechless.'

'We tossed a coin for it and guess who won, the lucky sod.' He glances towards his brother who's looking splendid in his flowing shirt, breeches and long boots. 'Never mind – he looks more like a girl than I do.'

I bite my tongue. I don't think so. I glance towards Olivia who is here, holding on to Scout. From her expression, I don't believe that she thinks so either.

'Thanks, little bro,' Robbie says.

'It's Leia, if you don't mind.' Dillon curtseys. 'Please sir, would you be so kind as to help me on to my horse,' he goes on in a falsetto voice.

'Now you're taking this too far.' Robbie smiles and Dillon vaults on to Scout's back. He gathers up the reins – the horses are wearing bridles and trick saddles today.

'What are we waiting for?'

'Sophia, I think,' Robbie says, mounting Diva, who's rolling her eyes at Scout in a threatening manner. 'She wants us down at the pond at two o'clock sharp.'

'It's ten past,' Olivia says, checking her watch.

'Let's go then.' Robbie squeezes his calves against Diva's sides and moves off. Dillon and Scout follow, trotting along the drive to the open space where a cedar tree stands, its boughs creating dark shadows, beneath which Sophia has lined up the Pony Clubbers to keep them safe from the sun. She greets the brothers and announces the demo before reminding everyone that they should always wear hats when riding, and that it's only highly trained stunt riders who are allowed to break the rule. I sit down along-side the children to watch the performance: the story of a beautiful maiden being rescued by the handsome prince.

The brothers walk and trot past each other, making their horses dance like the Lipizzaner stallions from the Spanish Riding School that my parents once took me to see as a birthday treat.

Robbie pulls Diva to a halt beside the pond. Dillon rides to the opposite side of the water, where he asks Scout to rear. He makes a play of clinging to his horse with his arms around his neck, almost falling out of the saddle and clambering back on. He slides to one side, ending up with his head beneath his ankles and his dress ballooning down over his chest, revealing a voluminous pair of white bloomers.

The children are laughing and Sophia is clapping and saying how marvellous it is, when he finally slips right off the horse backwards, landing behind his tail. He pats Scout on the rump. The horse canters away. Dillon pulls up his skirts and runs after him, tripping through the tufts of rough grass and falling flat on his face. Scout stops some way away where he turns and stands waiting.

Robbie gallops to Dillon's side. I can't keep my eyes off him as he rides Diva through the pond, sending up rainbow splashes from the surface.

'Fair maiden, I see you are crying. Pray tell me what's wrong?'

'My horse hates me.' Dillon rubs his eyes. 'He's run away, never to return.'

'What did you do to him? Did you say a rude word?'

'Oh no, handsome prince. I don't know any of

those . . .' Dillon winks at the audience. 'I'm an innocent fair maiden. I don't know any words like, like . . . bottom.'

'Maybe you are not as fair as you make out,' Robbie says.

'I ate too many cakes at Pony Club.' Dillon's falsetto voice grows shaky as he bites back a guffaw of laughter. 'He says I'm too heavy to ride him. It makes his fetlocks ache. And now I am stranded in this desolate place with no way of returning home.'

'Let me help you get him back. Give me your arm.'

Dillon offers his leg. Robbie leans right down and makes a show of trying to pick him up. At the third attempt, Dillon ends up hanging upside down from Diva's back. Robbie drops him so he lands on the ground on his hands, turns head over heels and lands in the crab position.

'I said, "Give me your arm!"' Robbie repeats, as Dillon struggles up, then quickly vaults on behind Robbie. Diva tenses, arching her back as if she's going to buck, but before she can do anything, Robbie pushes her into canter. He sends her all the way around the pond and back through it to pick up Scout, who canters along beside her, bringing the demo to an end to cheers and applause.

'Well done, and thank you to the Salterton brothers,' Sophia yells. 'Now run along and get your ponies.'

'Can we have a go now?' somebody asks.

'No, not today, not any other day,' Sophia says. 'I don't want to spend the night at A&E.'

The Pony Clubbers disperse, heading back to tack up their mounts for their next lesson while Robbie and Dillon return to the lorry.

'What did you think?' Robbie asks me when we are in the cab with the horses loaded, waiting for Dillon who's talking to Sophia outside.

'It was very funny and completely unexpected.'

'I thought you were going to tell me off for not writing it so that the princess rescued the prince. We tried it the other way round at home, but it just didn't work.'

'No, it was amazing and Diva was great.' I note the cut of Robbie's features and the shadow of stubble that adorns his cheeks. 'Perhaps she will be ready for the Country Show after all.'

'We'll see. She performed far better than I thought she would,' he says, his face flushed. 'Even Dillon behaved himself.' He lowers his voice. 'I'm not sure I can behave though, not with you around.'

'Just wait till tonight,' I whisper hoarsely.

'I've said goodbye to Maisie. I don't think we should waste time hanging around here any longer. As soon as Dillon's stopped talking, we'll go. He's going to come and collect Paddington later.'

Back at the yard, we throw ourselves into doing the horses, which involves giving them their afternoon feeds, mucking out the stables and turning them out for the night. The dogs 'help', walking up and down to the fields with us, and sometime later Sally Ann calls us in for dinner.

I look at Robbie.

'Do we have to?' I mouth.

'Mum, I'm cooking for Flick tonight. I told you.'

Sally Ann gazes at him. Her mouth curves into a smile. 'Your face. It's all right, you told me this morning.' She turns to me. 'Have a lovely evening, you *two*. I hope you survive the night – as far as I'm aware, Robbie's cooking hasn't advanced much beyond fish fingers and waffles.'

'Thanks a lot,' he cuts in cheerfully.

He cooks spaghetti marinara with green salad and garlic bread, served with bottled beer.

'What do you think?' he asks as we sit eating at the kitchen table with a lighted candle between us.

'It's delicious. You could be a chef.'

'I'd hate it. I couldn't do anything but work with horses.' He changes the subject. 'What do you think of my attempt at romance?'

'The meal?'

'The candle.'

'It's lovely.'

'I'm not sure I know what romance is.' He smiles. 'Dad says it's about hearts and flowers, while Mum tells me that it's the everyday, ordinary gestures that count.'

'I think it's about feeling appreciated and loved.'

'I feel loved when I'm with you,' he says quietly. He reaches out and covers my hand with his and suddenly I'm no longer hungry. He gazes into my eyes and clears his throat. 'Shall we go upstairs?'

I lean across and blow out the candle while the flames of lust ignite inside me.

On the way to the bedroom, we kiss and strip off each other's clothes, casting them aside until we're naked on his bed, but as we head for the heights of passion and surrender, Robbie's mobile rings.

'I'd better get this,' he says, fumbling for his phone.

'Oh, do you have to?' I sigh, but he's talking.

'Hi. What's up?'

Apart from the obvious, I think as I gaze at him,

301

hungry for his body, which is gleaming in the moonlight that streams in between the curtains. I get the gist of the conversation: the sleepover is in jeopardy.

'Yes, of course I'll come and get her straight away.' Robbie gives me a look as he cuts the call. 'Maisie thinks she can see a man in a black cloak lurking behind the bed. You told them the story of the black-smith and the Devil.'

'Young kids like being frightened. I used to.'

'Not when they're eight and staying away from home.'

'Mel suggested it.'

'He was winding you up. I'll be having words with him.'

'I don't believe it. It's just a story. Look at how brave Maisie is cantering about on Paddington and catching spiders the size of her hand. Who would have thought she'd be scared of a piece of fiction?'

Robbie rolls away from me and slides out of bed.

'Are you coming?'

'Not now,' I say ruefully.

'Ha ha. Very funny,' he says.

'I'll stay. I have an early start in the morning.'

He leans across and kisses me tenderly.

'Another time,' he says, and I watch him slip back into his clothes and go, my heart heavy with regret, my stomach churning with unrequited lust. Our night of passion has been brought to a premature end. Just one night, I think, rolling on to my back. Is it too much to hope for?

I stare at the ceiling, at the dark oak beams with their roughened edges and wormholes. I shouldn't be this upset. This is supposed to be a casual summer fling, a bit of fun, and it shouldn't matter that we can't share a bed tonight – but it does.

I return to my room, but I can't sleep. I count horses, grey ones and black ones, jumping one by one over a five-bar gate.

I'm still regretting telling the tale of St Dunstan and the Devil a few days later, because Maisie continues to maintain that she isn't ready to face a night alone. She sleeps in Robbie's bed while he has a mattress on the floor, which serves me right for not thinking firstly that Mel might be leading me on, and secondly that the story was inappropriate for seven- and eight-year-olds of a nervous disposition.

Chapter Seventeen

Nelson's Last Stand

On a wet Saturday afternoon a week later, Robbie has taken Maisie for a walk with the dogs in the rain, so I have peace and quiet for a while. I clean the kitchen – my contribution to tidying the house. I put the dirty dishes into the dishwasher, clean the spiders' webs and dead flies from the windowsill, and arrange some flowers that I cut from the garden in a vase that I find in the cupboard. I mop the floor and make tea and toast before sitting down at the table with the radio on low.

The cottage is like a living thing – the fabric of the building feels warm or cool to the touch, depending on the weather. I can hear the occasional creak of her bones as the timbers warp and bend, while I force myself to look through the paperwork that I've been saving for a rainy day. There's an invoice from Westleigh Equine for Rafa's annual check-up, dental treatment and vaccination, along with a bill from Overdown Farmers for a couple of bags of feed, and confirmation of renewal of his annual insurance for veterinary bills.

'What are you doing?' Maisie walks in with Badger and Tatt, one on each side.

'I have to pay the bills.'

The dogs stop and shake themselves, showering us with dirty water.

'Ugh!' Maisie shrieks and grabs a tea towel to wipe her face.

'That's disgusting,' I say, getting up to send the dogs outside. 'What are you doing, apart from traipsing mud all over the floor that I have just cleaned?'

'Oops.' She looks down, holding up her dress. 'I've forgotten to take off my wellies.'

'What will Daddy say?'

'He won't mind. Sometimes he forgets to take his boots off too.'

I shut the door, but it slowly swings back open and the dogs wander back inside and pad around, leaving muddy paw-marks. Devon mud versus clean cottage. It's a losing battle, I think, amused. The mud is winning. We need the rain, though. The first three weeks of May have been warm and dry; the fields are turning yellow, and much of the grass has been nibbled down to its roots.

'Where are you going?' I ask as Maisie kicks off her wellies and leaves them where they fall.

'I'm going to watch a DVD. Daddy says I can't ride Paddington now because he's got too much to do.'

'Paddington has?' I say, straight-faced.

'No, Daddy!'

'Okay. Well, I could come and help you with Paddington later.' Her eyes light up. 'Give me an hour or so, and I'll be with you.'

She skips away to the living room, leaving me to shuffle correspondence for a little while longer. I've had minimal income – the equivalent of Kerry's wage minus mine and Rafa's keep. Mel has paid me, and it's too late to ask for my job back even if I wanted to; Robbie says that one of the other local farriers is looking after Mel's clients until he makes a full-time return.

Where does that leave me, I wonder?

I can't stay here for ever. Eventually, the Saltertons will employ a permanent groom, which will mean I'll have to move on. That will mean getting into more debt to buy a van and find somewhere for Rafa and me to live.

I tot up some figures: the loan to buy and fit out the mobile forge; my monthly debt repayments; Rafa's keep (I can minimise it by doing everything myself, but I'll still have to rent a field and stable, because he hates living out in the winter); a deposit on a flat or rooms for myself; advertising. The list goes on.

I make a spreadsheet on my iPad and create a budget. My heart sinks to the pit of my stomach. What am I going to do? The answer is staring me in the face. I blank the screen quickly. I can't even contemplate it. I'd rather starve.

'Hi, Flick.' I look up to find Robbie at the back door, dressed in a green waxed jacket, jeans and navy wellington boots. 'Did Maisie and the dogs come this way?'

I point towards the floor.

'I see.' He makes to walk inside.

'Hold it right there,' I say, smiling. 'Boots off first.'

'I see that the house elf's been.' He leaves his boots on the step outside and walks into the kitchen. He glances around the room and leans down to kiss my cheek. 'Thanks. I've been meaning to tidy up for a while. Are you all right? You look upset.'

'I've been going through my paperwork, that's all.'

'Bills?'

'The usual.' I pick up the sheaf of papers and slide them into a folder.

'There's an auction in a couple of weeks' time – Dad's always on the lookout for bargain furniture for the holiday lets. He showed me the catalogue online – there are a couple of vans coming up, bailiff repossessions, so they have to be sold. I thought we should go and have a look.'

'I wouldn't mind looking, but I doubt I'll be in a position to bid.'

'I could lend you the money.'

'That's very kind of you, but no, I won't accept any loans. I'm in enough trouble as it is.'

He stands behind me with his hands on my shoulders, massaging the tension from my muscles.

'The problem is that you're trapped in a vicious circle. You can't work without a mobile forge, and you can't afford to buy one without working.'

I reach up and touch his hand. 'Tell me about it.'

'I like the way you're so proud and independent. I've always been determined to stand on my own two feet, but I've learned that it's fine to accept help when it's offered. It doesn't make you any less of a person.' I notice the humour bubbling up in his voice. 'Besides, I have a vested interest: the sooner you're set up, the sooner you can go back to being my farrier.'

'I know, but it's my mess and I need to sort it out,' I say stubbornly.

He leans down and plants a kiss on the side of my neck.

'The offer's open if you should change your mind.'

I thank him, but I have no intention of taking him up on it now or in the future. Robbie's going to need his money to buy another horse – or horses – for the team, if Nelson fails to come sound.

'The rain's clearing,' he observes. 'I have loads to do, but I wonder if you'd like to come out for a hack with me and Maisie. I want to take Nelson on the short route, so it'll only be about half an hour.'

'Are you sure? He hasn't had much time to break his new shoes in. It's like swapping from flats to heels.'

'I can't say I know anything about that,' Robbie says, smiling ruefully. 'It's all right. We'll only walk. I won't push him. I'm planning to take him to the beach next week to work him on the sand. Do you want to come? I'll take the lorry so you can bring Rafa along.'

'I'd love that,' I say, picturing myself galloping over the sand alongside Robbie in his flowing shirt.

'I thought we'd go on Wednesday this week.' He lowers his voice. 'Don't tell Maisie – she'll be at school.'

'What are you saying about me?' Maisie calls from the living room.

'How did she hear that?' Robbie exclaims before calling back. 'Flick's coming out with us.'

'Yay!' She comes cantering into the kitchen, tossing her head and neighing.

The three of us go for a quick ride through the puddles. Nelson and Rafa stride out, sticking to the soft verges where we can, while Paddington jogs along, breaking wind behind us. Robbie and I ride so close that our stirrups touch. I move Rafa away when

I glance over my shoulder and notice that Maisie is watching closely. I'm not sure how much she knows about the situation between her dad and me. What I do know is that it's becoming increasingly difficult to hide our feelings from her. The horses drift back together and our stirrups touch once more. We're like magnets, unable to keep apart.

Rafa has been a different horse since he's been living at the Saltertons', and in some ways I'm a changed woman. I'm more relaxed, after all the rushing about I was doing working for Mel. Living at Cherry Tree Cottage with Robbie is like having a breathing space.

I'm in a relationship again, albeit not one with long-term prospects, but so what? I'm having fun. He's good for me.

A delicious shiver of desire runs down my spine as I recall last night, the first occasion that Maisie decided she could sleep in her own bed since the St Dunstan episode. I remember the touch of his hands on my buttocks as he pulled me close, the 'what planet am I on?' sensation as he made love to me twice, with passion and tenderness, nothing like I've felt before, and the deepest, most satisfying sleep, lying in his arms, our breathing matched and our legs intertwined.

I woke and he had gone. I don't know what time he left, but it was before dawn and before Maisie would have been awake, which reminds me that I am still in effect his secret lover, not his girlfriend. As we ride, I gaze up at the dark green leaves of the ivy that clings to the side of one of the oak trees. Understanding his motives doesn't stop the tendrils of jealousy creeping around my heart.

Over the next four nights, despite the fact Maisie is sleeping in her room in the cottage, we can hardly keep our hands off each other. I creep across the landing to Robbie's bedroom, learning to avoid the creaky floorboards, and practising turning the doorknob without making it click. This morning, I woke at dawn to find us lying apart with just our fingers and toes touching because of the heat. I scurried back to my room and dressed in shorts and a white cotton top to take account of the forecast.

When I meet Robbie on the yard after he's dropped Maisie and Ashley at school, he's looking cool and collected in jeans and a khaki T-shirt.

Dillon doesn't turn up until nine, when Robbie is emerging from the barn with several hay-nets slung over his shoulders. He gives his brother a weary telling-off before handing over the load of hay.

'There you are. It's all yours for the next few hours. Flick and I are taking the horses to the beach.'

'I'll bring Scout,' Dillon says.

'No, you'll stay here – there's work to do in the office if you run out of things to do on the yard. Don't argue. You haven't been pulling your weight.'

'Who do you think you are?'

'I'm supposed to be your partner, but I feel more like your boss, and I'm inclined to give you the push.'

Dillon swears. 'How do you think it feels always being second to you?'

'Don't talk rubbish. You can't do any wrong. You're the golden boy, the younger son.' He hesitates, then turns and walks away towards the horsebox.

'What's eating him?' Dillon asks me when Robbie is out of earshot.

'He's worried about Nelson.'

'There's no need to take it out on me.' Dillon heaves the hay-nets on to his back.

'I know, but he's completely committed to everything he does, so it's hard for him to see you rolling up without a care in the world when he's been on the yard since seven thirty. Give him a break.'

'All right, seeing that it's you who's asking. You'll look after him today?'

'I'll try, but you know what he's like. He does his own thing,' I say, watching Robbie lower the ramp on the lorry. I admire his determination to be the best dad and the best stunt rider, but I'm not sure if he's trying hard enough to be the best boyfriend, because there is still the issue of Maisie. 'I have no control over him.'

'You have more than you imagine,' Dillon says. 'He'd do anything for you.'

'Even take me and my horse to the beach,' I say, smiling, as I turn my attention to Rafa, who is looking over his door. I walk across to give him a pat, but he turns and walks away to nibble from his hay-net. 'Sometimes I wonder if he's all that into me,' I observe.

'That's ridiculous,' Dillon says. 'Robbie adores you.'

'I'm talking about Rafa.'

'My mistake,' Dillon chuckles.

'I'd better get going. I'll see you later.'

Robbie and I load the horses. Before we set out, he takes off his shirt, rolls it up and lays it across his shoulders, and I worry that he'll stop the traffic.

'I had a great time last night,' he says, as we finally head off to the holiday resort of Talysands.

'It was fun,' I agree, 'although I'd have liked to stay cuddled up in bed with you. Do we have to continue this charade in front of Maisie?'

He glances across at me.

'Are you still intent on leaving?'

'Well, yes, but—'

'Then nothing's changed,' he says abruptly.

'I wish we didn't have to keep our relationship hidden, that's all. It makes me feel a little uncomfortable, pretending that we're just friends whenever Maisie is around. Other people have guessed what's going on. It won't be long before she works it out for herself.'

'I'd rather that she didn't. I'm sorry, Flick, but I can't do it to her, not after what happened to her mum and then with Rachel. I'll have to be in a long-term, committed relationship before I involve Maisie.'

'I understand why you feel this way—'

'You aren't a parent, though. You think you have some idea of how strongly I feel about protecting my daughter, but I can tell you, you haven't a clue until you've been there.'

'Are we having an argument?' I ask, trying to keep the conversation light.

'I prefer to describe it as a discussion.' He reaches across and squeezes my knee. 'I feel torn. I want to keep Maisie happy and I want to make you happy too. It's like walking a tightrope, trying to live life without hurting anyone's feelings.'

I love him, but sometimes I wonder about his decision-making. I know he worries about Maisie, but I wish he'd also think about himself and what he wants.

As we pass the sign for Talysands, Robbie drives on down the hill to the railway bridge. The road continues beneath the arch to reach the amusement arcades and shops but, before we get there, Robbie stops, braking slowly for the horses, and swears.

'I'd forgotten there was a height limit here.' He smiles ruefully as he lowers the window to give him a better view. 'Idiot!'

Inhaling the mixed scents of the sea, fresh doughnuts and chips, I reach across the seat and touch his thigh to reassure him that he is anything but.

He makes a six- or seven-point turn and drives back along the road until he finds a side turning into a car park behind the dunes. He picks a space for the lorry at the far end of a row of vehicles, parks and turns off the engine.

'Are you ready for this?' he asks.

'Of course. I'm very excited – I've never ridden Rafa on the beach.' I lean in for a kiss and the temperature in the cab is starting to rise to a dangerous level when we finally tear ourselves apart.

We unload the horses in front of a small audience of holidaymakers, who stand with armfuls of colourful bags, balls, parasols and beach towels. I fasten the strap on my hat and mount Rafa bareback from the step at the side of the lorry, while Robbie vaults on to Nelson's back, having moved the T-shirt from his shoulders to reveal his naked torso, and kicked off his shoes.

'Which way?' I say, looking in the direction of the sea.

He gestures towards a slatted wooden pathway that runs across the sand between spiky clumps of marram grass. There's a double-headed sign with 'Dogs Allowed' pointing one way, and 'Dogs Not Allowed May–Sept' the other.

'Away from the crowds.' He squeezes his calves

against Nelson's sides and we ride along the first section of the beach, negotiating encampments of sun-tents, windbreaks and deckchairs. The crowds thin out as we head towards the far end of the shallow bay, where red sandstone cliffs, scarred by waves and weather, border the shingle. Looking back, I can see the promenade and the steep stone steps down to the sand.

Rafa shies at the shells and strips of seaweed that lie strewn across the foreshore. I let him take Nelson's lead as we reach the water's edge where the waves caress the sand. Robbie rides straight in. Rafa hesitates as a creamy swirl of surf flows towards him. He makes to take a step back as the water touches his hooves, but I push him on in. He stops as the water begins to fall back again and starts pawing at the froth, digging a hole that the sea fills in when the next wave washes back.

'What are you waiting for?' Robbie yells. Nelson's black coat is gleaming wet as he stands belly-deep in the water.

I send Rafa forwards. Bemused, he jumps an incoming wave, and another, making me laugh.

'Your horse is mad,' Robbie shouts above the sound of splashing.

'He's loving it,' I call back, enjoying the touch of the cold water against my skin. 'Thanks for bringing us.'

'The more time I can spend with you the better.'

Squinting through the searing brilliance of the sun dancing on the water, I watch Robbie work with Nelson, asking him to break from walk to canter and back again in the surf. Horse and rider perform a pirouette. Nelson turns on his haunches with his hocks underneath him and his tail tucked in. The foam from his mouth mixes with the spray from the breaking waves and sweat trickles down his shoulders, blending with the saltwater that flies up as he plunges his hooves into the sea.

My belly tightens with longing as I watch them. My feelings for Robbie are no longer casual. They're deeper than the ocean.

With droplets of water glinting from his hair, he lets Nelson relax before asking him to rear up, a trick I've seen him do many times.

Nelson lifts his front feet high into the air, throwing up a mixture of glittering water and sand. The muscles down his thighs swell and ripple as he takes his weight on his hind limbs and propels his body forwards before slamming his forefeet down with a loud splash. He freezes momentarily – if you didn't know the horse, you might not notice how his ears drop just a little, and his expression changes from complete joy and exhilaration to confusion and pain.

In an instant, though, he hides his feelings. There is no way that he would continue to survive in the wild by showing weakness.

Robbie glances down towards Nelson's shoulder and gives an almost imperceptible shake of his head before turning and riding into the deeper water, where he slides off Nelson's back and swims with him. For a few minutes, I wonder if they're intending to return to shore or if they're going to carry on their journey to the horizon and beyond, where the blues of the sea and sky blend into one. Rafa shifts beneath me, growing anxious as his companion heads out towards the rocks in the middle of the bay, and the seagulls cry overhead.

He doesn't relax until Robbie and Nelson return, emerging from the surf side by side.

'He's done enough,' Robbie says. 'I thought I'd take the weight off his feet.'

I look away from the compelling sight of Robbie's lightly tanned chest adorned with goose bumps, to the expanse of sand and pebbles that exists between us and the lorry.

'It's a long way to walk. Here, jump on. We'll give you a lift.'

'Will Rafa be okay with that?' Robbie shields his eyes from the sun.

'There's only one way to find out.'

He vaults on behind me. Rafa flicks his ears back and forwards again as Robbie wraps his arms around my waist, but he's fine with the extra weight, and we return along the beach with Nelson ambling along beside us. I settle into the rhythm of the walk, leaning back against Robbie's chest.

'Thank you,' he says, leaning closer with his cheek against mine.

'What for?'

'For being here. For being you. I don't think I could get through this without you.'

'What do you mean?' My pleasure at being up close and personal with my man on a horse evaporates as it occurs to me what he's talking about. 'Nelson?'

'This was his last stand. It was a pretty long shot, but I was hoping that he'd be sound on the sand. That would have been a start, but it isn't to be. I'll never ride him again.'

'Don't say that! You can't be sure.'

'I know him too well. He tries his heart out to do

his best for me, but it hurts. I can't bear to cause him any more pain. It isn't fair.'

'I can't tell you how sorry I am.' My eyelids are gritty and I can taste salt on my lips. 'What will you do about the TV contract?'

'I don't know. I can't think about that just yet.'

'You can borrow Rafa if you think he's up to it. There's no way he'd be ready to join the team for some time, but you can have a go.'

'That's a kind offer. I could buy him . . .'

'I couldn't give him up completely.'

'I know.' He sniffs and clears his throat. He's crying, I think, as he goes on, 'I'll call Matt when we get back.'

I can't speak. There's nothing I can say to make him feel better. It's the end of Robbie's partnership with his beloved horse and, depending on what Matt advises, it could easily be the end of Nelson too.

Chapter Eighteen

My Kingdom for a Horse

For how much longer will I be able to take advantage of the Saltertons' generosity, I wonder, as I'm finishing breakfast in the kitchen of the big house a couple of days after our ride on the beach? Sally Ann opens the fridge door and a jug falls out, spilling milk across the floor.

'Oh dear,' she sighs. 'I've had better days.'

'I'll clear it up,' I offer, feeling a little guilty for sitting on my bottom at the table while she runs around tidying up.

'No, you stay there.' She mops the floor with a tea towel.

'Matt's coming out today, isn't he?'

'Yes, it's decision time for Nelson. Poor Robbie, I'm afraid he's going to be heartbroken.'

'I know.' He's been putting on a brave face since deciding to stop riding him, but underneath he's devastated. When you love a horse, part of his soul becomes joined with yours, and when you lose him, that part of your soul goes with him.

'He's very fond of you.' She changes the subject as I'm turning the colour of fried tomatoes. 'It's all right. I realise he's trying to keep it from Maisie, but it's pretty obvious to everyone else. I wish you'd consider making your stay in Furzeworthy permanent.'

'I can't because . . .' At this moment, with the scent of fresh coffee and horse drifting into my nostrils, and the sight of Robbie leading Diva across the yard outside, I can't think of a single reason for leaving.

'You have to follow your dream,' Sally Ann finishes for me. 'You just have to be sure that you're following the right one.'

'Thanks for the advice,' I say.

'Anytime.'

I head back outside and I'm sweeping the yard when I hear the sound of a vehicle turning up the drive.

'Is that Matt?' Robbie calls from the doorway into the tack room.

I pause to look as a familiar silver four-by-four pulls up beside the barn. The pile of shavings and horsehair I've been sweeping up outside Rafa's stable is caught by an eddy and whirls away across the yard.

'It is,' I call back as Robbie strides towards me. 'I'll let you talk to him.'

'No.' Robbie catches my hand as I make to carry on sweeping. I'd rather keep busy and wait until the last possible moment to hear bad news. 'Please, I'd like you to be here.'

Reluctantly, I lean the broom across the wheelbarrow and accompany him and Matt to Nelson's stable. Nelson puts his head over the door and breathes in Robbie's ear as he puts a bridle on. Robbie leads him out.

'Let's see him trot up on the concrete first,' Matt says. 'Flick, if you wouldn't mind taking the reins so we can both watch him move.'

I walk Nelson up and down the yard before trotting him past the two men.

'What do you think?' Robbie asks as I pull Nelson up and stand him nearby.

'I see what you mean. It's like you said on the phone. He's landing toe-first to avoid putting pressure on his heels,' Matt says. 'Is he still on bute?'

Robbie nods. 'It makes him feel more comfortable. Matt, I need you to be honest with me now. As his rider, I know that he isn't up to working at the level I require of him any more. A quieter life of light hacking isn't an option – I've walked him out on the road and ridden him on the beach and he can't take it. I can give him more time if you think that will do it, but . . .' He shrugs.

'I doubt that it will make much difference. He's already some way down the line and, as I said before, this is a progressive condition. There's a suggestion too that it's hereditary, so using him for breeding isn't the way to go.'

'I won't consider retiring him to stud then.' Robbie pauses before plunging on, his voice hoarse with an emotion that tears at my heartstrings. 'Is he suffering?'

'Only you can be the judge of that.' Matt clears his throat. I think he's suffering, having to deliver bad news. 'You're facing a stark choice: retirement or euthanasia.'

I shrink back. Robbie asked for honesty, but the statement rings harshly in my ears.

'I can't do that to him, not yet,' he says eventually. 'There's no need to rush into making a decision.'

'He's been my best horse, my friend, my rock.' Robbie sounds close to tears, and I want to hold him in my arms, but I'd hate to embarrass him in front of Matt when he's trying to be strong. 'Without him, I wouldn't be where I am today, and Eclipse wouldn't exist. He deserves a good retirement. I owe him that.'

'Would you be able to do that here?' Matt asks.

'We have plenty of space. I can keep him on bute and spoil him until the time comes when he's in too much pain.' He bites his lip.

'That sounds like a reasonable approach,' Matt says.

'I'll know when he's ready. I don't want to see him hobbling around the yard.'

'It would be better for Nelson to keep front shoes on – you have your own farrier on site so that shouldn't be a problem.'

'For now,' Robbie acknowledges. 'I'm afraid that he'll get frustrated and bored, watching the other horses work, but he likes being out in the field and he loves his stable. I hope he'll get used to it.'

I recall Nelson's proud bearing as he moved around the arena at the festival, the way he held his head high and his neck arched as he galloped fearlessly through the hoop of fire with his tail streaming behind him. He thrives on performing – like his master – and it's quite devastating to think of him being left behind in the company of the likes of T-rex and Paddington when the team goes out in the lorry.

321

'We'll see. He may well adjust to an easy life. I know I would.' Matt smiles ruefully.

'Are you busy at the moment?' Robbie asks, abruptly changing the subject.

'I'm rushed off my feet. It's that mad time of year when everyone is out and about competing. The boxes at the clinic are full to overflowing; one of the vets is on leave and we can't find a locum.' He yawns. 'I haven't slept for twenty-four hours. I'm off home to get some sleep right now.'

'So you don't want a tea or coffee?' Robbie says.

'No thanks, no more caffeine for me. Let me know how it works out with Nelson, and give me a shout when you need more bute.' He shakes hands with Robbie, then turns to me. 'It's good to see you, Flick. A couple of my clients have been asking after you. You have a few fans out there – you really should get back on the road.'

'I don't think it would go down too well with Mel,' I say.

'We're struggling to get hold of a decent farrier at the clinic. Mel says he's back on form, but in reality he needs a good week's notice before he'll turn up. I don't know if that's because he has too much work to catch up with, or if he can't cope.'

'I thought he had cover,' Robbie says.

'They fell out. You know what he's like – he's a one-man band. Anyway, I must go. Cheers.'

Robbie and I say goodbye to Matt. Robbie takes Nelson from me and leads him back into his stable, closing the door behind him. He doesn't emerge for some time. I don't intrude on his grief.

I return to my duties, filling hay-nets and scrubbing buckets while Dillon exercises Scout and Dennis in the arena. As he returns to the yard, I explain what Matt said and what Robbie has decided to do about Nelson.

'What's the point of keeping him, the soft git?' Dillon says, but later I notice him outside Nelson's stable, stroking his neck and whispering in his ear. I smile to myself. Softheartedness must run in the genes.

Towards the end of the afternoon, Robbie and I turn the horses out. We take Nelson out last, walking together to his field.

'Are you all right?' I ask.

'I will be,' he says quietly. He leads Nelson through the gate, turns him and removes his head-collar. Nelson waits for a pat, then spins on his hindquarters and canters off up the field, bucking, whinnying and stirring up his next-door neighbours. I link my arm through Robbie's as we stand at the gate, watching the horses settle down once more to graze.

'Silly bugger,' he says, turning to me. 'Thank you, Flick.'

'What for?' I frown.

'For your support today. It was a tough decision, but I'm glad I made it. It's a relief, a weight off my shoulders.' I kiss and hug him. 'But it leaves me without my lead horse.' He smiles wryly. 'I've had to call the TV people to let them know that he's out of the picture.'

'What did they say?'

'They were disappointed. Even though we haven't signed anything yet, they'd already decided that they could see Nelson as the lead actor's horse. They're still planning to watch us perform at the Country Show, though.'

'That's good news then.'

'Except that we're one horse short, unless by some miracle Diva's ready to take her place in the team.'

'She did pretty well at the rally,' I point out.

'That's true.' Robbie frowns. 'Whatever happens with her, though, I'm going to need at least one – if not two or three – more horses to secure Team Eclipse's future. We can't afford for this to happen again. We need trained and experienced spares. I've already done some research and ringing around because I've known for a while that retiring Nelson was on the cards. Delphi has one of her dressage horses up for sale, and there's an agent who imports Spanish horses like Rafa who has one that sounds as if it could be suitable. Would you like to give me your opinion of them when I take them for a test-drive this weekend?'

'Tomorrow?'

He nods.

'I'd love to, but are you sure about buying a horse from Delphi? Stevie at Nettlebed Farm had a couple of donkeys from there – they are little devils.'

'I know of her reputation. I'll err on the side of caution. The horse looks okay – she sent me a video.' He plays the clip on his mobile. Delphi is riding a dressage test that looks almost foot perfect. 'Does that meet with your approval?'

'The horse looks lovely, so what's wrong with it?'

'That's very cynical.' He rests his arm around my shoulders. 'Come on, let's get finished here, then I'll take you out for dinner.'

'What about Maisie? Is she coming with us?'

'Mum's having her for the weekend, so I'm free to look at horses, introduce Diva to the concept of working with rest of the team –' he pulls me close and looks deep into my eyes – 'and spend time with you.'

The next morning, I find myself back at Delphi Letherington's for the first time since Mel let me go.

'I feel like a traitor,' Robbie says as he picks up his riding hat from the back of the Land Rover. I can't help admiring Robbie's outfit of a white shirt and black jodhpurs with long boots.

'I don't think Nelson will mind you looking for another horse. When I last saw him, he had his head down grazing.'

'Well, I hope that the time I've spent choosing the shortlist pays off.'

I walk quickly to keep up with him as he strides through the first yard and into the second. I hadn't noticed before but there's a sign outside the tack room, reading 'Push for attention' and pointing towards a white button. Robbie presses it three times, bringing Delphi from one of the stables.

She greets us effusively.

'Let me get Ptolemy out for you.' I notice that she has a bridle slung over her shoulder, one with a fearsome twisted metal bit. 'A lovely horse like this won't be available for long. The first to try will buy.'

'Let's see about that,' Robbie says wryly. 'I hope you don't mind that I brought Flick along with me for a second opinion.'

'Oh, not at all. He'll pass muster with any vet or farrier. He has the most wonderful feet.'

'Have I shod him before?' I don't recognise the horse that she brings out of the stable. He's a tall bay animal with long legs, big knees and a white stripe down his face.

'Mel and his current associate put shoes on him last

week. He was a complete angel.' She stands him in front of us with a flourish of her hand. 'He's immaculate, as you can see: no scars or blemishes. He has paces to die for and his breeding is impeccable.'

She walks and trots him past us, elbowing him in the ribs when she thinks we aren't looking to make him appear more alert.

'His saddle's on the rail over there if you'd like to tack him up yourself,' she says, pulling him up. The horse stands, blowing slightly, and there's a trace of sweat across his chest.

Robbie throws the saddle on and fastens the girth. He puts on his hat while Delphi leads the horse through to the indoor school, where the air is cool and the sunlight slants between the vertical wooden slats of the walls, creating stripes across the sand surface. She moves the horse up alongside the mounting block and Robbie gets on. He gathers up the reins and sets off around the perimeter of the school at walk.

'Why are you selling him?' I look Delphi straight in the eye. She doesn't flinch.

'Sadly, he's surplus to requirements. I haven't got time for him and it seems such a waste to have him standing around when he's more than capable of top-level dressage or anything else you ask him to do.'

As Robbie reaches the corner of the school, a pigeon flies from the rafters. Ptolemy takes fright, giving a huge buck. Robbie hangs on, but only just. He sets his mouth in a straight line as he continues. I don't think he's enjoying the ride. He draws up alongside us as Delphi finishes giving me a long list of Ptolemy's merits.

'I'd like to take him outside now,' Robbie says.

'The outdoor school's free, but I'm afraid the jumping field is occupied. We're having some drainage put in and the diggers are here.' Delphi opens the gates to let us out. Ptolemy quivers as they scrape across the concrete apron. He's too much like Diva. I can't see him making a stunt horse.

Robbie rides him twice around the outdoor school. Ptolemy carries his head up, fighting the bit and walking sideways like a crab and getting more and more wound up. Poor horse, I think, as Robbie dismounts and hands the reins to Delphi.

'This one isn't for me,' he says calmly.

'He's young yet. He'll come right with time.'

'I haven't got time.'

'He's half-brother to Nicci's horse, Dark Star. He had a few issues at this age, but look at him now. He's a four-star eventer. You're making a mistake, walking away – this horse can turn his hoof to anything.'

'His temperament isn't right for me.'

'I should take some time to think about it,' Delphi suggests. 'If you want to come and try him again, do let me know. You're more than welcome – if he hasn't been snapped up beforehand.'

'When I say no, I mean no,' he says firmly. 'He's a good-looking horse, but he won't fit into the team. Thank you for your time and I wish you all the best with selling him.'

Back in the Land Rover, Robbie leans in and kisses me before starting the engine.

'I feel sorry for that horse – he's been schooled indoors to the nth degree until he can't think for himself.'

'He's scared of his own shadow. It's such a shame.'

327

'I should have known better than to take Delphi at her word. When I spoke to her on the phone, she said he was one of the bravest horses she had on the yard. I dread to think what the others are like.'

'I think she'd lunged him before we got there to quieten him down,' I say as Robbie drives back towards the main road. 'He was sweating before you put the saddle on.'

'I did wonder about that.'

'And as for the diggers in the jumping field – do you see any activity out there?' I gesture towards the nearby pasture where there's a course of show-jumps set up.

'I expect she'll trick some mug into buying him eventually,' Robbie sighs. 'Let's hope the next horse that we're going to see is suitable.'

We drive northeast and take the motorway.

The seller of the second horse is a man in his forties. He's an agent for the Spanish equine industry and imports into the UK. Tall, slim and tanned, he has something of the weasel about him. He wears a red shirt and chinos and stands puffing on an electronic cigarette as Robbie examines the horse's legs and feet, asking me for my opinion at the same time.

'He's clean-limbed and his feet look great,' I say, admiring the charismatic grey stallion, who reminds me of Rafa.

'He has a kind eye too,' Robbie says.

He is gorgeous, but when Robbie gets on to ride him, he turns into a firecracker. He snorts and jogs his way from the yard to the outdoor manège, showing off his magnificent flowing mane and broad chest. He flares his nostrils, revealing a flash of scarlet when Robbie asks him to trot in circles on the sand.

He's an impressive horse, and I'm beginning to wonder if this is it and Robbie was right that our search will be over today, when he jumps off and leads the horse to the gate.

As I open it for him, the stallion yanks the reins from his hands and canters away to one of the stables, where he proceeds to try to jump the door to get in with another horse, a black mare.

'He has his eye on the ladies, just like the rest of us,' the owner says, giving me a lecherous wink. He catches hold of the reins and tries to pull the stallion away from where he's nuzzling and nipping at the mare's neck, but the stallion, assuming that he's in with a chance, refuses to budge.

'I've seen enough, thank you. I'll be in touch. Let's go,' Robbie says, and we set out for home, not stopping until we arrive back at the cottage. Robbie lets the dogs out while I make tea and sandwiches, which we eat sitting next to each other on the sofa.

'What next?' I ask, looking out through the window to the garden, where the roses are blooming bright pink, salmon and red, and the yellow cherries on the trees are acquiring a carmine blush.

'I really don't know. Keep looking, I suppose. Delphi's was a dud and the stallion was far too driven by his hormones to be any good to me. I didn't think it would be all that hard to find another horse.'

'You must have known that it was a tall order, trying to replace Nelson.' I hesitate. 'I could try calling my parents to see if they know of anyone who might have a horse that would fit the bill.'

'One like Rafa, you mean?' Robbie's expression brightens. 'Would you? What will they think, though? I don't want to cause you any grief.'

'I guess I'll find out,' I say, smiling. 'As I've said before, they've retired from the industry, but they'll still have contacts.' I jump up.

'Where are you going?'

'To give them a call. There's no time like the present; the longer I wait, the less inclined I'll be to pick up the phone.' I wander outside and sit under one of the cherry trees. Watching the bees buzzing around the roses, I dial my parents' number.

'Hello, Felicity, how are you?' My father sounds cheerful, merry even. 'Did you get our text?'

'Yes,' I say guiltily, because I did, but didn't reply to it.

'So you know that we're home now, enjoying a bottle of Rioja to remind us of sunny Spain. Are you still in Devon, working for . . . what's his name?'

'No and yes. What I mean is that I'm in Furzeworthy, but I'm no longer working for Mel. It didn't work out . . . He sacked me,' I add in response to my father's questioning silence. 'It isn't what you think.' I refrain from mentioning the fact that I found him with his mistress. 'He accused me of poaching his clients. He thought he'd end up with no business if I carried on.'

'I'm sorry,' he says.

'Really? I thought you'd use this opportunity to advise me to get back behind a desk and earn some proper money.'

'This might surprise you, but all we've ever wanted is for you to be happy. Your way isn't the one we'd have chosen, but it's clearly right for you, otherwise you wouldn't have stuck at it like you have.'

'I wish you hadn't doubted me.'

'Being totally honest, knowing from bitter experience how dangerous horses are, we tried to put you off becoming a farrier because we didn't want you to get hurt, but you've survived so far.'

I don't mention my accidental self-harming with the knife and nailing myself to a horse. What the eye doesn't see and all that.

He sighs. 'The wine must be making me mellow.'

'Thanks, Dad.'

'What are your plans now?'

'I'm staying with a family called the Saltertons, who've been very kind, giving me and Rafa board and lodging in return for doing some yard duties while I look for another job.'

'Mum and I could help you if you'd let us.'

I know what he's getting at – he wants to assist me financially with a gift or loan, but I can't accept. My pride won't let me.

'It's all right, thank you.'

'I understand why you feel that you need to do this yourself. I admire you for that, but it works both ways. My health isn't as good as it was, and time is slipping away. Your mum and I are beginning to feel old and useless.'

'Less of the old, Nigel,' my mother's voice cuts in sharply.

'What we want more than anything is to be needed,' he goes on.

'You might be able to help me then,' I say, wishing I'd tried harder to break the ice between us before. 'I'm staying with one of the sons of the family – he's a friend of mine. I met him when I was shoeing his horses.'

'Sarah mentioned you were seeing someone,' Dad says.

'Let me speak to her. Nigel, give me the phone.'

Mum takes over. 'We went to see the baby the other day. She's such a darling. Now, what's this about a boyfriend? I assume from the fact that we haven't met him that your father and I wouldn't approve. He isn't another farrier like that dreadful Ryan? We never did like him.'

'Rosa, keep your opinions to yourself,' I hear my father say in the background.

'Robbie's an expert in horses as therapy, using the healing power of horses to help people with learning difficulties.'

'So he's almost medical then.' My mother sounds more cheerful.

'He's a stunt rider too. He works in TV and film,' I go on.

'Wow.' For once, she's impressed. 'Who knows who he might introduce you to? That Johnny Depp is rather gorgeous.'

'Mum, he's far too old,' I groan. 'Anyway, Robbie has just been forced to retire his lead horse through lameness and he's looking for another one. We went to see a couple today, but they aren't suitable and there isn't much around. I wondered if you had any contacts who have horses for sale – something like Rafa.'

There's some muttering as my parents confer before my father comes back on the line.

'Let me have a think and come back to you on that one. I'll do some ringing around,' he says.

I thank him and cut the call before returning inside to find Robbie, who's almost asleep on the sofa with Badger sprawled across his body.

'How did it go?' he says, opening one eye.

'Much better than I expected. Dad's going to call

some of his contacts and let me know the outcome.'
I perch on the arm of the sofa and reach down to
stroke his hair. 'I think we've come to an
understanding.'

'Better late than never,' he murmurs.

I smile in agreement. My father is getting old and
we shouldn't waste any more time on past differences
of opinion. Life is short.

Over the next week, we see several more horses, but
they are too old, too crippled, too big or too small to
fit into the team. The one we like best is built like a
drum horse and no good for tricks. My father gets
back to me with a promising contact, but the two
horses available are too young. Robbie keeps them in
mind, but our horse-hunting comes to a stop.

Robbie arranges for Sally Ann to babysit one
evening so we can spend a couple of hours at the
Talymill Inn. We sit at the table beside the water
wheel, watching it turn. I look up.

'Robbie, I've been thinking about the offer you
made for Rafa. Is it still on the table?'

He gazes at me, a glimmer of hope in his eyes.

'Have you changed your mind?'

I nod. 'I've hardly ridden him recently.'

'Flick,' he says in a low voice. 'You don't have to
do this. I know how much he means to you.'

'I can see how much it would mean to you to have
a new lead horse, and I know he won't be ready for
the next show, but he could be for the filming in the
spring, if you get the contract.' My voice breaks. 'It
would be better for him to have a settled home where
he can work and fulfil his potential. I wouldn't let
him go to just anyone. I know you'd look after him.'

'I would, I promise. You can see him, ride him, whenever you like. I'll pay you what I think is a fair price.' He mentions a sum.

'That's very generous. Too generous. You aren't offering over the odds?'

'Definitely not.'

'Are you sure?'

'He's worth it. He's a fantastic horse.'

'It doesn't feel right talking about Rafa in terms of money.'

Robbie reaches across the table and rests his hand on mine.

'That's why I don't want you to rush into a decision. Take your time.'

Waiting won't make any difference, I think. I'm caught between a rock and a hard place. I need the money to get myself out of the financial abyss I've ended up in.

'Will you have Matt out to vet him?' I ask. 'I have nothing to hide. He's never been anything except one hundred per cent sound.'

'I will do, if you agree to sell him to me. It's nothing personal. It's just after what I've been through with Nelson, I don't want to find out that he can't cope with what I'm asking of him a few months down the line.'

'It will be a bit of a shock to him at first. His life's been one long holiday so far.'

'It's good that he's low mileage.'

'Let's drink to it.' I hold up my glass, a half-pint.

'You mean . . .?'

'Yes, he's yours, subject to a clean bill of health.'

'I don't know how to thank you.' Robbie touches his glass to mine. I pour the remaining beer down my throat. 'Let me get you another one of those.'

'I'll have a pint this time, seeing as you're buying.' I force a smile. I've done it. I've as good as sold my best friend. How can anyone do that?

The pint goes down quickly, followed by another as I drown my sorrows and try to get used to the new normal. I am no longer part of that exclusive club of horse owners. I will no longer have to worry about where I'm going to buy the next bale of hay, find the money for the vet bills, or watch the weather at least twice a day to decide which rug Rafa needs. He will be Robbie's responsibility.

'I'm feeling a little under the influence.' I gaze at him across the table. 'Would you mind taking me home – I mean back to Cherry Tree Cottage – now?'

'Not at all.' He stands up, moves round and picks up my jacket from the back of my chair. He supports me as I get to my feet, then places it around my shoulders. He holds my hand on the way out to the car park and drives me back to Furzeworthy, where there are bats swooping across the sky and silhouetted against the vast orb of the full moon.

'Hey, Sleeping Beauty, we're here.' Robbie's voice nudges into my consciousness.

He helps me out of the Land Rover, puts his arm around my back and guides me to the door, takes off my shoes and helps me up to bed, his bed.

'What about Maisie?' I stammer.

'Don't worry about her. She's asleep – Mum's been babysitting.' Slowly, he undresses me and puts me to bed, pulling the duvet up over my breasts. 'I'll get you some water.'

'I'm all right.' My voice sounds distant, as if the words are coming out of a disembodied mouth on

335

the far side of the room. I touch my forehead. 'I'm going to regret this tomorrow.'

'You aren't going to change your mind about selling Rafa?'

'No, I'm talking about the beer. I shouldn't have had that last pint.' I feel wretched. Robbie fetches a glass of water, a packet of plain biscuits and black coffee, but the only thing I want is to feel his arms around me as we lie skin-to-skin in his bed. I want to be enveloped in his warmth and scent. I want to forget what I've done, but I can't. I don't think I've ever felt so guilty and sad. I've sacrificed a lot for my career, but I never imagined I'd have to give up my beautiful horse.

Chapter Nineteen

The Wrong End of the Stick

Over the next few days in June, Matt vets Rafa and passes him as sound in wind and limb. Robbie transfers the money to my account. I borrow the Land Rover to take Rafa's passport with the change-of-ownership details to post in Talyton St George on the morning of the auction. I drop Maisie at school at the same time.

'Daddy always buys me sweets on the way,' she says earnestly. She sits on her booster seat beside me, with her book bag on her knees and satchel on the floor.

'I don't think so.' I can't help grinning. 'You are so cheeky.'

'If you don't ask, you don't get,' she says as I pull in around the corner from the Talyton Primary. I let Maisie out and walk to the school gates with her clutching my hand.

'Hello, Maisie,' a boy calls from the pavement on the opposite side of the road.

'Who is that?' I ask when she waves back.

'That's Finn – he's my boyfriend,' she says confidently. 'We aren't getting married yet because we're too young.'

'I should say so.' We join a queue of children and their parents and carers at the gates. 'Do I leave you here?'

'You have to take me to my classroom.'

'Are you sure about that?' I notice that the older primary school children are in the playground without their parents. It's the younger ones, whose uniforms seem far too big for them, who are walking up to the classrooms with their significant adults.

She nods. 'Haven't you heard of stranger danger?'

'Yes, but you're quite safe here.'

'This way.' She pulls me towards the covered walkway at the front of the grey stone building, on to which the classrooms open via doors painted yellow. She releases my hand and struggles for a moment to open the door marked 'Class 3'. I follow her inside.

A young woman looks up from where she's sitting marking a pile of exercise books at a table beneath the arched windows at the back of the classroom. She's about twenty-seven, with freckles and flame-coloured hair tied back in a ponytail, and her clothes – an emerald blouse with a blue-and-green scarf, a pair of linen trousers and sandals – are as bright as the artwork on the walls.

'Hello, Maisie,' she says. 'Why aren't you waiting outside?'

'Miss Fox, this is Flick. Flick, this is my teacher.'

'Hi,' I say. 'I'm sorry for disturbing you. Maisie said it was okay.'

'Flick is going to be my mummy.'

338

'Oh, that's lovely news,' Miss Fox says. She seems rather distracted.

'That isn't right,' I say gently as Maisie looks up at me. Her lip wobbles and a tear wells up and rolls down her cheek. 'I'm a friend of the Saltertons. I've been staying with Maisie's father – I mean, lodging with Maisie and her dad for a while. Someone's got the wrong end of the stick.'

'Never mind.' Miss Fox stands up and walks over to rest her hands on Maisie's shoulders. 'Let's have a chat about this while we're getting the exercise books and number lines out ready for Maths today.' She gazes towards me. 'I'm afraid this happens quite a lot. Our lovely Maisie is always on the hunt for someone she can call "Mummy", even though she has a wonderful daddy and devoted grandparents ... She'll be fine,' she adds for my benefit, because I'm gutted for her.

I understand why Robbie is so protective. He's right to keep our relationship from her while we're working things out. As it is, she's going to be sad when I leave Cherry Tree Cottage, but it would be ten times worse for her if she'd built us up in her imagination into one happy, forever family.

On my way back to the Land Rover, I run into Louise, who is leaving the school at the same time.

'Long time no see,' she says. 'I missed you when I brought Ash for his latest therapy session with Robbie. I thought I'd catch you on the yard.'

Okay, I was hiding, I think, but I don't fess up.

'How is he?' I ask.

'He's very well, thank you. Mel took him to play crazy golf the other day – it doesn't sound like much, but it means everything to me that Mel's taking an interest in him.'

'I think you're a great mum.'

'You do what you have to do when you're a parent. Do you want children?'

'I'm not sure,' I say slowly, wondering at my change of opinion. What has happened to the woman who used to say, 'No, never'?

'Your mind will turn to babies once you have your business up and running.'

'There's a lot that has to happen first.'

'Robbie's a decent man,' Louise says, her eyes sparkling with humour. 'You could do worse than settle down with him.'

'I do like him very much, but it's complicated.'

'So I shouldn't buy my hat just yet,' she teases.

'Ha ha,' I say wryly. 'No, seriously, we're keeping it low-key, partly for Maisie's sake and partly for ours.'

'I think it would be a shame if you had to move far from Furzeworthy, but don't tell Mel I said that. I know we warned you off taking Mel's clients, but the truth is that he has more than enough work – if you settled here, he could have an easier life, and Ash and I would get to see more of him. Have you got yourself a van yet?'

I shake my head. 'Robbie and I are going to the local auction house today.'

She wishes me luck and gives me a brief hug, and I'm glad that I didn't say anything about Mel and Gina because it would have made things between us very awkward.

After lunch, Robbie and I make our way to the local auction house, F. Oak and Sons Auctions, which is based in an industrial unit on a nearby farm.

'Are you sure about this?' I say, as we walk across the tarmac towards the building, passing crates of scrap metal that Robbie assures me are engine parts, a rubber dinghy, and a stone nymph that appears to have been modelled on some surgically enhanced celebrity. One of her generous breasts is covered by her stone robe, while someone has stuck a numbered sticker to the other.

There are people – mainly men dressed in fleeces, camouflage jackets, jeans and heavy boots – wandering around looking at the items for sale. Most of the potential buyers appear bewhiskered and dusty, much like the lots on view.

'How do we know that this van is any good?' I go on.

We walk on through the building where the auction is already under way. The auctioneer stands on a lectern, holding a gavel tucked into his palm, and speaking so quickly that I can hardly catch what he's saying. Behind him is a screen with the current lots highlighted. In front is his audience, some seated on benches and chairs, some standing.

'Sh, otherwise he'll think you're bidding,' Robbie whispers as he catches my hand. 'I don't think you want a parachute, although it might come in useful to slow your fall when you next come off Rafa.'

'Hey, I can see where Maisie gets her cheek from.'

We head on through to the yard, beyond where there is a row of vehicles: two vans, one white, one blue; an ancient grey tractor, a motorbike and a silver saloon car.

'It's the blue one,' Robbie says. 'The keys are inside.

I checked with the guy in the office when you were registering to bid. He says we can run it.'

'It isn't the same as a test-drive, is it?'

'What else do you suggest? The guide price is within your budget. It might go for less, in which case you'll have bagged yourself a bargain, or it might spiral out of your reach, in which case we'll have to keep looking.'

'We?' I look at him.

'Of course.'

'I love the way you talk about us as a team.'

He smiles softly. 'We are, aren't we? You sold me your horse, and in return I'll make sure you find a van.' He guides me towards it and opens the driver's door. 'Jump in.'

I adjust the seat and turn the key in the ignition. It starts first time and runs smoothly, apart from a slight rattle. We check the outside and investigate the back. I'm no expert but it looks sound for its age.

'It's exactly what I need,' I say to Robbie. 'Oh-mi-God, it sounds so manly getting excited about a van.'

'You aren't manly in the slightest.' He laughs and gives me an affectionate squeeze. 'I reckon this one will do if you get it for the right price. Gary will service it and make sure it's safe.'

I'm already picturing the furnace and aluminium fittings in the back, and 'F. Coleridge, Farrier' printed along the sides. I've placed an order for the fixtures that I need and I'm waiting for them to be delivered to the garage.

'What time is the auction for these?'

'Four thirty. There's plenty of time for a burger and tea first. Louise is having Maisie after school and

Dillon is doing the horses with Dad – I could get used to this.'

We sit on plastic chairs outside the refreshment van, with drinks and cheeseburgers with extra onions. The chairs have tatty stickers on them, as if they didn't sell at previous auctions. Robbie stretches his long legs out in front of him. I rest my feet against his.

'Thanks for taking Maisie to school this morning. Was she all right?'

'She tried to tell me that you bought her sweets every day.' I smile, then grow serious again. 'She also dragged me into the classroom to meet her teacher, Miss Fox.'

Robbie sighs fondly. 'I'm not entirely surprised.'

'She introduced me as her future mummy.'

'Oh dear.' He sips at his tea and takes a mouthful of cheeseburger. A string of fried onion dangles from his chin.

'You have a . . .' I say, reaching across to point it out.

'Thanks,' he says, flipping it into his mouth. He gazes at me, his eyes twinkling with humour. 'I can see where she's coming from – that was quite a mumsy thing to do.'

I'm not sure whether to be offended or flattered. I go with the latter. My cheeseburger remains untouched in the cardboard tray on my lap.

'I'll have a word with her. She's spent much of her life looking for a mum, even though I've done my best, with the help of her grandparents, to keep Carla's memory alive for her. Maisie doesn't remember her, of course, which makes it much harder.'

'It's made me realise why you're so protective over her,' I say. 'She was in tears – I left Miss Fox looking after her.' I don't reveal that I wanted to take Maisie straight home and mother her.

'She'll be fine. She's pretty resilient – she's had to be.' He changes the subject. 'When you get a van and Gary's kitted it out, you'll be able to shoe our horses. Dennis is desperate for new shoes – one of them is only just hanging on.'

'Much as I'm enjoying being your groom, I'm looking forward to getting back to what I love most.' I've missed the sounds and smells, the hollow ring of metal against metal and acrid scent of smoking hoof. I've missed the sheer physicality of pulling shoes and hammering nails. 'I can't wait to get back out there.'

'Which is good news, because we've found someone to work for us. Dad told me this morning that he'd had an approach from a woman who's relocating from Yorkshire with her fiancé. He's got a job with Stevie as their marketing manager at Nettlebed Farm, while she's looking for yard work. She's very experienced – she's been working with racehorses for the past two years, so we're hopeful that she'll cope with us.'

'I'm sure she will – I did.' I'm smiling, but in my heart I'm confused at my reaction to his revelation. It makes the fact that I'm moving on soon all the more real. When the new groom arrives, the Saltertons won't need me any more. It won't be long before I have to move out of Cherry Tree Cottage and throw all my energies into setting up my business. 'When does she start?' I ask.

'A week on Monday. Mum's booked the builders to come in and redecorate the flat.'

'Good. That's great.' I pick at the cheese in my burger – it's cold and congealed.

'You'll be able to stay on,' Robbie says. 'Flick, this is all working out. You get your van and set up your business here, starting with our horses. You'll soon pick up clients. Remember what Matt said about people asking for you. It's perfect.'

'I'm not convinced that I can find enough work in this area though.' When Louise said that there were plenty of potential clients, I don't think she meant there were enough to provide a living for two full-time farriers. 'I need to be out there earning.'

'But you won't have so many outgoings now that you've let Rafa go.'

'I know,' I say, as another wave of sadness hits me. 'Here, have this – I don't want it.' I hand him the cheeseburger.

'I shouldn't,' he says, but he does. He eats it in three mouthfuls. 'You can stay at the cottage. I'm more than happy to support you while you're building up your round.'

'No, absolutely not,' I say quickly.

'I thought we were friends.' He leans closer and rests his hand on mine.

'We are, and I don't want to be beholden to you, to anyone.'

'This is because of your ex, isn't it? I completely understand why you want to keep your independence, but I'm not asking you to give it up. Why can't you see that I'm offering you help so that you can stand on your own two feet in the future? Okay, I have an ulterior motive, I'll admit that. I'm falling in love with you, and I can't bear the thought that you're going away and I'll never see you again.' He takes a breath before plunging on. 'We could have a wonderful life here with Maisie and the horses, if you'd give

345

it a chance. All you have to do is agree to stay and we can carry on as we are.'

'As we are,' I echo. 'Well, it wouldn't be, would it? I'd be a kept woman—'

'For a while,' Robbie says. There's a small smile on his lips, as if he thinks I'm joking about it.

'And we'd still be creeping around behind Maisie's back?'

'Until we're certain that we're going to stay together. Until we're sure that you aren't going to disappear off to the outer reaches of the universe to shoe horses.'

I sit back. He's done it again. If this really could be love, he wouldn't keep doing this, hinting at commitment, then backing off. I look at him, really look at him, and I'm torn between love and despair. I adore this man, yet – apart from the practical obstacles – there is this one element of his character that keeps coming between us and the happy-ever-after: his fear of upsetting Maisie.

'So, what are we going to do?' he asks me. The muscle in his cheek tightens as he awaits my answer. His expression is gentle and supplicating, reminding me that he's also a good man – generous, kind, fit, gorgeous . . . I could go on.

'We'll carry on as we are for now,' I say.

'Thank you,' he breathes. He leans across and kisses my cheek. 'You won't regret it.'

We sit quietly for a while before going to wait near the vehicles for the auctioneer to get started. Two of his minions bring his lectern. Dressed in a cream linen suit, tie and white shirt, and shiny brown loafers, he takes the stand. He adjusts his half-moon spectacles, and peers over the top of them into the gaggle of people who have assembled to watch the sale.

The white van goes for a couple of thousand pounds, then the auctioneer runs briefly through the details of the blue one. My pulse starts to flutter and I can feel my fingers crushing the rolled-up catalogue that I carry in my hand.

'Who would like to start me at fifteen hundred?'

No one, it seems.

'One thousand. Come on, ladies and gentlemen, this is worth at least double the price.'

Robbie gives me a nudge. I hold up my hand.

'One thousand, thank you,' the auctioneer says. 'Eleven hundred, new bidder.'

My heart feels as if it's about to jump out of my chest and into my throat as the price steadily rises. The second bidder drops out but, just as I begin to dare think that the van is mine, a third bidder leaps in, pushing the price up to match my limit. I hesitate, glancing towards Robbie.

One of the rules of auctions is to set a budget and stick to it, but I'm within touching distance. Another one hundred pounds and the object of my desire could be mine. The auctioneer looks in my direction. He raises one eyebrow. I nod and he registers my bid. My opponent goes in with another. I beat it and then that's it. I have to stop. If I bid any higher, I'll never be able to afford to have the van kitted out.

I'm trembling as the auctioneer turns to my opponent.

'Any advance?' He names the figure. 'Going, going –' the gavel comes down – 'gone.'

'It's yours.' Robbie elbows me in the ribs.

It takes a moment for it to sink in. I turn and throw my arms around his neck. 'We got it!'

'Well done,' he says. 'You held your nerve.'

'Now what? I've never been to an auction before.'

'You have to go to the office to pay, get it taxed, and call your insurance company so you can drive it away.'

We don't get very far. I take the key out of the ignition and put it back in – it snaps in half.

'Don't ask me why I did that,' I groan.

'I'll call Gary and ask him to pick it up tomorrow.' I sit in the driver's seat while Robbie's on the phone, arranging for his mechanic friend to kit out the van within a week. My mobile rings at the same time as I fish out a pound coin from a small tear in the upholstery. It isn't a number that I recognise.

'Hello, is that Flick?'

'Yes . . . ?' I say.

'This is a little embarrassing. I hope you don't mind me getting in touch with you. Mel gave me your number.' There's a pause. 'It's Gina.'

'I don't think I have anything to say to you.'

'Please hear me out. I'm sorry for being a bitch. I shouldn't have said those things about you. Mel has pointed out the error of my ways.'

'Has he, indeed?' The skin on the back of my neck prickles with antagonism.

'He reminded me of all the times he's had to come and put one of Rambo's shoes back on again. Anyway, I was wondering if you'd be able to look after my horse's feet from now on.'

'I don't know. I'm not sure that I can.'

'Please, Flick. I'm not seeing Mel any more,' she says, which makes the decision a little easier for me.

'I'm having my mobile forge kitted out at the moment, so I could drop by sometime next week.'

'Thank you. That's perfect. I'll let my friends know that you're back on the road.'

'There is one thing,' I point out, not making any effort to keep the humour out of my voice. 'You'll have to pay in cash on the day.'

'I've learned my lesson,' she says, sounding contrite. 'I'll see you soon.'

'Who was that?' Robbie asks when I come off the phone.

'My second client,' I say, grinning. 'Let's go back to the cottage and celebrate.'

However, when we get back, Dillon is behind schedule, and the horses are kicking at their stable doors, demanding their evening feeds. Robbie goes to speak to his father, who's putting the quad bike away in the barn. I head for the feed room, where I line up the black rubber bowls, and scrutinise the list of horses and their requirements on the white board that's on the wall above the row of metal bins.

It's complicated. Each horse has a different dinner containing various mixtures of proprietary foods, chaff and supplements, such as biotin for good feet or garlic for the blood. I put herbs to calm the difficult mare in Diva's feed, and a sachet of bute in Nelson's. I pour water from a scoop to soak all the feeds, and stir them before I load them on to the hand trolley and haul it outside.

'So you're the trolley dolly tonight,' Neil says, joining me to help.

I give him a frown as we stop beside Diva's stable. 'Less of the dolly, thank you.'

'You are a hard woman, Flick.'

'Someone has to keep you in order.' I smile fondly as I post Diva's feed through the door. I'm getting used to his ways. 'I would describe you as a dinosaur, but that would be ageist.'

'Thanks for selling Rafa to Robbie. It's got him and Dillon out of a bit of a spot, having a second horse to work on before next spring. I hear you bought a van at the auction. I didn't bother to go in the end.'

'I expect Robbie has told you that I broke the key in the ignition before we could bring it home.' Home? There, I've said it a second time, and I'm sober on this occasion. 'Gary's going to sort it out tomorrow. He'll fit the forge and storage cabinets at the garage in Talyton St George. I'm really excited about it.'

'I'm not sure if that's a good or bad thing. I expect you'll be making plans?'

'I guess so.' I take the rusting handle of the trolley and pull it further along the yard. When I'm here with the horses, I don't want to talk about moving on.

I collect the empty bowls later, pausing to speak to Rafa on the way. He nuzzles through my hair as he always does, but something between us has shifted, or is it my imagination? Does he know that I've sold him, that I've exchanged him for a van? Does he realise that we're no longer exclusive?

I try to look on the bright side. He'll forge bonds with other horses in a permanent home, and fulfil his potential with someone who has both time and expertise. I trust Robbie to care for him, although he'll never be able to love him as fiercely as I do. I blink back a tear as I stroke his face. He's my once-in-a-lifetime horse. I'll never have another one like him.

Chapter Twenty

One-Trick Pony

Gary works to Devon time, so the van isn't ready until the following Friday, when he delivers it to the cottage, kitted out, washed and waxed. I forgive him for the delay because he's done a great job. The rust spots have gone, the engine purrs, and I have not one but two new keys. I load it with my order of shoes and nails, which arrived earlier in the week, and drive it straight round to the yard to show it off.

'Hi,' Robbie says, walking over with Dillon and the dogs to where I've parked near Dennis's stable.

I jump out and open up the back.

'It was worth waiting for,' Dillon observes.

'I'm going to christen it now. Is Dennis ready for his new shoes?'

'He's in, and more than ready. I need him shod for the show tomorrow,' Robbie says. 'As you can see, I've put your trolley and anvil outside his stable ready for you.' He leads Dennis out and ties him up.

I'm back where I belong, I think, smiling as I give him a pat and pick up his foot. I raise the clenches and remove the old shoe – he's pretty well worn it out.

Later, I test the furnace, placing new shoes into its glowing interior. It works perfectly, softening the metal so I can shape the shoes over the anvil to fit Dennis's feet. When I give his hooves one final rasp, I straighten up and look around for someone with whom I can share my joy and triumph, but it isn't the same as when I first shod the Saltertons' horses. No one is watching. I realise that they're busy getting ready for the show tomorrow, but there was a time not so long ago when they would have dropped everything. I am no longer a curiosity.

I put my tools away and give the back of the van a quick clean.

'How did it go?'

I turn to find Robbie behind me.

'Well, thanks.' I lean up to receive his kiss. 'I'm off to shoe Rambo next.'

'It's all go then.'

'Not really. Are you managing without me?'

'Dillon and I have everything under control. There's no need to feel guilty because you've abandoned us today of all days. You carry on with what you're doing.'

'I'm not sure what I'll do this afternoon. Polish the van, maybe? Sharpen my knives? Help you out?'

'Don't despair. Word will soon spread and your phone won't stop ringing. Nothing's impossible – remember that.' He pulls a wad of cash from his pocket and tries to hand it to me.

'What's that?'

'Your first earnings.' He grins. 'I hope you've registered for tax.'

'No, I mean, I can't take it. I owe you far more in board and lodging.'

'Don't be silly. Take it,' he insists, but I can't. The more he tries to persuade me to accept it, the more stubbornly I refuse. 'Okay,' he says eventually, and he walks past the van, dropping the money through the open window on to the driver's seat. 'Sometimes, Flick, you can be very annoying.'

I bite my tongue, hurt that he refuses to respect my feelings on the matter. As I've said before, I will not be dependent on anyone.

As I drive away, I stuff the notes into the glove box where they're out of sight and out of mind, but I'm still smarting when I arrive at Nethercott Farm. I relax a little when I see the goat waiting at the gate.

Gina lets me through.

'Nice truck,' she says, greeting me. 'Would you like a coffee? Cappuccino or latte?'

'A latte, please.' I'm going up in the world, I think, when she brings me a mug of proper coffee while I'm shoeing Rambo.

'I'm sorry about what happened,' she begins as she leans against the stable door and scratches the goat's back. The goat nibbles at a loose thread on her ripped designer jeans.

'Forget about it. I have.'

'My friend – I think you might have seen her when we were at the pub. Anyway, she has a horse called Maverick and she's asked me to find out if you'll be her farrier. He'll need shoeing in the next couple of weeks, if that's okay.'

'Yes, I can do it.' I'm not sure Mel will be too happy about it, but that's his problem. I don't feel as though I owe him anything.

'I'll get her to give you a call. It will put her mind at rest knowing she has someone she can trust.'

I refrain from mentioning that I'm not sure how long I'll be available for. I feel as if I'm walking on a knife edge. Will I stay or go?

Gina pays me in cash and I return to the van. I drive back towards Furzeworthy, stopping in Talyton St George to buy dinner for tonight. I check my phone several times. Robbie has sent a text.

I'm sorry about earlier. Come back to the yard when you're free. We'll teach Rafa a trick, or two xxxxxxxxxxxxxxx

Sarah has left a voicemail about catching up sometime soon. Baby Isla is well – she's putting on weight.

There are no other messages, nothing from Gina's friend. I know it's early days and I'm expecting too much because I've only just left Nethercott Farm, but I'm still disappointed. I need to go out and look for more work.

I meet Robbie back at the yard, thinking that spending time with him and Rafa will take my mind off my problems.

'I'm going to play with your horse, I mean, my horse. Oh, what am I saying? *Our* horse. If you stay, he'll be ours. I'm happy to share,' Robbie says.

'What are you planning to do with him today?' I'm slightly apprehensive. What if he's being overoptimistic? What if Rafa doesn't live up to his expectations?

'I'm going to teach him to lie down.'

'That'll be interesting. How on earth are you going to persuade him to do that?'

'Watch and learn,' he says. 'I've cut off a corner of the arena to create a small area to work him in.'

We fetch Rafa from the stable and take him out on

a head-collar. Robbie leads him to the arena and lets him off in the section he's penned off. I sit on the fence to watch. Rafa gazes at me as if to say, 'What's going on here?'

'Go on, my boy,' I murmur. 'Please be good.'

Robbie makes friends with him, running his hands over Rafa's muscular body. I smile to myself. As I've mentioned before, he's good with his hands. Rafa looks amazing. His silken mane and tail gleam in the sunlight. His eyes are bright and alert, and his ears pricked forwards. I don't think I've ever seen him looking so well.

Robbie sends him away, using body language to direct him. Rafa trots around the pen before return-ing to await further instructions. I notice with a pang of regret how he returns to Robbie without a second glance in my direction. Robbie sends him away again. After a couple of circuits, Robbie calls out, 'Whoah!' and Rafa comes to a halt. He lowers one ear and grinds his teeth, listening for the next command.

Robbie sends him away again at a canter, making him work on the circle until he's sweating lightly.

'That was great,' I say grudgingly.

'He's a fast learner. I could well have him trained up in time for next spring, which will tie in with the filming of the TV series – if it goes ahead.'

'Tomorrow is decision day, isn't it?'

'Yeah.' He runs one hand through his hair. 'I'm not usually nervous, but . . .' He shrugs. 'We'll see. If we don't get the contract, I'll be able to look back and say that I did my best. Dillon and I did a dress rehearsal at lunchtime and it went well. Diva behaved like a pro, so I'm hopeful.' He holds up his hands, crossing his fingers. 'Let's hope that no one has stage fright in front of the TV people. You are still okay to hold the fort here for the day?'

'Of course. I'd love to have come along to watch, but I expect Neil or Sally Ann will video it.'

'I'll make sure someone does.'

'What about this trick?' I ask.

'Patience,' Robbie smiles. He catches Rafa and takes him to the tap, where he hoses him down before he leads him, his coat dripping, on to the grass in the nearest paddock. He encourages him to lower his head, rewarding him with a treat from his pocket when he starts to paw the ground. I can see what he's doing now, rewarding the behaviour that he wants. Rafa wants to lie down and have a good roll, but he isn't sure about going ahead while Robbie is invading his personal space.

He begins to sink to his knees, but changes his mind. Robbie rewards him again. He keeps him moving, making clicking sounds in his throat.

'The cue I use is "down",' he says.

Rafa lowers himself to the ground.

'Good boy,' Robbie says, letting him go on to roll and cover himself with dust and grass stains. He stands up and shakes himself. 'I'll keep doing this over the next however long it takes for him to respond to the verbal command. Would you like to put him away?'

'Yes, I'll do it.'

'And if you have any more spare time, I'd be very grateful if you could help by getting the horses' gear ready for tomorrow: travel boots, rugs, water, et cetera.' He checks his watch. 'I'm off to collect Maisie from school. I'll catch you later.'

'I've bought dinner,' I say, but he's already on his way at a run.

I collect up the equipment that the team needs for the show the following day and load some of it into the lorry. When Robbie comes back with Maisie, I notice how Rafa looks out over his stable door and whinnies in recognition of his new master.

In that moment, my heart shatters, because his reaction confirms that our special bond is broken. I turn towards the barn where my van stands gleaming in the sunshine, but it's no consolation. My horse has transferred his allegiance to Robbie and I don't think I can bear to stay and watch their bond develop.

All in all, it hasn't been the best of days. I've realised that building a business here in this area will take a very long time; in the interim, I'll be dependent on hand-outs from Robbie. I can't even claim that I'd be working on the yard in return when the new groom starts on Monday. Robbie's right that we could overcome these challenges in time, but there's the underlying deeper issue that lies between us – the apparent inability of either of us to commit. He thinks I'm flaky because I've kept going on about leaving Furzeworthy, while I can't help feeling that he's using Maisie as an excuse not to fully commit to me. We have deep-rooted differences: my stubborn refusal to compromise on my independence and his inability to communicate what he's really thinking.

It's time for me to go.

It isn't hard to set my plan into action when it's been at the back of my mind for a while. I stand in the tack room counting out eight sets of travel boots and tail guards. I'll pack my belongings, call Sarah to ask if I can stay for a couple of days to see the new baby, and find a place to rent while I set myself up. I've done my research and there's an area not far from where Robbie and I saw the randy stallion – I'm talking about the horse, not the owner – where one of the local farriers has recently retired and no one has yet stepped in to fill his shoes. I'll get a load of flyers printed and blitz every yard, riding school and tack shop.

The thought of starting afresh is exciting, daunting and devastatingly sad. I won't be taking Rafa with me this time. I'll be completely alone, with no one to care for except myself. I bite back tears as I step outside and make my way back to the cottage.

I kick off my boots and go upstairs to my room, Carla's room, where I start to throw a few things into a suitcase as what sounds like a herd of elephants comes charging up the stairs. The door flies open, revealing Maisie dressed in her school uniform.

'Hello,' I say.

'Hello, I had sausages and baked beans for dinner,' she says.

'I can tell – you have half of it down your front.'

She glances down and smiles. 'Miss Fox told me off because I said a rude word.'

'Oh dear. I won't ask you what it was,' I say, but Maisie is going to tell me anyway, except that just before it slips out, she presses her hand to her mouth and bursts into a fit of giggles.

'Where are you going?' she asks, running in and bouncing on to the bed.

'I'm heading off to stay with my friend Sarah.'

'When are you coming back?'

I gaze at her. She sucks on her upper lip, making it disappear.

'I don't know,' I say quietly. I don't want to upset her, but I don't want to lie either.

'Aren't you going to live with me and my daddy any more?'

'No,' I say, turning away to hide my anguish.

'But I'll miss you,' she cries. 'I miss you already.'

'I'll miss you too.' I turn back to find her holding her arms up to me. I give her a hug. 'I'm sorry.' I can feel my shirt growing damp. 'I'll come back and see you sometimes.'

She sniffs. 'And Paddington?'

'And Paddington,' I confirm.

'And Daddy?'

'Yes.' I release her and she slides off the bed on to her feet. She gives me a long teary stare before turning and stumbling out of the room. 'Where are you going?' I call after her, but she doesn't respond. I hear the sound of voices downstairs, Maisie and Robbie having a discussion, and my heart sinks even further than I thought possible. I should have broken the news of my plans to Robbie gently before exposing Maisie to them. I close my suitcase and snap the catches shut as the tread of heavy footsteps grows closer. I've been a thoughtless bitch.

The bedroom door is thrown open so hard that the brass handle hits the wall.

'Robbie? I'm sorry. Where's Maisie?'

'I've given her some crisps and sent her to watch a DVD. Luckily, she's still obsessed by *Frozen*.' He moves across and stands at the end of the bed with his arms folded. 'What's all this about? Please, tell me that she's got it wrong.'

'She hasn't,' I say, shaking my head miserably.

'This is exactly why I insisted on protecting her,' he

exclaims. 'What do you think you're doing? She's devastated, and so am I that you've decided to leave us. When were you going to mention it to me?'

'This evening. I didn't mean for Maisie to find out before I'd spoken to you.'

He sits down at the end of the bed. 'I can hardly believe it,' he says gruffly. 'I thought you were staying on, at least for a while.'

'I have to go where the work is,' I say in a small voice.

'Sometimes you come across as being very selfish,' he says, his tone like iron. 'I suppose that comes of being an only child.'

'I'm not selfish,' I say, annoyed at being judged, especially because I know that he's right.

'When are you intending to go?'

I can hardly breathe, let alone speak. 'As soon as I can,' I mutter.

'I'd appreciate it if you could stay until after the weekend.'

'I'll stay until Monday. I wasn't planning to leave you in the lurch.'

'Well, that's very considerate of you,' he says, his voice laced with sarcasm. 'Flick, I wish I knew what was going on in your head. Is this about Rafa?' He moves closer and gazes at my face. I can't bring myself to look at him. It's too painful. 'Your eyes are red.'

'I got some saddle soap in them earlier.'

'Please, tell me the truth.'

'Okay, I'm upset because he's transferred his affections to you.'

'You're jealous?'

'A bit,' I confess. 'I know that sounds stupid, but—'

'I've been the stupid one,' he cuts in. He rubs at his neck, raising a red rash. I can feel the anger radiating from his skin. 'You used me! I took you in and helped you out, and now you've kicked it all back in my face. Did you plan this all along? I didn't realise you could be so cold and calculating.'

'I did nothing of the sort.' Part of me wants to throw my arms around him and hold him tight, while another part of me wants to punch him.

'I thought you cared about me and Maisie. I thought you loved me!' he exclaims.

'I do. Of course I love you.'

'I adore you. I'd have done anything for you.' He stands up, his shoulders slumped in defeat. 'I knew this would happen. I knew you didn't love me enough and that one day you'd walk out on me.' He hesitates as he reaches the doorway.

'You can't have known that in advance,' I call after him.

He glances back towards me, his face etched with anger, frustration and grief. My heart aches because I never intended to hurt him.

'It was inevitable. The people I love the most always leave me in the end.'

'Robbie, come back,' I shout as he disappears on to the landing and his footsteps fade down the stairs. I jump up and follow him to the living room, where he sweeps a protesting Maisie out of her chair and away from the adventures of Elsa and Anna.

'Daddy, where are we going?' she says.

'To Uncle Dillon's,' he says harshly.

'I was going to make dinner,' I say.

'Do whatever you like,' he says. 'It's what you always do.'

361

'We need to talk. Give me a few minutes. Please.'

'I'm done with talking. I need to focus on the show tomorrow.' He sits Maisie on the bottom step in the hall and helps her put her sandals on. He slips into a pair of battered shoes and whistles for the dogs, who follow him and his daughter out of the front door. Through a blur of tears, I watch them walk down the path between the cherry trees where the fruits have ripened to the colour of deep burgundy.

Why hasn't he said any of this to me before? And what stopped me from speaking up? Suddenly, I realise that we are as bad as each other, and if we are to have any chance of making our relationship work, one of us will have to give. And it looks as if it will have to be me. A flicker of hope emerges from my despair. I just hope that it isn't too late.

Chapter Twenty-One

Negotiate with a Stallion, Tell a Gelding, and Ask a Mare

At dawn on the morning of the third Saturday in June, the day of the show, I find myself wading through rivers of silver dew, leaving green trails through the horses' fields. There's a lake of white mist lying across the Taly valley and the veils of cloud are slipping aside to make way for the sun that's rising from behind the hills.

I lead the horses in two and three at a time – apart from Diva, whom I bring in on her own. Paddington and T-rex are waiting at their gate, as are Rafa and Nelson. I take a quick selfie of me and Rafa. He nuzzles my face, then takes the peak of my cap between his lips and pulls it off my head. I jam it back on before catching Scout and Dennis.

'I'm sorry, guys,' I say as I lead them past the others. 'You're staying out today. There's nothing doing.'

Once I've got all the horses that are needed on the yard, munching on their morning feeds, I turn on the radio for some music. I pick out their feet and give each one a quick brush. I rinse the grass stains off the greys and make sure there are no knots in any manes or tails.

I'm grooming Scout when Dillon makes an appearance at seven, half an hour before we're due to load. He looks slightly the worse for wear.

'You look like you had a heavy night,' I observe lightly.

'I feel a bit rough.' He yawns. 'I took the Robster out for a few drinks to try to cheer him up, and Maisie was still up when I got him home. I stayed to babysit the both of them while Mum went back to the big house to sleep. Robbie was up all night. Flick, he's really cut up about you leaving.'

I don't know what to say. I run my fingers through Scout's tail, picking out an imaginary tangle.

'I understand your reasons for pushing off, but isn't there any way you can compromise?' he goes on. 'Can't you hang around for a little while longer? Give it another month or so and see how you feel then? You're perfect for Robbie . . . and we're all fond of you – me, Mum and Dad. It won't be the same without you. We haven't known you long but you're already part of the family.' He groans. 'Oh God, I feel sick.' He turns on the tap and drinks from the end of the hose. 'That's better.' He wipes his mouth and forces a smile. 'What about your horse? Won't you stay for him at least?'

'He isn't my horse any more,' I say flatly. My Rafa, my fifty shades of grey, is no longer mine. 'It's hard for me to watch him bonding with Robbie.' I bite back a sob, but Dillon has noticed. He moves up to me and rests his arm across my shoulders.

'I'm sorry,' he says.

'When he was a foal, I promised him he'd be mine

for ever.' I recall a memory of wrapping my arms around his neck and whispering in his furry ear. 'That makes me feel even worse. I've betrayed him.'

'Surely it's better to be able to see him every day than never see him again?'

'You don't understand.'

It's agony, I think, like having a nail driven into your heart.

Dillon shrugs and changes the subject. 'You've brought Diva in?'

'I have, but are you absolutely sure that you want to take her?'

'We have no choice. Rafa isn't ready, while Diva has half an idea of what she's doing.' He smiles. 'She was fine yesterday, but I'm still a little worried she'll do a comedy routine and do her own thing. Robbie's going to work with her – he can persuade her to cooperate, whereas I can't. She's a witch.'

'Go and make yourself useful then. There's a summer sheet, tail guard and set of boots outside each stable.'

Within half an hour, all the horses are ready to travel. I don't make a bad groom, even though I say it myself. The horses look stunning and I wish I was going to the show too.

Robbie brings the lorry on to the yard and parks with the ramp down. Sally Ann and Maisie take cool-bags and plastic crates of kit up into the living quarters, while Neil stands talking on his mobile. Robbie waits beside the ramp while Dillon and I load the horses one by one, leading them into the lorry and tying them up. He fastens the partitions between them so they don't kick each other on the journey. Scout tries to take a chunk out of Dennis, who retaliates with his ears pinned back and baring his teeth.

'Hey, stop that,' I tell them. Dennis tosses his head as if in defiance, but they soon settle down. It's like two brothers having a scrap. They do that now and again, and I think of Robbie and Dillon, who can love and hate each other at the same time. My heart aches when I try to catch Robbie's eye as he slips the pin into the ring to secure the partition. He's avoiding me.

The last horse to load is Diva. Dillon fetches her from her stable. She prances about as he leads her to the ramp, where she stops, plants all four feet and refuses to move.

I scratch my head, wondering how best to approach the problem. There are seven horses on the lorry. Diva is the eighth member of the equine team that Robbie and Dillon are using today to entertain and enthral the audience, and impress the TV producer who is making a special journey at Robbie's invitation. He's done so much work, devoted so many hours to making the display perfect, that Diva must go in. The show has to go on.

Dillon turns Diva away, chivvies her and makes to run up the ramp. She trots alongside him. She stops at the bottom, but Dillon doesn't. The rope tightens under her nose with a jolt. She tosses her head, breaking the clip attaching the rope to the head-collar.

Robbie fetches a knotted halter that applies pressure to various points on the mare's head, to encourage her to move up the ramp, but she hates the sensation and rears almost upright.

'Take that thing off,' Robbie says. 'I don't want her going over backwards.'

'She has to get used to it,' Dillon argues. 'You can't let her win.'

'It isn't about winning. You can negotiate with a stallion and tell a gelding, but you have to ask a mare,' Robbie says. 'Take the halter off. And the boots. She doesn't like the travel boots.'

'For goodness sake,' Dillon snaps. 'You're always pandering to them. Who do you think you are? Monty bloody Roberts?' he says, naming a famous horse whisperer.

'I'd rather whisper at her than shout,' Robbie says.

'Walk on, you silly mare,' Dillon yells. Diva rolls her eyes and paws the ramp in a threatening manner.

'Let me have her.' Robbie snatches the lead rope from his brother. 'You're too bloody impatient. You're winding her up.'

'Hey, that isn't fair. She has to learn to fit in. We can't have this palaver every time we load the horses.'

It doesn't help that neither of the brothers is cool and calm. Everyone is on edge this morning. Diva's putting on a performance of entirely the wrong kind.

Robbie changes the halter for Diva's usual head-collar before walking her away to the hedge on the drive to let her pull a few mouthfuls of herbs. I fetch a bucket of feed and two lunge-lines. Robbie holds the bucket in front of her nose while Dillon and I tighten the ropes around her bottom, pulling her into the lorry. As Dillon and I look across at each other, wearing triumphant smiles, she shoots backwards. (Who says horses don't have a sense of humour?)

'What the . . . ?' Robbie exclaims as he half trips, half runs back down the ramp with her. 'What do you think you're doing, Dillon? Why did you have to go and have a hangover today of all days?'

'I didn't plan it.'

'You never do. That's your trouble – you don't take life seriously. If this goes on, I'm going to look for a replacement.'

'You'll never find another brother like me.'

'I mean a new team member.'

'You can't do that.' It dawns on Dillon that Robbie means it. 'We've always worked together. We built the team up from scratch. We choreographed the stunts. You can't go and replace me.'

'Oh, I can and I will. I've had enough.'

'Okay, I'll go then.' Dillon drops the end of the lunge line.

'No way. Not today.'

'Why not? You've just told me I'm no good.' Dillon turns away.

'Where are you going?' I can hear the panic in Robbie's voice as Dillon responds, 'Back to bed.'

Robbie swears. I feel sorry for him, but not as sorry as I could be, because he's not handling the situation with any tact. This isn't the time.

'Come on, guys, let's try again,' I say, intervening. 'You should be on the road by now.'

Dillon walks off across the yard, with Robbie staring after him, open-mouthed.

'What the hell's he doing?'

'What did you expect?' I say. I can't imagine the new groom will be impressed with her employers when she turns up on Monday.

Robbie leads Diva up the ramp. She goes straight in, perhaps overwhelmed by the change in mood. I shove the gates closed and fasten the bolts, without giving her the option of reversing out again, then step away to help him close the ramp.

'Well, she's in, but we might as well start unloading,'

he says. 'I can't do much without Dillon. I don't know what's got into him.'

I'm afraid that I do know what's got into Robbie – it's my fault that he's like this. I should have done things differently.

'Let me go and speak to him,' I say, annoyed that Dillon is showing no consideration, when he knows what Robbie's going through.

'I don't think that'll do any good.'

'I'm going to try. Give me five minutes.' I run to the cider house, the converted barn in which Dillon lives, and bang on the door. 'Open up!'

'What do you want?' he says gruffly, pushing it open. He has a glass in his hand and is still wearing his boots. 'Did *he* send you?'

'I came of my own accord. Listen to me. Don't blame Robbie. He's upset and it's all my fault. You need to get yourself back to that lorry and go, or you'll miss your slot, the Eclipse team will never ride again, and you'll lose any chance of that contract.'

'I don't give a—'

'You don't now, but you will tomorrow,' I interrupt. 'You and Robbie have everything to gain. You're a great team, the best. It would be completely devastating to throw it all away in a fit of temper.'

'It isn't me.'

'It's both of you.'

'Well, I'm not doing it.' He crosses his arms and scowls. I don't know what it is – the pout, or the way he's looking through his unkempt hair – but he reminds me of a little kid.

'Okay, you can be as stubborn as you like. It's your choice. Just remember that you're not only wrecking your life, but you're ruining Robbie's and Maisie's.

How will her dad support her? How will you feel, knowing that your brother won't be able to provide for your niece? Some uncle you are.' I turn to walk away.

'Flick. Wait.'

I look over my shoulder. 'What?'

'I'll do it. I won't apologise, but I'll do the show.'

'I should think so too.'

'Thank you,' Robbie says quietly when Dillon climbs into the passenger side of the cab, ready to leave.

'No problem. I'll see you later,' I say, the words catching in my throat.

'It won't be until eight or nine o'clock.'

'That's okay. I'll be here. We'll talk.'

Robbie drives while Neil, Sally Ann and Maisie travel in the car. I watch them go and the yard falls silent, apart from the swallows chattering in their nests in the stables, and the distant sound of church bells. Someone is getting married, I think, and the aching sense of emptiness intensifies.

I fetch the quad bike and muck trailer and drive it up to the fields, whizzing along with the wind in my hair. I have plenty to do to keep me occupied, but my mind and heart are overflowing with thoughts of Robbie. I continue to clear all the fields and scrub every trough and bucket until my muscles hurt. On my way back to the yard, I have a chat with Paddington, who stands with his head growing heavy in my arms. What am I doing? Don't I want to stay here with my lover more than anything?

Paddington utters a sigh of contentment as I rub his face. The wound on his nose has healed completely and his coat is sleek and shiny.

'I'm sorry, I'm going to have to disturb you. You'll have to hold your own head up. I've got lots more to do.' Sally Ann's left instructions for the dinner tonight, and there's plenty of tack cleaning to get on with. 'Onwards and upwards,' I say bravely, but as I return the quad bike to the barn, there's a call from Robbie.

'Is everything okay?' I panic, wondering what I've forgotten to pack.

'Diva's pulled a shoe on the lorry. I've tried to take it off, but there are a couple of nails that won't come out and she's a bit sore. I'd ask another of the farriers who's on site, but you know what she's like. The other option is to leave her on the lorry and work with seven, but it won't look so good. Or you could drop everything and drive here in your fancy van and save the day.' From his tone, I'm not sure if he's being sarcastic or defensive.

'How long did it take you to get there?'

'An hour, with the queue to get on to the show-ground. You could be here by twelve. We're on at one. It's cutting it fine, but I can't see any other way.'

'Give me the address for the satnav. I haven't got time to get lost.'

'Thanks. You wouldn't believe the stress,' he sighs. 'This has to go well today, but everything seems to be conspiring against us. Badger's been sick on Dillon's cloak and we've run out of mascara.'

'I'm on my way.' I lock up the feed and tack rooms as we are speaking. 'Is there anything else you want me to bring?'

'A bottle of vodka for me and a couple of tubes of sedative for Diva. Only joking. I'll see you soon.'

'I'll be as quick as I can.' I cut the call, and run

across to the cottage to collect my keys and wash my hands and face. I head for my shiny new dark blue van and drive to the showground, following an ice-cream van. Eventually, I reach the entrance, where an elderly man in a fluorescent jacket tied around the middle with baler twine directs me towards the public parking.

'I need to be in the lorry park.'

'Have you got a pass, my lover?'

'No.'

'In that case, you need to go that-away. I can't let people park willy-nilly and all over the place. It's more than my life's worth. The organiser of this show is like a ruddy Rottweiler.'

'I'm the stunt team's official farrier.' Okay, I've promoted myself. It's becoming a habit. 'One of the horses has pulled a shoe. You must know the saying: No foot, no horse.'

'Indeed I do.' He rubs his chin, which is covered with silver stubble, as he ponders the options.

'Oi, hurry up, we're going to miss our class,' someone yells from the horsebox behind me. Someone else sounds an air-horn, but nothing will hurry the man at the gate.

'Patience is a virtue,' he says. 'More haste, less speed.'

'We're holding up the traffic,' I point out.

'Where are you from, maid? You aren't from round here.'

'I'm from Hampshire.' I start to worry about fixing Diva's shoe in time. 'Can I go now?'

'I suppose so. I can't understand why everyone's so impatient nowadays. Slowly but surely, that's my motto.'

One of many, I think, amused as I drive on. I park beside the Saltertons' lorry, where Robbie is already made up and dressed in a black vest, leggings and boots. Maisie is with him, wearing a blue sundress, hat and sandals, accessorised with smears of strawberry ice cream. She greets me, and one of the dogs who's lying in the shade of the lorry barks in welcome.

'Maisie, go and sit on the ramp, please,' Robbie says. 'I don't want you to come to any harm.'

'But Daddy, I wanna watch Flick shoe Diva.'

'You can watch from the ramp. Don't move . . . or else.'

'Or else what?'

'I don't know. I can't think of anything at the moment. Please, just for once do as you are told and without arguing.'

'Daddy's in a bad mood,' she explains as she skips up the ramp and perches on an upturned bucket at the top.

'I'm not,' he says quickly.

'Oh yes you are.'

'Oh no I'm not.' He smiles suddenly. 'This isn't a pantomime – I haven't got time for this right now.' He turns to me. 'Do you think there's time for this?'

'It depends on what mood she's in.' I take out the anvil and trolley from the back of the van, along with a shoe in Diva's size. Robbie unties her from the lorry and leads her towards the trolley. She snorts and gives me a look that means, 'Don't you dare touch me.'

'This isn't going to be easy.' Her coat is dark with sweat and I can see that she's pulled one of her front shoes – the nails are still embedded in the hoof, a potential danger to her and the other horses.

'Let's try. If it doesn't work, we'll go for plan B.'

He means the seven horses.

I approach Diva and let her sniff my hand. I stroke her neck and shoulder and bend down to pick up her foot. She strikes out, but I'm prepared, staying well to one side. Robbie shakes the rope and whispers something in her ear. When he gives me the nod, I have a second go when she lets me go as far as pulling out the remaining nails before she decides she's had enough.

'Do you want another shoe on?' I ask.

'It's tempting to leave it, but she's slightly footsore. I don't want to risk our reputation by taking a lame horse into the arena. Someone's bound to notice.'

I don't put the new shoe in the furnace. I check it cold against her hoof, but she still leaps upwards like a cat, knocking me sideways. Robbie gives her a stern telling off, which surprises me. I've never heard him raise his voice to a horse before.

'Are you all right?' He holds out his hand to pull me up.

'I'm fine.' I limp back to the anvil where I hit the iron into a better shape. 'How much longer have we got?'

'About ten minutes at a push.' He calls his brother over. 'Can you grab my cloak? It's in the lorry.'

'Let's leave the mare here,' Dillon says, striding across. 'She's a right pain in the arse. She'll make us look like idiots. Don't take the risk.'

'I don't take risks. You know me.'

'I'm ready,' I interrupt. 'The shoe will fit well enough.'

I pick up her foot. Diva tenses. Robbie growls at her. She settles and lets me hammer in the nails, clench them and rasp them smooth while he fastens his cloak.

'She's ready to go,' I confirm, and he leads her to join the other horses. Neil and Dillon have three each, while Sally Ann has Scout.

'I'll look after Maisie,' I offer, and we follow the rest of the family down to the arena, to where the crowds are milling around beneath a cloudless sky, waiting for the display to begin. The brothers trot the horses in circles in the collecting ring, working them in pairs and fours from the ground as a warm-up.

'Daddy says I can have an ice cream,' Maisie says hopefully as we find a vantage point near one of the flagpoles that line the side of the arena. I take a deep breath of burgers, beer and baby wipes. I feel much calmer now.

'Another one? Did he really?'

'Yes,' she says slowly.

'We'll see.'

'That means no,' she says sadly.

'It means maybe. Let's watch Daddy and Dillon first. We don't want to miss them.'

I look down. Having spotted the horses lined up at the entrance to the arena, Maisie is trying to clamber over the post-and-chicken-wire fence.

'Here they are,' she calls excitedly. 'That's my daddy. Go, Daddy.'

As the commentator introduces the Eclipse stunt team, I cross my fingers that the TV people are watching from the hospitality box and that the performance is a hit. I hope that they don't decide that Nelson's absence is a deal-breaker.

The music begins – it's dramatic, like a Wagnerian opera – and the brothers run in with the horses behind them. Robbie keeps Diva close and, as Dillon sets the others off, trotting circles and weaving between each other, Robbie has Diva rearing and showing off her moves. Gradually, the display builds in complexity and skill, and the music becomes more dramatic. Robbie and Dillon vault on to the backs of their horses, from where they guide four at a time around the arena. They turn from each end, bringing their horses to a halt and, sitting astride now, they encourage Diva and Scout to rear up and the others to jostle and throw up their heads.

The crowd gasps in awe. To the inexperienced eye, all looks well, but I worry about the mare. She flares her nostrils, exposing their cherry-red lining. A white foam of sweat, saliva and fear adorns her chest. She rears for a second time, going up so high that for a moment my heart is in my mouth, afraid that what Robbie predicted about her going over backwards is about to come to pass. He clings on with his powerful thighs, the effort of staying there etched across his face as he challenges the force of gravity. Diva brings her front legs down and I start to breathe again. Can she hold it together in the arena for the last few minutes?

Maisie slips her hand through mine and holds on with hot, sticky fingers. I glance down. She smiles and I smile back at a little girl I've grown fond of. Although we did our best not to involve Maisie, it's inevitable that I've become part of her life, and she's become part of mine.

I turn my attention back to the arena at the sound of a drum roll. Robbie and Dillon are at opposite ends of the arena. With a shout, they send their horses off at full pelt towards each other, their hooves thundering across the ground.

I know it isn't dangerous, that the moves are

choreographed and the team has practised over and over again, but my pulse beats faster and Maisie's grip on my hand tightens. As the two teams of horses charge towards each other, Diva seems to change her mind. I don't know what distracts her – a bee, a balloon, something in the crowd – but she slows, gathers herself up and bucks with her head down and hind legs high in the air. Time stops. My heart stops. The scene in front of me travels in slow motion: Diva tipping Robbie over her shoulder and him flying through the air.

Even now I'm sure he'll be all right. He'll land on his feet like a cat, like he always does, take a bow and vault back on to wild applause. But he is catapulted headfirst towards the ground. He holds out his hands, but he's going too fast, flailing, running through the air, trying to right himself. The music continues into a crescendo of stringed instruments, horns and drums as his head hits the ground. The music stops. His body buckles, and crumples into the grass, and then . . . then nothing . . . no movement, just an awed and uncertain silence.

'That is part of the show, I take it,' one nearby spectator mutters.

'Daddy's fallen off,' Maisie observes in a tiny voice.

The mare gallops away to the exit, running straight through the rope, pulling up stakes and dragging them along with her. The people in the crowd try to get out of the way, screaming and crying. Maisie starts screaming too.

'Stay here with me,' I tell her as I hold her back from climbing the fence to join her father in the arena. I can see Dillon cornering the other horses in the collecting ring with the help of some of the stewards, and Neil

and Sally Ann running across to where Robbie
has fallen. 'Maisie, please wait,' I beg as I pull my
mobile phone out of my bag and start to call the emer-
gency services, but the commentator announces that
someone is organising an ambulance so I put it
away again. Dr Nicci turns up at the scene and I'm
not sure what to do when every fibre of my being is
telling me I should be there at Robbie's side, yet the
best thing I can do for him right now is to look after
Maisie.

Dr Nicci is kneeling on the ground at Robbie's side.
Neil's face is ashen and Sally Ann is crying.

'My daddy's hurt,' Maisie says.

'The doctor's looking after him.'

Dillon and the stewards have head-collars on all
the horses, including Diva, who has returned to rejoin
her friends. Dillon is examining her legs. I think she's
bleeding where the rope has cut into her flesh.

'Please will the duty vet make their way to the main
arena,' comes an announcement over the loudspeakers as the sound of a siren grows closer. The
vet – Matt – arrives in his four-by-four at the same
time as an ambulance comes bumping across the
arena. Two paramedics in green jump out to assess
Robbie's injuries. After they've had a conversation
with Dr Nicci, there's another flurry of activity and a
steward is sent to the commentary box.

'Daddy's bumped his head,' Maisie says. 'He
should have been wearing a hat, shouldn't he? Sophia
says we must always wear our hats when we ride our
ponies.'

'That's quite right,' I say distractedly.

'Can we clear the arena immediately? All stewards
to the collecting ring to help move the horses back to

the lorry park,' the commentator says. 'The air ambulance is on its way.'

'It sounds like your daddy's getting a trip to hospital in a helicopter.' I'm trying to stay positive for Maisie's sake, but it isn't working.

'I want to see my daddy.' Her voice rises to an ear-splitting, heart-wrenching wail.

'Neil,' I call, waving to catch his attention.

He looks across and whispers something to Sally Ann before walking over to us.

'I'm sorry. She wants to see her dad. I don't know what to do,' I say as Maisie reaches her hands out to her granddad, who lifts her over the fence and gives her a hug.

'You come too, Flick,' he says, holding Maisie on his hip and offering me his hand to help me over the fence. I walk with him to the small crowd that's assembled around Robbie.

'Daddy's very sleepy,' Neil says. 'We're waiting for the air ambulance to come and take him to hospital where the doctors can find out what needs to be done.'

'I wanna see him,' Maisie repeats.

'You'll have to promise you'll stay with me, because the doctor is looking after him, and we mustn't get in their way.'

'I promise,' she says.

'This is Robbie's daughter, Maisie, and his girlfriend, Flick,' Neil says, ushering us through.

Some girlfriend I've turned out to be, I think, looking down at his upturned face as he lies on his back on a stretcher. He's deathly pale, and there's blood congealing at his temple. There's a pulse at the side of his neck – I recall kissing him there, pressing my lips to that very spot. His eyes are open and staring as if he's in shock, and I remember the shot of electricity that ran through me when we first touched, mouth to mouth. I want to throw myself down by his side and hold his hand and tell him everything is going to be all right. I want – no, I *need* to be with him. A tear trickles down my cheek. I brush it away.

The paramedics put a brace around his neck.

'Clear the arena immediately. All non-essential personnel, please clear the arena,' announces the commentator as the sound of a helicopter comes thrumming through the air.

My heart lifts a little because the people who can save his life are here, yet in the next breath I'm swamped with despair that he is beyond help. I watch his eyes. His eyelids flicker then grow still, taking me back to when he fluttered them against my cheek, like the kisses of a butterfly.

'Flick.' Someone – Neil, I think – gives me a gentle nudge. 'We need to move. Can you take Maisie home, please? Sally Ann will go in the air ambulance if she's allowed and I'll drive to the hospital. We'll keep Dillon updated with any news.' He lets Maisie down, I grab her hand, and we run towards the collecting ring as the red air ambulance lands at the opposite end of the arena. Tripping across the grass, she sticks a finger in her ear at the rhythmic throb of the engine. The draught from the spinning propeller makes the flags flutter on their poles and a stray balloon jerks across the ground.

I turn to see the crew with a stretcher and kit, heading towards Robbie, and all I can do is pray that he'll be all right.

'Come on, Maisie, we have to go home and look after the horses. Paddington will be wondering where you are.'

When we return to the lorry, all the horses are loaded, including Diva, which is a relief and one less battle to fight.

'What's happening?' Dillon asks me. 'I heard the helicopter . . .'

'He's unconscious. He has a head injury, but they won't know how bad it is until they've got him to hospital. I'm assuming they'll do a scan.'

'He's hurted his head,' Maisie says, reverting to baby talk.

'Your dad asked me to take Maisie home. He and Sally Ann are planning to go to the hospital. From there, he'll keep you updated with progress.' Note that I say 'progress'. I have to remain optimistic, for everyone's sakes, because no matter how much the brothers have fallen out and in with each other, Dillon is clearly distraught. 'Are you okay to drive, or should we find someone else?'

'I'll do it,' he says firmly.

'I'll give you a hand with the horses when we get back.'

He runs his hands through his hair and swears out loud. 'What happened? Robbie's always so careful. If it wasn't for that monster he bought—'

'I'm not sure it was her fault.' I touch his arm. 'Let's not play the blame game now.' One of the horses starts kicking the inside of the horsebox. 'Let's get these guys home.' I just hope that Robbie comes home too, and soon, so I can say everything I want to say. I don't know what I'll do, how I'll ever recover if he doesn't.

Chapter Twenty-Two

Life is a Bowl of Cherries

It's the longest evening of my life. Dillon and I feed and turn the horses out with Maisie's 'help' on our return to the yard. They seem unconcerned by their stressed-out human carers. Most of them have a good roll before dropping their heads to graze. Diva stands quietly nibbling at the hedge and flicking the flies away with her tail as the sun begins to set behind the hills, hailing the onset of dusk that falls like a curtain on the day's theatre.

Dillon and I spend a few minutes watching them. Maisie clings like a limpet to her uncle's leg. Louise called when she heard the news through the family grapevine, offering to have Maisie for however long we wanted, but Maisie insisted on staying at home, and I couldn't see any reason why she shouldn't.

'I'd better take you home so you can have tea and go to bed,' I say. 'Would you like to eat with us, Dillon?'

'I'm going to meet Mum and Dad at the hospital.

I'll give you an update later, unless there's any news beforehand.'

'Give Sally Ann and Neil my love, and –' my voice fractures – 'make sure you tell Robbie I'm thinking of him.'

'Will do,' he says.

Maisie and I walk back to the cottage, holding hands. I unlock the door and push it open. Maisie turns the light on. There's a jacket hanging over the banister. It's Robbie's. I reach out and touch it as I pass on my way to the kitchen, swallowing a lump in my throat at the realisation that he isn't here.

I cope by keeping busy. I feed the dogs and hens under Maisie's supervision and dig around in the freezer for chicken nuggets, chips and peas for dinner. I'm not hungry, but Maisie finds an appetite. We sit down on the sofa in the living room rather than in the kitchen to break the normal routine. Robbie likes her to sit at the table.

'My mummy went to heaven when I was a baby. Is my daddy going to die?' she says, as she squeezes ketchup on to her plate.

I choke on a chip and burst into tears.

'It's all right.' She reaches out and rubs my back with the ketchup bottle. 'Don't cry.'

I take the bottle and make an excuse that I need to put it back in the fridge. Maisie seems to be dealing with the situation better than I am, but when I return to the living room, the dogs are staring at an empty plate on the floor, and she is curled up, sobbing into a cushion.

'I really want to see my daddy,' she cries.

'Nanny is with him,' I try to reassure her, but she won't calm down until I call Dillon for an update.

Even then, Maisie insists on interrogating him personally when he comes home after ten, way past her bedtime.

'Thanks for dropping by,' I say, offering him a mug of tea.

He sits down on the sofa with Maisie on his knee. 'He's had a scan,' he says. 'That's all good – there's no sign of any fractures or bleeding.'

'That's a relief. Is he awake?' I ask.

'Not yet.' Dillon frowns. 'That's a bit of a worry. He's still unconscious, but the consultant is optimistic for a full recovery. All we can do is wait and hope for the best.'

'Are we going to cross our fingers?' Maisie says.

'That's a good idea,' Dillon says.

'I'll get Paddington to cross his hooves for Daddy too.'

I notice how Dillon's Adam's apple bobs up and down, not once, but twice. He clears his throat and gets up to leave.

'I'll let you know how he is in the morning. If you can look after Maisie, I'll make sure the horses are fed and watered. We'll do the minimum necessary until the new groom arrives on Monday to take some of the strain.' He gives me a hug before he goes outside. 'He's going to be okay, Flick. My big brother is one of the bravest and toughest people I know.'

I hope so, I think, as I close the door behind him.

'Maisie,' I call softly. 'It's bedtime.'

'Oh,' she calls back, 'I wanna make fairy-cakes.'

'Another time,' I say wearily.

Neither of us sleeps well, and I wake the next morning to find Maisie lying alongside me on top of my duvet. She has her thumb in her mouth and the unicorn tucked under her arm. I don't wake her.

I go downstairs and sit in the kitchen with a mug of tea, and watch the chickens foraging through the flowerbeds. Neither of the dogs eat their breakfast and both jump up with a low bark and trot through the hall when they hear a knock, only to be disappointed when they find Dillon, not their master, on the doorstep.

'How is he?' I almost fall out of the door I'm in such a hurry to find out.

'He's awake.' Dillon is smiling. 'He can remember everything except what happened at the show, but Mum says he's very tired. He fell over when he tried to get out of bed, going against his doctor's orders. I'm going to see him again this afternoon – they've said I can take Maisie for a short visit. I hope she isn't giving you too much trouble.'

'She's no trouble. I'm just so glad he's awake.' I change the subject. 'How are the horses?'

'I'm leaving them out today. I'll hitch the trolley to the quad bike to transport their feeds. The fields can wait.'

'What about this afternoon?'

'I'll do them when I get back.'

I'm pleased to see that Dillon is stepping up.

'I'd like to visit Robbie sometime soon. Can you let me know when it would be convenient? I don't want to overwhelm him if he needs to rest.'

'He'll want to see you. Don't worry. According to Mum, the first thing he did was ask after you and Maisie. The second was to ask when he could come home.'

When Dillon and his niece are out visiting the

hospital, I wander out to see the horses. I take a wheelbarrow, mini-rake and scoop with me, thinking that I can clear a couple of the paddocks to save the new groom some work tomorrow. I decide to make a start with Rafa's field. He wanders over to greet me and check out my pockets for treats. When he's satisfied that there are none, he takes the handle of the scoop between his teeth and lifts it off the barrow.

'I'll have that,' I say, smiling as I extract it from his mouth. 'It's kind of you to help, but I can manage.' As I move along the hedge, poo-picking, Rafa walks with me, stopping now and again to nudge the handles on the barrow. I reach out and rub his neck. He turns his head towards me, lifts his front leg and lands his hoof in the front of the barrow, which tips forwards.

'No!' I exclaim, trying to wrestle it away, but it's too late. It's on its side with its contents spilled across the grass.

'Thank you for your help,' I say dryly. 'Are you going to pick that up? Silly question. Of course you aren't, when I'm here to wait on you hand and foot.'

As if contrite, Rafa moves up close and rests his chin on my shoulder. I reach my arm up around his face and lean back into his embrace, enjoying his warmth and the sunshine.

'So you do still like me,' I murmur, thinking of Robbie lying in his hospital bed. 'Maybe you can learn to love us both.'

When Dillon returns to drop Maisie off, he lets me know that I'm welcome to visit Robbie the following day, before he rushes off to do some admin and make sure that the flat is ready for the arrival of the new groom and her fiancé. Maisie and I make fairy-cakes.

She dips her finger into the mix to taste it.

'Daddy's getting better, so why can't he come home yet?'

'Because the doctor has to say he's well enough.' I dampen a piece of kitchen roll and wipe a blob of sponge mixture from the tip of her nose. She screws up her face.

'Will it be tomorrow?' She picks up a wooden spoon and sticks it in the mixture so it stands upright.

'I don't know.'

'Will it be the next day? Will it be the day after the next day? Flick, answer me.'

'Maisie, I can't, because I really don't know. I'm a farrier, not a doctor.'

'When Finn's mummy wasn't very well, he didn't have to go to school.'

'Miss Fox will miss you if you don't turn up. Who will hand out the exercise books and number lines if you aren't there?'

She ponders for a moment, leaning on the spoon, which suddenly slips, sending a substantial volume of the sticky mix splattering across the table and on to the floor.

She laughs out loud. 'Don't worry. The dogs will lick it up.'

'I'm worried that there won't be enough left to fill all the cases in the tin.'

'We can make some more.'

'I think we'll make do with what we've got. I shouldn't eat too much cake.' I pat my stomach.

'Are you getting fat?' Maisie asks.

'No, I don't think so. Come on, keep stirring. What shall we add next? Chocolate chips or glacé cherries?'

'Both,' she says. 'Do you love my daddy?'

I stop halfway through emptying the packet of chocolate chips into the bowl. What kind of question is that?

'Lots of people love your daddy,' I say diplomatically. 'Your granddad, and Nanny, Dillon . . .'

'What about you? Are you going to marry him?'

I shake my head. 'I have no plans to get married.'

'I'll ask him to ask you when he's better,' she says.

'There's no need to do that, thank you. It isn't up to the man to propose. If I wanted to get married, I'd ask him.'

Her eyes widen like saucers and I realise that she's jumping to the wrong conclusion.

'Maisie, I'm not going to marry your dad – or anyone else, for that matter. Is that clear?'

She pops a chocolate chip into her mouth and nods.

The rest of the day passes quickly. I make sure that Maisie's uniform is washed and ironed, and that she's done her homework. We ice the fairy-cakes and add pink sprinkles that Sally Ann drops round, having torn herself away from the hospital for a few hours. Maisie decides that she'll sleep in her own bed, which means that we both have a good night and feel refreshed in the morning.

I drop Maisie at school, promising Miss Fox that I'll pick her up if she becomes distressed about her dad being in hospital, and then I return to the yard to find Dillon showing the new groom around. He introduces me to her. She seems friendly and I warm to her straight away. Although she's petite at no more than five foot tall, she has a presence that even Diva respects. As we're talking, my mobile rings.

'I'd better take this,' I say, apologising. 'Hello?'

'Good morning. Is that Flick?'

It takes me a moment before I recognise Delphi's voice.

'It is.'

'I've heard that you're taking on new clients and, as I can't pin Mel down to a time to come and shoe my horses, I wondered if you'd be happy to take over with immediate effect.'

'Well, yes, I'd be delighted. Would you like to make an appointment?' I put the mobile on loudspeaker and open the diary.

'Today would be useful.'

'Today? How many?'

'There are two whose shoes are falling off, and another three that I'd like done by the weekend.'

'Let me do the two urgent ones this morning and we'll go from there.' I'm keen to build up my business, but visiting Robbie is my priority.

I shoe Delphi's horses, two of the riding school ponies, and drop back to the cottage to shower and change before I drive to the hospital in the van.

A nurse waves me through the ward to Robbie's hospital bed, where he's sitting propped up against a couple of pillows. His face is pale, his hair messed up, and he has a purple bruise on his temple. He looks drawn and exhausted, yet my heart skips a beat at the sight of him and my chest hurts as if I'm about to go into cardiac arrest. Even though it's been less than forty-eight hours since I last saw him being airlifted from the arena, I've missed him more than I can say.

'Hello,' I say, unsure what his reaction will be.

'Hi, Flick.' His expression brightens. 'Thanks for coming to see me. I'm bored out of my skull. Maybe not the most appropriate comment for someone on the Neuro ward, but never mind.'

'At least you still have your sense of humour.' I pull up a chair and sit down. 'How are you?'

'Much better for seeing you.'

Mindful of what Dillon said about his memory, it occurs to me that he might not recall what passed between us in the days before the show.

'I wish I hadn't put everyone through this,' he goes on. 'My parents seem to have spent almost every minute here at the hospital. Did you see me hit the deck?'

'Maisie and I were watching. We saw everything: Diva bolting from the arena; Dr Nicci rushing to your side; the air ambulance.' I shudder at the memory. 'Can you remember what happened?'

'Not much. I've gleaned some of the details from other people.'

'I'm sorry if I had anything to do with it . . . if I contributed in any way.'

'What do you mean?'

'I thought maybe . . . well, you were upset because we fell out the night before. I wondered if that had made you less careful.'

'I admit I was preoccupied. I didn't take a moment out to prepare because we were running late, what with Diva not loading and then the incident with the shoe. I didn't have time to breathe, empty my mind, and visualise the performance like I normally do. It sounds odd, but it does work.' He pauses. 'Please don't blame yourself. I made an error of judgement by including Diva in the team, especially as I was expecting her to fill Nelson's shoes. It was too soon. I've been lucky, though. I'm still here.'

'Thank goodness,' I sigh.

'I've been waiting for you, even though I didn't really think you'd turn up. You didn't have to.'

'Hey, don't worry about it. I wanted to.'

He reaches out and touches my hand and the familiar surge of electricity darts between us. It's still there – I look into his eyes; I guess it always will be.

'I'm sorry,' I repeat.

'As I've said, it's entirely my fault. I knew I was under par, but I wanted to impress the TV people. Have there been any calls, or messages? Has Dillon heard anything?'

'He would have said if he had,' I respond as Robbie goes on, 'I should have been able to put the personal stuff aside that day.' He smiles weakly. 'It just shows what a wreck I am when I think of not seeing you again.'

'But you will see me. Robbie, I don't think this is the best time or place to discuss it but, suffice to say, I've had second thoughts about leaving. I wanted to talk to you about it, but you didn't come back from Dillon's that evening, and you weren't exactly in a receptive mood on the morning of the show.'

'You're going to stay on?'

'If you'll have me.'

'Of course I will.' A smile lights up his face. 'Flick, will you pinch me? This feels like a dream.'

I pinch the spare flesh on the back of his hand.

'Ouch!' he says.

'Again?' I ask.

'No, that's real enough.' He strokes my fingers. 'What made you change your mind?'

'Are you sure you're up to this?'

'What, talking? I'm ready to get back out there with

391

the horses, but they won't let me.' He flexes one arm, revealing his bulging muscle under his hospital gown. 'So, where are we at?'

'It was something you said – two things, actually. You told me I was selfish and it's true. I've been so driven by the idea of achieving my dream of having my own farriery business that I haven't considered the people around me. I've sacrificed my personal life and relationships, and hurt people like my parents, Maisie and you on the way. I need to let you help me and not try to do everything myself . . .' My voice trails off. I wonder if he knows how much effort it's taken for me to acknowledge that I need his support. 'It isn't about money,' I continue. 'It's about knowing that you are at my side. When you're with me, I feel that anything is possible. I'm sorry for what I've put you through.'

'You don't have to apologise. I'm partly responsible. I've had time to think while I've been lying here in bed and wondering where we were going wrong, and I've realised that I have to face up to the fact that I've been using Maisie as an excuse not to fully commit to someone, as in you.'

'I did wonder,' I say. 'You were scared that I would abandon you, just as your biological mother and Carla did.'

He nods, his eyes filled with pain. 'It became a self-fulfilling prophecy.'

'I'm not going to leave. I made my mind up after we argued the other night. I want us to take the next step and commit to each other for the long term, if you'll have me.'

I wait, holding my breath for his reply.

'What does "long term" mean?' he asks tentatively.

'That sounds like another cop-out, doesn't it? What I'm saying is that I want us to be together for ever, for the rest of our lives.'

'Oh, Flick, darling.' He sits upright and slides his legs to the side of the bed so he can reach his arms around my shoulders. I lean in close and press my lips to his in a long, lingering kiss.

Someone clears their throat from the periphery of my consciousness. We turn our heads to find a nurse holding on to the curtain.

'Should I pull this around the bed to give you a bit of privacy?' she teases. 'My patient isn't allowed any excitement – he's recovering from a head injury.'

Robbie blushes as he slides back into bed, strategic-ally rearranging the sheet across his middle. I can't help giggling as the nurse walks away, the soft soles of her shoes squelching across the floor.

'Can I get you anything, do anything for you?'

'Ah, you could, but not here.' He sinks against the pillows. 'I'm fine now, Flick. The only thing I need is you.'

I gaze at him. The feeling is entirely mutual. I can survive perfectly well on my own, but Robbie makes me complete.

'Why don't I take you for coffee in the canteen?' I say.

'I'd rather be outside, if that's possible. I could do with some fresh air.'

'Can you walk?'

'I don't think they'll let me walk that far. I'm still having these funny turns.'

'I'll see if I can find a wheelchair.'

'If you could, that would be great. I just want to get out of here.'

'It won't be long before they let you out. They need the beds.' I get up and look for the nurse. It takes a few minutes because she's busy, but she sets us up with a wheelchair and I push Robbie out of the ward and along the corridor towards the restaurant. As I move him aside to let a trolley pass, the wheelchair bumps against the wall.

'Can you drive this thing?' Robbie says.

'It isn't that easy to manoeuvre.'

'I suppose I should be grateful that I'm still in one piece. This is a cheap way to get your thrills.' He glances down at his fingers, gripped tight around the arms of the wheelchair, and chuckles. 'It's a white-knuckle ride.'

'I can make this move a bit faster if you want a bit more excitement.' I give the chair a good shove and let it roll on ahead of me. He makes to jump out. 'No,' I yell at him. 'No stunts.'

He's laughing. I'm laughing.

'You haven't done a risk assessment,' I gasp, clutching my stomach with one hand. My muscles are aching. 'There isn't much wrong with you.'

But later, when we're having coffee and chocolate-and-almond cookies on the balcony outside the day room, he grows pale and quiet.

'It's time I took you back to bed.' I can't stop flirting with him. He's irresistible.

'Our bed,' he says, 'the one in our room at Cherry Tree Cottage. We can buy a new one if you like – it can be a symbol of our fresh start.'

'Take it easy,' I say. 'We can make plans when you get home.'

I take him back to the ward, where I help him settle back on to the hospital bed before saying goodbye.

'I love you,' I say, reluctant to walk away.

'I love you too,' he says, reaching out for my arm as if to stop me leaving. 'I want you by my side. I want to kiss you goodbye in the mornings and hold you in my arms at night for the rest of our lives.'

I press my lips to his cheek.

'I thought you said you didn't know how to do romance,' I say. 'That is the most romantic thing anyone has ever said to me.'

Chapter Twenty-Three

Another Bite at the Cherry

Towards the end of the week, Robbie is allowed home on condition that he takes life easy for a few days at least. I bring him back in the Land Rover on the Friday morning, when Maisie has special dispensation to have time off school to welcome him. When I arrived at the hospital, he was up and dressed in a shirt, jeans and jodhpur boots.

'Thanks for coming to rescue me,' Robbie says as I drive along the lane to Furzeworthy, with his hand on my knee and the aphrodisiac scent of his aftershave filling my nostrils.

'It's no trouble. I couldn't wait to have you back. I can't believe how much I missed you.'

'And to think you were going to walk out on me!' he exclaims.

'Are you going to hold that against me for ever?' I say lightly.

I turn up the drive and head straight to the yard, where Maisie, Sally Ann, Neil, and Daisy, the new groom, and the dogs come rushing over to greet

Robbie. Maisie fumbles to open the passenger door to let him out.

'Daddy, Daddy,' she shouts.

'Hush, Maisie.' Sally Ann puts her hands over her ears. 'Keep the noise down – you'll frighten the horses.'

Robbie hugs and kisses everyone before looking around.

'Where's Dillon?' he says.

'We got it!' As if on cue, Dillon comes running out of the tack room, waving his mobile in the air. 'The TV contract!'

'Yeeesss!' Robbie throws himself at his brother and clings on to him, almost knocking him off balance. Neil and Sally Ann clap and cheer. The horses disappear behind their doors, except for Paddington, who watches with great interest.

'Steady on, bro.' Dillon catches hold of him by the waist, letting Robbie slide to his feet.

'I thought they'd walk away after the fiasco last Saturday. The sight of your stunt rider being airlifted to hospital partway through a performance isn't the best way to inspire confidence. What did you say to convince them?'

'I managed to persuade them that it was a one-off. I sent photos and videos of our new lead horse.'

'Rafa? He isn't ready.'

'Filming doesn't start until next spring. I've been working with him for the last few days – he's going to be as good if not better than Nelson. I also negotiated a better deal, on the basis that they'll employ both of us.'

'I can't believe it.'

'Yeah, I'm glad you're here. I didn't fancy the idea

of having to call them to tell them the deal was off because you'd pegged it.'

'That's an awful thing to say,' I cut in, but both brothers are laughing.

'What a great result. Dillon, I'm sorry for the arguments we've had recently.'

'Perhaps this will prove that you can trust me, and I'm not completely useless.'

'Let's put this behind us.' Robbie steps towards him and shakes his hand. 'We're equal partners from now on.'

'I know how you feel now, trying to run the team pretty much singlehanded at times.'

'This calls for a celebration,' Neil announces. 'I'll fetch the champagne.'

'It isn't even eleven o'clock yet,' Sally Ann says.

'I don't think there are any rules that restrict bubbly to a particular time of day,' Neil says.

'I'll come and get the glasses,' she says with a smile.

We have a glass each to celebrate Robbie's homecoming and Dillon's achievement in securing the team's future. I can feel the bubbles popping on my tongue as Neil makes the toasts, and Robbie's hand on my back as he stands beside me. I notice how Maisie is watching us, her eyebrows raised in an as-yet-unspoken question. I smile at her and she smiles back.

'Do you always have champagne on a Friday morning?' Daisy jokes as we disperse. Maisie accompanies her grandparents into the big house, and Dillon and Daisy continue with the yard work and exercising the horses, leaving Robbie and me gazing at each other.

'What next?' I say.

'I'm going to see how Rafa's doing as he's going to be our star horse. Are you coming with me?'

'Why not? I haven't got any more horses to shoe until next week.' I put a few flyers beside the till in Tack 'n' Hack when I was at Delphi's the other day, and I've had a couple of enquiries, but nothing concrete yet.

'I didn't think.' Robbie breaks his stride as we walk towards Rafa's stable. 'You don't have to – I know it upsets you.'

'It's fine. I can deal with it now. I spent some time with him while you were in hospital and you're right – we can share.'

I watch Robbie getting Rafa ready for Dillon. He bends over, revealing his taut loins, to pick out each of his feet, letting the mud fall into a bucket. Then he picks up a brush and runs it across Rafa's skin, head to tail in sweeping strokes. The horse stands quietly, enjoying being groomed.

Robbie picks up the saddle and lays it on Rafa's back. He smooths out the saddlecloth underneath, drops the girth and lifts the saddle flap to fasten it. When he pulls the girth up to secure it, Rafa flicks his ears back. Robbie gives him a moment to become accustomed to the grip of the girth around his middle before tightening it a little more.

He drops the reins over Rafa's head, removes the head-collar, slips the bit into his mouth and the head-piece behind his ears, before fastening the throatlatch and noseband. He picks up a hat from where it's been left balanced on top of the grooming kit and puts it on his head.

'You aren't riding?' I say quickly. 'You aren't allowed to—'

'Don't make a scene,' he whispers. 'Please, I'll go mad if I can't ride.'

'You've had a head injury. You were completely out of it for hours.'

'I'm well aware of that.' He points to his hat. 'I'm being careful. All I'm going to do is walk and trot around the arena. You can come with me to make sure I'm safe.'

'I'm not happy about this,' I say as he fastens the chinstrap, but I realise that there's nothing I can do to stop him when horses and riding are in his blood.

Dillon is schooling Diva. He makes no comment about whether or not Robbie should be back in the saddle when he joins him in the arena.

It seems as though Robbie is making up for lost time. Having ridden and put Rafa away, we walk arm-in-arm to the cottage, the dogs ambling along behind. We pass through the gate where the brambles are beginning to overtake the geraniums in the border and wander up the path between the cherry trees. Robbie stops and plucks a ripe fruit. He turns towards me and pops it into my mouth.

'What do you think?' he asks.

'It's delicious,' I say, spitting out the stone as discreetly as I can and wiping the juice from my chin.

He leans down and kisses me. 'I've been dreaming of this.'

I pull away and pick a cherry for him to try.

'That is the sweetest one I've ever tasted,' he says. 'Everything is better with you.'

'I've been thinking about what we talked about the

other day, about how you want to hold me in your arms every night for the rest of our lives . . .'

'And?'

'I think we should get married.'

'Making the proposal is supposed to be my role.' I stare at him. His expression is deadpan, but the longer I stare, the more his mouth twists and his shoulders shake. 'I'm winding you up. I don't mean that at all. You're perfectly entitled to go down on one knee.'

'I'm being serious.'

'I know you are. I'm sorry for being a prat.'

Standing beneath the boughs of the cherry tree, I take both his hands.

'As we're going to live together openly from now on, it makes sense to get hitched, as a sign of our commitment to each other, and to Maisie. I've appreciated her company over the past few days and I'd be honoured to be her stepmum. I want us to be a family.'

'You don't have to do this for Maisie,' he says.

'It isn't just for her. I'm doing this for you. You've told me how you're afraid of being abandoned and I want to give you some kind of assurance that I'll do ' everything in my power not to let that happen to you again. I'm willing to make a formal promise in front of our families and friends to love and respect you for as long as we both shall live.' I take a breath and gaze into his eyes. 'Robbie Salterton, will you marry me?'

My heart starts to pound like a hammer as I wait on tenterhooks for his answer. It seemed like such a good idea at the time, but the more I think about it and the longer he keeps me in suspense, the more off-the-wall my proposal seems. I wouldn't blame him, or be at all surprised if his response is a no.

'Yes, of course I'll marry you,' he says eventually, his voice breaking with emotion.

It takes a moment for his response to sink in, but when it does, I'm overwhelmed with tears of joy.

'Don't cry,' he says, pulling me close and smothering my face with kisses. 'I love you more than you'll ever know. I'm going to do everything I can to make you happy.' Eventually he takes a small step back and rests his hands on my waist. 'I'm a traditional guy at heart, so I'm going to buy the ring. No argument.'

'I can go along with that.' I turn towards the cottage, but before we reach the door, the sound of Maisie's voice holds us back.

'Daddy and Flick, there you are.'

'I'm sorry,' Sally Ann says, sounding slightly short of breath as she marches up the path following her granddaughter. 'She wanted to come and find you.'

Robbie kneels down in front of Maisie.

'We have some special news for you,' he says.

'Yay!' She raises her hand. 'Flick is having a baby.'

'Whoah there. No, no, no, I'm not pregnant.' I look towards Robbie. 'Not yet, anyway.'

'Where did you get that idea from?' Robbie asks.

Maisie presses her finger to her lips and looks skywards. 'I can't remember.'

I recall how she asked me if I was getting fat when we were making the fairy-cakes. She must have jumped to the wrong conclusion.

'What is it then?' she says.

'Flick asked me to marry her, and I said yes.'

'Wowzer,' Maisie says, beaming. 'Am I going to be a bridesmaid?'

'Of course,' I say.

'Can my dress be purple?'

'I'm not sure about that.'

'Can Paddington be there? And Badger and Tatt?' She turns to Sally Ann. 'And Nanny?'

'Oh, I shall be there. I wouldn't miss it for the world.' She bursts into tears. 'I love a good wedding.'

Robbie stands up, holding his arms out to her. 'Come here. Let me give you a hug.'

Sally Ann embraces her stepson and congratulates us both on our engagement before she rushes away back down the path.

'Mum, where are you going?' Robbie calls.

She stops briefly. 'To tell the others and fetch another bottle of champagne. This definitely calls for another celebration.'

Maisie runs off after her, leaving me and my fiancé alone together.

He takes my hand. I can feel his fingers wrapped around mine, gentle with repressed strength and power. I can feel the heat in his skin and read the desire in his eyes as he draws me closer.

'I want to be worthy of you, Flick,' he says. 'I want you to let me be your hero.'

I close my eyes, picturing him in his dark breeches, leather boots, and one of his flamboyant and rather ridiculous cheesecloth shirts, galloping his proud black stallion around the Devon countryside.

I recall his endless patience with Maisie when she refused to sleep in her own room, his respect and appreciation for Nelson and Rafa, his kindness in taking me in when Mel kicked me out, his enthusiasm for helping Ashley begin to communicate through the healing power of horses, and his willingness – with a little persuasion from me – to give a funny little pony like Paddington a forever home.

I lean up, press my lips to his ear and whisper through tears of love and happiness, 'Robbie, my darling, I've looked up to you since the very first time we met. You *are* my hero, and always will be.'